# RING OF
# SWORDS

# RING OF
# SWORDS

>>>

## ELEANOR ARNASON

A Tom Doherty Associates Book
New York

This is a work of fiction. All the characters and events portrayed in this book are fictitious, and any resemblance to real people or events is purely coincidental.

RING OF SWORDS

This book was originally published as a Tor® hardcover in August 1993.

This book is printed on acid-free paper.

An Orb Edition
Published by Tom Doherty Associates, Inc.
175 Fifth Avenue
New York, N.Y. 10010

*Edited by David G. Hartwell*
*Design by Lynn Newmark*
*Cover art by Roger Loveless*

Library of Congress Cataloging-in-Publication Data

Arnason, Eleanor.
    Ring of swords / Eleanor Arnason.
        p.    cm.
    "A Tom Doherty Associates book."
    ISBN 0-312-89016-8
    I. Title.
    [PS3551.R4853R56    1995]
    813'.54—dc20                                    94-38162
                                                    CIP

First Orb edition: January 1995

Printed in the United States of America

0  9  8  7  6  5  4  3  2  1

For the Yard sisters
& their families

## ACKNOWLEDGMENTS

The following people read this novel in manuscript (or heard me read it). I thank all of them for their comments.

Eugene L. Baryngton III
Ruth Berman
David Cummer
Terry A. Garey
David G. Hartwell
P. C. Hodgell
Virginia Kidd
Mike Levy
Sandra Lindow
K. Cassandra O'Malley
Laurel Winter

I also want to thank Albert W. Kuhfeld, Ph.D., who answered a couple of questions re science at the last minute and designed a new and wonderful starship for me over the phone in the course of a ten-minute conversation. I can't get the starship into this novel, but I am definitely going to get it into the sequel.

Everything has consequences, inaction as well as action. But as a rule, it's better to do nothing rather than something and a little rather than a lot.

*Hwarhath* saying

If you must act, act decisively.

*Hwarhath* male addendum

# CONTENTS

A Note on History                                              11

Memo                                                           13

Part I: Nicholas the Liar                                      15

Part II: The Rules of War                                     131

Part III: Returning                                          321

Appendix A: On Time                                          365

Appendix B: On Rank                                          367

Appendix C: On Theater                                       369

Appendix D: On the Social Theories of Tsai Ama Ul            371

Appendix E: Miscellaneous Facts about the People            379

Appendix F: On the Pronunciation of the *Hwarhath*
    Main Language                                            383

# A NOTE ON HISTORY

In the first decade of the twenty-first century, a group of remarkable thinkers changed the basis of physics. By 2015 it was evident that an FTL drive was possible; by 2030 the drive was built. Humanity, which had believed itself trapped on Earth and doomed to stew in the poisons it had created, went suddenly out into the galaxy.

Or rather, some of humanity went. Most people (there were nine billion of them by 2070) stayed on the home planet and tried to deal with the terrible consequences of environmental collapse: the greenhouse effect, ozone depletion, acid rain and the seemingly endless series of plagues that swept the planet, all caused to one degree or another by pollution.

Explorers found a multitude of planets, many habitable, though none inhabited by intelligent life. The problem was: the life already there was not compatible with life on Earth. In some cases the native life was toxic; in others it was simply not nourishing. Almost always, in these alien environments, life from Earth did not thrive. There were many voyages of exploration and many research stations, but only a few planetary colonies.

In spite of this, the ships continued to go out, traveling distances that were close to incomprehensible, often in competition. (Nations did not go out of existence until the end of the century.) They searched for two things: planets that were habitable for humans, and other intelligent life.

## MEMO

RE:      Negotiations Coming-Forward
FROM: Sanders Nicholas, information-holder attached
        to the staff of First-Defender Ettin Gwarha
TO:      First-Defender Ettin Gwarha
FOR HIS EYES ONLY

The problem, as I see it, is an information gap. The People know far more about their enemy than the enemy knows about them. This is due mostly to the difference in the two cultures, but also to pure dumb luck.

For a long time, this was an advantage, and most of the Men-Who-Are-in-Front think it still is.

I disagree.

The enemy is continuing to gather information. At some point, they are going to know enough to mount an attack on the Weaving. (That point is near. All the models run in the past year have looked bad.) Whether they will decide to attack is uncertain, and how much damage they would do is equally unclear.

What does seems clear to me is this: the enemy does not know enough to act intelligently.

There are worse things than an ignorant enemy. (A stupid enemy. An enemy who's smart and crazy.) But ignorance is bad enough to frighten me.

The other side cannot judge consequences. They simply do not know what kind of behavior is unacceptable or disastrous. They could destroy us all by accident.

It seems to me imperative that the Weaving begin to look for ways to share information. Not, obviously, military information. We have discussed this over and over. I refer you to your memory and to previous memos.

I realize that most of the other frontmen do not agree. They think no change is necessary. The People can continue as they always have. This war—with a strange new enemy—can be fought like all previous wars, and there is no special danger in fighting a people who do not know what they're doing.

I realize as well that prudence and honor require that you do nothing without the agreement of the other front-men.

This makes a trap that is large enough to hold all of us: me, you, the Frontmen-in-a-Bundle, the Weaving and the People. I can see no way out. Maybe you should think about the situation. Keep in mind the computer models. They do not look good.

# PART I

## NICHOLAS
## THE
## LIAR

# I

➤➤➤ THE PLANET WHERE Anna was stationed was in Earth position: 148 million kays out from an ordinary G2 star not visible from Earth. Farther in was a double planet, one of those anomalies just common enough to drive theoreticians crazy. Both worlds had atmospheres, thick and poisonous and brilliantly white from a distance. On Anna's planet they were the morning/evening star, that waxed and waned as the pair rotated around one another. At their point of farthest separation the star became two stars, shining side by side in the blue-grey sky of twilight or dawn.

Farther out—beyond her planet—were four gas giants, all visible in the night sky, though none was as bright as the Twins. No one had bothered to name the giants. There was nothing special about them.

That was it, except for the usual bits of space debris: comets and planetoids, moons and rings and the dark companion that traveled around the G2 sun a good long distance out. It was a singularity, and it made the system a transfer point.

The planet she was on was habitable by humans. The atmosphere was remarkably like the old preindustrial atmosphere of Earth. The ocean was $H_2O$. There were two continents. One lay in the southern hemisphere and was shaped, very roughly, like an hourglass; the other, far bigger, stretched from the equator to the north pole and looked something like a boomerang.

Her station was in the middle of the hourglass, on the

east coast of the narrow waist. Until recently, it had been the only location on the planet with for-certain intelligent life.

Now there was another base on the planet: on the south coast of the boomerang, right at the bend. It had been established by the aliens who called themselves *hwarhath*. Humans called them "the enemy"; and her station—her nice quiet biological survey station—was full of fucking diplomats.

# II

>>> DARK CLOUDS BLEW in off the ocean. There were whitecaps on the bay. Anna fastened her jacket as she came out of the main building, then started toward the beach. The local form of ground cover—it was something like yellow moss—had sent up spore stalks in the past few days. They were tall and feathery and bent in the wind.

Early autumn. The ocean currents would be starting to change, bringing her particular area of study up from the cold waters around the pole. In bays like this one they would gather, signaling each other with elaborate displays of light, then exchange genetic material (carefully, carefully, the mating tendrils stretching out from among the many stinging tendrils), and then produce young. After that, if they were in the mood, a few would hang around and chat with the humans.

She climbed on the dock, which extended, long and jointed, into the bay.

This was her favorite part of the day. Moving over the narrow segments was a kind of microjourney. As on all journeys, she felt (for a time) outside her life. She was not the person who had left the research station, nor the person who would arrive at the research boat; she could consider past and future with an equal mind.

Mostly she noticed the present. The dock rose and fell, responding to her weight and the motion of the water. The wind blew cold and fresh.

On Earth, a day like this would be full of gulls and the

noise they made; but this planet had no birds, and the native bugs had been driven into hiding by the weather. She listened, hearing only water and wind and the creaking metal sound that the dock segments made as they rubbed against each other.

The boat was at the extreme end of the dock. Beyond it, anchored in the middle of the bay, was a communication float: ten meters long and white, called (inevitably) Moby Dick.

She climbed on board and ducked into the cabin. Yoshi was there, drinking tea and looking at the screens. He glanced at her. "Red-red-blue came in last night, flagella beating and making good time."

"Three weeks early," she said.

Yoshi nodded.

"The usual routine?"

He nodded again, which meant the alien had flashed a series of lights that meant "greetings—welcome—no aggression."

"I replied. The lights on Moby all work fine. Red circled a couple of times, then made the signal for recognition and moved away." He tapped a screen with a glowing dot. "That's Red. Close to the entrance and not moving. Waiting for someone who is more sexually interesting than Moby."

After five years, the aliens—her aliens—knew Moby and knew Moby did not exchange genetic material. Until they had finished mating, they would have no interest in the float.

She looked out the window at the grey-green bay. There were drops of water on the plexy: spray or the start of rain. The *hwar* subbase was out there, on an offshore island that would have been just barely visible on a clear day, close enough so the *hwarhath* could commute to the diplomatic compound, but far enough out so they could be reasonably sure of privacy.

"They'll be flying in and out daily," she said. "Right over the bay. I hope that isn't going to be a problem."

"I don't think Red and company are going to have anything on their minds except sex and fear, if they have minds." He got up and closed his thermos. "Have fun, Anna."

She settled in for eight hours, her thermos open, coffee steaming in a cup. As soon as Yoshi was gone, she turned the audio system up.

Yoshi found the noises produced by the animals in the bay faintly irritating. But she liked them: the moans and whistles of the various kinds of fish, and the bursts of clicking that came (they were almost certain) from creatures sort of like trilobites that lived in the muck on the bottom.

Ah! Today it was the whistle-fish. She drank her coffee and listened, checking the screens from time to time.

At ten hundred hours, she heard the sound of an engine, got up and went on deck. There it was—the *hwarhath* plane—coming out of the east. A fanwing, she saw when it passed over. Perfectly ordinary-looking, a little stubby maybe, blunt and inelegant like the alien ships. Though maybe she was reading in; we see what we expect to see. Rain fell steadily. A lousy day for the first meeting between humanity and the only other known starfaring species.

She went inside and turned on her communication unit. There, as promised, was the landing field, a wide strip of concrete with rain pounding down on it. A dozen figures stood on the field amid pools of water: the human diplomats. They were all civilians, dressed in long dark coats and holding umbrellas, and all men. The aliens had insisted. They would not negotiate with women, which did not speak well of their openness of mind. But maybe there was an explanation other than bigotry; it was always a good idea to suspend judgment when dealing with a really foreign culture.

The human military people were off-camera, and everyone else was in the station. The field was off-limits until the official welcome was over and the aliens were all safely inside the diplomatic compound. But as a gesture of courtesy, a camera had been set up and hooked into the station comm system. Every human on the planet could watch the moment when history was made. She poured fresh coffee into her cup.

The plane landed. Water rose in clouds. The long coats flapped, and the umbrellas tried to escape, rising like coal black kites. One turned inside out. Anna laughed. Ridiculous!

The plane door opened. She paused, her cup halfway to her mouth. A stairway unfolded, and people came out. They were broad and solid-looking, humanoid, as grey as the sky and the mist. No coats and no umbrellas. Instead, the aliens wore close-fitting clothing the same color as their fur.

They moved into the rain as easily—as casually—as if the weather did not matter, as if the rain did not exist. The first ones out carried rifles, a strap over one shoulder, one arm resting on the barrel, keeping the muzzle pointed down. They looked relaxed, but they moved (she noticed now) precisely, though not with a military precision. Like athletes or actors.

Very nice, she thought. Very impressive. The aliens had a sense of drama.

They spread out to either side, leaving a passage between them. Now the important people came out: more stocky grey bodies and, among them, one body that was much taller and thinner, with shoulders hunched against the rain.

For a moment—who was operating it?—the camera zoomed in. She saw a face without fur, long and narrow, hair dripping and eyes half-closed. A human.

At that point the transmission ended.

She started punching buttons, trying first to get the picture back and then to reach someone at the station. No use. Her unit was still on. She could hear it: a faint low hum. But nothing came out of it, except the hum. The entire system must be down.

She went out on deck. The diplomatic compound was on top of the hill that rose in back of the research station. It was a cluster of prefab domes, barely visible through the rain. The landing field was beyond the compound, entirely hidden.

She could see the research station, and it looked the way it always did: low buildings set in a landscape of yellow moss. Lights shone from the windows. A person came out a door and hurried across an open space, then ducked in through another doorway. Not running, she told herself, merely hurrying because of the rain.

She went back in and tried the CU again. Still nothing. What was going on?

She tried to keep her mind focused on the problem at hand, but it kept going back to the landing field and the man coming down the stairway, out of the alien plane.

Humanity had encountered the *hwarhath*—when? Forty years ago? In all that time, no one had ever changed sides, at least as far as she knew.

They were the other, the unknowable, the people in ugly stubby faster-than-light vessels that came into our space and ran if our ships found them or fought and were destroyed. After forty years of skirmishing and spying, humanity knew what about them? One of their languages. Something about their military capability. We had mapped the edges of their space, but never found a settled planet, only ships and more ships and a few deep-space stations. (She had seen a holo of one: a huge cylinder turning in the light of a dull red sun.)

Everything was armed. As far as humans could tell, the aliens had no civilian society. There had never been a human culture—not Sparta, not Prussia, not America—so entirely devoted to war.

So what was this man—this perfectly ordinary-looking human, pale face and lank sandy hair—doing among the aliens? Was he a prisoner? Why had they brought a prisoner along with their negotiating team?

She went back out on the deck. Nothing had changed. Maybe she ought to go over and ask what was going on. But if there was trouble, she would rather stay out of it; and if there was trouble, wouldn't she see a lot of people running and the flash of gunlight?

For the next hour or so, she paced back and forth between the cabin and the deck. Nothing happened, except that the whistle-fish moved into deeper water and she could no longer hear them. Shit. Shit. If she had wanted to be in a war, she would have joined the military and gotten a free education.

Finally, at thirteen hundred hours, the comm screen came back on; she saw Mohammed's face, dark and thin.

"What happened?" she asked.

"We had a temporary interruption of power," he said carefully. "It's not likely to happen again. I have been assured of that."

Mohammed was their expert on the comm system. He wouldn't go to anyone else about a technical problem; so the problem hadn't been technical. Someone had pulled the plug.

"What about the aliens?"

"They went to the diplomatic compound, as planned."

She opened her mouth, and he raised a hand. "I know nothing else, Anna."

She turned off the CU and settled down to watch her other screens.

At fourteen hundred, one of Red's buddies came into the bay. She picked it up on the sonar, swimming rapidly through the narrow entrance channel and then stopping when it noticed Red. The aliens did not use lights during the day. Instead, they communicated with chemicals excreted into the water. None of her instruments could pick up the chemicals at this distance. She could only watch the two dots on her screen. They remained motionless for a long time.

Finally the new alien moved on. It did not approach Moby Dick, though there was no way it could have missed the float, and Moby bore a superficial resemblance to an alien. Good enough to fool Red, at least at first. But this fellow showed no interest at all, which seemed to indicate that it had gotten information from Red.

She imagined a conversation.

*Is anyone else here?*

*Just that funny creature that can talk like us, but never tries to eat anyone or to screw.*

*Oh. Well. There's no point in even bothering to say hello.*

The alien stopped midway down the bay. At fifteen hundred Maria arrived.

"You're late."

"I got hung up at the station. It's going to drive you crazy, Anna. One hundred field-workers, all speculating at once, and none of them with enough information to say anything that makes sense."

"Great. Red has company. It just arrived, and it didn't try to check out Moby. If they are not intelligent, they're giving a very good imitation."

Maria shook her head. "What we have here, Anna, is a bunch of very big jellyfish with funny nervous systems. An intelligent species is like those people up the hill."

"Maybe," said Anna.

She walked back to the station slowly. The rain had turned to mist, and the evening animals were emerging from their holes. Most were one species: long and segmented and many-legged. Their backs shone in the light of streetlamps. (Was that the right name for things that stood tens of light-years from the nearest street?)

Hunters, she knew, looking for the worms that would be driven to the surface by moisture, and not in any way intelligent, though splendidly suited for what they did. Her aliens were different. They had brains, as many as ten in a single animal, all interconnected; though Red and its buddies out in the bay had maybe five brains at most. They were half-grown. The big fellows, with tendrils a hundred meters long, never mated or came in from the deep ocean.

Maria was right about the station. The dining hall was full of people, and the noise level was far higher than usual. She got food and went looking for Mohammed. He was at a table in a corner, people sitting all around him, looking intent. Obviously they wanted to know what had happened to the communication system.

Anna stopped, her tray in her hands, and Mohammed glanced up. "I did not want to talk over the comm system, Anna. There was a military fellow with me during the broadcast of the landing. When he saw what was coming out of the plane, he turned off my power, and he wouldn't turn it back on for over an hour. Crypto-fascist! I was angry, I can tell you."

"Does anyone know what happened to the man?" asked someone at the table.

"He must be in the diplomatic compound, mustn't he? He isn't in the station, and they could not have left the poor fellow out in the rain and dark."

Anna grinned. It was typical of Mohammed. He'd use a word like "fascist" as if he knew what it meant, and at the same time he believed that people were civilized. There is a right way to behave; you cannot leave a member of a diplomatic mission out in the rain.

Someone else said, "They aren't going to be able to get away with this, are they?"

She didn't know who "they" were—the *hwar?* The

human military? And she wasn't interested in listening to speculation. She nodded to Mohammed and turned away, looking for a table with room.

Later, on her way from one building to another, she heard the low roar of the alien plane and looked up. There were its lights—white and amber—moving above her, heading out to sea.

# III

➤➤➤ THE ALIEN PLANE flew in the next morning and left in the evening. This seemed to indicate that the negotiations were continuing as planned.

The compound said nothing officially. The talks were secret; they always had been, with no coverage on any of the nets. The station people had been given a little information out of courtesy and because they were too close to be kept entirely in the dark; now they were shut out, too.

After three days, she got the first unofficial news. It came from Katya, who was screwing one of the dips: a very junior man who talked too much. Katya extracted information from the dip—who was named, of all things, Etienne Corbeau—and then told selected friends, people who could be trusted to stay quiet. It would be a pity if the other dips found out.

"They are using the man as a translator," Katya said. "Their chief translator. According to Etienne, the first day he introduced the main *hwar*—he's something like a general—and then said, 'My name is Nicholas. Don't make the mistake of thinking that my loyalties are in any way divided, and don't think that what I say has anything to do with me. When I speak, the general is speaking.' Or something like that. Etienne likes to improve his stories. The MI people have sent a message probe out of the system. They want to know who this fellow is."

"What's happening in the talks?" asked Anna. "Are they getting anywhere?"

Katya smiled sweetly. Most of her ancestors had come from Southeast Asia; a few were African. She was small and dark and fine-boned and the loveliest woman Anna had ever seen outside a holo. She was also a first-rate botanist; no one knew more than she did about the yellow mosslike ground cover.

"Etienne won't tell me. That information is confidential; but it's all right to tell me gossip. He's fluent, really fluent, in the main *hwar* language."

"Is this still the mystery man?" asked Anna.

"Of course. The translators say he is using at least one other language—not often and not for long and only when he's talking with the general. Our people don't know what it is. We are recording everything, of course, but the translators say they aren't getting enough of the other language. They aren't going to be able to break it."

Anna wasn't sure how interested she was in any of this. She didn't share Katya's passion for intrigue, which Katya said she got from studying plants. "They are wonderfully complex and devious, a constant inspiration to me. Those who cannot run must find more interesting ways to survive."

All of which had nothing to do with the man who called himself Nicholas.

The weather changed; they had day after day of sunlight Indian summer, it would have been called at home. The wind dropped. Now and then, there were whitecaps on the ocean, but not in the landlocked bay. Red and its companion floated quietly, doing almost nothing that showed on the instruments. Saving energy, Anna figured. They would not eat until the time for mating was over.

No other aliens joined them. No one had any good theories why. Maybe the weather. She sat in the cabin of the boat and caught up on her reading—the latest professional journals, brought in by message probe—or wrote letters back to Earth.

The letters were all short, in part because of the security restrictions—no one could say anything about the negotiations—but also because she did not have much to say. How could she explain anything about her life to people who lived among nine billion other humans? They knew nothing about darkness or emptiness or silence or strangeness. To them, reality was humanity. There was nothing else near them. The *hwarhath* were legendary, and the creatures she was studying were incomprehensible. She had more in common with soldiers, at least the ones who were out here on the edge.

One morning she inflated a small rubber raft, attached a motor and puttered onto the bay. It was a perfect fall day: bright and still and warm. The planet's primary was overhead; she had no trouble looking down into the clear, barely moving water.

She went after Red, approaching slowly, watching on a portable sonar. The alien did not move. When she got close, she stopped the motor and drifted the last few meters. There it was, floating just under the surface.

The top of the animal—the bell or umbrella—was three meters wide and transparent; it rippled gently. Inside, dimly visible, were feeding tubes and clusters of neurological material. At the lower edge of the bell were tentacles. She could make out three varieties: the long, thick ones that Red used for swimming; the sensory tentacles, which were shorter and thinner; and the light-producing tentacles, which were little more than stubs. Everything waved gently, keeping time with the motion of the bell.

She could not see the rest of the animal: the stinging tendrils, twenty meters long, and the mating tendrils, even longer. These hung under the bell.

Around her were the sky blue bay and the low hills, covered with golden vegetation. Next to her was the animal, as clear as glass and pulsing like a heart. She felt a tremendous sense of happiness and rightness: this was what her life was about.

After a while, she fastened a sample bottle to a cord and lowered it into the water—very slowly, very carefully. Red noticed. All along the side nearest her boat, tentacles stretched out. The mouths at their ends opened and gulped water, testing.

A flicker of light went around the bell. Interesting. Red would have used chemicals if it had been talking to another pseudosiphonophore. But it must have realized she would not get a message delivered that way, so it was trying the night language.

*Red-red-blue,* the lights said. (The first color was actually a deep rose pink, and they had considered calling the animal Rose. But the name didn't fit. The animal was too big and far too dangerous.)

The first message went around the perimeter of the animal twice. Then it was followed by a second message: *Orange-orange-orange.*

Orange was a distress color.

*I am Red-red-blue,* the animal was saying, *and I don't like what you are doing.*

She pulled up the bottle, and the animal subsided into muttering: a colorless flicker of light that went round and round the bell. She waited a bit longer. Red went dark. Now it was safe to restart the motor. She puttered away at the lowest possible speed, remembering the long stinging tendrils—down there, out of sight, in the water like a net of silk.

# IV

➤➤➤ AFTER THREE WEEKS, the rest of the animals began to
arrive, swimming in through the narrow entrance to the
bay. Now her real work began. Anna changed her hours.
Most of the valuable information came at night, when the
creatures floated close to the surface of the water, flashing
messages back and forth. At times (and this was behavior
that had only been seen during the mating season) they
would all repeat the same message, either in unison or in
sequence, so the pattern of lights swept back and forth
across the bay.

Only the comparatively big animals came into the bay.
They had tendrils of more or less equal length and were
safe from one another. Other pseudosiphonophores—there
were hundreds of them—floated in the ocean beyond the
entrance channel, drawn by something, most likely a
pheromone, but reluctant to go in.

"There is no evidence of intelligence here," said
Maria. "The little ones fear the big ones; that is nature; and
everyone is attracted by the possibility of sex. That also is
nature."

Anna didn't argue. She was too tired and busy. She
knew the negotiations were continuing—the plane kept
passing over—but by this time she had lost track of what
might be happening.

One morning after work, she climbed the hill above the
station. The sky was dark and clear, and the morning/

evening star shone over the water: two brilliant points of light.

The creatures had started signaling just before she quit, and now they were really going at it. Pulses of blue and green light went back and forth across the bay, then out through the channel into the ocean. The rhythm—the pattern—stayed the same, but the colors changed, becoming paler. Here and there she saw a flash of orange. In this context, the color was probably an indication of sexual frustration. For some reason, which no one understood as yet, the creatures only mated in bays, never in the open ocean. (More evidence that they were not intelligent, said Maria; one sign of intelligence was flexibility.) The little animals knew they were not going to breed this year, and they sparked like so many fires. Farther out, away from shore, the animals were less common, but there were still a few, dotting the dark water all the way to the horizon, flashing in time with the big guys in the bay.

An amazing sight.

After a while a pair of very polite young soldiers came out of the compound. Marines. The name hadn't changed, though the ships they rode now traveled to the stars. They wore dress uniforms, and their heads were shaved except for a narrow strip of hair that went down the middle from front to back. The boy's hair was white-blond, straight and fine; the girl's hair was dark and tightly curled.

"The hill is off-limits, mem," the girl said. "You'll have to go."

The boy looked down at the bay and ocean. "What *is* that?"

"Animals," she said. "This is their mating season. It's like frogs singing or like Verdi. We don't know yet if they're intelligent."

"Why not?" asked the boy. "Whales are. And dolphins."

He was wrong, but she didn't want to argue. "I came up here to watch."

"It is really *something*."

"It will go on for weeks."

"Hey," he said. It was an exclamation of joy.

The girl said, "Mem, you have to go."

The next day the plane did not leave at its usual time. Katya told her the *hwarhath* had been invited to stay for a party.

"Etienne says they are trying to establish a more comfortable relationship, now that the question of the furniture has been settled."

"The furniture?" asked Anna.

"Don't ask me," said Katya. "Etienne clammed up. That is confidential information."

"Huh," said Anna, and went to work.

It was after dark by the time Yoshi left the boat. Anna went out on deck. The bay was still. The aliens floated motionless, not signaling.

Three people walked toward her along the dock. One strolled ahead; the other two followed. She couldn't see any of them clearly, until they reached the light at the end of the dock, next to her boat.

The first was human. She barely noticed him, because she was looking at one of his followers: a stocky person, dressed in grey. It had a broad flat face, covered with grey fur, and its eyes were entirely blue; there was no white at all. Its pupils were horizontal bars, broad at first, then narrowing rapidly in response to the light.

The alien gazed at her directly for a moment, then glanced down.

The other follower was a marine: the boy she had met on the hill. He carried a rifle, as did the alien.

The man in front was unarmed, or at least she could not see a weapon. His hands were in the pockets of his jacket, which was plain and made of some kind of tan fabric and looked vaguely wrong, as if it had been made by someone who didn't really understand human fashion. The rest of his clothing was similar: plain and tan and not quite right.

Was that one of the prices of treason? she wondered. Bad tailoring? Being out of fashion?

The man said, "A direct stare is a challenge. It's one of the things that is the same in both species. That's why he looked down. He's indicating that he isn't interested in a fight."

"Good," she said.

"I was told that you are the person I should talk to about the lights in the ocean."

She nodded, still looking at the grey man.

"Could I come on board? I'm afraid they come with me, and they're going to want to check to make sure there's nothing I can harm or that can harm me."

She looked at him directly. He was as ordinary as the first time she had seen him on the comm screen. This time his hair was dry; it curled, and there was a lot of grey in the sandy brown. His face was very pale, as if it had been years since he'd spent time in the sun.

"You're the translator," she said, figuring that was more polite than calling him a traitor.

He nodded.

What the hell? Why not? She might never get a chance to be this close to a *hwarhath* again. She nodded.

He spoke to the alien. The two soldiers climbed on board and searched.

"Be careful," Anna called after them. Nicholas added something in the alien language, then swung himself on board. He leaned on the rail, looking out at the bay. One of the pseudosiphonophores began to flash, yellow, green, white, yellow: a name, almost certainly. *I am me. I am me.*

"Okay," he said. "What are they?"

She told him, then added, "The trouble is—we know their intelligence is related to size. We figured that out from studying the little ones. These fellows are half-grown and half-bright, most likely. The really big ones stay out in the ocean, and we haven't figured out how to reach them."

The soldiers came out of the cabin and stood, watching each other and Nicholas. The boy—the marine—looked nervous. She could not read the expression on the alien's face or even be sure that he had an expression. The posture of his body indicated alertness but no tension. He wasn't worried, but he was paying attention, though he never looked anyone straight in the face.

"That's all very interesting," said Nicholas. "But I can't see any reason why you'd think the animals might be intelligent."

Half a dozen were flashing now. Tonight the messages were all different. Not a chorus; maybe a sextet, or maybe random noise.

"What can I tell you? It's easy to decide that a species is intelligent when it's like us. Your buddy over there, for example. No one ever had a question about the *hwar*. From the first time we saw one of their ships—from the first time they took a shot at us—we knew."

He glanced at her, but said nothing.

"These fellows here"—she waved at the bay—"are *seriously* alien; and we aren't sure what constitutes evidence for intelligence in a seagoing animal that doesn't use tools. Why are you asking, anyway?"

"I'm curious. We've been leaving after dark the last few days, and when I look down, there they are, flashing; and they're visible from the island—patches of light, bobbing in the ocean. Those are the little ones, you said.

"And I have time to kill. They are trying a social event tonight. A crazy idea, but the general is curious. He has never seen a group of humans having fun. I don't think it's going to work. The *hwarhath* don't eat as a recreation; for them it's either a necessity or a sacrament. They do drink as a recreation, but their drinking parties are nasty. I avoid them as much as possible." He paused for a moment, looking out at the bay. "I had a horrible fantasy of watching the general trying to make cocktail-party conversation or deal—for the first time—with a canapé."

"How are the talks going?" she asked.

He shrugged. "It's early days, and my area of competence is not diplomacy."

She wanted to ask him how he had gotten into this situation, but there didn't seem to be a way. How *does* one betray one's species? She talked some more about the animals in the bay, formally known as *Pseudosiphonophora gigantans*. Then she wound down into silence, and they stood together looking at the bay.

He seemed relaxed, leaning on the rail, his hands clasped loosely in front of him; but she had a sense of tension and loneliness. The sense of tension would come from something in his body, so slight that she wasn't noticing it consciously. She had no idea why she thought he was lonely. Reading in, maybe.

He pushed himself upright. "Time to get going. If I know the general, he'll be getting bored by now and maybe toxic. Alcohol does absolutely nothing to the *hwarhath*. But he brought his own stuff along." He paused. "Thank you for the information. There's a line from an old book—I don't remember the name—about learning. It's the one certain source of pleasure, and the one consolation that never fails." He grinned. "All I have been learning about lately is furniture. Believe me, it is not adequate."

He left, the two soldiers following. She stood watching, till the men vanished into darkness. What an odd conversation.

# V

➤➤➤ RAYMOND CALLED HER in the morning as she was leaving work.

"Please come to my office, Anna." He saw the expression on her face and added, "It's important."

She grabbed coffee and a muffin at the dining hall, then went, feeling angry. She did not like Ray at the best of times, and she certainly had not voted for him in the last election. But, in fairness, he was a perfectly adequate director of the station, and he knew how to get along with the dips and the military. At the moment, this was a useful ability.

There was someone with him, sitting opposite the big desk, a woman in uniform. Her skin was the same dark color as Anna's coffee. She had the regulation haircut, and her skull shone as if polished. Her hair, the regulation narrow band, was bleached pure white. Earrings made of little glass beads dangled from her ears.

Ray said, "This is Major Ndo."

"Please sit down," the major said.

Anna obeyed, feeling uneasy. There were crumbs on her shirt and pants. She brushed them off, then looked for a place to set her cup down. There was nothing except the floor.

The major said, "You had a conversation last night with Nicholas Sanders. I want you to repeat it for me. Please be as accurate as possible and explain the biology."

"Why?"

Raymond said, "Anna, please."

She did it.

When she finished, the major nodded. "Very good. It's very close to the recording, except that you have gone into more detail. Do you have anything else to add? Any observations?"

She liked the man, but that was nothing she was going to say to the military. "No. Who is he?"

The woman hesitated. "There is nothing I can tell you, Mem Perez. All the information is sensitive. Not protected, but definitely sensitive."

"I don't want to sound like a kid, but that doesn't seem especially fair. I've just given you everything you asked for."

The major nodded. "You're right. It isn't fair. I'm not going to give you the line about life not being fair, because I've always thought the line was stupid and un-useful.

"Your problem isn't that life is unfair. Your problem is that *I'm* unfair." She grinned. "It's always a good idea to make a clear distinction between the armed forces and the universe.

"All I can tell you is the obvious. The negotiations are important; the situation is sensitive; this fucker is right in the middle; and he's protected by diplomatic immunity."

Ray said, "Thank you for your help, Anna."

She left, forgetting her cup. It was still half-full. With luck, Ray would knock it over.

The next time she saw Nicholas, he was at the door to her room, sunlight shining around him. He wore the same kind of clothing as before, made of tan fabric and oddly cut. In the sunlight, his hair looked much more grey than brown.

"How did you find me?"

"I stopped a man and asked." He grinned. "I didn't know your name, but I said 'the woman who talks endlessly about those things in the bay.' That was sufficient. Would you like to go for a walk?''

"What about the negotiations?''

"I asked the general for a day off. I'm not the only translator, and I am really tired of sitting. He knows what I'm like when I don't get enough exercise.''

She thought for a moment. "Okay.''

"The Twins come with.'' He moved slightly, and she looked past him. The marine was there, the boy, and an alien. She didn't know if it was the same one.

"Give me a moment.''

He stayed in the open door, leaning against the frame. The tension in his body had a manic quality. At first she thought he might be kiting. But his eyes were moving and focusing normally. The irises, she noticed, were an odd dark green, the color of New World jade. She had never seen eyes that color before. She didn't know any drug that affected the color of irises, though of course drugs were not her specialty. In any case, the expression on his face was alert. The man was not on drugs. He was happy.

She got a jacket. They started away from the station.

"Up the hill?'' asked Nicholas.

"It's off-limits.''

Nicholas looked back at the marine. "Corporal?''

"Yes, sir, it is to station personnel.''

"But not to me?''

"I'm not sure. I think you could go up. But not with the mem.''

"That doesn't make sense.'' He looked around. "I want to get up on top of something high and stare into the distance. There.'' He pointed to another hill at the south edge of the human settlement. "Is that okay?''

"I have no orders about that one, sir. It ought to be okay.''

The day was bright and very windy. The hill was steep, and there had been a heavy frost, which was melting now, making the ground cover wet and slippery. They went slowly, the two soldiers having the most trouble, since they were carrying weapons.

"Hey," the boy called finally. "Slow down."

She looked back, as did Nicholas. The soldiers were well behind and below them.

"We'll wait at the top," said Nicholas and went on.

"Sir!" The boy scrambled forward and slipped. A moment later, he was rolling and sliding toward the bottom of the hill, still holding his rifle.

Nicholas called in the language of the *hwarhath*. The other soldier scrambled after the boy.

"Sloppy," Nicholas said. "They really ought to train them better. Of course, they train them to obey orders, not to think; and his orders are probably a bit contradictory. I don't think the people in the compound have come to any kind of agreement about me."

"What is the distance on a recorder?" she asked.

The boy had stopped rolling. He had finally let go of the gun. The alien picked it up and held it out, waiting for the boy to get up and take it. The body of the alien expressed indifferent courtesy.

"Like the one the corporal has? It might still be picking us up." He looked around. "Goddess, what a lovely day! Everything is gold and blue. I really miss the out-of-doors. If you are worried about recorders, I have one. Don't say anything you don't want analyzed by the *hwarhath* security people."

"This sounds like a really tedious way to live." They were high enough up to have a good view of the ocean. Whitecaps dotted it. Nicholas was right: a truly lovely day.

"At the moment, I'm finding it kind of amusing. That's probably the weather and the fact that I'm not sitting almost motionless for hours in a room that has no windows."

The two soldiers climbed up to them. The boy's face was flushed. His uniform was rumpled and stained.

"Don't ever do that again, sir."

"What?"

"Go on ahead, when I ask you to wait. I might have had to shoot you."

Nicholas shook his head. "Think a long time before you do that, Corporal. Hattin is along to keep me alive. He has very clear orders in that area."

The boy looked stubborn. "I'll do what I have to."

The alien watched them with an air of detachment. As usual, he did not look anyone directly in the eye, but she had a strong sense that he was seeing pretty much everything.

"He doesn't know any English, does he?" Anna said.

"No, and he doesn't want to. Hattin is a very sweet kid, but lacking in curiosity. He has no interest at all in foreign deviants."

"And he never meets anyone's gaze."

"I'm senior to him. The *hwarhath* men pay a lot of attention to hierarchy. A junior man simply will not stare at someone who is his superior in rank. The corporal is his equal but also his enemy; if you stare at an enemy, you are inviting a fight; and I told him that you are a woman. *Hwarhath* men do not look at women, unless the women are members of the same lineage."

They started climbing again. The soldiers kept close. When they reached the top of the hill, Anna said, "What do you mean by foreign deviants? Is that like foreign devils?"

"Sort of. Hattin is—how can I describe him?—traditional. He knows right behavior when he sees it; it's the kind of behavior he learned at home as a child. Anything different is either boring or disturbing. Look at the view!"

On one side of them were the bay and the station, the compound above everything. Its domes had been treated with something that made them corrode quickly, at least on the surface; they were copper green, rust red and a dull, rough-looking gold.

On the other side, the hill sloped down to a wide beach and the ocean. The bottom was shallow. Waves broke in long white lines.

"How *did* you get into this situation?" she asked.

He laughed. "That's the kind of question the *hwarhath* would ask. They're very direct, as a group. If they want to know something, they ask and don't worry much about politeness. If you don't want to answer, you say 'I will not talk about that.' "

He paused for a while and stared at the ocean. "They don't lie much. Remember the line about the ancient Persians? It's probably in Herodotus. They taught their men to ride and shoot a bow and tell the truth. The *hwarhath* are like that, except the weapons they learn to use are a lot more impressive."

"Does that mean you don't want to talk about it?"

He paused again. "Not at the moment."

They walked along the crest of the hill. The spore stalks had released all their spores and were no longer feathery. They bent in the wind like reeds.

Very nice. Very relaxing. Or maybe that wasn't the right word. Happy-making. The wind carried away ennui and lassitude.

After a while Nicholas said, "I don't want you to get the idea that the *hwarhath* are all like Hattin. They vary as much as humanity, though over a different range. The general, for example, is much less conservative and much more curious."

"Who are you talking to?" asked Anna.

He grinned. "You, among other people. Let's go back down. I want to learn more about your animals."

They went to the bay, the soldiers following. When

they reached the boat, Nicholas paused and said something to the alien. Anna went into the cabin.

"We have company, Yosh."

Nicholas came in, ducking under the rather low doorway. Yoshi stood, polite and a little uneasy. He was never entirely comfortable around strangers.

"This is—" Anna hesitated. "Do you have a title or rank?"

He nodded. "A literal translation would be 'holder.' It's roughly equivalent to captain."

"Captain Sanders. Dr. Nagamitsu Yoshi. The captain is interested in our guys in the bay."

Yoshi looked puzzled. He was trying to place Nicholas and not managing. Someone from the compound, obviously. There were no strangers at the station. But he wasn't getting any further. She could almost see his mind working, trying to recall which human community used a title like holder.

"Why don't you explain the equipment, Yosh?"

He did: the sonar and radar, the underwater cameras and mikes, the equipment that measured the flow of water in the bay. He explained how samples were taken and analyzed. Finally he explained about Moby.

All this time, the soldiers remained outside. The boy was visible in the doorway. (Yoshi glanced at him from time to time, bemused.) Anna did not see the alien.

"You're talking to them, using the float," said Nicholas.

"We are communicating," Yoshi said. "There is no question about that; but we are not certain that we are having conversations. For one thing, they don't seem to have much of a grammar. Our tendency is to think that any intelligent creature must have a way to make statements of relationship, to speak about cause-and-effect.

"We say words to them. They say other words back, or sometimes the same words. They can act like parrots, especially during the mating season. You must have seen the displays the last few weeks. Have you been here long?"

"Since the *hwarhath* arrived," said Nicholas.

"Ah," said Yoshi. He still hadn't figured out who the other man was.

She was watching a really fine example of Watsonian thinking, called that (of course) in honor of Sherlock Holmes's companion, a man much maligned. The good doctor wasn't stupid. He simply did not make certain kinds of connections—like Yoshi at the moment, who was going on to explain how they had taught the animals to sing "Mary Had a Little Lamb."

"We translated it into the international emergency code and flashed it on Moby—this was during mating season, of course—and they picked it up. We could not get them to do it as a round; they kept wanting to synchronize. A splendid sight, but not the behavior of an intelligent species."

"Why not?" asked Nicholas. "You're talking about singing in chorus. Humans do it, and so do the *hwarhath*."

"They do?" said Yoshi. "I did not realize." And still the international monetary unit did not drop. "It's the parroting I mean. They do far too much repeating—with us and with one another. This is not a sign of intelligence."

"Isn't this a fake problem?" asked Nicholas. "Intelligence is a slippery word, and so are most of the words that might be synonyms. Understanding, consciousness, apprehension in the old sense, reason. To what extent is it meaningful to talk about intelligence in any kind of being? Humans or the *hwarhath,* computers, dolphins and whales? And anyway, why do you care?"

Yoshi looked reproachful. "We want someone to talk to. Someone who understands."

"Then talk to the fellows up the hill, though I wouldn't bet money on how much they're going to understand." Nicholas looked at the corporal. "Do you have the time?"

The boy glanced at the butt of his rifle. "Fifteen hundred fifty."

"I'd better get going. The plane leaves early sometimes." He turned to Yoshi, whose mouth was open. "Thank you, Dr. Nagamitsu. Goodbye, Anna."

He ducked out of the cabin, and Yoshi said, "That is the man—"

"Uh-huh," said Anna. "I kept waiting for you to figure it out. Didn't you notice his clothes?"

"I thought maybe something had happened to fashion on Earth, or maybe it was some kind of uniform. I don't pay much attention to the military. There are so many of them, and they come in so many different varieties. Who can possibly keep track? What have you gotten yourself into, Anna?"

"Nothing that matters. The people at the compound know what's going on. He's not running around loose. He isn't going to do anyone any harm."

# VI

➤➤➤ THE GENERAL'S OFFICE (the current one, on the island) has the bleak, spare look of something meant to be temporary: grey walls, grey wall-to-wall carpeting, a work-table and two chairs.

There are no windows. A tapestry hangs opposite the table. It's large and simple and has the look of something that belongs in a public space. I've never seen it in any of his rooms. He must have gotten it out of the main ship storage: something to cover an empty wall.

In the middle of the tapestry is a fire, done in red and orange and yellow. Colors radiate out, less intense than the colors of the fire, but still bright and warm, as if the fire is lighting the ground around it. As the distance from the fire increases, the colors begin to dim and turn a little grey. Finally, halfway to the edge of the tapestry, the radiating colors meet the swords, which are definitely grey—a cold hue that looks hard. They are arranged in a circle, laid point to hilt, touching one another, so the circle is continuous. It would make better sense for them to be pointing out, I've always figured. But this works visually. Beyond the swords, the tapestry is black, dotted with white: space and the stars.

The Hearth in a Ring of Swords. As far as I know, it's the oldest emblem for the People, though this version is obviously comparatively recent, created after the People realized their world—their hearth—was surrounded by darkness. **[Yes.]** For them the image has great power. To me it has always seemed—how can I put it? Like a ball made of the seeds of a valuable food plant grown in central North America on Earth. [?]

Every couple of days I go to the office. The general sits quietly at his table, looking at the tapestry. I try to sit quietly in the other chair, though I think better when in motion.

We discuss the negotiations, taking them apart, trying to figure out what the humans are thinking, analyzing the reactions of the other people on the *hwarhath* team. Some of them have close ties to other frontmen. Their loyalty is not entirely to him.

If the general gets involved in the discussion—seriously interested, thoughtful—then he is likely to pick up a stylus and turn it in his hands. It is a human gesture, though the hands are considerably different: the little finger much longer than it would be on a human, the thumb also very long and narrow. There is fur like grey velvet on the backs of the hands. The fingernails are narrow, at least in comparison to human nails, and thick. If they aren't clipped, they start to curl under, turning into claws.

I can go for days and weeks without really seeing him and—all at once—there he is, real and solid and alien.

I said, "The kid, the human soldier, told me he was willing to kill me."

The general waited, his hands folded.

"You made it very clear that I had to be persona grata, and the human diplomats agreed."

He asked me to explain "persona grata."

"It means they aren't supposed to kill me. I think we may have mis-estimated the balance of power between the diplomats and the military people. That kid takes his orders from the military. If he was telling the truth, and he does not look the least bit like a liar, then the military people are not listening to the diplomats."

He looked irritated. "Can humans do nothing in an

orderly fashion? Why did they send two different groups of people to handle one set of negotiations? We are talking about war and the rules of war. There ought to be no one here except people who know how and why to fight."

"At the moment, I'd rather deal with diplomats. The soldiers make me uneasy."

He sat looking at the tapestry for a while. "There isn't enough here. You have brought me ten words, spoken by a carrier. We don't know if he spoke correctly or understood his orders. We don't know what is in the minds of those in front of him."

I opened my mouth. He held up a hand. "I'm not going to throw this information away, but I am going to put it to the side. We'll continue as before and see what happens."

He was speaking in his public voice, which meant the time for discussion was over. I stood up.

He said, "Find out more about the animals in the ocean, the ones that may be intelligent."

"They're no good at all as enemies. They are not likely to ever have any kind of technology, and they are certainly never going into space."

He made a noncommittal noise. It is always worth looking for new enemies. **[True.]**

The base is in the middle of the island. (If the *hwarhath* want to look at an ocean, they turn on a holo.) After I left the office, I went to the shore. The tide was out, what little tide there is. I walked along the narrow gravel beach.

I've met some of the people who take care of the action for military intelligence. (Not among the *hwarhath*. They've been careful to keep me away from those areas. But among the humans.) I don't like them. There is too much plotting, too much posturing—especially about toughness—too much secrecy, too much fascination with technology, too much unnecessary elaboration.

Dangerous people. Eaters of rats and poisoners of socks. **[?]** They are here on this planet, I am almost certain.

I've seen people who have the look in the corridors of the diplomatic compound; and when they look at me, they look hungry.

I went all the way around the island. A good idea. The wind blew, waves foamed, and I got a considerable amount of exercise.

At one point, on a beach of black sand, I found something that looked as if it belonged in the Field Museum of Natural History in Chicago, in one of those lovely ancient dusty exhibits. *Life in the Devonian.*

It was about a meter long with a narrow segmented body and a very wide head, shaped approximately like a hammer. The damn thing was moving slowly up from the ocean on many little legs, moving its awkward head from side to side, obviously hunting. I couldn't see a mouth or any eyes.

I stopped. It went past me, a few centimeters from my shoes. Apparently, I didn't matter: wasn't edible, did not represent a danger. It kept going slowly over the wet black sand, head moving back and forth. I went on.

From the journal of Sanders Nicholas,
information-holder attached to the staff
of First-Defender Ettin Gwarha
CODED FOR REVIEW BY ETTIN GWARHA ONLY

# VII

➤➤➤ SHE GOT ANOTHER call from Ray in the morning. He looked tired and worried.

"The same thing again?" she asked.

He nodded.

She went to his office. The major was in the same chair as before. This time her earrings were silver: little bats, their wings spread, shining in the early-morning sunlight.

Anna sat down and leaned forward, taking another look.

The major said, "I belong to an organization that is devoted to the conservation of bats."

Bats? thought Anna.

"They're useful and interesting animals, and God knows how many species have become extinct in the past two hundred years. We have done terrible things to Earth, Mem Perez." She paused for a moment, obviously thinking about something that angered her. "Nine billion people! How could we?" The major glanced at Ray, behind his wide impressive desk as if behind a barricade. "You can go, Sab Medawar. Thank you for your help."

Ray opened his mouth, closed it and got up.

After the door shut, the major looked at Anna. "Nicholas Sanders came looking for you."

"Yes."

"Do you have any idea why?"

She thought for a moment. "I can tell you what he told

me. He wanted information about my research, and he wanted company on a walk."

The major moved her head, dismissing the problem. "People don't always have good reasons for what they do. They certainly don't always have reasons we can understand. I am going to ask your help in dealing with this man."

"Why?"

"It's possible he won't visit you again. If he does, we'd like you to carry a recorder and to report back to us. You make your living by observation; we'd be interested in what you think you see."

"Why should I help you?"

The major looked down at a screen, which lay on one knee. She tapped a button. "I like to make lists of everything. There are three reasons which have occurred to me. You will be helping your government and your species. Your field is nonhuman intelligence; and the only unquestioned example of nonhuman intelligence is—" She paused and listened. "—flying over us right now. The *hwarhath*. Most of the information about them is protected. I can get access to some of it for you. You won't be able to publish, but you will know."

"That is very tempting," said Anna.

"Reason number three is your jellyfish." The major paused. "We are facing a dilemma in this area. If Sanders is interested in them, then the people he works for must be, and if that is so, then maybe the information about them is strategic. Though we can't imagine how. Still and all, maybe the information ought to be protected."

"Wait a minute," Anna said.

The major raised a hand. "Don't get angry yet. Our inclination is to leave that situation as it is. We are much more interested in Sanders."

"What I think I am hearing," said Anna, "is I should work for you in order to protect the status of my research.

If I don't, *you* might protect it, and I won't be able to publish.''

The major nodded. ''That's right. A threat, a bribe and an appeal to patriotism. That is what I am offering.''

''I need to think.''

''Of course,'' said the major.

She headed for the door. Behind her the major said, ''We know you told Sanders about the recorder Corporal Ling has been carrying. If you decide to help us, Mem Perez, remember that your loyalty must not be divided.''

''Okay.'' She opened the door.

The day was mild with very little wind. She walked along the narrow gravel beach that edged the bay. Little bugs hurried among the stones, and the morning sunlight was hitting the water at just the right angle. Here and there, she could make out something gleaming under the surface. A bell undulating. A tentacle waving. By this time the pseudosiphonophores had begun the slow and careful ritual of reassurance and— She hesitated. Was it right to call it seduction?

The animals were close enough to touch each other now. The stinging tendrils would be kept down, twitching now and then. It was very hard for these animals not to attack one another. At this point, she was almost certain, the mating tendrils were still safely curled. But soon—in the next few days—they would be extended. The actual exchange of material was very brief; and then there was the long slow process of disengaging—not physically, that was easy and over almost at once, but emotionally. Again, she was using loaded words, reading in.

For days after, the animals would repeat their messages of reassurance and their statements of identity. *I am me. I mean no harm.* Gradually, the colors would fade; the rhythms would slow; the patterns would become more erratic; one by one, the pseudosiphonophores would move out into the ocean.

She stopped and looked out at the bay. She loved the animals. She could not bear the idea of not publishing. Who was Nicholas to her? A stranger, a traitor. She would tell the major yes.

She walked back to her room quickly, afraid that she would change her mind, and called around until she found the major.

When she gave her answer, the dark face broke into a smile. "Good. Come up to the compound this evening. There is someone I want you to meet. I think you'll like him. And mem—from this time on, from the point of our conversation this morning, everything I say to you is protected."

Anna nodded.

She went to bed and lay unable to sleep. This was not a good situation. She was getting into something that was ethically ambiguous and possibly stupid and certainly over her head. After a while she dozed and had nightmares, involving the research boat and lots of tentacles.

Her clock woke her. She got up and took a shower, got dressed and went to the compound. Nightfall was coming early now, and the sky was dark enough for stars. The center of the galaxy shone above her, a band of pale light. A couple of the gas giants were visible: one directly above her (ruddy), the other above the compound (yellow).

The guard at the door had her name. Another soldier led her to the major's office: a good-sized room, paneled in something that could not be wood but looked convincing. On one wall was a holo of Earth, taken from space, white clouds swirling and the whole planet very slowly turning.

There was no desk, only a circle of four chairs, low and comfortable, around a little table. On the table was a silver tea service and three china cups. It was pretty close to the last thing Anna had expected. Maybe she hadn't just entered the world of espionage. Maybe this was Wonderland or Oz.

She looked at the major. She had not changed into the Mad Hatter or the Scarecrow, and the little man in the next chair over was perfectly ordinary.

"This is Captain Van," said the major. "He's one of our translators."

He rose. They shook and sat down. The major poured tea. It was dark brown. Indian. There was a plate of tiny sandwiches. The major handed them around.

Captain Van said, "The major has an odd sense of humor. If you're going to be working with us, you had better know that. It does not affect the quality of her work."

The major smiled and ate a sandwich, then picked up a screen computer. "Everything I am going to tell you and the captain is going to tell you is protected. Formally protected, using stamps and file-locks and 'for your eyes only' codes. Now in some cases this should never have happened. The material is not sensitive and never has been. In other cases, the material was sensitive twenty years ago, but isn't any longer. In a few cases, we are going to tell you information we really do not want let out. In all cases, you are going to be all the way up shit creek if you talk. Is that understood?"

Anna nodded and took another tiny sandwich. It was delicious.

The major turned on her screen. "Okay. There was a ship called the *Free Market Explorer,* which vanished twenty years ago." She grinned. "The name makes it sound like a freighter. It was a very fast long-distance ship, the best we had at the time, and it vanished in *hwar* space. We have always assumed that it was destroyed.

"One of the people on the *Free Market Explorer* was a man named Nicholas Sanders. He was a captain in military intelligence. He should not have been. He did not have the right personality. But he was, at that point, one of the few people really fluent in the main *hwar* language."

"The man here," said Anna.

The major nodded. "We don't have a positive identification, but I'm almost entirely certain. Sanders was twenty-six when his ship vanished. He would be forty-seven now, and I think that's approximately the age of our Nicholas. He has lived for twenty years behind enemy lines."

"Would you like more tea?" asked Captain Van.

Anna nodded.

The captain poured, and the major went on. "I'm going to have to explain something about the problem of gathering information in this—what can we call it? A war has never been declared, and we have never fought a real battle. For close to forty years there have been voyages of exploration, spying missions, now and then a skirmish."

She looked down at her screen. "There are several problems. To begin with, the immensity of space and the nature of FTL travel. We have no guarantee that the aliens come from anywhere near here. We think—though we are not certain—that they have expanded very rapidly from their home system, as have we. We think we're looking at two enormous and almost empty spheres that have come into contact, that are touching lightly. I have said the spheres are empty. They are full of stars—thousands, maybe millions; and we are looking for maybe a dozen inhabited worlds."

A good speaker, thought Anna, though she still had the feeling that she was at a mad tea party. It was the combination of enormous distances and tiny sandwiches, and the little captain sitting quietly, almost sleepily. He was starting to look like a dormouse.

"That is one set of problems," the major said. "Problems of scale. The other set of problems has to do with psychology.

"The aliens are paranoid or careful or maybe something else that we don't understand, something genuinely alien. The first time we met them, they were ready for war. They expected us or some other enemy. Their ships and stations were armed *and* booby-trapped. We have never captured a ship with its navigational system intact.

"And there have always been problems with questioning the aliens, the few we have managed to capture. At first, we did not have a way to speak to them. We managed, finally, to decode—would that be the right term?—their main language. Nicholas Sanders was on the team that did that. He's very good at languages."

The little captain nodded.

"At the same time we had another problem, and this one we have not been able to solve. The aliens die easily. If you give them any chance at all, they will kill themselves. If that isn't possible, then they will refuse to eat. If they are force-fed, they fail to thrive."

So would almost anyone, thought Anna. She felt mildly ill, thinking of people like Hattin strapped down somewhere with tubes running into them. It was a kind of rape.

"It's been difficult keeping the few we have managed to capture alive long enough to learn anything.

"Maybe the first ones—the ones we could not speak to—had information that would have been really useful; but they died before we could question them; and the ones we have been able to question—" The major looked frustrated. "They haven't known the things we really want to know. This may be due to chance. How many experts on military engineering are there in any population, even the population of an FTL ship? And how many experts on navigation? And what are the chances of getting one of these people alive?

"Or maybe, once they knew we were here, the enemy moved the people with sensitive information back to safety, wherever that may be." The major grinned. The grin was nasty. "There are times I think that's all I ever say: 'I don't know. We don't know. They don't know. Nobody knows.' "

"What does this have to do with me?" asked Anna.

"After close to forty years of trying, all we know is a little about their military technology and a little about their culture. Now, here in front of us is a man who has lived among the aliens for twenty years. God knows what he has told them. God knows what he has learned."

"What are you going to do?"

"Try to get him back. He's been turned once. Maybe he can be turned again."

"You want my help."

The major nodded.

"I don't think I'd be any good at playing Mata Hari."

"Who?" said the little captain.

"A spy," said the major. "Out of Western history, a woman who got information by seducing men."

"Ah." The captain set down his teacup. "I think I had better tell you some more about Sanders. What I have learned in the course of the negotiations." He sat for a moment, obviously considering. "I am going to have to tell you something about the *hwarhath* main language. I apologize for this. The major has already given you a lot of background."

She got the sense that the captain thought she had been given too much information already. Why? Did he think it was sensitive? Or irrelevant? It wasn't, as far as she could tell, anything she didn't know or couldn't have figured out, except the material about the alien prisoners. She did not like to think about them dying.

"The language has fifty-six forms of the second-person singular," said the captain. "The variables are the sex of person being addressed, the comparative rank of the two people involved, the degree of relationship, if any. Are they close relatives? Distant relatives? Or not related at all?

Finally there is the degree of emotional closeness. Is this a good friend? Is this a person one loves?

"Sanders has been doing most of the translating. He is always very formal, very deferential to the *hwarhath*. His title—holder—is not a high one."

"It's the one thing about this situation that makes me happy," the major said. "He was a captain twenty years ago, and he's still a captain now. Changing sides did absolutely nothing for his career."

Captain Van nodded. "When he addresses the *hwarhath*, he always uses the form of 'you' which indicates that he is speaking to a male of higher rank, not related to him and with whom he has no emotional relationship. And they—almost every time—have replied using the reciprocal form, indicating that they are speaking to a junior male, unrelated and a comparative stranger.

"However, the *hwar* act strangely around him." The captain paused. "I have to go cautiously here. I'm talking about something other than hard facts. They are—except for the general—too courteous. It's in the way they move around him. They give him a lot of room, and they pay attention to where he is and what he's doing. They don't expect him to get out of the way; and they do not meet his gaze. Sanders has been among these people a long time. He ought to have learned to keep his eyes down. But he forgets occasionally, and only the general will stare him down. The others glance to the side.

"He acts—and they act—as if he is more important than he seems.

"Which leads to a second consideration. He and the general sometimes talk in a language which is not, apparently, known to the other *hwar*. It is almost certainly a *hwarhath* language, though it is not closely related to the one we have learned. My own feeling is that it's the general's language. I don't think he is a native speaker of the language we know." Captain Van smiled. "He is easier to understand than the other *hwarhath* or than Sanders.

"After I had noticed all of this, I began to pay very close attention to Sanders and the general. I'm not our main translator. I did not have to spend my time thinking about technical problems of language. Instead, I could concentrate on the aliens as people.

"Once, at the end of a very long day, the general switched languages. He said something in his language, then went to the other language, and I think what happened is that he did not change his thinking quickly enough. He addressed Sanders, and he used the intimate form of 'you.' The truly intimate form of 'you,' which says nothing about rank or familial relationship. It indicates only the sex of the person being addressed. Gender is always important to the *hwarhath*.

"As far as we can tell, this form is used for members of a person's immediate family, for very good friends—who are usually friends from childhood—and for acknowledged lovers.

"I checked the recording later," the captain said. "I heard the general correctly, and I was able—then, looking at the recording—to examine the other people on the *hwarhath* negotiating team. They froze. A couple had expressions that might have been discomfort or embarrassment. I have a hard time reading *hwar* expressions. Their language is easier, and so is their body language.

"What interested me was Sanders. He did not react at all, and I would have noticed it if a human had been shocked or embarrassed; and when he answered the general, he used the general's full title. Not First-Defender, which is what he almost always uses, but Defender-of-the-Hearth-with-Honor First-Ahead."

"I'm not sure I'm following this," Anna said.

"I think the general was using the form he habitually

uses with Sanders, most likely the one he had been using a moment before in the other language.

"When Sanders used his full title, he was reminding him, 'That is not appropriate here.' "

Anna thought for a moment. "What you are telling me—what I think you are telling me—is that Nicholas has a sexual relationship with a person who is covered with grey fur."

"Well," said the major. "He isn't part of the general's family, and he isn't a friend from childhood, and as far as we can tell, the enemy do not have what we would call a normal sex life. Not any of them."

Anna laughed. "What do you mean?"

"I mean exactly what I am saying. We have found an entire culture, maybe an entire species, that does not practice heterosexuality, except maybe—we are not certain about this—as a perversion."

"How do they reproduce?"

"How do you think?" The major was obviously uncomfortable. Funny, she had no trouble talking about war and people dying. "Modern medical technology. Artificial insemination."

That made sense. But how had a culture like that developed? And why? And what had it done before the development of modern medical technology? Anna opened her mouth to ask the first of many questions.

"I went back over Sanders' file," the major said. "There was nothing in it—absolutely nothing—that indicated any problems in relation to sexuality. All his psychological tests were fine. He never married, but a lot of people in MI find it hard to form long-term relationships."

How do you test for a willingness to get sexually involved with aliens? Especially if no aliens are available? Anna tried to imagine a new version of the MMPI.

Answer yes or no:

"I find grey fur sexually exciting."

"I have fantasies about people with bright blue eyes and horizontal pupils."

She put her teacup down. "I think I've gotten as much information as I can handle at the moment; and I'm late for work. Could this be continued?"

The major looked at the captain, who nodded. He seemed uncomfortable, but Anna had a sense that it wasn't the aliens who were bothering him. It was the major. He had obviously been trained in one of the behavioral sciences. Most likely he was less disturbed by the variation to be found in people and their cultures.

Anna stood up.

The major said, "Remember, none of this information is for public consumption."

She wasn't inclined to run down the hill and grab someone and talk about the sex lives of the aliens or Nicholas Sanders, or the fact that she had gotten herself into something that was seriously weird. "Don't worry, Major. All I want to do right now is go and watch a bunch of creatures, who are all of them both sexes, negotiate their one and only annual fuck. Good night."

She had an excellent view of the bay as she went down the hill. It was ablaze with light, as were the channel and the ocean. At first, she felt stunned more than anything else; then she started to think about the *hwar* culture. This was interesting. This was going to be fun. After a while, she felt a need to laugh and did.

# VIII

➤➤➤ I SPENT THE evening in the general's quarters, watching a hero play. Gwarha was drinking—not quickly, but steadily, which meant he would be toxic by the end of the evening. This is a problem that is not getting better. **[Thank you for the warning.]**

I had wine. He'd brought half a dozen bottles back from the party on the mainland. I wasn't drinking much. I'm no longer used to alcohol, and if both of us got drunk we'd end by arguing about either the play or the negotiations.

He'd set up the holo against the far wall, facing the couch, which was long and low and not especially comfortable. *Hwarhath* furniture is not designed for people my height. When he turned on the machine, the wall vanished; there was the stage with two men on it, dressed in brightly painted armor. Long feathers were attached to their helmets and bobbed and waved with every slight motion. It ought to have been funny, but it wasn't. The men stood almost facing one another, and their gazes crossed at an angle, like swords at the beginning of a duel. There was music, the strange *hwarhath* noises that I am finally—after twenty years—able to hear as music. The piece was new, but retold a very old story, and the instruments were deliberately antique: chimes, a bell, a whistle and a drum.

Gwarha got the intent look he does when he settles in to watch one of these damn fool things. **[?]** I got ready to not listen.

The music stopped. The men faced one another directly, and the play began.

I used to be interested, back when I was first learning about the *hwarhath*. The costumes are always splendid, and the works themselves can have the spare beauty of a Noh play. They are almost never longer than half an *ikun*. They almost never have more than five characters. The speeches are brief, and the sets are close to nonexistent. They are always about men who have to deal with a horrible ethical problem: a conflict between two kinds of honor, a conflict between two equal and opposing loyalties.

Personal honor set against a lineage.

A lover set against a lineage.

A lineage set against the People.

Impossible choices, which have to be made in a little over an hour. And most of the time you die at the end, no matter what kind of choice you made.

I stayed interested a while longer in the plays that involved women. (The female roles are played by men, of course. This is an entirely male art form.)

What does a man do when he discovers that his mother is a danger to the lineage? Now, there is a scary problem. There is no way for any sane *hwarhath* man to offer violence to a woman or a child. But the lineage—like women and children—must be defended.

A serious dilemma.

I stayed interested, I think, because it was so hard to find out anything about *hwarhath* women—for me at least, living on the perimeter. (Gwarha wasn't about to take a human home to visit the sacred family and the aunts.) **[I think I will not make a comment here.]**

In the same category as plays about women, or maybe in a slightly different category, are the plays about heterosexual love. They have always struck me as funny. My response is shocking to the *hwarhath*. For them these plays have a sick fascination. Children are never allowed to see them; and at times, when the mood of the Weaving is conservative, they have been banned entirely. They are always violent and often verge on serious ugliness. They always end in craziness and blood.

Often, at the end, after the bodies have picked themselves up and walked offstage, the main character will return and speak an epilogue. (The *hwarhath* love morals.) This is what happens when the violence of the perimeter is brought into the center. Everything is destroyed. The family cannot survive.

There is one final kind of hero play, which does (I guess) still interest me. The plays about the *rahaka:* the men who will not die, who keep on living when any normal person would have chosen the option.

For example, a man whose lineage has been destroyed: the men killed except for him, the women and children integrated into another lineage. Every connection he has to the world has been broken, but he struggles to survive. Toward what end? Why? It is a problem that fascinates the *hwarhath.* They die easily, compared to human, and they don't understand what makes some people continue without any good reason. Most of the time they figure it is some kind of defect in character; but sometimes they suspect it is another kind of heroism.

There is an old and famous play about a warrior who is slowly dying of some terrible disease. He sits on the stage. Ghosts and people visit him. They talk. He is offered the option. He does not take it. Instead he continues slowly to die. Late in the play (it is longer than usual) he lies down, too weak to sit up any longer. At the end of the play he's still just barely alive.

Taken all in all, I prefer comedy.

From the journal of Sanders Nicholas,
information-holder attached to the staff
of First-Defender Ettin Gwarha
CODED FOR REVIEW BY ETTIN GWARHA ONLY

# IX

➤➤➤ SHE WENT BACK the next day and got a recorder. It looked like a wristwatch, and, in fact, it did keep time. She tucked it in a pocket. Nicholas might have noticed that she never wore any kind of chronometer.

Several days later Nicholas called and set up a meeting at the boat in the late afternoon, a couple of hours before she was due at work. The weather had stayed mild and still. They sat on the deck. This time Nicholas wore a grey *hwarhath* uniform, cut to fit his body. It looked all right. Apparently the problem was not *hwar* tailoring; it was the *hwar* sense of human fashion. He'd gotten a pair of human sunglasses: frames made of narrow gold wire and lenses that shone like the back of some kind of beetle, iridescent green.

Hattin wore *hwar* sunglasses, which were rectangular with black lenses and very heavy black plastic frames. They looked fine on his flat alien face. They would have looked awful on a human.

"It's not just a question of style," Nicholas said. "*Hwarhath* ears are set higher on the head and the nose is much wider and flatter than a human nose. I can't wear them. I could get a pair custom made, but it doesn't seem worth it. I spend most of my life inside."

He put his feet up on the rail and looked out at the bay, shining in the low, slanting light. "In theory I am here to ask about your creatures. As I think I told you, the general has a wide-ranging curiosity. He is interested in alien intelligence—human, mostly, but anything he can find. I think I'm in the mood for something other than gigantic, possibly intelligent jellyfish. Why don't you tell me about Earth?"

The human soldier moved uneasily. It was a new person this time: a stocky boy with features belonging to no ethnic group that she knew. From around the Black Sea, maybe? His narrow band of hair was cut short and dyed brick red, a color that went very nicely with his light brown skin. She couldn't tell the color of his irises. They were covered by jet black contacts.

"Nothing of strategic importance," Nicholas added after a glance at the soldier.

She needed some time to think about what constituted strategic importance. "Do you miss it?"

"Earth? Sometimes." He paused for a moment. "I don't believe in regret. There are emotions that trap you, that make your life stop where it is, and regret is one. I prefer to stay in motion, which means I try to think about the situation I am in right now and what I can do about it." He glanced over, light flashing off his glasses, and grinned. "I don't ever believe in letting well enough alone.

"I miss ordinary practical things mostly. Decent human contact lenses. Coffee. There are days—still, after all these years—when I think I'd kill for a cup of coffee."

"That can be taken care of." She got up and went into the cabin and asked Maria to make a pot.

"I hope you know what you are doing, Anna," Maria said.

"Maybe." Anna went back out, sat down and told him about her last visit to New York, which had not changed much since his time. It was still huge and dirty and rundown and splendid. As always, it was in the process of construction. The monstrous glass towers of the late twentieth century, crazy eaters of energy, were almost all gone.

(A few had been saved for historical reasons.) The latest architectural style was Gilded Age Nostalgia.

"They call it that?" asked Nicholas.

She nodded. "Brick or stone walls. Air shafts. Windows that open. Gargoyles."

"What did you do, take an architectural tour?"

She nodded. "And a tour of the dike and levee system. They finally had to close the harbor off entirely. It was the only way to keep the ocean out of the city. It's no longer a port."

"Now, that is a pity."

Maria brought the coffee out and set it down, then stood by the cabin door, listening. She was from Central America and almost pure Indian with copper-brown skin and lovely long straight black hair.

Anna told him about the plays she had seen on her visit. Surely there was nothing strategic about *Revenge of the Wolf Man* or *Measure for Measure*?

"Now, that is a play I wouldn't mind seeing again," he said. "Remember the speech the duke gives to Claudio, when that poor fool is in prison, condemned to die for fornicating? It's the one that begins 'Be absolute for death.' What a wonderful ringing line! And then he goes on with one argument after another for why life isn't worth holding on to.

" 'Reason thus with life:
If I do lose thee, I do lose a thing
That none but fools would keep.'

"What beautiful language! And what a crock of shit!" He tasted the coffee. "This isn't the way I remember it."

"That is good coffee from Nicaragua," Maria said. "And I know how to make it."

He raised a hand, a gesture of apology. "It's been a long time, mem. I'm sure that I've forgotten."

"Have you remembered that passage from Shakespeare for twenty years?" Anna asked.

"No. The *hwarhath* have picked up a lot of odd little pieces of human culture, including the complete plays of William Shakespeare and a lot of Chinese literature in translation. I wonder if this is strategic information? Does it tell you anything useful about the *hwarhath,* if you know that they've never had the chance to read Ibsen?"

The conversation drifted for a while, then ended at fashion. Nicholas had only a mild interest in the subject, except for the new military look. That, he said, was kind of fascinating. "And it makes me glad I changed sides. No way in the universe would I get a haircut like the one on Maksud."

The human soldier frowned.

"Let's stick to the new civilian look," said Anna. "It can't possibly be of any strategic importance."

"It isn't even attractive," Maria said. She had a magazine in the cabin of the boat, not on fashion but on popular culture. "It comes to the same thing, especially up north. The yanqui have always gotten style confused with life. It comes of having no real politics or religion."

"Where are you from?" Anna asked.

"Originally? The dust bowl. Kansas. I got out as soon as I could. I remember reading an interview once with someone—I can't remember who—a writer from Kansas. She said when she was a kid she loved *The Wizard of Oz,* because it told her that it was possible to get out of Kansas." He grinned. "I've always liked that story."

Maria brought out the magazine. Nicholas turned it on, moving slightly so the screen was in shadow. (By this time the sun was low, almost behind the diplomatic compound.) Bright colors flickered and there was a burst of music, which he turned down.

She couldn't see the images from where she sat. It didn't matter. She'd rather watch Nicholas. He looked down at the magazine for a moment, then sighed and took off his sunglasses. "You haven't experienced hell until you've had to wear alien bifocals," he said, and pulled a new pair of glasses out of a pocket. They were clearly *hwar* work: rectangular lenses and thick metal frames. "These are custom made. They fit all right, and the lenses do the job they are supposed to, but look—" He put them on. They were absolutely awful. Maria put her hand to her mouth.

"I keep hoping the *hwarhath* will capture a ship with an optician, but no luck so far."

"Are they really bifocals?" asked Anna. "I've never seen you wear glasses before."

"I need—thank the Goddess—almost no correction for distance vision. It's easier to do without them, except when I'm reading." He hit Play on the magazine. More colors flickered. Now and then he said, "No kidding."

Hattin looked over his shoulder. The human soldier averted his eyes, which meant—almost certainly—that he belonged to a conservative religious faction.

After a while Hattin spoke. Nicholas looked up and grinned. "He says that everything is either ludicrous or disgusting. It's too bad that he and Maksud don't share a language. They could hold a lovely little indignation meeting, until they discovered how their cultures differed."

The human soldier frowned again. Hattin looked as serene as ever, though he no longer watched the magazine. Instead he gazed out at the bay, dismissing human popular culture without even a shrug. Of course, she had no idea if the aliens shrugged or had any kind of equivalent motion.

"What does Hattin think of you?" she asked.

"He's a member of the general's personal guard, and he's very loyal. If Ettin Gwarha says I'm okay, that is enough. His not to reason why. If you'll excuse me, I'm going to finish this article. Who would ever name a singing group Stalin and the Epigones?"

He read hunched over, looking intent. Anna glanced at the sky above the compound. It was streaked and dotted with little clouds.

An odd day. She would have enjoyed it, except for the recorder in her pocket. She felt like a traitor, though she was the person being loyal.

Nicholas finished the article, then played the sample recording of Stalin and the Epigones that was included. "Nasty, but then—if I understand the article—it's supposed to be." He turned off the magazine and handed it to Maria. "Thank you. Does anyone have the time?"

She did not pull the recorder out. Instead Maria went into the cabin to check.

Nicholas took off the alien glasses and put them away. "The next time I'll ask about your creatures. How are they doing?"

"Very nicely. The next week or so ought to be the height of the light display. Then it's going to slow down and dim."

"Amazing to watch. I've taken to walking along the beach at night. It's not half the sight the bay is, of course. But still, the ocean is dotted with flashing lights as far as I can see." He paused for a moment, thinking. "I suppose I ought to add the island has very good perimeter defenses."

He left, the soldiers following.

Maria said, "You have the strangest friends."

"I wouldn't call him a friend. An acquaintance."

"Whatever he is, I can see why you like him. But there isn't any kind of future in knowing him."

"That's for sure."

The next evening she went up to the compound and reported to the major in the office full of fake dark wood. Earth continued to turn on the wall; the cloud cover was heavier than before.

When she was done the major said, "Unfortunately,

Sanders is right about the defenses on the island. The only way to get to him is here." She paused for a while. "And there is a question about how much longer the negotiations will go on." The woman stared at Earth.

Captain Van poured tea. "They were meant to be very preliminary—to find out if we could actually meet each other face-to-face and to set up a procedure for further negotiations and to settle a number of minor details. The furniture, for example."

"That's the third time I've heard about the furniture," said Anna.

The captain smiled. "The *hwar* like to sit closer to the floor than we do, and they did not want us to be looming over them; so we had to negotiate a height for the chairs in the conference room. And they wanted us to get rid of the table. They said people can't have a serious conversation with a great hunk of plastic in between them; their term for talking heart-to-heart is 'talking knee-to-knee.' "

The major finally looked away from the turning planet. "Keep on as you have, Mem Perez. And thank you."

She left the compound. The light show in the bay was really spectacular tonight. She went down the hill to the station, thinking all the while about Nicholas walking on the island, at the dark edge of the brilliantly flashing, blue-green and orange sea.

# X

➤➤➤ MOST OF MY journal is elsewhere: at the Tailin station or on the ship. (The *Crossing-Great-Distances Hawata*. A lovely name, though I just realized that I am not entirely sure what a *hawata* is. There are things about the People I still don't know, and some of them are ordinary and obvious.) **[Yes.]** All I have down here is the entries I've made since we arrived on this planet. I can't do a search and find the line of argument that led us to the current situation. All those conversations took place earlier, on the ship or at Tailin. So I've been remembering. The general would say it's a waste of time. We have made our decision. There is no new information, no reason to rethink. Better to think about something else entirely. I figure, what the hell. It doesn't do any harm that I can see.

**[I will make no comment.]**

The idea was simple. To make a little—a very little—change in the situation that existed in re the humans. To try and get a little information to the other side.

The general wasn't sure how far he wanted to go in this direction. **[Yes.]** And I don't like complicated plans. They work in the holo, but in real life they come back and hit you between the eyes. There are too many variables in reality.

A small action is better. Do it. See what happens. Then do something else.

Our small action was bringing me to the negotiations. This wasn't entirely easy. The other frontmen (some of them at least) wanted to keep my existence a secret. But the general was able to convince them. I am first-in-front as an expert on humanity.

There was—is—an element of risk, which bothers me more than it does the general. But it had to be done. It is such a lovely way to convey information!

Dramatic. We knew the humans would pay attention.

Quick. It would only take a moment—one look at me—to get across everything we wanted to say.

And public. The general does not want to deal with the enemy in private.

All I had to do was step off the plane into that downpour.

We told the enemy it was possible for humans to live with and among the *hwarhath*.

We told them it was possible for humans to cut deals with the *hwarhath*.

We told them it was possible for humans to work with and for the *hwarhath*.

(This last is ambiguous. But it seems to me that employment, oppression and enslavement are all relationships between beings that are—at least to an extent—similar. One doesn't employ or enslave a great white shark or a tree. One ignores or destroys that which is truly alien.)

(This is a bad argument. I can tell already. What about cats and dogs? Cows? Sheep? Herbaceous borders? Yeast? Forget it.)

**[Please explain everything immediately in front.]**

We drew their attention to the general, as someone with an unusual interest in and knowledge of humanity, and we drew attention to me. We told the enemy there was someone who is not alien, someone they can—without question—understand, living among the *hwarhath*.

With luck, the diplomats got the message. MI is another question. They are the reason I worry.

\* \* \*

I looked up *hawata*. It is a large predatory flying animal similar to a bird, which lives on the *hwarhath* home planet, on two of the three northern continents. It used to occupy all five continents, but civilization has decreased its range. It shows up in folktales and in mythology, though only in the northern hemisphere. It has—apparently—been extinct too long in the south.

According to legend the *hawata* is able to carry off babies and small children. (This is only a legend. According to the scientists there is not one authenticated case.) In the usual form of the *hawata* myth or story, a child is carried off but not eaten. Instead he or she is rescued by people from another lineage and raised as one of their own.

In time, of course, the child's true line of descent is discovered, either through an artifact of some kind (a piece of jewelry that the child was wearing when the *hawata* got him) or through a physical peculiarity. The child has strange eyes or a dark stripe along the spine.

If the story is a comedy, the discovery leads to a reconciliation of some kind: enemy lineages end their war, when they discover they share a son or daughter. Often, however, the story is tragic. Lovers discover that they are siblings, and their love is forbidden. A man discovers on the eve of battle that the enemy are his true kin. Now he must choose.

For some reason the *hawata* never turns up in any animal play, and as far as I can discover there has never been a hero play that uses abduction by *hawata*. It seems like a natural. I can even imagine the awful final scene.

I'd better send a message to Eh Matsehar.

From the journal of Sanders Nicholas,
information-holder attached to the staff
of First-Defender Ettin Gwarha
CODED FOR REVIEW BY ETTIN GWARHA ONLY

# XI

➤➤➤ SHE DIDN'T HEAR from Nicholas for over a week. Okay by her. The mating ritual in the bay was reaching its apogee. Was that the right word? She'd check a dictionary when she had time.

By day the water was flooded with chemical messages, some of which were picked up by sensing devices that hung under small floats or buoys. Yoshi had set these out one morning when the migration was just beginning. They dotted the bay. There was no way to reach them at the moment, without disturbing the courting animals; but they sent out analyses every few hours by radio.

The animals were using visual signals as well. This was not so much for communication, she thought, as out of excitement. On bright days, the signals were barely visible. But most of the days were overcast. The grey water gleamed and flickered under a sky full of dark grey clouds.

At night, of course, the display was spectacular: rose red, green, blue, yellow, pale orange and white. The colors filled the bay and spread out into the ocean. On a couple of occasions, when the clouds were especially low, lights gleamed above her in the night sky: reflections, dim and pale and difficult to see, but there. She got very little sleep.

One afternoon, Nicholas called. "The general's going to another party. More booze and canapés. I want nothing to do with it. Can I come down and bother you?"

Shit, Anna thought. Her eyes didn't want to stay open, and her head seemed to be full of grey fuzz.

"At sixteen hundred," she said. "I ought to be awake by then. Meet me at the boat. It is the animals you want to talk about this time?"

"They'll do." He smiled briefly and signed off. She went back to bed.

Half an hour later the CU rang again. She cursed and crawled out from under her blanket.

This time it was Major Ndo. "Can you come up here? As quickly as possible."

Anna opened her mouth.

The major frowned. "This is important, Mem Perez."

"Okay."

"Good." The major gave her a broad, toothy grin. Predatory, Anna thought.

She dressed and went up the hill. The sky was cloudy. A cold wind blew, bending the bare reddish spore stalks and tugging at her hair, making it flip around the sides of her face. Now and then she felt a drop of rain.

Captain Van waited at the entrance to the compound, looking worried.

"What's going on?"

He put his finger to his lips: the international symbol for quiet.

She nodded, and he led her to an elevator. They went down one floor and out of the elevator into a hallway. Tubes on the ceiling cast a pale harsh institutional light. The air had a sterile aroma. Of what? she wondered. Metal and concrete.

"What is this?" she asked.

"A basement."

They went through a grey metal door and down a flight of stairs, then out into another hall. This was more and more curious. Why did a temporary building need a sub-basement? At the end of the hall was another metal door. He stopped and pressed a button in the wall. She heard a

whir and looked up. A camera, tiny and black, turned
slowly, then stopped and pointed its red light at her.

The door slid open; the captain waved; and Anna went
in.

She had trouble taking in the scene. It was too complex. A room with concrete walls, a grey metal desk and
the major, sitting behind the desk: that was the first image.
Next was a man standing on the right side of the desk. He
was tall and thin, dressed in tan pants, a tan shirt and
jacket. Nicholas, she thought for a moment, cutting a deal
with Earth.

Then she saw three people on the left side of the room,
against the wall. A man in a chair, his head down, his
arms resting on his knees and his hands loosely clasped.
A pair of soldiers, both human, stood on either side of
him. One was Maksud. The other, a short dark South
Indian, was unknown to her.

The seated man lifted his head. Nicholas. His face was
mottled red and white, and there was the oddest look in his
eyes. She couldn't read it. His gaze flicked from her to
Captain Van to the major, then to the door, which had
closed.

He was terrified. That explained the change in his coloring and the look in his eyes.

"What's going on?" Anna asked. "And where is the
other guard? The alien? Hattin?"

"It ought to be obvious what's going on," the major
said. "This is our best chance to get Sanders. The *hwar*
won't expect to see him until this evening late. We have
five hours, maybe six or seven, to get him away from here.
We need your help."

"Why?"

"A diversion," said the major. "We want you to go
down to the boat with Lieutenant Gislason." She nodded
toward the man who looked like Nicholas. "Take the boat
out. We want the *hwar* to look in the wrong direction. We

want them to think that Sanders may have taken off on his own. He's shown an obvious interest in you."

"You're crazy. There's no place to go on this planet. It's empty. And he isn't interested in me. For God's sake, you told me the *hwar* general is his lover."

All this time, she was watching Nicholas at the edge of her vision. He was making small nervous motions, looking up, then down, shifting, getting ready to run, then hesitating. There was no place for him to go, no hope of getting out the door. Clearly he knew that, but he couldn't keep still. The fight-or-flight response was too strong.

The major said, "According to our records, he was a perfectly ordinary heterosexual male twenty years ago. Maybe he's reverted. How would the aliens know? They can hardly be experts on human sexuality; and we don't much care what they think is going on—a joyride, a romantic weekend—so long as they are looking on the ocean." She paused and stared at Anna. "We can't pass up this chance. There's twenty years of information in this man. We have to take him."

Anna said, "They aren't going to believe he ran off on his own. Think who this man is! They aren't going to let him disappear. They'll take apart the compound."

The major shook her head, light sliding over the bald dark skull. "Thanks to Sanders, the *hwar* know more about us than we do about them, but we've learned a few things. They will do anything to protect or rescue women and children. But to them all men are expendable. Our people are very clear about this. They believe—the aliens, I mean—that it's the nature of men to quarrel and make war. It is the fate of men to die by violence. When it happens, it happens. *Que sera sera.* As the Goddess wills. General Ettin is not going to risk ending the negotiations because of a man."

"Nick? Is this true?"

He lifted his head, that strange blank look still in his eyes. "Yes," he said after a moment.

"We don't have time to discuss this any further," the major said. "Will you help us, Mem Perez?"

"How much choice do I have?"

"None, if you want to publish your research, and if you want the boat to get away safely without damaging any of your animals. We're going to take it out, Mem Perez, with you on it or not."

Their story—the romantic weekend—required that she vanish. Anna had a sudden sense that if she refused, she'd stay in this room, a prisoner like Nicholas.

So that was the choice. On one side was her freedom, her research and the safety of the animals in the bay. On the other side was only her personal integrity and her hatred of being used. Nicholas was not a consideration. There was nothing she could do for him. If she refused to cooperate, the major would find some other way to get him away from the compound.

She glanced at him. He was looking at her, his gaze steady, which it had not been previously, and tension obvious in his body. He was holding himself motionless by an effort of will, using his gaze to plead with her. For what?

She nodded to the major. "Okay."

Nicholas looked down.

"Good," the major said. "Yoshi Nagamitsu is on the boat at the moment. Call him and tell him you're coming in early. Tell him he can leave."

She took a step toward the desk.

"Not here," said the major. "Gislason will show you to another room. Once you leave this level of the compound, be careful what you say. The *hwar* have some really remarkable listening devices. Not because of us. Apparently, they spy on one another."

Huh, thought Anna.

"Thank you for your help, Mem Perez. It will be remembered."

She left with Gislason. As the door slid open, she glanced at Nicholas one final time. He was staring at the floor, his shoulders hunched: the pose of a man who had received—what? A sentence of death?

The door closed. Gislason said, "This way, mem," and led her down the hall to a room like the first one: light grey concrete walls, a grey carpet and a grey metal desk with a comm unit on it. She called Yoshi.

Usually he was meticulous about staying to the end of his shift, but this time he was eager to go. She wasn't sure if this was good luck or bad. If he'd been unwilling to leave the boat, she might have escaped from this stupid plot. But maybe not. The major seemed determined. She turned off the CU and looked at Gislason.

He wasn't really that much like Nicholas. The height was the same and the general body type, also the coloring. He had the same pale skin and sandy-grey hair. His eyes were green, though much lighter than Nick's. But his face was very different: strong-boned and nordic. Handsome, though not in a way that she especially liked.

"What will happen to him?" she asked.

"Sanders? You will have to ask the major." He had a very slight Scandinavian accent.

"He was terrified."

Gislason shrugged. "Do you expect courage from a man like that? We're on a tight schedule, mem. We have to go."

# XII

➤➤➤ THEY WENT UP to the ground floor, meeting no one on the stairs or in the elevator. Was it the party, the dip reception? Was everyone there? Or did these people quit work early?

They didn't go back the way she had come with Captain Van. Instead Gislason led her down another hall to a door marked EMERGENCY EXIT ONLY, ALARM WILL SOUND. He opened it. Nothing happened, except that a cold wind blew in, bringing rain.

He gestured. Anna fastened her jacket, pulling up the hood, and stepped outside. The sky was beginning to darken, and the temperature was falling, along with the rain, which came down steadily. A lousy evening.

He followed her out, closing the door.

"We really shouldn't take that boat out in bad weather," she said.

He put a finger to his lips. They went around the compound, following a trail beaten in the thick and spongy mosslike vegetation. In front of the main entrance, their trail joined the path that led downhill. This had been properly made: cut by machinery and paved with gravel from one of the beaches. The stones were round and slippery, the footing treacherous. She went slowly, Gislason behind her.

The more she thought about it, the more uncertain she was about the plan. Nicholas knew a lot more about MI than she did. She didn't think his reaction was simple cowardice. He knew what they were going to do, and it terrified him. She had never seen anyone so frightened.

She thought about the secret services in modern history: the SS, the CIA, the KGB and others with names she no longer remembered, since she'd heard them only in a college course on atrocities. In theory, things had gotten better. Did she know that for certain?

It occurred to her now, slipping down the hill toward the yellow lights of the research station, that she had no evidence that any of the diplomats were involved in this kidnapping. If they weren't, if the major was operating on her own, then she—Anna—was betraying her government, as well as Nicholas and herself.

This was deep shit.

They reached level ground. It was easy going now. The path led between the buildings of the settlement, past lit windows. She could see people inside, working in labs and offices. One large window opened onto a lounge. The people there were having predinner drinks. She could see the glasses and imagine what they contained: sherry, wine, some kind of fancy water. God, it looked comfortable!

Out here rain fell around the streetlights and shone like silver. Creatures like furry blue worms wriggled on the path among the gleaming black pebbles.

"What are those horrible things?" asked Gislason.

"Worms, basically. The fur isn't hair, and it doesn't serve as insulation. They use it to feed."

"What?"

"Yasmin—the woman who is working on them—is calling the fur 'cilia' at the moment, though she doesn't think the name will last. The cilia produce enzymes that digest food, and they absorb the food once it's been digested. The animals have a gut, but no mouth, only an asshole. The food goes in through the cilia and out the ass."

"What do they eat?"

"Anything they can find, according to Yasmin. The bulk of their diet is microorganisms in the soil; but they also scavenge, and she thinks they may eat the roots of living plants. They live in tunnels in a kind of nutrient soup that is made of their digestive juices and whatever they have digested. It's as if they are living inside their own stomachs. Wonderful creatures!"

Gislason made a noncommittal sound.

"They're up here because of the rain. Their tunnels are flooded."

The worms became more numerous. Anna stepped carefully around them, silent because she had to concentrate on where she was putting her feet and because she had to think. She didn't want to take the boat out at night in rainy weather, and she didn't want to be involved in an international incident. She also—irrationally—did not want to be involved in harming Nicholas Sanders.

What could she do? Run? Yell? Gislason was right next to her, tall and formidable. She imagined him grabbing her, choking her or knocking her out with some kind of esoteric martial-arts blow. She'd wake up a prisoner with the major very pissed, and the boat would leave anyway. She imagined it ploughing through the bay, frightening her aliens, ending the fragile mating peace.

If she managed to attract attention, it would be the attention of human scientists. How would they fare, against MI?

They passed a final building. Ahead of them was the bay, entirely dark at the moment. Her aliens had not begun their evening signaling; or, if they had, their messages were hidden by the rain. The light at the dock shone brilliantly, though, and she could make out the dim shape of the boat.

She led the way onto the dock, moving carefully. There were no worms here, but the metal surface was slick with rain. In the water nearby a light flashed, faint and pale. She couldn't tell what color it was. One of the aliens was identifying itself, but without authority or conviction. *I am me. I think—I am almost certain—I am me.*

Gislason was immediately in back of her. No way to escape. She certainly wasn't going into the water. Stinging tendrils filled it.

Yoshi waited on the boat, at the door into the cabin, holding an umbrella made of bright yellow oiled paper.

As soon as they climbed on board, he said, "This is really very fortunate, Anna. I'll explain later. Good evening—ah, Holder. Isn't that right?"

"Yes," said Gislason. She glanced at him. The hood to his jacket was up. It shaded his face, and there was no way to tell him from Nicholas.

"It's all yours. Have fun." He opened the umbrella and went past them, nodding to Gislason.

She entered the cabin. A moment later, Gislason followed. "He's gone. We can cast off."

"We have to disconnect the cables to the float," Anna said. "And I have to warn the pseudosiphonophores."

"What do you mean?"

"The bay is full of them, and they've reached the point where they aren't paying attention to anything except one another. We might hit them. We'll certainly cut across tendrils."

He frowned. "How do you warn them?"

"There are lights on the float, the big one in the middle of the bay, and we have a program that translates English into light signals. That's how they communicate—the animals—by flashes of light."

He shook his head. "No."

"I am not going to take the boat out unless I'm able to warn the creatures in the bay. They may be intelligent. They are certainly vulnerable. I will not be responsible for harming them."

His pale green eyes examined her, and the long face

was thoughtful. He was considering options, weighing consequences, and she had a sense—a very clear one—that some of the options would be unpleasant for her.

Finally he said, "All right. Send your message. But I'm going to watch you."

She nodded and turned on the computer, punching through to the translation directory. There were two programs there. One translated English into the language of light. The other had been set up by Yoshi, when he decided to teach the animals "Mary Had a Little Lamb." This program translated English into the international emergency code.

She pulled up the second program. It was labeled "LP2—IEC." She tried to think of an explanation for the letters glowing yellow on the screen; but Gislason did not ask her about them.

"I'm going to type in eight words, which the program will translate into colored light. The message is 'Danger. Strange friend.' The boat is the strange friend." She typed the words in. "The rest of the message is 'Act now. Go toward shore.'"

"Will that be adequate?" asked Gislason.

"Uh-huh." She finished typing in the message and hit Enter. Questions appeared at the bottom of the screen. What color should the message be? How often should it be repeated and how rapidly? She answered quickly, hoping Gislason would not realize that the questions indicated that the message was not being translated into the language of the pseudosiphonophores, and then hit Enter again. The screen cleared, except for the cursor, flashing in the upper left corner.

"We can decouple now. The float is on automatic. It will continue signaling on its own."

"I hope I'm doing the right thing," Gislason said.

"You are."

They went on deck. It was entirely dark by now, and

her aliens had begun their evening conversation: pale tentative flickers of blue and green, made dimmer than usual by the rain. Moby Dick floated in the middle of the bay, lit up like a luxury airship coming into port. The entire surface—above and below water—flashed first orange, then pale blue.

"Come on," said Gislason. "We really are pressed for time, Mem Perez."

They began to uncouple the cables that led to Moby.

The message itself—the pattern of dots and dashes—was meaningless to her aliens, but they ought to understand the colors. Orange was anger or danger; blue meant nonaggression. It was a friendly warning. There was danger, she was telling them, but no malice.

When the boat's engines started they would know the source of the danger. They knew boats were dangerous. When human first came to the planet, boats had been used to hunt them. That had been the first indication that the animals might be intelligent: how quickly they learned to fear the boats and how rapidly the fear of boats had spread through the entire species.

Any other time of the year, the sound of the engines would have been enough of a warning; but at the moment, they were focused on mating. They might not pay attention to the boat, or alternatively they might become panicked, flailing around with their stinging tendrils and harming one another.

The message was not for them. She wasn't entirely sure who it was for. Nicholas had said the *hwarhath* general was interested in the pseudosiphonophores. It was possible he had told the general about his conversation with Yoshi. Maybe the *hwar* would realize the float was sending out a new kind of message. Maybe they would be able to decode it.

A very long shot. Her real hope lay with Yoshi. He would certainly recognize that the message was in the international emergency code, and he would certainly translate it. There was a good chance that he wouldn't understand it. But he'd tell Maria Luz, and Maria did not suffer in the least from Dr. Watson's disease. She would figure out what the message meant. *My strange friend is in danger. Act quickly, and don't look on the ocean. Look on shore.*

Maybe she ought to have shouted as they passed through the station or tried to run, though she was a lot shorter than Gislason and had never been good at running.

The last cables went into the water. "You cast off," she said to Gislason, and climbed into the pilot's chair. Part of the roof extended over the instrument panel and the chair. In theory, this would keep the instruments and the pilot dry; but she was already thoroughly wet, and the cold wind blew rain in the open sides. In front of her was a windshield, streaked with rain, and the roof of the cabin and prow. A limp pennant hung from a flagpole on the prow: the flag of the expedition. TO THE STARS FOR KNOWLEDGE, it said.

Anna hit a switch. The instrument lights came on. A deep, warm masculine voice said, "Good evening, and welcome to the wonderful universe of power boating! I am your Mark Ten Marine Mind computer. If you need any information on how to operate your new Star Craft Model Seven Hundred powerboat, please leave me on. Otherwise, hit the red button to the left of the wheel."

She hit the red button.

"I will now remain silent," the voice said, "unless something occurs that requires a warning or some other kind of output."

She started the engines.

Gislason called, "Everything is untied."

She increased power. The boat edged forward; and she turned the wheel, bringing the boat out from the dock, then around, so it pointed into the bay.

Most of the animals were still flashing blue or blue-green, but the rhythm of their messages had changed. It was rapid and staccato now, the rhythm of the code. Here and there she saw a quick burst of orange like an exploding bomb.

"There is some kind of obstruction in front of you," the boat computer said. "Please check your sonar screen."

She glanced down. The screen showed many little dots, all glowing green: the animals. As she watched, they began to move left and right toward the edges of the screen. She looked up. A lane of darkness was opening in front of the boat.

"Jesus," said Gislason.

The entire bay flashed deep orange and pale cool blue: *Danger. Strange friend. Danger.* In spite of the rain—falling on the water and streaking the plexy in front of her—she could read the message.

"They really heard you," the man said. "Saw you, I guess I mean. Understood your message."

"They are not stupid."

The lane of darkness led past Moby Dick toward the ocean. She guided the boat along it. The windshield wipers flicked back and forth. The raindrops they missed shone like jewels: orange and blue.

"And they have good memories," she added. "Some of them must have been here on some other occasion when the boat went out. You see the path they're clearing? They know where we're likely to go." She paused. "Or maybe they have eaten someone who was here before."

"They eat one another?" asked Gislason. He sounded horrified.

"That isn't the right word. I ought to say cannibalize. They capture one another. Usually the big ones capture the little ones. The victor or predator paralyzes the victim and disassembles it and uses it for parts."

"Does everything on this planet have disgusting habits?"

By this time they were in the channel that led out of the bay. The water was dark, and the sonar showed no animals ahead of the boat.

"Life has disgusting habits," Anna said. "There are animals on Earth—mites and parasitic wasps, especially—that have blood-chilling ways of reproducing."

Gislason made a noise, a grunt that meant nothing to her. Agreement? Repulsion? Indigestion, maybe. She concentrated on guiding the boat, until the sonar told her that they were out of the channel. Not that she needed the equipment to tell her when they reached the ocean. The air changed; a vigorous breeze blew out of the east; she could taste salt and feel spray. The boat was rocking, as it rode up and down over good-sized waves.

"And the sex lives of humans are not always attractive," said Anna, finishing her train of thought.

"That is true," said Gislason. His tone was definite, and she got the impression he was thinking about Nicholas Sanders.

Her aliens were all around them. The ocean was dotted with flashing lights that bobbed up and down: blue, green, yellow, orange, pink. Some of them had picked up her message. Others continued to send their own messages: *I am me. I intend no harm.*

Gislason said, "Turn south, mem."

She brought the boat around. In back of them and to the right was darkness: the land. The ocean lay ahead of them and to the left. Most of the animals were directly outside the entrance to the bay, held there by the chemical messages that flowed out from the larger animals preparing to mate; but lights flashed to the south and east: single animals floating in the darkness and, here and there, patches of light where the animals had gathered into groups.

She decided to go back to cannibalism. She had a feeling it was less controversial than human sexual behavior. "They're colonies rather than single organisms."

"What are?"

She waved at the luminous ocean. "The various parts retain a lot of their original integrity. It isn't such a big deal for them to disassemble. One chemical paralyzes the animal that has been captured, but without doing any permanent harm, and then another chemical—or more likely it's a series of chemicals—tells the parts to separate from one another and join the new animal. As far as we can tell, they do most of their growing this way; and we know from experiments that the parts retain their memories. When a pseudosiphonophore eats a relative, it gets the relative's past. We don't know how big the animals can get or how long they can live or how much they can remember. Maybe centuries, maybe millennia. The history of the species may be out there, floating in the deep ocean."

She was lecturing again, the way she had about the worms. Why? Fear maybe. She was certainly afraid.

"At this point," said Gislason, "I can take over the boat. I know where we are going."

She slid down off the seat, and he climbed up.

# XIII

➤➤➤ THE BOAT CONTINUED south through the rain. According to the instruments, they were traveling roughly parallel to the coast, though the coast was out of sight, hidden by darkness. The aliens appeared less and less frequently: a gleam of blue in the darkness that flashed and vanished; then, later, another gleam of green or blue or very rarely orange. *I am me. Danger.* (Or possibly *Anger.*) *I intend no harm.*

She stayed next to Gislason. The roof overhead sheltered her from most of the rain, which was easing up now. It was mostly spray that flew in.

"We need that cloud cover," he said. "I hope it doesn't lift."

"Why?" she asked.

"There's an enemy ship above us, mem, and it has very good detection equipment. The clouds are some protection."

Two ships, Anna thought, in synchronized orbit. One had brought the human diplomats. The other had brought the grey-furred aliens. On clear nights they were visible in the sky above the station, and her colleagues—the astronomers, amateur and professional—had pointed them out to her: two stars that never moved. The *hwarhath* ship was in the east, over the ocean. The Earth ship was above the diplomatic compound. They paced each other and the station, never changing position.

His remark did not make sense to her. If the *hwarhath*

equipment was so good, it ought to pick up the boat, maybe not on the visible part of the spectrum, but somewhere. It wasn't, after all, any kind of fancy spy machine. It had no shielding. Heaven knew—she didn't—what kind of radiation it emitted, but certainly something that the *hwarhath* would be able to spot, and they couldn't possibly mistake it for anything else. It was the only boat of any size on the planet.

She glanced at her companion. His long thin face was lit from below by the instrument panel. It shone pale green, like something out of a ghost story. Not a reassuring apparition. She decided to ask no further questions and turned back toward the ocean.

Time passed. She was very cold, but she stayed above deck, unwilling to leave Gislason alone.

They passed one final group of aliens: little fellows, who must have been afraid to come any closer to the bay. They floated on the east side of the boat: a great patch of light that rose and fell, riding the waves. Colors rippled across it: blue and blue-green mostly. There were sparks of orange and yellow: anger, frustration, excitement, a warning. Once, for a minute or so, the entire cluster turned an extraordinary purplish shade of pink. What was that about? She couldn't read the message. Was it a variation of the reassurance the big fellows sent to one another? *I am me. Do not be afraid.*

Streamers of light went out from the cluster, and other much smaller clusters floated around it. That much she could see, in spite of the darkness and rain. If only she had a plane and a clear sky! She needed to look down from above.

"What's going on there?" asked Gislason.

"I don't know. We've never paid much attention to the fellows who are too small for mating. We may have been wrong. I wish I knew what triggers that kind of behavior. I don't think these fellows are even in sight of other aliens, so I don't think they are reacting to a light display. And I wish I knew the purpose of the gathering. They're not going to exchange genetic material. They're much too young." She paused, looking out at the bobbing, flashing lights. "And I wish I knew if their action is mindless, or whether they know what they're doing."

The cluster of aliens vanished. The boat continued south and east for another hour. No more aliens came into view. God, it was cold out here! And scary. White foam showed atop the waves, barely visible in the dark.

"Excuse me," a warm voice said finally. "This is your Mark Ten Marine Mind computer, intervening a second time. If you will check your radar screen, you will notice an object directly in front of you, estimated distance, a thousand meters. The object is solid and floating on the surface of the water. It is not moving. If you do not wish to make contact with the object, please change course. If you do wish to make contact, please slow down."

Gislason hit the red button.

"You have indicated that you wish to handle this situation on your own. I will now remain silent."

"Asshole," said Gislason.

The boat slowed.

Anna peered forward. She couldn't see anything. "What is it?"

"A plane," said Gislason. "We get off here."

"We what? This is the middle of the ocean."

"The enemy can track this boat, mem. Surely you realize that. We can't stay on it. I am going to let the Mark Ten Marine Mind carry on by itself. It ought to be clever enough."

"This is the only boat within light-years, and it's full of research equipment. We can't abandon it."

"We aren't, mem. Mark seems eager to take over. We're going to let him."

"No," said Anna.

"Mem, you have no choice."

She saw lights ahead, moving up and down above the surface of the ocean. There were three of them, small and dim and clearly artificial.

The boat slowed further. She made out the dark shape of the plane. The lights marked its nose and tail and wing.

"We can't do this," said Anna. "I could lose my job."

"Believe me, Mem Perez, you will be in far worse trouble if you don't cooperate with the major."

The boat turned sideways, rocking more violently than before as Gislason edged it toward the plane. When they were close, almost touching the plane's dark side, a door opened; yellow light shone out; Anna blinked and saw a person in the doorway, silhouetted by the light. "Lieutenant?" The voice was male.

Gislason said, "We're going to have to tie up here for a while. Help Zhang, and then get on the plane."

She opened her mouth to argue, but the look on his face made her keep quiet. Not at all a nice person, she thought as she helped the man in the doorway fasten the mooring lines. When they had finished, the man reached down and handed her across the narrow expanse of water into the plane. Now she could see him clearly: a tall East Asian, dressed in a uniform. He had the usual mohawk, dyed turquoise blue. His eyebrows were the same color, exotic as hell. She wondered what Nicholas would think of it. Not that he was likely to be thinking about anything, except the trouble he was in.

"Welcome on board the *Shadow Warrior*." The soldier waved at a long narrow room. At one end was a row of seats, facing a metal wall that was blank except for a closed door. The seats looked as if they belonged on a rocket plane or an interurban maglev back on Earth; though there would have been no seat belts on the maglev. Except for the row of seats, the room was empty. A cargo plane, thought Anna.

"I'm afraid that we have no amenities, and I have to deliver a package to Lieutenant Gislason. If you'll sit down, I'll get you coffee in a couple of minutes."

She went to the row of seats and sat down, facing the wall. It was only a meter away. The brightly lit room frightened her more than traveling on the open ocean.

A couple of minutes later, the Asian soldier reappeared. He went through the door in the metal wall and came back out almost at once, holding a mug. It was heavy ceramic and entirely plain. "It will have to be black, I'm afraid; and as bad as the coffee is, the tea is even worse."

She took the mug and drank. The coffee was truly awful. "Don't you ever clean the pot?"

"It's not a high priority. If you'll excuse me." He left.

She drank more coffee—only a little—and stared at the metal wall.

After twenty minutes or so, Gislason came on board. He sat down next to her and fastened his seat belt. "That's it. Mark is on his own."

The Asian soldier closed the outside door, then took her coffee cup and went forward. She got no sense of what lay beyond the inside door. A coffee machine, the cockpit.

Engines started.

"Are you strapped in?" asked Gislason. "The takeoff is going to be rough."

It was, and she remembered that she had never much liked flying. She grabbed the arms of her seat. Beside her Gislason put his hands to his face.

For a moment Anna was terrified. "What is it? Are we in trouble?"

The plane bounced a few more times and then was airborne, rising smoothly. Gislason looked up. His eyes had changed color. They were blue, a color so intense that they seemed lit from within.

"Jesus Maria," said Anna.

He grabbed hold of the lock of hair that fell over his

forehead, pulling up and back. "Shit! That hurts." The hair came off. Underneath was a pale skull, bare except for the usual mohawk, as yellow as butter.

He rubbed the mohawk, brushing the yellow hair upright. Now he looked entirely like a Scandinavian and a soldier, not a bit like Nicholas.

The plane was turning; she could feel the cabin tilt.

"Where are we going?"

"We have a place the enemy doesn't know about." He tossed the wig into the seat next to him. "You might as well settle back. This is going to take a while."

She leaned against her seat, trying to relax. Not easy to do. She had no idea what direction they were going. East over the ocean? West or south to land? If they went south, they would be going over a part of the continent that had not—as far as she knew—been explored. There were aerial pictures, of course, and her colleagues in biology had taken a few samples of life. The pictures showed low bare mountains and plains covered with the yellow mosslike plant. Here and there were forests of large bushes and/or little trees. An animal that looked like a cross between a crab and an armadillo grazed on the mossy yellow plains. It was two meters long from the tips of its front claws to the end of its armored tail: the largest land animal on the planet. No internal skeleton, and the creature was as dumb as shit, according to her colleagues; but it had a fascinating respiratory system.

After a while Gislason pulled something out of a pocket and unfolded it as if he were unfolding a piece of paper: once, twice, three times.

A chessboard, standard size. He tapped the edge. All at once the board was solid: a single unbending piece of metal and silicon. The red squares began to glow a soft rosy color. The black squares remained dark, like windows into space.

Impressive, thought Anna.

He tapped the chessboard again. The pieces material-
ized, though that wasn't really the right word. They were
hologrammic, made of light, not matter.

Two rows of Chinese warriors. Behind them were elephants and counselors, generals on horseback and a pair of
splendid emperors standing next to their slim and elegant
wives. One emperor was dressed in red; the other wore
white and silver.

"Do you play?" asked Gislason.

"I know the moves."

"That isn't adequate." He touched the board. One of
the warriors drew a sword. The tiny blade glinted. He
waved it over his head and then strode forward.

How could she resist? She watched the game. The warriors flourished swords and banners. The elephants lum-
bered. The horses of the generals pranced. The counselors
slid as if on bearings. The emperors stepped forcefully, and
the dangerous queens moved forward with a curious sway-
ing and tottering gait.

Very impressive, though clearly a hologram. The colors
were too pale. The reds and whites both had a pearly iridescent quality, and the figures lacked solidity, though they
looked three-dimensional and were beautifully detailed.
Now and then they flickered or vanished for a moment.

A pair of ghost armies, thought Anna. Fighting over
what?

"Isn't that very expensive?" she asked.

"The board? Yes. But there isn't much to spend money
on in space. I like chess and expensive toys."

He kept on, until the plane began its descent. Then he
turned the board off. The tiny ghostly figures vanished. He
folded the board and put it away as the plane landed—in
water, she was certain. It slowed, turned, and finally
stopped. The door in front of them, the one that led to the
coffee machine, opened. The soldier with blue eyebrows
came out.

"We have to move quickly, Lieutenant. The cloud cover is starting to break."

Gislason nodded and rose. "Mem?"

She followed the two of them to the outside door. Blue-brow opened it and jumped into darkness. She heard a splash.

"A meter deep," he said. "And cold."

"Mem," said Gislason.

She jumped and hit the water, then the bottom. Sand slid under her foot. She started falling, and the soldier grabbed her.

"All right, mem?"

"Yes."

They waded to shore, Gislason behind them. Once she was on dry land, she looked back. Another soldier was in the doorway, a woman this time. She closed the door, and the light from the plane vanished. A moment later another light appeared in the hand of the blue-browed soldier. He directed it ahead of them, over a rocky beach.

"Come on."

Again she followed, as in a dream. The flashlight revealed stones and then the mosslike plant. They moved up a slope. There were objects around them, about the same height as people, but motionless and silent. What? thought Anna. The soldier lifted his flashlight, playing its beam over a stubby tree. A thick fuzz covered the trunk and branches. There were no leaves.

"Where are we?" she asked. "On the southern half of the continent?"

"I'm afraid I can't tell you," Gislason said.

If there'd been daylight, she could have looked for large armored animals with claws. But the animals were diurnal. They and their predators needed the heat of the sun.

The flashlight showed a cliff ahead of them, low and made of dark, rough stone, with an opening, which they entered: a shallow cave. In back was a door. She would have missed it, even in daylight. It was that well disguised.

The soldier pushed, and the door swung open. Beyond was a corridor made of concrete, with lighting tubes on the ceiling. The light they cast was pale and had a tinge of blue.

"Welcome to Camp Freedom," the soldier said.

# XIV

➤➤➤ THEY ENTERED, ANNA first, then Gislason, then the soldier, who closed the door. On this side it was metal, and there was a wheel. The soldier turned it, as if he were locking an antique bank vault.

Gislason said, "Go straight down the corridor."

Their footsteps echoed slightly. Otherwise she heard nothing except the hum of an air-circulation system. After a hundred meters they came to another door. The soldier opened it. On the other side were bright lights and the sound of music. Anna knew the song. It had been a hit when she first came out to the edge of the Confederation: "Living on the Edge of the Con." She no longer remembered the name of the group. They'd come and gone like a comet. But this one song was terrific: the best description she had heard of what it was like to live "Where no one's been before me/And all the rules are new" and "The messages from home turn into noise."

At the moment, though, the music was too loud, and she couldn't make out the words. A less-than-great sound system.

"What's going on?" asked Gislason.

The soldier with blue eyebrows shrugged.

This new hall was lined with doors. They went past several, all closed, then came to one that was open. Gislason took her elbow and guided her in.

An ordinary office, with an ordinary-looking woman sitting behind a desk. She didn't even have a mohawk; her

hair—thick and curly and black—stuck out all over her
head. She wore business clothes rather than a military
uniform: a navy blue vest and a silver shirt with a high
collar. Her tie was dark and narrow and fastened with a
silver pin in the shape of a dolphin.

Gislason shut the door. The music became just barely
audible. "Why are you generating all that noise?"

"We're having trouble with soundproofing," said the
woman. "Between the rooms and the corridor. Nowhere
else. You can't hear from one room to another, and there's
no leakage of sound to the exterior. That I made sure of.
But—all things considered—music seemed like a good
idea." She paused for a moment. "And it helps morale. It
reminds us that we are fighting for human civilization.
You must be Mem Perez."

"Yes. I'd like to know exactly what I've gotten myself
into. Where am I? What is this place? And what's going to
happen to my boat? Aren't the enemy—the *hwarhath,* I
mean—going to be able to track it down? What are they
going to think, when they find it empty?"

"I'm not going to answer all your questions," the
woman said. "I will tell you about the boat. By this
time—" She looked at her wrist. "—it ought to have
sunk."

"What?"

"All the enemy will find is wreckage, too deep to bring
up easily. If they reach it or bring it to the surface, they will
find evidence of what?" She looked at Gislason.

"A fire, starting in the galley," he said. "Defective
wiring in the coffee maker. The fire reached the fuel tanks
and—boom."

"You son of a bitch," said Anna.

"You have no reason to believe that Lieutenant Gislason's mother is in any way responsible for his present
behavior," the woman said. "The enemy won't find any
bodies, of course. That happens in the ocean. The current

takes them. Who knows where they end up? Though it's always possible that the bodies will turn up later."

"What?" said Anna.

"One body," said the woman in a reassuring tone. "Not yours, of course. Sanders'. We'd prefer to keep him alive. Still and all, it ought to be possible to get most of the information we need out of him in a week or two or three. After that, we could dispose of him, if it proved necessary."

Who *was* this person? She went quickly through famous monsters of the past two centuries. No one had ever proved for certain that Dr. Mengele was dead. But after 190 years . . . And Colonel Peterson was lying underneath a black granite monument, after having devoted his life (the inscription said) to the Cause of Public Health in America.

"He will reappear only if the *hwarhath* insist on evidence of his death. Well, if they insist, then his body will float up on some beach or another." She paused. "Not in the best condition, but recognizable and with enough left so they can determine that he died by drowning."

Jesus Maria, this person was actually enjoying the idea of murder; it was evident in her voice; and she was enjoying the idea of frightening Anna Perez.

"If we can stall them, if they are willing to believe in the accident, you and Sanders will leave the planet. But not for a while. For the time being, Anna—may I call you that?—you are stuck in Camp Freedom."

"Is that name serious?"

"It's the only place on the planet we are free of enemy surveillance." The woman paused. "And free of civilian interference. Yes, indeed, Anna, the name is serious." She stood up. Now Anna could see the neatly tailored navy pants that completed her suit. "I'll show you to your room."

They left Gislason in the office. The woman led the way farther down the corridor. A new song was playing, one

Anna didn't know. The music was still too loud, and she still could not understand any words, though they sounded as if they were in English.

They turned into a side corridor. The noise level dropped just a little.

"Here," the woman said, and pushed a door open.

Another perfectly ordinary room. This one looked at if it belonged in a dormitory. A table, a chair, a storage chest, a bed, a second door that led into a little bathroom. No windows, of course.

"There are towels in the bathroom, along with the usual necessities—toothbrush, comb and so on. The chest contains extra clothing. There's a computer in the table. I've ordered dinner for you, a vegetarian curry with rice. I'm afraid that all our food is vegetarian. I hope you won't mind."

She found herself answering, "No, of course not. I almost never eat meat."

"Good." The woman smiled. "The door will be locked. We really cannot have you wandering around the camp. Please go in."

She did without a protest, then turned and opened her mouth. The door shut. There was the click of a bolt going home.

She sat down on the bed. She was a prisoner, held by people who had deliberately destroyed the only research boat within light-years, the property of the government that employed them. What kind of criminal assholes were they?

Murderers, she thought after a moment. This certainly explained why Nicholas had looked so frightened. He must have known.

She had done the right thing by sending the message.

What if it didn't get through? What if no one acted on it? She pushed her hair back and then rubbed her face. All the muscles felt tense. What if Military Intelligence learned about the message? That was possible, maybe even likely, she realized now.

Her body would float up on a beach, and maybe then they wouldn't have to kill Nicholas. If her body was found, that might convince the *hwarhath* that the accident was real.

They might not need to learn about the message. Maybe she was doomed already. She had done what they wanted. She was of no further use, and she knew—as the holoplays said—too much.

Nicholas, on the other hand, was extremely valuable. It made sense to kill her first.

She began shaking. How had she managed to get into this mess?

By talking to a pleasant man. By taking someone as she found him. By liking someone because he was curious and asked good questions.

The door opened, and the soldier with blue eyebrows came in. "Dinner," he said, and put a tray on the table. "Is everything okay? Is there anything you need?"

"I need to get out of here."

"Sorry, mem. I'd better tell you, this room is under observation. That might save you some embarrassment." He smiled. "We all do things we'd rather not have other people see. Have a good evening."

He left. Anna got up. She wasn't hungry, but there was a half bottle of white wine on the tray. Hardly adequate for the day she'd been having, but she would have to make do. She opened it and filled a glass, sitting down again. It was slightly sweet. A Chardonnay?

After she finished the wine, she decided that it was too early for panic. She didn't know enough. Her advisor in graduate school had told her that was her great failing. She formulated theories and drew conclusions before the data was in.

She opened the chest and found a nightgown: full

length and genuine flannel with a perfectly darling floral print.

What kind of people were these? And what did the nightgown mean? Was it possible to kill someone after providing them with a flannel nightgown?

Yes, she decided after a moment. It was possible, but it wasn't fair.

She took the nightgown into the bathroom and ran a bath. The water was hot, and bubble bath had been provided. This was the nameless woman, the head—apparently—of Camp Freedom. It had the feel of her: the perfect hostess. This place belonged in *A Guide to Country Inns and Concentration Camps*. Anna used the bubble bath. It foamed in a truly satisfactory manner.

Afterward, she brushed her teeth and went to bed. For a long time she lay in darkness and thought about the possibility of death, then finally drifted into an uneasy sleep, waking often. Her dreams were fragmentary and unpleasant. Things chased her. She couldn't run.

She woke a final time and heard music, loud and blurry. The door to her room was open. The soldier with blue eyebrows stood in the doorway. "Sorry to disturb you, mem. I'll be gone in a minute." He set a tray down on her table and picked up the old one from dinner. "And I'd better apologize for the breakfast as well. We're having some trouble in the kitchen. The doctor wants to see you when you're done."

"Who?"

"You met her yesterday."

The woman with curly hair.

He left and she got up. The tray held black beans and rice and black coffee. Not bad, actually. The coffee was much better than the stuff on the plane. After she finished eating, she got dressed in her own clothes. They were grubby and stiff with salt, but she wanted as little as possible to do with Military Intelligence.

Bluebrow came back and led her to the office of Dr. No Name. The doctor was there, sitting behind her desk. Today she wore a flame red blouse and a black vest. Her tie was silver mesh. Gislason leaned against a wall, his arms crossed, looking—what? Sardonic? Anna wasn't even sure what "sardonic" meant. But something was wrong; she could tell from his expression. Captain Van was in a corner, hunched in a chair, looking unhappy.

"Please be seated," the doctor said.

Anna took the last chair.

"A problem has developed," said the doctor.

"What?"

Gislason spoke. "The enemy hit us last night, just a little while after you were escorted to your room."

She opened her mouth, and he held up a hand. "Not here, mem. At the moment this is the only spot on the planet that is held by human beings. They took out the landing field with rockets and dropped combat troops into the compound and the station. Very quick. Very neat. Our people had time to get out one message. The next thing we heard was an announcement from the *hwarhath* that they had everything and everyone. They are holding the entire human population of the planet hostage. Your friends, my friends, the diplomats."

No shit.

"They want two things: Nicholas Sanders and enough time to get out of here safely. If they do not get both, they will kill every human on the planet. Male *and* female, they said."

"I think they're bluffing about the women," said Captain Van. "But they will certainly kill all the men, military and civilian. In their culture there is no such concept as a male civilian. All the men are soldiers; and they have no objection to killing soldiers."

"What happened to your plan?" asked Anna. "The story about me and Nicholas?"

"We don't know," the doctor said.

"They must not have believed it," said Gislason.

"So now we have to decide how to respond," the doctor said.

"Give them what they want," said Anna.

Gislason grinned without humor.

Captain Van said, "There is a third thing they want, Mem Perez. You. In good condition, they said. Unharmed. Why, mem?"

The message, of course. The aliens had gotten it. But she couldn't tell this trio of villains that she was the person who had foiled their plan. "I have no idea."

"You know," said Gislason.

"We think you found a way to betray us," the doctor said.

She kept quiet.

"Does it really matter?" asked Captain Van.

The doctor nodded. "Of course it does. If we are right, Mem Perez is guilty of treason."

"Don't you think you'd better decide what to do about the *hwarhath* ultimatum?" Anna asked.

Gislason unfolded his arms and straightened up. "We know what we are going to do. We have no means of transportation here. That was an error, but we wanted the planes as far away as possible, in case the enemy had a way to track them. So we are stuck. We can't go anywhere; and there are people at the compound, people in the hands of the enemy, who know about Camp Freedom. Someone is going to talk. I think we have another day or maybe two before the enemy arrives."

"If we fight," said Captain Van, "hundreds of people will die."

"We thought of killing Nicholas Sanders," said the doctor. "Then, at least, he would not be of any more service to the enemy."

Gislason made a face. "You saw what he was like

yesterday, Doctor. He was acting as if we were tearing him apart, and we have barely touched him.''

"A few drugs," said the doctor to Anna. "Nothing more. They should have made him responsive to questioning. Instead—" The doctor frowned. "It must have been a paradoxical effect. He became more agitated rather than less. He seemed to be hallucinating."

"The man is no use to anyone, human or alien," Gislason said. "The only thing they ever got out of him was information, and he must have given them everything he had to give many years ago." He looked at Anna. "We're not going to fight, mem. There is no way to get Sanders off the planet or even away from the camp. So we have lost him and whatever information he has about the enemy. I can see no point in killing him, nor can the captain here." Gislason looked at Van, who was still sitting hunched over, looking miserable. "Today we will call the enemy and negotiate an exchange: you and Sanders for everyone else. But we'd like to know what you did."

The doctor leaned forward. "We can find out, mem. The drugs that frightened Nicholas Sanders work on any human."

This was like being in a bad halo. At any moment, one of these maniacs was going to begin twirling a nonexistent mustache. "Aha, me proud beauty. I have you now!" But they were serious. That was the frightening part. They meant what they said, when they talked about drugs and murder. There was a line, which she couldn't remember, about the banality of evil. An old line, most likely from the twentieth century, a century that was hard to beat for evil. Her mind was wandering. What in fuck was she going to do?

"I guess you'll have to use the drug," she said. "That's the only way you're going to believe that I did nothing. Maybe they want to know what happened. Maybe I'm getting pulled in for questioning."

"Well, then," said the doctor.

Captain Van said, "This is ridiculous. I'm the ranking officer here, and I will not allow you to question her any further. We will deliver her in good condition to the enemy, as they requested. I will not endanger the lives of hundreds of people in order to satisfy your curiosity, Doctor."

He looked at Gislason. "Please take Mem Perez back to her room. Then—" He sighed. "—we will decide what we are going to say to the *hwarhath*."

# XV

➤➤➤ SHE SPENT THE rest of the day in her room. A soldier—a Latin American woman—brought her lunch: a cheese sandwich and coffee. Anna asked for news.

"I can tell you nothing," the woman said in Spanish.

After she was done eating, she got out the computer and looked at the directory. It had an all-purpose entertainment program: chess, checkers, bridge, the new editions of Monopoly and Revolution, a quest and half a dozen novels. She looked at the list of novels. She had always meant to read *Moby Dick*. Why not now?

She began.

The Latin American soldier brought her dinner, which was stir-fried vegetables and rice. She ate and took a shower and went to bed early. This time she had no trouble getting to sleep.

In the morning she went back to reading. She was into the chapter on whiteness when the door opened. Breakfast, she thought; and it was late.

A *hwarhath* stepped in: short and trim, wearing the usual grey uniform. His fur was dark grey, almost black.

She looked up, surprised. He dropped his gaze at once.

"Anna Perez?" he asked.

"Yes?"

"My name is Hai Atala Vaihar. My rank is watcher one-in-front, and I am attached to the staff of First-Defender Ettin Gwarha. I have been sent to rescue you."

"Your English is really excellent," she said.

He showed teeth briefly. Was it a smile? "I learned from a native speaker, though Sanders Nicholas tells me that he is not entirely happy with my accent. My own native language is tonal, and I cannot seem to lose the lilt."

She turned off the computer, picked up her jacket and put it on. After a moment's thought, she stuck the computer in a pocket. *Moby Dick* was getting interesting. "Can we go? This room gives me the creeps."

"I beg your pardon?"

"It makes me uneasy."

"Yes. We can go. Please precede me. We are going straight out. I have instructions to get you and the holder back as quickly as possible."

She remembered the way to the entrance and took it, the alien close behind her.

"How is Nicholas?" she asked.

"At the moment, he is heavily sedated. The enemy did that. They said he became upset, and they could not get him to calm down."

"They tried to question him."

There was silence; then the *hwarhath* said, "Sanders Nicholas is famous for not liking to answer questions."

There was no one in the halls, either human or alien. The music had been turned off. She heard only the gentle whish and hum of the air-circulation system, and their footsteps, echoing between the concrete walls.

What had happened? Were the aliens in control here as well?

They passed an open door. She glanced in and saw a *hwarhath,* leaning over a computer, punching keys with deft rapidity.

That seemed to answer her question.

Through into the outer hall. The rods in the ceiling were as dim as before, but at the far end the lock was open, and there was sunlight, blazing in.

As she stepped out into the sunlight, Anna drew a breath. Ah! Fresh air! A wind blew. The sky was dotted with little clouds. Around her the hills were bright yellow. Below her a round blue lake lay in the middle of a shallow valley. Trees grew at the edge of the water. They were all (as far as she could tell) the same variety: dull orange with short thick trunks and clublike branches. None of them had leaves.

The alien paused beside her and gestured. Off to the right was a level space. Two planes sat there: *hwarhath* fanwings, VTLs.

"Where are we?" asked Anna.

"I still have trouble with human distances," the alien said. "Though I have finally learned how you measure time. We are two hours south and west of the human research station. Sanders Nicholas is already on the plane. Please go forward, mem."

She walked over the plant like yellow moss—it was thick and soft and springy, and the air smelled of its faint dry aroma—then up a flight of metal stairs, entering a cabin that was very like the cabin of a human plane. An aisle went down the middle, between rows of seats. Well, how many ways were there to transport large numbers of humanoids?

The seats were larger than the seats on any human plane: wide and very low to the floor, with broad armrests and lots of room for legs. Odd, considering that the aliens were—as a group—smaller than human. There were no windows. Curious. Didn't these people like to know where they were going?

The alien waved toward the front of the plane. She went in that direction. Halfway up she came to Nicholas. He was in a seat next to the cabin wall, slumped down with his head leaning to the side, touching the wall. A blanket had been wrapped around him. His face was sheet white, and his eyes were closed. Next to him sat a *hwarhath*.

"Nick." She stopped.

The alien next to him glanced up briefly, then looked down again.

"Nicholas."

He turned his head slightly and opened his eyes. She had the impression that he couldn't see her. After a moment he spoke in a language she didn't recognize. His voice sounded tired.

Her alien said, "I do not think he knows who you are, mem. He is speaking our language."

"What did he say?"

"That he knows nothing. I think we should continue toward the front."

She took a seat several rows farther on. Her alien—what was his name? Vai something?—sat down next to her and explained how to fasten the seat belt.

A couple of minutes later the engines started. The plane took off. Anna got out the computer she had taken from her cell, turned it on and finished reading about the whiteness of the whale.

The alien sat quietly, hands folded, doing nothing at all.

Two hours later, by the clock in the computer, the plane began to descend. She turned off *Moby Dick*. The plane slowed. The sound of the engines changed. It stopped in midair, then settled down. A very nice landing; she barely felt it touch the ground. Everything these people did seemed competent. It was an inhuman trait.

The engines went off. She undid her seat belt.

"Please stay were you are, mem. Sanders Nicholas will be taken off first. May I ask what you were reading?"

"It's a story about a man who became obsessed with hunting and killing a large marine animal."

"Did he succeed?"

"The animal killed him."

She heard the door open and felt air blow in, damp and

smelling of the ocean. People moved in back of her. One of them spoke softly in the alien language.

"It's a famous story," she added.

"Is it decent?" asked the *hwarhath*.

"I think so. I don't really know what your people think is decent."

"Stories about men or women. But not stories about men and women. We have found it difficult to study your culture. You seem obsessed with activities that are contrary to the will of the Goddess."

For some reason his careful voice reminded her of Nicholas's guard, the young alien named Hattin.

"One of your people was guarding Nicholas. What happened to him? Is he all right?"

"We found his body. His ashes will be sent home. That is important. We like—in the end—to go home."

The alien glanced toward the back of the plane. "We can leave now, mem."

She followed him out into a fine, cold misty rain. As soon as she got a look around, she said, "This isn't the station."

"Your station? No."

The buildings around her were square and grey and featureless. There were no windows and no architectural detail, only flat blank walls. There must have been doors, but she did not see them.

"Why am I here?"

"The first-defender wants to talk to you."

"Why?"

"I am not an important person, mem. The first-defender does not tell me what's in his mind."

She stood for a moment longer, looking at the square grey buildings, then shrugged. "Tell me where to go."

"There." He pointed.

When they got close to the building, she made out a door, flush with the wall and barely visible. He opened it, and they went into yet another corridor. This one had grey metal walls. The floor had carpeting: a slightly darker shade of grey. Boy, these people liked that color. The air had a funny aroma. Like what? Some unfamiliar kind of animal. Two aliens with rifles stood just inside the door. One spoke to her guy. He answered. The alien who had spoken first moved his head slightly. A nod?

"Mem?" said her guy.

They walked down the corridor. There was a lot of activity here. Aliens passed them, moving quickly and with the athletic grace that seemed characteristic of the species. Weren't there any klutzes among the *hwarhath?* No one looked at her directly, but she had a sense of being watched, of people glancing sidelong. About half the aliens were armed, mostly with rifles, though she also saw what had to be handguns, tucked in holsters.

They reached another guard point. Her fellow talked to another guy with a rifle. This one was large and stocky, with pale grey fur that had a definite blue tinge. His eyes— he raised them briefly—were the same color as his fur. He nodded finally. She and her alien went on.

Was the guard a freak or did the *hwar* come in different colors? Most of the people they passed were various shades of medium grey, but her fellow was almost black, and she had seen another man with fur that was two-toned: dark at the tips and silver underneath.

A third guard point. Another conversation and nod. Again they went on and came to the end of the hall. There was a door with a symbol on it: a flame inside a funny spiny ring.

Her guide touched the door and it opened. "Go in, mem. You are expected."

She did. The door closed behind her. In front of her was a table. An alien sat behind it, broad and solid-looking; she got the impression that he was shorter than was usual for his people. His fur was a hard, almost metallic grey. He lifted his head. His eyes were blue, and they looked directly at her.

"Perez Anna." His voice was deep and soft. "It is difficult for me to look anyone in the eye, unless of course they are a relative or a friend. But Nicky tells me among your people a direct stare indicates honesty and an honorable spirit. So I will try. Please sit down." He tilted his head, indicating an empty chair in front of the desk.

She sat down. "You speak English."

"I have known Nicholas for almost twenty years. This is his native language, and it is the language of my enemies. Of course I have learned English." He picked up an implement, a narrow piece of metal, and turned it in his hands. What was it? A kind of pen? "Why did you send the message?"

"You got it."

He was silent for a moment. "Not directly, and not at once. We discovered it this morning, when we were questioning—what is the word? Your comrades or compatriots? Your fellow workers?

"We had already acted, mem. You message was clever and—I think—brave. It was not necessary."

"Then why did you ask for me, if you didn't know about the message?"

"You are a woman. I thought you might be in danger. I did not trust the humans to treat you with respect."

He tossed down whatever he'd been playing with and leaned back in his chair. "I don't mean to be insulting, but why does your species give power to idiots? And how could those products of a badly considered insemination think—for even a moment—that I would believe their story? Nicky, go off on a boat with a human and a woman? Why?"

"I told them it wouldn't wash."

He frowned. "I don't understand."

"I told them the story wasn't plausible."

"You were right. We pretended to believe the story, of course. We had to, until we could get back to our base; and those amazing fools believed our pretending. They let us get away." He looked and sounded angry. After a minute or two, he relaxed. She saw the shoulders drop slightly. A furry grey hand reached out and touched the metal implement. "Why did you send the message?"

She was quiet for a while, trying to figure out exactly why she had acted. "I like Nicholas, and I don't much like the people in Military Intelligence. They forced me into working for them. I really did not like that; and I saw Nick after they captured him. He was frightened. I don't think I've ever seen anyone so afraid. One of the MI people said that Nick was a coward. I didn't think so. I thought, He knows these people, and he knows what they're going to do to him, and it is something really awful."

The first-defender looked thoughtful. Was that right? Was she reading his expression correctly? "You are right that Nicky isn't a coward. Hah! That is an ugly word! But you may not have understood what you were seeing. They were going to question him, mem. He must have known that. It was obvious. He does not like being questioned." Again he paused and looked thoughtful. Then he leaned forward, resting his arms on the table in front of him. She had a sense that he had made some kind of decision.

"When we captured him twenty years ago, it was the first time we had gotten hold of an enemy who was fluent in our language. We knew that he could understand our questions, and that we could understand what he told us in reply. It was our chance to get a great deal of information that was unambiguous.

"Nicky was irreplaceable. We could not try anything on him that was in any way experimental. We had to— how do you say it?—play safe. We had to use the oldest and best-established and safest methods of interrogation.

"Remember how long ago this was! Now we have

drugs that make it hard for your people to lie or evade questions. Now we have equipment that will tell us whether or not a human is telling the truth.

"Then we did not, and there was a great deal we did not know about human physiology." He hesitated a moment. "We used pain. It is simple. It is reliable. It is the great universal."

She was beginning to feel queasy, and the man behind the table looked more and more inhuman. It was like the remarkable transformation in *Return of the Wolf Man,* when Lewis Ibrahim turned—right there onstage in front of the eyes of the audience—into a hairy monster.

The soft voice continued. "He was very responsive to the methods we used, and we got a lot of information. Most of it was new, and there was no way to check it. But we were able to check some of the information, and we found out he was lying. So we had to ask him again; and when we checked the new answers, we found new lies. It took a long time before we were certain that we had gotten the truth; and somewhere along the way, we became more interested in Nicky than in the information. We wanted to see how much more he could handle and what he was going to try next. We told each other that we were learning something valuable about human psychology." He paused, looking at the implement he held: the long narrow piece of metal.

"We stopped finally. I think we got almost everything he had to tell, though I am not entirely certain. He is the best liar I have ever met.

"He still has dreams about the questioning. Sometimes when he wakes, he doesn't realize where he is. His eyes are open, but he is still in the dream, and he is very frightened. I have to—what is the phrase?—talk him back. Make a path of words that will bring him to what is real."

"You keep sounding as if you were there, when all this happened."

"Twenty years ago? When Nicky was questioned? I was. I have always been interested in humanity."

She felt as if she was standing at the edge of an abyss. If she looked down, she would see things twisting in the shadows. *If* she looked down? Hell, she *was* looking down. What on Earth—what in the universe—held these two people together? Most likely, she did not want to know.

"I can read human expressions much of the time," the first-defender said. "You look disturbed. You ought to be. You have interfered in a struggle between men. By doing so, you have caused a problem and created an obligation.

"The problem is this: you have jeopardized your standing among your own people. You did it in an attempt to help Nicky. This creates what your people, who seem to think of nothing except procreation and the activities of the marketplace, would call a debt. My people would call it—" He paused, his blue eyes remote. Odd that she could tell when those eerie long pupils were looking beyond her. "—a reciprocal obligation. That will do as a translation.

"Or maybe I ought to say, your action may have created an obligation.

"You acted, as far as I can tell, out of honor and compassion, but your action was unnecessary and inappropriate. Does the fact that your action was unnecessary make it meaningless?

"What you did was contrary to the will of the Goddess and to all good sense. But you didn't know that. How can I judge the behavior of an alien, a person from a culture that does not seem to have the first idea of what is decent?"

He paused and drew in a breath, hissing softly. "Does intent matter or only the action? Does action matter or only the result?

"This is like a situation in a hero play. Right and wrong are so tangled that there is no way to pull the different strands apart. You tug on a bright thread and find you have drawn out something dark.

"I do not know for certain whether I owe you any-thing."

After a moment Anna said, "I can't tell you."

"I did not expect that a human could advise me on a matter of ethics." He looked past her again, his blue eyes unfocused. Finally he said, "I will do what I can for you, though I don't have much time." His eyes returned to her. "There were two human ships, as you may know. The one at the edge of the system got away. We think we know how long it takes to reach your nearest important base. We have been watching the message probes come and go. We need to be off planet in another day.

"So." He paused. "I have two alternatives, Perez Anna. You can choose. I will offer you asylum. If you want, you can come with us when we leave."

"No," she said without thinking.

"Are you certain?"

He was asking her to step into the abyss.

"Thank you for the offer. But no."

"Very well. I will move to the second alternative. As far as I can determine, this entire absurd plot was devised and carried out by the soldiers who came with the diplo-matic team. The diplomats seem to have known nothing, though they may be lying. There isn't time to find out.

"Nicky warned me that there were two groups, and that they were not working together. And he warned me that the soldiers were dangerous. I should have remembered that this is his species.

"I am going to speak with your diplomatic team and suggest to them that this need not be the end to negotia-tions. This mess can be blamed on the military. The diplo-mats—if they are clever—can extract themselves without dishonor. I will ask them to make sure that you get out as well."

"Thank you."

"It may not work." He shifted in his chair and looked

at something on the table. "There is one more thing, Perez Anna. I want to ask you for a favor. You don't have to say yes. We are taking advantage of the present situation to appropriate anything in the compound or at the station that might prove useful. Information, mostly." She saw the gleam of teeth. That was definitely a smile, and the alien teeth—like human teeth—were square and white. No werewolf fangs. How reassuring. "We would like to get as much human food as possible. As you may know, we don't share the human interest in eating, and the food we eat does not nourish your species. In some cases, it kills them. Our laboratories are able to feed our—here I lose my grasp of English—our guests? our prisoners? But according to Nicky, our human chow does not provide the level of entertainment that his people expect from food."

She couldn't tell whether the alien had a sense of humor or was a self-righteous prig. She couldn't imagine Nicholas living with someone who lacked a sense of humor. But then again, she couldn't imagine Nicholas living with a torturer.

"You want me to tell you which foods to take."

"Yes."

She considered for a moment. Why not? She was already in horrendous trouble. Why not go for broke? And she was touched maybe by the thought of human prisoners eating something like the balanced and nutritious foods that pets got. Human chow, the alien had called it. It had an ominous ring.

She nodded. "I'll do it."

He touched something on his table and spoke in another language. The table answered back. The first-defender looked up. "Watcher Hai Atala will escort you to the human kitchens. Thank you for your help."

A dismissal. She got up. "Will Nicholas be all right?"

"I think so. He is resilient."

She had one more question. "The MI people thought

you wouldn't do anything, even if you figured out what was going on. They said that in your culture men are expendable."

"Hah," said the alien, a long exhalation. It sounded thoughtful, considering. Most likely, she was reading in.

After a moment he said, "We believe that it is in the nature of men to fight. Those who fight risk injury and death. We have to accept the consequences of what we are and do, Perez Anna. We know that our lives are likely to be short. We know that we are likely to lose one another.

"But it is not easy for us to lose our relatives and friends, and I would never use the word 'expendable,' especially for Nicky. The people one loves are never expendable."

That seemed like a good parting line.

Her alien, Hai Atala, was in the corridor, standing upright and managing to look both alert and comfortable, as if he could easily spend the day waiting and not get restless or miss anything important. Like a good outfielder. Would it be possible to teach these people baseball? Would they be interested? Watching them move, she thought football was entirely out. They were too graceful and too smart.

They walked back to the entrance of the building.

"I thought about *Moby Dick*," Anna said. "All the important characters are men, and the story is about hunting and killing and God and craziness. There's a good chance that you would consider it decent."

"Maybe I will read it," said Hai Atala. "Thank you for your advice. It's not easy to study your literature. You are obsessed with reproduction. No wonder there are so many of you."

They left the building. Rain still fell, fine and misty. It dimmed the low rolling yellow landscape of the island and made the black landing field shine.

They walked together to the plane.

# XVI

➤➤➤ BY THE TIME I got out of sick bay, the *Hawata* was on its way out of the system. The first gas giant was behind us, and we were gaining speed. The corridors were starting to take on the feeling they did on trips. I'm not sure I can find the words for it. The function of a ship is to travel, and when a ship is traveling, the people on it are doing what they are supposed to. They move toward their proper goal; they rest at the center of their lives. There is a concentration and a confidence that is missing when they are killing time or doing the less important parts of their job.

But the *hwarhath* are the worst maniacs for work I have ever met.

I reported to the general in his office as instructed. It was smaller than the office on the planet, though that wasn't evident at once. He had a hologram on, and one wall had turned into a row of tall narrow windows. Beyond the windows was a landscape: rolling hills covered with a low pale yellow vegetation. I had seen the plant up close. It looks like grass, until you notice that there are no seed stalks and no seeds, only the long narrow flexible leaves, faded gold like maple leaves at the end of autumn. Trees dotted the hills. They were large and leafy—shaped like maples, come to think of it—and yellow: a bright and brassy hue. Large dark animals grazed on the hillsides. The sky was a deep clear blue.

The land of Ettin. The view was almost certainly from one of the houses held by the women in his lineage. **[Yes.]**

I sat down. The general paced, which was very unlike him. Now and then he stopped at his worktable and fiddled with something on it: the statue of the Goddess in her guise as the Keeper of the Hearth or the long dangerous-looking knife that was the emblem of his rank.

He asked me how I was. I said fine.

"You warned me about those people, and I did not listen properly."

"We all make mistakes."

He looked at the hologram. "I do not like to."

This is true.

"We emptied their computers. As soon as you are able, I want you to begin looking through the information. It is going to keep you very busy."

"No problem."

"I will let Shen Walha explain how he got you away from the humans. Everything went smoothly, except for the harm done to you. And I do not know what is going to happen to the human woman. Your species is incomprehensible to me. It is possible they will do something to her. A punishment, a revenge."

With that as a lead-in, he told me about his conversation with Anna.

Afterward I said, "Why did you tell her that story?"

"About the first year you spent among the People?"

I nodded. He picked up the statue of the Goddess and held it for a moment, then set it down. "She does not belong on the perimeter. No woman does. But your species mixes everything together. Nothing is safe. No one is protected.

"I don't know if you owe her anything. She tried—as she understood it—to save your life and, so doing, put herself in danger. I was trying to make her understand that she must not involve herself in the affairs of men."

"So to speak."

He looked puzzled and went on. "I was trying to make

her understand something about the violence on the perimeter. Your people must lie to each other constantly about the nature of everything, but especially about the nature of violence. I really don't think she understood what she had gotten herself into. I wanted to give her some idea. I wanted to frighten her and make her feel disgust and horror.''

"You probably succeeded.''

"Good. As I say, I am not sure that we owe her anything. But if we do, I would like her out of this mess.'' He picked up the dagger. The hilt was gold with a gemstone in the pommel that shone reddish-purple with flashes of green. An alexandrite, I was almost certain. The blade was thirty centimeters long, the edge razor-sharp.

"There were women in the compound. We killed one, though fortunately we did not find out until afterward, and no one knows who did the killing. It has not been necessary for anyone to ask for the option.

"We told the human ship we would destroy it, if it moved out of orbit. I know there are women on board. We held the entire human population of the planet hostage, making no distinction between the men and the women; and we have left missiles behind us, to keep a watch on the planet till we are gone. Their programs have been altered. They no longer make discriminations. They cannot be reasoned with. They will spare no one.''

"Jesus Christ,'' I said.

"I did this because I could not see an alternative; but now I must go to the other frontmen and ask them how we are going to fight an enemy like this. There is another question I will not ask them, since I do not trust them to give me a good answer; but I will ask you, Nicky. I have known for a long time that I am *rahaka*. I will not take the option, if there is any way to avoid it. How am I going to live with what I have done?''

You will live with it, because you have to, you damn fool. **[Ah.]**

After I left him I went to visit Shen Walha, the general's chief of operations. The first time I saw this man I knew he was a Wally. He is big and broad and soft-looking with fur that is close to pure white. There are spots over his back and shoulders and on his upper arms. The spots are like those of a snow leopard: large fuzzy rings, empty at the center and often broken. They are very pale grey.

A big, wide spotty fellow who looks a bit like a teddy bear. Of course he's a Wally. I've got almost everyone using that as a nickname, even the general.

He's from an island far to the south on the *hwarhath* native planet. The weather there goes from rain to sleet to snow and back again, and the people have long thick fur. They all look large and soft and cuddly. They have a reputation for extreme toughness.

He sat in his office, dressed in his invariable costume: a pair of shorts. Poor Wally is always hot. His hands were folded over his broad furry belly. He looked at me with pale yellow eyes.

"I understand I have you to thank for my life."

"Your freedom. I don't think the humans would have killed you. Sit down, if you want to." He scratched his chest, then yawned, giving me a good view of his four stabbing teeth. In most of the People, these teeth are about as prominent as human canines; but Wally's stabbers are long and pointed, and he yawns a lot. He claims the heat makes him sleepy. I think it's a form of display.

"The first-defender said I ought to ask you about the operation."

"He came to me twenty days ago and said you were worried, and he thought it was nothing. But it might be a good idea to have a contingency plan, which you were not to know about."

"Why?"

"I can't give you Ettin Gwarha's reasons. As for me, I don't trust you. I never have."

"Oh yes. That."

"So I began to bring men and weapons from the main base in the north: a little every day or so on the regular flight. The humans did not notice. They were too busy sneaking around in their undetectable planes to their hole-in-the-ground secret bases. We found two planes and two bases after we took over, and there are almost certainly more of both. Useless folly! But it kept them occupied.

"We put everything—men and weapons—in the high-security portion of the base."

Where I was not permitted.

"And when the enemy made their brilliant move, we were able to retaliate.

"It was simple enough. Take out the landing field. Destroy the shuttle on the ground. Drop men into the compound and the station. Wave guns and shoot a few of the enemy, those who are unusually stupid or brave.

"Tell the ship in orbit that we have deployed intelligent missiles. A large number, too many to find and stop. If it does anything, if it begins to move, we will destroy it and every human on the planet. There is no threat like a big threat, Nicky."

He frowned and scratched his wide, flat furry nose. "There was only one problem. The second human ship. I told the first-defender I wanted to destroy it. It was too close to the transfer point. I thought it would make a run. He said no. He wanted me to bluff. This was wrong, Nicky. If I had gotten that ship, we could have taken our time on the planet. Gone through all the data systems slowly and questioned the humans.

"The first-defender thinks he can rescue the negotiations. He wanted no more violence than was necessary. It is always stupid to be moderate in war."

"There were almost certainly women on that ship. You would have destroyed it anyway?"

"Yes. Of course." He leaned forward and rested his thick arms on his table. "These perverted aliens are not the first people who have ever tried to hide behind women and children. They are not the first people who have broken the rules of war. We have known in the past how to deal with such offenders against the Goddess."

The usual technique is to form an alliance. Old quarrels are put aside, at least for the time being. Bitter enemies unite, and everyone moves against the offending lineage.

If possible, the women and children are not harmed, at least directly. But if the criminal lineage cannot be stopped without harming women and children, well, then it happens; and the men who do the harming take the option as soon as it's convenient. (One of the things I really like about the *hwarhath* is you can break almost any rule, so long as you are willing to commit suicide afterward. They feel that this keeps people from developing bad habits.)

No one will negotiate with a lineage that has broken the rules of war, and there is only one ending: a final solution. The offending lineage is completely destroyed. The men are killed, and the women and children are not taken into any other lineage. They become wanderers and pariahs. As the male children mature, they are killed.

If the women have new children, which used to happen sometimes in the past, though the *hwarhath* do not like to admit this, the new children receive the same treatment as everyone else. They have no place among the People. They, too, are criminals.

In the end, the lineage vanishes. It may take a generation or two or even three. There is no forgiveness ever. The *hwarhath* believe in consequences and in genetics. There are certain traits they do not want to retain.

Wally said, "We have two alternatives. We can declare

that humans are people who have broken the rules of war. Or we can declare them not people."

"What do you mean?"

His pale yellow eyes stared at me. He outranks me. I glanced down. "We can say that humans are very clever animals, who can mimic the behavior of people, but lack the essential quality of personhood. They cannot distinguish between right and wrong. They lack judgment and discrimination.

"I think there is a good argument for this, and if they are animals, then we can deal with them as animals. We do not need to worry about the rules of war."

"Wally, you frighten me."

He yawned again, showing off his teeth. Then he smiled. "We are not friends, Nicky. I never forget what you are. An alien. An enemy. A betrayer-of-the-lineage. In the end, I think, you will betray Ettin Gwarha."

"I don't think so."

"Maybe not intentionally; but you have a spirit that goes in two directions, and like all humans you are easily confused. Everything is mixed up together. You cannot tell right from wrong."

A pair of cheerful morning conversations. I went off to practice *hanatsin* and then to check the supplies that the general had lifted from the humans.

From the journal of Sanders Nicholas, etc.

# PART II

## THE
## RULES
## OF
## WAR

# I

➤➤➤ THE TRIP WENT as planned. They made the first transfer, following directions given by the enemy, and arrived in the middle of nowhere. A *hwarhath* ship met them and gave them a new set of directions. They moved on. The *hwarhath* ship stayed and made sure no one was following. This happened two more times and then, after four transfers, they came to the enemy station.

The singularity it orbited (at a good safe distance) produced no useful light, and the station was visible only as a computer graphic. It turned on a screen in the observation room: a blunt, squat cylinder that looked more than anything else like a can of soup.

As had been agreed, their ship stopped a good safe distance from the can of soup and waited for an alien shuttle to arrive. Anna packed. It had not been easy to decide what to bring from Earth, and now she had to make more decisions. What should one wear to the first-ever negotiations with an alien enemy in their own space?

Comfortable clothing with a lot of versatility. Clothing that was easy to wash and did not require pressing.

But also—as well—one outfit that would dazzle the dull blue eyes of the aliens, or if not the aliens (who knew what would dazzle them?) her colleagues on the diplomatic team, or Nicholas Sanders, he of the pleasant smile and the not so pleasant history. Though she had no assurance that he would be involved in the new set of negotiations.

When she had finished packing she went to the observation room and watched the soup can turning, spinning around its long axis.

One of her colleagues was there, a young diplomat named Etienne Corbeau.

"I don't understand," he said. "These stations can look like anything. Why do they make them look ugly?"

"Maybe they see them differently. Beauty is in the eye of the beholder."

Etienne shook his head. "I believe in aesthetic absolutes. Morality is relative, but there is truth in art."

"Bullshit."

"You are going to have to learn a new vocabulary, dear Anna."

Why? She was on this trip for one reason only. The enemy had asked for her by name. The *hwarhath* knew she wasn't a diplomat. They weren't likely to expect her to speak like Etienne.

The enemy sent out their shuttle, and the diplomatic team got on: broad-beamed human men settling into wide alien seats. She was the only woman; the *hwarhath* had specified.

The air in the shuttle had a strange aroma. The *hwarhath*, thought Anna after a moment. She had forgotten about their scent over the past two years, but it came back to her now. It wasn't unpleasant, merely inhuman.

The shuttle crew wore shorts and sandals. They were courteous; she remembered this quality from her previous encounter with the *hwarhath*, on the planet of the *pseudosiphonophores;* and they moved with the deft grace that was apparently characteristic of the species. They looked more alien than they had before. Maybe it was their new costumes, which made it clear how furry they were. Or maybe it was their nipples. They had four, arranged in two sets of two, large and dark and clearly visible on the broad furry chests.

Anna wondered about the number of children in an

average *hwarhath* birth. She'd done all the research she could, but so little was known about the aliens! Especially, so little was known about the alien women.

"These people have always given me the creeps," said Etienne. He sat down next to her.

"Why?"

"The eyes. The hands. The fur. And their violence. You weren't in the compound when it was hit."

No. She had been a prisoner of human Military Intelligence.

She felt a jolt: the shuttle disengaging from the human ship, the *Envoy of Peace.* A moment later their gravity changed, and she checked to make sure her belts were fastened.

The trip was nothing special. The engines went on, then off, then back on. The gravity kept changing. There was nothing to see, except the windowless cabin. Did the *hwarhath* use nothing except industrial colors, and why were their industrial colors the same as industrial colors on Earth? Of course, she knew nothing about alien optics. Maybe these blank walls were actually covered with festive patterns not visible to her. Maybe when the aliens looked at the various shades of grey, they saw—who could say? Colors as vivid as fuchsia.

Around her the diplomats chatted nervously. They said nothing important. The aliens might be listening. In front of her the assistant ambassador talked about his gladioli, and Etienne described his last visit to the Museum of Modern Art in New York.

After an hour there was another little jolt. The shuttle had docked. Doors opened, and the team floated out, helped by the aliens, who were not floating. There must be something on the bottom of their sandals that held them to the floor.

It was like arriving at a human station, thought Anna. An elevator carried the diplomatic team from axis to rim.

When the elevator stopped, they were no longer floating. They filed out with dignity, and *hwarhath* crewmen guided them down a corridor and into a room: large and brightly lit with greyish tan carpeting. The air was cool and smelled of machinery and aliens; half a dozen stood waiting, dressed in knee-length shorts and nothing else.

"I don't understand the costumes," said Etienne.

She missed the close-fitting uniforms that the *hwarhath* had worn before. But they did look more comfortable now, though less like space-age warriors.

There was an official greeting, spoken by a large alien with a thick accent. Not the first-defender. Where was he? The human ambassador replied. Anna was far enough back so she had trouble hearing, and she wasn't much interested anyway.

She looked at the *hwarhath* and noticed that one of them seemed familiar: short and dark and trim. He glanced at her, his eyes meeting hers for only an instant. After he looked back down he smiled, and the smile was definitely familiar: brief and glinting, lasting no longer than his glance. Hai Atala Vaihar.

When the speeches ended, he came over. "Mem Perez."

"Watcher Hai Atala."

"You remember me. I'm pleased. Though I ought to tell you that I've been promoted. I am now a holder."

"Congratulations."

He smiled his glinting smile. "As you know, it was agreed that you would have proper quarters away from the men. I will escort you."

She spoke with her colleagues. Etienne looked worried. The assistant ambassador said, "I'm not entirely happy about this, Anna." The chief of security told her to be careful. Hai Atala waited in courteous silence.

A couple of minutes later the two of them were walking through a corridor just like the ones in the *hwarhath* base:

large and bare and grey and full of aliens, moving quickly and with their usual air of assurance.

"I read *Moby Dick* as you advised me," the holder said. "A very good book and almost entirely decent. I have been—what is the word?—harassing Sanders Nicholas to read it. I want to discuss it with a human. Maybe while you are here—"

They turned a corner into another corridor. She glanced ahead. A tall, thin figure stood facing in their direction, arms folded, one shoulder against the grey wall of the corridor. His feet were crossed, and all his weight was on one leg. Absolutely typical. Her memory of Nicholas was of him always slouching and lounging, except at the end.

He straightened and stepped away from the wall, unfolding his arms and holding them out from his sides. This had to be a formal gesture: arms straight, hands flat, the palms held forward. His fingers were together, and his thumbs pointed up. What did it mean? "I have nothing in my hands or up my sleeves"?

Hai Atala stopped and made the same gesture.

"Hello, Anna," said Nicholas, and smiled. He looked almost the same as he had two years before. A little older, maybe. There was more grey in his hair.

Hai Atala said, "Nicky will take over as your escort, mem. I have no relatives in the women's part of the station. I really should not go in. Nicky, at least, is the same species as you, and he tells me that he is from the same region on your home planet."

"Are you?" asked Anna.

"I read your file. You grew up in the Chicago area. I grew up in Kansas. Two Midwesterners. It makes us almost relatives. Can I take your bag?"

"I'm supposed to keep hold of it. The enemy might put something in. A listening device, a bomb."

"We can listen perfectly well with the devices in the walls," said Hai Atala. "And no one would set off a bomb

in his own space station." The alien paused. "Not a large
bomb, anyway. I hope to see you later, mem." He turned
and moved off. Anna watched him go. "Am I seeing
things or does he move even more beautifully than the
other *hwar?*"

"They like to make up names for each other," Nicholas
said. "Especially the men. Usually the names are jokes,
and often the jokes are nasty; but his nickname is The
Graceful Man. It isn't only the way he moves. He is socially graceful, and he has a graceful spirit; and he's a lot
more open-minded than most of the People. A very good
young man, who's going to be very important, if there isn't
a serious war. If we end up fighting the Confederation, you
will have the dubious pleasure of dealing with Wally
Shen."

"Do you have a nickname?" she asked.

"A couple. The Man Who Does Not Like to Answer
Questions and The Man Who Hates Carpeting." He scuffed
at the carpet that covered the floor with a sandaled foot. "I
have lived with this stuff for twenty years, and it still
moves me to invective."

He was dressed in a long-sleeved tan shirt, pants of the
same color and the sandals. As before, his clothing looked
not quite right, as if made by a tailor who was not entirely
sure what he was trying to make. Two round badges were
clipped to his belt: enameled metal with emblems she did
not recognize and stuff that was almost certainly writing.

"Let's get going," he said.

They walked. His hands went into his pockets almost
at once and his pace was a stroll, nothing like the quick
graceful motion of Hai Atala.

"What happened to the uniforms?" she asked after a
while.

"What you are looking at is the usual *hwarhath* costume for men. Remember, the People are covered with fur,
and the men—to a very considerable extent—live in places

that have artificial climates. Why would they need clothing? They need pockets and a place to hang their ID badges, and they need enough of a covering so the People who come from modest cultures are not disturbed. And that is what you're seeing."

"The uniforms on the planet were fake," said Anna.

"Costumes," said Nicholas. "As for a play. I told the general that the humans might find it hard to take people wearing shorts seriously. So we had the Art Corps design space cadet uniforms. Very nicely done, I thought. I especially liked the high shiny black boots, though I can't imagine what they would be for. You don't ride horses in a space station, and you don't do a hell of a lot of hiking. The snakebite problem is minimal. Maybe you use them to kick subordinates, while uttering guttural curses in an alien tongue." She had forgotten the sound of his voice. It was tenor, light and pleasant and full of amusement.

"Do they do that kind of thing?"

"Kick subordinates? No, and they don't curse much, either. There are no obscenities in the *hwarhath* main language, none at all. You can't tell anyone to fuck off. You can't describe anything as a crock of shit. There are times I think this explains a lot about the *hwarhath*."

They turned another corner. Ahead was a tall double door, framed by a pair of soldiers holding rifles. Midway up the door was an emblem, spreading out from the line that split the door in two: a cluster of flames about a meter tall, in relief and gilded.

"The Hearthfire," said Nicholas. "It represents the Goddess and the Home World, the Center of the Lineage, and Women or possibly Woman. I can hear the caps on all those words." He glanced at one of the soldiers and spoke. The soldier turned and touched something. The doors opened.

Inside was a wood floor, pale yellow and shining.

Nicholas stepped through the doorway. Anna followed, and the doors shut in back of them.

The walls of the room looked to be plaster; they were white with a faint blue tinge. There were tapestries in rich colors, showing *hwarhath* doing things she did not understand. A long wide rug ran down the middle of the floor. Like the tapestries, it was richly colored: red, dark blue, dark green, deep orange and bright yellow.

"Jesus Maria," said Anna.

Nicholas laughed. "I had lived among the *hwarhath* almost ten years before I saw the inside of any women's quarters. Then a couple of the general's aunts decided that they wanted to find out more about the companion that their darling nephew had chosen, and they came out to one of the stations." As he spoke he led her down the hall, over the richly colored rug and past the tapestries. "They called the general and me in for an interview. I'd heard by then that the women's quarters were different. But still, I was impressed."

She looked ahead. At the end of the hall were three people, dressed in robes of red and yellow. They stood waiting with the usual *hwarhath* calm. Big people, broad and solid.

Nicholas went on speaking, his voice soft. "It takes a lot to make *hwarhath* matriarchs leave their home planet. But the general was being a weasel. They had asked him to bring me to Ettin, and he kept finding reasons not to. So they came after him. They are a very ambitious lineage, and the general is the most important Ettin male of his generation. The aunts were not about to have anything happen to their chief representative in the world of men."

They reached the three people. Their robes were made of long narrow panels, sewn together at the shoulders. Further down the panels were separate, connected here and there by fine gold chains. When the people moved, the panels would shift and maybe even flutter, but the gaps between them could never grow large.

The material reminded Anna of silk brocade. Each robe had a different pattern. One looked like flowers; another was geometric; the last might have been animals, though what kind Anna could not tell.

Nicholas stopped. His hands were out of his pockets and at his sides. His usual restlessness had ceased. He stood quietly, looking down. Even with his head bent, he was taller than the aliens by something like ten centimeters, but their massive bodies made him seem frail.

These were almost certainly women, though the faces—broad and blunt-featured and covered with fur—did not look feminine, nor did the barrel-like torsoes, nor did the arms, bare from the shoulders, heavy and furry. They all wore bracelets: wide and thick and plain, made, Anna was almost certain, of gold.

"Don't look directly at them," said Nicholas softly.

Anna looked down.

One of the aliens spoke in a deep—very deep—voice.

"I am to introduce you," said Nicholas. "The woman on the right is Ettin Per. Next to her is Ettin Aptsi. And on the left is Ettin Sai. They are sisters and the current leaders of the Ettin lineage. Ettin Gwarha is their nephew."

The third woman—Sai—spoke in a voice that was less deep, a baritone rather than a bass.

"She understands English, though she doesn't usually speak it. She has asked me to tell you that she understands you meant no discourtesy by staring. Human customs are different."

The first woman—Ettin Per, the one with the very deep voice—spoke again.

Nicholas said, "She's welcoming you to the women's quarters. They look forward to speaking with you. They have become interested in humanity and especially in human women."

"Tell them I am glad to be here," Anna said. "And I look forward to speaking with them. Is that why the general asked for me?"

"Yes," said Ettin Sai.

The third woman—Aptsi—spoke. Another baritone.

Nicholas lifted his head and looked directly at her, answering in the alien language. Aptsi reached out a grey furry hand and touched him lightly on one shoulder.

"We have been dismissed," said Nicholas. "Come on."

They left the three women, standing like statues of the Three Fates. Nicholas led her down another hall, narrower than the first one, but made of the same materials. There were no tapestries here. They reached a door made of a silvery metal. A square plate—also metal, but darker and duller—was set in the wall next to the door.

He gestured toward the plate. "Put the palm of your hand there. Press in firmly. Good. Now it's set to open for two people only: you and me."

Beyond the door was a large square room. The floor was pale grey wood, and there was paneling made of the same kind of wood covering the lower half of the walls. It had an odd iridescent shimmer. Like what? The scales of a fish? Mother-of-pearl?

Anna touched the wood. It felt like wood, but it really did look as if it had come from under water. Pale colors shifted and gleamed on the cool polished surface.

"Do you mind if I sit down?" asked Nicholas.

"Go ahead." She set down her bag and glanced at the door. It had closed.

He settled into a large low chair and stretched out his legs. "I have known the aunts for over ten years now. I'm still not entirely comfortable with them. Aptsi is the easiest one to get along with. She was asking me how I was and saying it was good to see me." He glanced up at her, smiling. "They passed me after that interview ten years ago. Aptsi and Per. They decided Gwarha could keep me. I felt like some kind of not very attractive pet. You know, the mutt the kid brings home. 'Just remember, Gwarha, you have to take care of him, and if there's *any* trouble at all—' "

"They are very big," said Anna.

"Yes they are. Maybe at some point I will explain about sexual dimorphism among the People, but not now. You have a kitchen and a bathroom. I supervised the installation. The fixtures may look strange to you, but they all work and can be used by humans. There is food in the kitchen, part of the haul that the general made at the end of the last set of negotiations. There are voltage converters at all the electrical access points. If you have anything that needs to be plugged in, you can do it with confidence.

"There's an intercom system. I've written out instructions on how to operate it and how to get hold of me, as well as the rest of your team. And I have translated the instructions on what to do in the event of an emergency: loss of power, loss of gravity, loss of atmospheric pressure."

"Does this happen often?"

"Never, in my experience. But read the instructions and memorize them.

"If anything does happen, this is the safest place to be. The *hwarhath* have made sure this part of the station is very solid. All the systems have a lot of redundancy, and the rescue teams will come here first. The *hwarhath* are serious about protecting their women.

"This might be a good time to explain about the station. It was built for this set of negotiations. It isn't close to anything that matters to the *hwarhath,* and they don't normally use this transfer point. There is very little useful information here. If your colleagues decide to play spy games, they will only—what is the line from the old joke?—waste their time and annoy the *hwarhath.*"

"The station is huge," said Anna. "They built it for one set of negotiations?"

He shrugged. "It's mostly empty at the moment. If the negotiations succeed, the People will almost certainly need the extra room. If things don't work out—I imagine the explosive charges are already in place."

Anna didn't want to think about a culture that could build something this big in less than two years, and in the knowledge that they might have to destroy it. She changed the topic.

"There aren't going to be any spy games. The people in MI have been told to keep their ugly sticky hands off everything."

"Turn around," said Nicholas.

She did. There was a rectangle made of lights on the wall above the paneling: three across and five down. All the lights were on. All were colorless, except two in the bottom row, which shone amber.

"That is your security monitor. If all the lights are colorless, that means your doors are all locked, and your intercom is off, and no one is listening or watching. If any one of the lights is amber, you are not secure."

"Are you telling me the truth?" she asked.

"My reputation as a liar is exaggerated. You've got bugs, Anna, and they are not alien. The general's security people came through and did a check this—morning, I guess I can say. In the first *ikun*. These rooms were safe, before you came into them."

"I think I'll use the bathroom."

He pointed, and she went through a door.

He was right about the fixtures. They were definitely odd, but they worked and a human could use them. The toilet paper was the kind she would have found in how many places on Earth? Was this something else that the general had taken?

She washed her hands and face, then looked in the mirror.

A stocky woman, of average height for a human. Her skin was brown. Her hair was short and black and wavy. She wore pants and a jacket of dark blue cotton, a kind that was meant to crinkle. Her blouse was white and made of the same crinkly cotton. She wore no jewelry except a string of lapis beads. Her mother had bought them on a visit to the Islamic Socialist Republic, back when there were still genuine independent nations on Earth.

Was this the look of a person who had traveled a hundred light-years from home? Was this the look of someone who had just used an alien toilet?

Yes, and it was also the look of someone who—at this distance and amid all this strangeness—could not escape from fools.

Huh! Her expression was angry! She did not like those lines around her mouth or between her eyebrows.

There was a pen in her jacket pocket. Thank God for being old-fashioned. She did not think she could trust her computer. She tore off a piece of the toilet paper and wrote, "Get rid of the bugs." Then she made a face at her reflection and went back to join Nicholas.

He was standing now, holding a pair of wineglasses. Each was half-full of a pale yellow liquid. "Your file said that you liked white wine. This is a Pouilly Fume. Not bad, I think, though I have to say I've lost track of such things."

She took one of the glasses and in return handed over the piece of toilet paper. He looked at it, nodded and lifted his glass. "To peace and friendship."

They drank. The wine was cold and good.

He set down his glass. "Nothing is planned for tonight. You can get some rest, and you look as if you could use it. Tomorrow is the formal opening of the negotiations, a lot of speeches that don't mean much of anything. I'm giving it a miss; but you ought to attend. I'll come by in the morning. You shouldn't go anywhere without an escort, Anna, and the escort should be someone you know. Me or Hai Atala Vaihar. I'll introduce you to the third man tomorrow. Eh Matsehar. He's a member of the Art Corps on temporary assignment with the general. His English is excellent, and I guess you ought to be able to tolerate his manners."

She didn't want to be left in this place with no company except human devices for spying, but she couldn't think of anything to say.

"There is more wine in the kitchen, and food, as I said. No one can get in without your permission. I don't think the aunts will bother you, but if they do, remember they are very senior to you. Treat them with respect, and treat them directly. Don't lie and don't try to be evasive. If you don't want to answer a question, say so. All the People respect honesty, and the people of Ettin are famous for being blunt.

"There is a love song that begins—" He paused and looked at the wall in back of her, his expression remote.

"Like the hill folk of Ettin
I will plainly speak my mind.

"That's a close enough translation. I've always liked the words to that song, and nowadays I even like the music. It took years before I could hear it as anything except alien noise." He walked to the door and touched the wall next to it. The door slid open. Nicholas looked down at her. "If you get lonely, remember the intercom. You can always talk to one of the dips. Good night. Don't look so angry, or so worried. This is not a bad situation." He smiled. "Believe me, I have been in a number that were worse."

The door closed behind him. Anna sat down in one of the chairs. It was deep and soft, covered with upholstery that matched the pale, intricate pattern of the rug covering the floor. She drank more wine, then kicked off her shoes and put her feet on a table made of the mother-of-pearl wood. The legs of the table had been carved into twisting monsters. At least, she thought they were monsters. They looked the part: scales and spines and claws and teeth.

She looked up. There was a light in the middle of the ceiling, made of grey metal and a material like frosted glass. It reminded her of something from Earth. Art deco, a style that had dominated Western art in the middle of the twentieth century. Now, that was curious.

But maybe she was doing what humans always did and trying to make the strange familiar. You meet a guy with grey fur and big ears and horizontal pupils and you say, "I got a cousin just like you in Schaumberg, Illinois."

Did Nicholas ever say that?

What would it be like to live utterly alone among aliens?

What would it be like to dream of being tortured?

In the dream the creatures who torture you are not human. You wake from the nightmare and discover that someone is comforting you. Someone is giving you reassurance. What was the phrase the general had used? Building a road of words that will lead you back to reality.

That person is inhuman and your torturer.

The abyss, thought Anna.

She finished her glass of wine and then the one that he'd left almost untouched. After that she went and found the bedroom.

A bare floor made of pearlwood, bare walls made of the material like plaster, a bed that was a rectangular block with a thin mattress on top. Only the pillow looked entirely ordinary, and it didn't feel quite right. Too soft. The ceiling was open to the stars.

My God, she thought, looking up. There were blazing

single suns, and distant clusters, clouds of glowing gas, all possible colors.

It must be a hologram. The station was turning, and this was motionless. Anyway, they had seen nothing like this coming in.

If it was a hologram, it was by far the best one she had ever seen.

She got undressed. A blanket lay at the foot of the bed, neatly folded. She spread it out and lay down on it, looking up at the splendid vista, until her eyes were no longer able to focus. The stars blurred together. Anna pulled the blanket over herself and slept.

# II

▷▷▷ THE GENERAL WAS in his office, the latest in a series that stretched (in my memory) over twenty years and across I don't know how much space. They are all more or less alike. This one had a new hologram.

It replaced the wall opposite his worktable. There were no windows: nothing to frame or mediate. The carpeting stopped. Beyond it, greenish waves broke against a beach of grey-green sand. The sky was stormy and almost the same color as the water. In the distance, cliffs rose and flying creatures soared. The creatures did not look familiar.

"Where is it?"

"One of the settlement worlds." The general paused and corrected himself. "One of the worlds we are trying to settle."

I told him about the bugs.

"They listen to women. That is contemptible."

"I told you they did and would."

He reached toward his intercom. "My aunts should know."

"I have told Ettin Per."

"Hah." The long exhalation. "What did she say?"

"She's angry. I told her the devices would be gone tomorrow by the end of the first *ikun.*"

He looked past me at the hologram. "We should not have asked the humans to send Perez Anna. We are introducing human behavior—human disrespect and dishonor—into places that should always be kept safe."

"Tell that to your aunts. They're the ones who decided that the Weaving needed to find out about human women."

The focus of his eyes changed. He was looking at something in the hologram. I turned. One of the flying creatures had landed on the beach. It had claws on its wings, and it crawled batlike over the sand: a big creature with a scaly skin, dappled grey and green and tan. Its beak had many narrow pointed teeth.

"Anna makes sense. We know her. We know she isn't entirely hostile to the People; and she's direct, First-Defender. She isn't likely to enrage the women of Ettin. If I didn't know better, I'd say that thing was a pterodactyl."

"What?"

"An animal on Earth. They have been extinct for—if I remember correctly—sixty-five million years. No one's ever been able to figure out how they took off and landed."

"Like that, possibly," said the general, as the animal leaped up and flapped and rose.

From the journal of Sanders Nicholas, etc.

# III

➤➤➤ SHE WOKE TO the smell of bacon.

Above her the stars had vanished, and she was looking at a plain white ceiling.

The bathroom was next to her bedroom. Anna gathered clothing, went in and washed and dressed in another pantsuit, this one grey (the favorite *hwarhath* color) with a yellow blouse and a string of agate beads, striped gray and tan. Gold stud earrings. No other jewelry.

Today her reflection looked less tired and angry, maybe even happy. She grinned at herself. Remember, Anna, her mother always said, a smile makes everyone look prettier, and if you smile you will *be* happier.

Breakfast was on one of the tables in the main room: a mug full of coffee, a knife and fork, a plate that contained a slice of bread (toasted) and three pieces of bacon, cooked to crisp perfection. The last thing on the plate was square and gelatinous and pale green.

Nicholas stood leaning against a wall, holding a coffee mug.

"What on Earth." She poked her fork into the green thing.

"Mostly protein. Very nutritious. The taste won't bother you. It tastes like nothing."

She took a bite. He was right about the taste.

"If you want some carbohydrates, I have something that's yellow and—" He paused. "—thick. I guess that would describe it. I've never been able to figure out the taste. There are days when I think it might be cardboard, but I haven't eaten cardboard in years."

"This is human chow," she said.

He grinned. "The bacon is real and the coffee and the bread; but I thought you might be interested in what most of the humans eat, who are—what is the general's lovely term?—our guests."

She ate. He watched and drank his coffee.

"I'll clean up later," he said when she was done. "We ought to get going."

They walked through the women's quarters, seeing no one, and went out through the big double doors.

A *hwarhath* stood waiting in the corridor: big and gaunt and grey, dressed in the usual shorts. He stepped forward. There was something wrong about the way he moved. He was awkward, and the People never were.

He held out his left hand and looked at it. "Is this correct? I am trying to shake hands."

"Other hand," said Anna.

He reversed, and they shook.

"How was I?" the *hwar* asked.

"Too vigorous. Let's try it again."

They did, with Nicholas watching. His expression was restless and amused. "We have to get going, Anna."

They turned and walked together. There was no question about the way the alien moved; he was the first *hwarhath* she had ever met who was uncoordinated.

"Mats forgot to introduce himself," Nicholas said. "This is Eh Matsehar. He's an advancer, which means he outranks me, and he is temporarily assigned to the general's staff. That is mostly so he can study humans. Most of the time he works for the Art Corps. He's the best playwright of the present generation."

"The best male playwright," said Eh Matsehar. "Amit Asharil is very fine, and it is possible that she is as good as

I am, though it isn't really possible to compare the work of men and women.''

''Apples and oranges,'' said Nicholas, sounding genial.

''I actually know that phrase,'' said the alien. ''They are two kinds of fruit native to your home planet, and for some reason that is not clear to me, they cannot be compared.''

''Uh-huh,'' said Nicholas.

''And you''—the *hwarhath* inclined his head, looking at her sideways—''are Perez Anna, the latest of Nicky's victims.''

''What?''

''We can talk about this some other time,'' said Nicholas.

''Why not at present?'' asked Eh Matsehar.

''I don't know who is listening.''

''Out here?'' The alien looked around. ''Not much of anyone, I should imagine. What are they going to hear? Corridor gossip.''

''Maybe,'' said Nicholas.

They had been going through a series of hallways, all close to identical: bare walls and tightly woven carpeting, everything (as usual) grey. The air was cool, almost cold. It smelled of metal and the aliens. *Hwarhath* passed them, not so many as on the day before. Had the human delegation arrived at shift change? Did the *hwarhath* organize their work in shifts?

They reached a corridor guarded by two soldiers with rifles.

''This is the Talking-with-Enemies station,'' said Nicholas. ''That's what its name means; and this is the Talking-with-Enemies section of the station. Matsehar will take you on from here. I have to take care of other business.''

She went with the alien. He led her to a room occupied by the members of the human negotiating team and left her there. The chief of security—a thin, very dark man in civilian clothes with a civilian haircut—said, "Did everything go all right?" He had a lilting Caribbean accent. Captain McIntosh.

"Fine. I met some of the women."

"Oh yes?" said the assistant ambassador. "Are they any easier to deal with than the men?"

"I think not," said Anna.

The assistant ambassador frowned. "I'm not certain I wanted to hear that, Anna. You're going to watch the meeting from here. We couldn't get them to budge on that. They don't want you in the actual meeting room, even though they asked us to bring you all this distance."

Okay by her.

The rest of the team filed out. The door slid shut after them, and Anna looked around: another grey room with carpeting. There was one chair, which faced a blank wall. As usual, the chair was large and low and overstuffed. She sat down, and the wall she faced vanished. She was looking at another room, larger than the one she was in and containing two rows of chairs, identical—as far as she could tell—with her chair. They went down the middle of the room, facing one another. Aside from the chairs, the new room was empty. The walls were the usual color, blank and windowless.

Odd, she thought as she settled back. The People seemed to go back and forth between a truly bleak kind of functional design and the kind of furnishings she had seen in the women's quarters: rich, ornate, beautifully made. Was it entirely a question of male and female? Were the men doomed to battleship grey, while the women lived among rugs and tapestries and wood that shone like mother-of-pearl?

People began to enter the big room, the hologram: humans first, coming in from a door she couldn't see and filing around one row of chairs. When they were all in position, they stood waiting. All of this had been negotiated and agreed upon: how people entered and where they sat.

The *hwarhath* came in from the other side. They had put on their space-warrior uniforms. The boots were tall and black and shiny and really did look powerful, arrogant, military. Much more impressive than sandals.

The first man to come into view was noticeably shorter than the men who followed him. He moved around the end of the second row of chairs and down it to a chair in the middle, then stopped and stood facing the humans: a stocky fellow, broad through the chest. He held himself very upright, as did they all; she had never seen any *hwarhath* slouch. And he had the usual alien ease of movement and stance, but with something else added. What? she wondered. Confidence? Definition? Was that the right word? The quality of being definite. The other *hwarhath* filed in on either side of him. She recognized Hai Atala Vaihar, taking the place immediately to the left of the short man and a little in back. All the *hwarhath* were keeping very close to the row of chairs, making sure that the stocky man was out in front, alone.

He glanced to the side briefly to make certain his people were in position, then glanced at the human ambassador and nodded. They all sat down, aliens and humans, and the introductions began.

The short man was Defender-of-the-Hearth-with-Honor First-Ahead Ettin Gwarha. Nick's general, leaning his head very slightly toward Hai Atala Vaihar, who was doing the translation, but otherwise upright and regarding the humans with an air of tranquility or maybe of indifference. When he finally spoke, in the alien language, she recognized his voice: deep and soft with a little roughness. He gave no indication that he understood English, though by this time everyone knew he did.

After the introductions came speeches.

Maybe she wasn't the right person for the job. Her tolerance for this kind of thing was not great. At least she wasn't in the meeting room. She could fidget and think about something more interesting. The bugs in her luggage, interior decorating among the aliens, the number of children in an average *hwarhath* birth. Funny that she'd been able to watch the creatures in the bay for hours and not get bored or restless. Maybe because, as far as she could tell, they were not speaking any kind of untruth. They really were caught between fear and a desire to mate. They really did want to reassure one another.

God, she missed that place! She hadn't been back since military intelligence pulled her off the planet. She closed her eyes for a moment and imagined herself back with poor old Mark, who still lay—as far as she knew—at the bottom of some kind of undersea trench; blue sky above her; golden hills around her; the clear water of the bay full of pseudosiphonophores and the light just right, so the transparent bodies were visible.

The meeting lasted four hours. Finally everyone rose and filed out in the manner agreed upon. The hologram vanished. The door to her room slid open. Eh Matsehar stood in the doorway.

"Why weren't you in there?" she asked, and waved at the now blank wall.

"My skill is not negotiation. I am here to observe and try and understand. If you'll come with me, Perez Anna, I will take you to the place where your companions are going to eat and talk to one another at the same time. Nicky tells me that this is a common, almost universal, practice among humans; and I have read about it in your plays. The banquet scene in *Macbeth*, for example."

They walked together down the corridor to yet another room. This station was like a maze or a house of mirrors.

Another door slid open. Eh Matsehar said, "I'll return

for you in half an *ikun*. That is something over two hours, as you measure time."

"Have you read *Macbeth?*" she asked.

"Yes. In the original and in Nicky's translation. I thought I could do something with it. The heterosexuality is irrelevant. The woman—that wonderful and horrible woman!—can be turned into a mother or sister. Then the story is about ambition and violence, which are decent topics that will not disturb anyone in the audience.

"But I haven't managed to do anything yet. Maybe after I see more of your people." He paused a moment, then added:

" 'Will all great Neptune's ocean wash this blood
Clean from my hand? No, this my hand will rather
The multitudinous seas incarnadine,
Making the green one red.'

"Now, that is good writing." He gestured toward the door. Anna went in.

The room was full of her colleagues, already seated around a long and too-low table. Their chairs were low as well. The ambassador, a portly Southeast Asian, struggled upright and said, "Mem Perez, please come over here. I need to know about the alien women."

She sat down between him and the assistant ambassador, who was as tall as Nicholas and folded uncomfortably into his chair.

Sten and Charlie. She told them about her encounter with the women of Ettin, while eating mock duck with lemon grass.

After she was done, Charlie laid his chopsticks across his bowl and leaned back. "Nicholas Sanders is here. I wonder why they're not using him in the negotiations."

"Does it matter?" she asked.

"I really can't say. I'm not going to worry about it. You

know from your previous experience how useful it has been to worry about Sanders. If MI had kept their hands to themselves, we might have a treaty by now; and we ought to be grateful to him. He's the reason, I am almost certain, that we have a usable kitchen. Everything labeled in English, copious and clear instructions. Maybe the man should have become a technical writer.''

"What do I do next?'' asked Anna.

''Exactly what you are doing. Talk to the alien women. Talk to Nicholas Sanders. Report back. At some point, I assume, we will begin to understand why the aliens asked for you and what role these quite amazing-sounding women play in the negotiations.''

"What concerns me,'' said Sten, "is the man's claim that this station was built for these negotiations. Is that possible, Captain McIntosh? Could we do it?''

"I don't know, and if I did know, it would be protected information.'' He paused for a moment. "If it is true, it's an impressive achievement. I think I can say that, and also— It's hard for me to believe the station is mostly empty. If I had this kind of room, I'd find a way to use it.''

Sten looked worried.

Charlie said, "Let's try to avoid speculation. What the *hwarhath* do with their station in their space is not our business.''

She left at the end of the meal, after the flan and the strong Asian coffee, mixed with sugar and condensed milk.

Eh Matsehar stood in the hall. He was as calm and patient as any other *hwar*. It was only when he moved that she noticed, once again, the un-*hwar*-like clumsiness. They walked back through the station.

At one point, midway there, she asked, "What did you mean by saying that I was Nicky's latest victim?''

"If he doesn't want me to talk in the corridors, I won't,'' the alien said. "Though I think he's wrong. He doesn't understand the rules for spying. Everything has rules, though you humans don't seem to understand that. It must make your lives very difficult.''

He left her at the tall double door. She went in and down the great hall hung with tapestries to her quarters.

Nicholas was in her main room, talking to an alien. He glanced up as she came in. "Anna. This is the general's chief of security. He'd like to check you for surveillance devices, with your permission, of course.''

She nodded.

Nicholas spoke, and the alien lifted one hand. It held something that looked like a handgun, silver in color, with a flared barrel like an old-time blunderbuss. A row of lights on the top flickered dimly. He ran the gun over her, never touching her and never raising his head high enough so their gazes would meet. The thing made a couple of chiming noises. The lights on top flickered more brightly and rapidly.

A wonderful show, thought Anna. But what was happening?

"Could you give him your belt? And your shoes? They're bugged.''

She took the belt and shoes off, handing them over.

There was some more conversation between Nick and the alien, who was the same height as the general and even stockier. His chest was barrel-like. His arms and legs were short and thick and powerful. A crest of hair ran over his head and down his back, longer and darker than the rest of his fur, and very distinctive.

Finally the alien turned to her and spoke, his gaze down.

"He thanks you for your consideration and cooperation. Your rooms are now secure.''

"Good.''

The alien left, carrying her shoes and belt.

After the door slid shut behind him, Nicholas said, "Do

you remember the guard I had the last time we met? The kid?"

"The one who was murdered."

He nodded. "His name was Gwa Hattin. The fellow who just left is his elder brother, Gwa Hu. Every time I hear that name, I think of the ancient American war cry."

She looked at him, puzzled.

He grinned. "Wahoo. The Gwa have been allied with the Ettin for over three centuries, and they exchange genetic material on a regular basis. The general's minor lineage, his male lineage, is Gwa. He usually has one or two men of Gwa on his staff."

"You're saying that military intelligence killed one of Ettin Gwarha's relatives."

"Yes. The advancer has removed your bag, your toothpaste dispenser and your computer. They'll be returned as soon as possible. The computer may take a while. The best place to hide a tree is in a forest."

"There was a bug in my toothpaste?"

He grinned. "So it seems. If you need a computer, I can provide one, a human model; and if you like games I have a really fine quest. It's the only one I've ever been able to tolerate."

She nodded. "Okay."

"Now." He paused and turned, looking around the room. "The general has decided that I'm going to be your liaison. There really isn't an alternative. There are no women on his staff, obviously, and I'm the only person who can claim even a remote relationship to you. He's told the other frontmen that we come from regions that are close to one another and that have often exchanged genetic material. Kansas and Illinois. Like Gwa and Ettin. That gives me the right to come in here. If you want, I can change the door so only you can open it; but there are going to be times—like today—when it will be convenient if I can get in."

Anna shrugged. "Leave the door the way it is."

He nodded. "Your team wants you back for dinner. The women of Ettin would like to speak with you tomorrow. I'll get you the computer and the quest. I should have taken hotel management in school, as well as all those classes on language."

He left, and she took a shower, then got a glass of wine from the kitchen.

So, she thought, sitting down and putting her feet up on one of the pearlwood tables. What questions was she going to ask Nicholas, now that her rooms were secure? She made a list, beginning with Eh Matsehar's remark.

# IV

➤➤➤ THE BUSY LIGHT was on in the general's anteroom. I waited there, pacing, till Vaihar came out and the general told me to enter.

The hologram still showed the beach of grey-green sand. The waves breaking on it were taller and more turbulent now. The sky was darker, and no animals soared on the wind. A storm blowing in.

"Sit down," the general told me. "And try to stop fidgeting. What is wrong?"

"Gwa Hu went over Anna's rooms. He found eight surveillance devices."

The general grimaced.

"Only five are human, First-Defender. The other three were made by the People."

He made a hissing sound.

"They are the very latest kind. No ordinary person could have gotten hold of them."

"*A'atseh Lugala Tsu,*" he said.

"Almost certainly."

He tossed down the stylus he was holding. It bounced and rolled off the table. I stood, picked it up and handed it back to him.

"That fool has never belonged in front. The Lugala should have found someone else to push forward. A lineage that size must have some male who is competent. But my aunts always told me the women of Lugala—" He stopped, before he said anything impolite, and looked at me angrily. "This is the effect of humanity. We know the humans are out there. We know they live without rules, and the Goddess does not destroy them. The knowledge frightens us and leads us to ask questions. Now we see the result."

"Are you going to throw the stylus around anymore? If you aren't, I'll sit back down."

He nodded toward the chair. "You don't agree."

I stretched out my legs and crossed them, then took a moment to breathe deeply and exhale. It's never a good idea for both of us to be angry at the same time. "This has a lot more to do with *hwarhath* male ambition than with humanity, and with stupidity. You've never thought that Lugala was especially bright, and now we know that his chief of security is as stupid as he is. The chief ought to have known his devices would show up if there was a thorough check of the room. Though they didn't show on the security monitor. Gwa Hu said he found them because his equipment was acting just a little bit oddly, after he found and removed the human bugs, so he kept looking.

"I told—I asked—Advancer Gwa to speak to your aunts. Their rooms ought to be checked as well."

For a moment the general was silent. Then he said, "I remember when it was announced that we had found another people who could travel between the stars, and that they had fired on us. Some of my uncles were home. I remember the rejoicing. We finally had an enemy, after a century of looking. Our problems were solved! We should have remembered that the Goddess has a very strange sense of humor."

"Does that mean you're sorry that the People encountered humanity?"

"Aren't you ever?" he asked.

"No. Absolutely not. Whatever I might have been doing, if our two species had not met, it would have been less interesting than what I'm doing now."

And I would not have liked to miss knowing you, Ettin Gwarha.

**[Hah.]**

From the journal of Sanders Nicholas, etc.

# V

>>> SHE SPENT THE evening with her colleagues, in part talking shop, in part continuing the slow process of getting to know them. Sten told her about his garden, which was on an island called Gotland in the Baltic, in his wife's care now. She didn't have a green thumb, and he wasn't certain what would be left when he got home.

The ambassador—Charlie—talked about the previous set of talks with the aliens, and his opinion of the general.

"A clever man, though odd, I think. Certainly in human terms and also, I suspect, in terms of the alien culture. What kind of person develops a sexual relationship with a member of another species? A species with which his own species is at war. Though he certainly has a valuable tool in Nicholas Sanders."

She ended by talking with Captain McIntosh, whose passion was cricket and who was missing the test matches.

"The things we give up, Mem Perez, in order to serve humanity and to have a career. Of course, if I had been good enough at cricket, I would not have been here."

She grew tired finally. The captain escorted her to the entrance of the human quarters. Nicholas waited there, talking to one of the alien guards. He turned and saw her and smiled, then saw the captain. The expression on his face changed, growing remote.

"Holder Sanders," the captain said, and held out a hand.

Nicholas looked surprised, then shook.

"I'm Cyprian McIntosh. Mac to most people. I find Cyprian a bit of a burden. The things that parents do to their children! Though as I was telling Mem Perez, I will be forever grateful to my father for giving me my first cricket bat. That may balance Cyprian. Good night, mem. Holder." The captain nodded and went back inside.

Nicholas watched him, looking thoughtful. "Military," he said finally. "What kind?"

"Regular army, I think."

"Then why doesn't he have the haircut?"

"I don't know. Do you want me to find out?"

He shrugged. They walked back to the women's quarters in silence.

The hologram was on again in her bedroom. She went to sleep looking at stars and woke, as on the day before, to the smell of cooking bacon.

Today she put on a dress: full length and made of African cotton, a traditional print of yellow, blue and brown. No jewelry except a pair of dangling earrings, made of coral and coin silver, another gift from her mother. She went into the main room and found breakfast and Nicholas in a chair, a mug of coffee on the table next to him.

He looked at her and nodded. "Good. The women of Ettin will approve. I may have overcrisped the bacon, though I've been practicing, mostly because the aroma brings back such strong memories. We always had bacon for breakfast on Sunday when I was a kid. I don't much like the taste any longer.

She sat down. The bacon looked fine. There was toast as well and something that was square and very bright yellow. Like what? Corn bread that had not risen. She took a bite. It tasted like cardboard. More human chow. "There's something I've been meaning to ask you."

"Yes?" His voice sounded guarded. The Man Who Does Not Like to Answer Questions.

"What am I supposed to call you? I've been sticking to

Nicholas, because I don't really know you very well; but the aliens all seem to call you Nicky."

"You've been meeting my friends. I don't give many people permission to use Nicky, and only a few people use Nicky without permission. Nick is fine or Nicholas." He smiled. "I knew you were starting to change sides when you called me Nick in that room in the basement of the compound; you hadn't done it before; and that was close to the last rational thought I had for a while. 'Maybe this stupid and frightening plan is going to fall apart.' "

"I have not changed sides, Nick."

"It was a poor choice of words. I knew you felt some sympathy for me, and that gave me a little hope. Is that better?"

"Yes."

She ate. He drank coffee in silence. They went off to meet the women of Ettin.

The meeting room was inside the women's quarters. There were tapestries on the walls, and a huge crimson rug covered most of the floor. The furniture was the usual kind. Rich dark brocades covered the chairs. The low tables were made of a wood as dark blue as indigo.

There were four women this time, standing together in the middle of the room. As before, they were dressed in sleeveless robes.

"You're senior," Nicholas told her softly. "Make sure you keep a little in front of me. Good. Now, stop."

She paused. The women turned toward her. Nicholas made the introductions.

She had met two of them before: Ettin Per and Ettin Sai. Now, in comparison to other *hwarhath,* she could see how really large they were: tall and big-boned with broad shoulders and thick round torsos. Their robes were similar, made of panels of dark red brocade, fastened with fine silver chains. Per rumbled a greeting in the alien language. Sai told her good morning in English.

The third woman was much smaller. Next to the Ettin she looked almost slim. Her fur was black, and the panels of her robe were grey and silver, a pattern of leaves and flowers.

"Tsai Ama Ul," said Nicholas. "Her field of competence is social theory, especially theories on how the People evolved the culture they have now. Once they discovered humanity, they realized—some of the People realized—there is more than one way to be."

The woman spoke briefly. Her voice was high, an alto.

"The woman of Tsai Ama says this meeting is very welcome. She looks forward to learning."

The last woman was the shortest and the most massive. Almost fat, thought Anna. The panels of her robe were covered with embroidery: twisting animals, done in green, gold, silver and blue. The chains that connected the panels were multicolored, gold or silver links alternating with links enameled green or blue.

The costume was impressive, but not lovely. There were too many colors, too much shiny metal, too much opulence.

"Lugala Minti," said Nicholas, speaking very softly. "She is the foremost woman of the Lugala. I think that's a fair evaluation."

"Yes." Spoken by the deep quiet voice of Ettin Sai.

"Her son Lugala Tsu is a frontman, the only frontman at this station aside from Ettin Gwarha. A very important woman with an important son. Treat her with respect, Anna. One does not fuck around with the Lugala."

"Yes," said Ettin Sai.

The fat woman spoke. Her voice was as deep as Ettin Per's.

"The woman of Lugala says you are welcome. This meeting is important. The fate of many families may depend on what happens at this station."

Eek, thought Anna. She didn't want that kind of responsibility.

They sat down, Nicholas next to her. The room must have been set up for this meeting, the furniture arranged so the women were in a circle in huge broad chairs, facing one another, while the man sat in a smaller chair that was set back, not quite in the circle.

Ettin Per spoke first.

"The woman of Ettin says, 'We do not spy and listen the way men do. But this meeting is—as the woman of Lugala says—important. Therefore we'd like your permission to record it openly and honestly.' "

Anna glanced at Nicholas. He spoke in the alien language.

Ettin Per answered him.

"The *hwarhath* will give you a copy of their recording, together with the equipment to play it. Go ahead, Anna. Your people will be interested."

She hesitated, then nodded.

The small woman—Tsai Ama Ul—spoke next.

When she finished, Nicholas translated. "We have learned a good deal about human women from the information we have captured and from Sanders Nicholas. But the information is incomplete, and Nicholas is a man. We wanted to see for ourselves what a human woman is like. We wanted to find out what it feels like to be a woman among your people."

Lugala Minti interrupted, speaking at length in her rumbling voice.

"The woman of Lugala wants to know how you have gotten so mixed together. Surely you understand how dangerous it is to have men in the house, except briefly for a visit. How can you let people trained in violence near your children? How can you let people capable of murder and rape live in your houses day after day and year after year? Surely you realize that something terrible will happen sooner or later? Sorry, I've made a mistake, Anna. The word isn't 'murder.' It's the intentional killing of other people, but it isn't necessarily a crime. The moral content of the act is dependent on circumstances. It's almost never wrong to kill an enemy male. It's usually wrong to kill a male who is a relative or ally. The same thing is true of the word that I've translated as 'rape.' It means sex with violence and without the consent of the other person, but it isn't invariably a criminal act, unless, of course, the victim is a woman or a child."

Anna tried to explain that most men were harmless. The alien women did not look convinced, though she wasn't really sure what was going on behind those broad fur-covered faces.

"No," Ettin Sai told her finally, speaking in English. "This cannot be right. We know—we have felt—" She stopped and switched to her own language; and Nick translated.

"We have felt the violence of humans. Your people are not harmless, Perez Anna. Two of my brothers were on a ship that was blown up by the humans, and my sister Aptsi has lost a son. Your men can kill just as well as the men of the People. But you have not been able to separate your violence from everything else, as we have done, at least to a great extent. You have no safe places. Your children must grow up in fear. Your women must live in fear, unless they become like your men; and who is there then to raise the children?"

Lugala Minti spoke loudly.

"The woman of Lugala says that humans are horrible and perverse, a shame to any other intelligent species and an insult to the Goddess, all praise be on her name. And hey, Anna, we haven't even gotten to the sexual habits of humanity."

"Yes," said Ettin Sai in English.

Tsai Ama Ul spoke again.

"This is not courteous, the woman of Tsai Ama says, and it does not lead to knowledge. We must not ask Perez Anna to defend her people as if they are criminals. Tell us about your childhood. Tell us what it is like to grow up a woman among the humans."

So she did. The women asked questions. What was it like to have a male parent in the house? How did she get along with him and her brother? Did her father threaten her? Was he violent?

He was a mild-mannered historian, whose crime as a parent was his inability to pay attention to the current century. The fourteenth was so much more interesting, though there were similarities: terrible plagues, a collapsing society and a vast universe just starting to become visible; the entire world waiting for explorers, and the skies about to open to astronomers.

"Indifference," said Ettin Sai. "That is not good. But there are women who are not interested in their children. In a large family, that does not matter. There are always enough mothers in a great house."

Why did human beings have such tiny families? Hadn't she felt lonely without a multitude of cousins? Hadn't she felt cramped in a handful of rooms?

No, she told them. It was ordinary, the life she knew. She had not been lonely. Her family apartment had seemed roomy. Her parents, after all, had been professional and made good money.

The women listened gravely, but she did not get a sense that they understood. The questions continued. What was it like to live in a sea of people, not connected by lineages, but all broken apart? Tiny families like waves that crest and vanish, leaving nothing behind them except an empty space where another wave—another family—can form.

Nine billion people! It was incomprehensible! And half of them men, always present. The streets of the cities, the frighteningly huge cities, full of male violence. How did it feel for the woman of Perez to walk among men who were not related? Without any protection, if what Nicholas had told them was true?

She found herself telling the truth. It could be frightening to walk in Chicago, especially in the areas where the people were poor. Poverty made people angry, and angry men were dangerous, especially if they had nothing to lose.

When she finished, there was a silence. Then Ettin Per spoke.

"You have too many people. There isn't enough to go around, and because you are all broken apart, you cannot share what there is in a decent manner. But even if you did share, there still would not be enough to go around. Here it comes, Anna. The speech on the evils of heterosexuality."

Tsai Ama Ul leaned forward and spoke.

"She says you must be getting tired, though she doesn't know the symptoms of fatigue among humans. Still, we are all flesh, the woman of Tsai Ama says."

Anna looked at her chronometer. Three hours gone. She felt as if she'd lost a fight.

Ettin Sai spoke. "It will end now. Thank you, Perez Anna."

They left. Once they were out of the meeting room, Nicholas sighed. "Jesus Christ! You did well, Anna; and I'm exhausted."

They walked back to her rooms. He palmed the door and, as it opened, looked down at her. "You look beat. Why don't you lie down? If you want to go somewhere later, give me a call."

A dismissal. He needed to be elsewhere, most likely with his general.

The hologram in her bedroom showed a green sky full of enormous cumuli. They were like a landscape: white mountains and shadowy grey-green valleys, angled plains, rifts and billowing slopes that looked forested. She lay on her bed, too tired to do much thinking. Above her the clouds changed shape. The mountains flattened into plains or divided, creating valleys. Valleys closed. Low hills rose and became towering peaks. Nothing remained the same.

In the evening she went to the human quarters and reported on the meeting.

"I'm not getting a good sense of this culture," said Sten. "Who's in control? The men or the women? And what is this obsession with violence?"

"From the way the women talked, their population must be considerably lower than ours," said Captain McIntosh. "That might turn out to be a disadvantage for them. Though Jah knows that we have not found our population especially advantageous."

"We are in an enemy station," said Etienne, sounding nervous. "Are we certain that they can't hear us?"

"Yes," said Captain McIntosh.

Charlie said, "Let's continue the negotiations in good faith. We know exactly how useful it has been to scheme and second-guess the *hwarhath*."

# VI

➤➤➤ THERE WAS A new hologram in the general's office: a plain covered with snow. In the distance was a line of small sharp mountains, most likely the wall of a crater. The sky above the mountains was almost entirely filled by a planet: a yellow gas giant with rings and half a dozen moons, made visible by the shadows they cast on the planet. The sky—what little I could see—was dark blue, which meant some kind of atmosphere.

A line of prints went across the snow, starting where the general's carpeting ended and going diagonally back across the plain, until they vanished in the distance. The prints had been made by a single pair of large wide boots.

"You aren't trying to settle that?" I asked.

"No. Most likely there was an observation station or maybe a single landing."

I nodded and sat down.

"So." He picked up his stylus. "Perez Anna meets with the women one time only, and the humans have learned something of strategic value."

"The bit about population," I said.

"Yes. I don't know to what extent this can be controlled, and I don't know how wise it is to use you as the translator. Why did you explain the exact meaning of the words that you translated as 'rape' and 'murder'? I thought, when I saw the recording, that you were going to tell the woman of Perez that we do not kill women and children."

"I helped write the first dictionary for your language, and those definitions were in it. I was not telling Anna anything that the humans do not already know." I glanced down briefly, then back up, meeting the general's gaze.

"Language is my one great skill. I would like to use it honestly. As much as is possible, I am going to be clear." (I was using the *hwarhath* main language. The primary meaning of the word is "transparent.") "If this is a problem, then pull me out. But how can you negotiate in any serious way, if the lines of communication are tangled?"

He made a low unhappy noise and laid his stylus down. "I spent last evening with Lugala Tsu. He has never known how to drink. It's another reason why his lineage should never have pushed him ahead. I won't describe everything he said. Toward the end it was not coherent. But two things emerged that are important.

"He is hoping that the time has finally come for me to fail at something. He is hoping that I will make a serious mistake in this set of negotiations.

"And." He picked up the stylus again and turned it in his hands. "He made the suggestion—he hinted at the possibility—that you are not entirely reliable. Some of the men in back of him were sober enough to realize what was happening. Hah! You should have seen the expressions on their faces! But they didn't know how to make him stop. That is what happens when you pick your staff the way he does."

I'd heard the general on this subject before. Good looks are fine, and it does not hurt to consider a man's lineage, but these should not be the only criteria.

"Who did you take?" I asked.

"Hai Atala Vaihar."

The perfect choice. Vaihar drinks enough to keep in touch with the rest of the party, but he never gets toxic, and he always knows what to do in a difficult situation.

"I can't give you the exact words that the son of Lugala

used. This was toward the end of the evening, and it was not entirely easy to follow what he was saying. But he mentioned that you were human, and that humans were different in many important ways, and who could predict for certain how you would act, now that you were around a human woman, who might or might not be related to you."

In other words, I might be a traitor to the People, and I might be a pervert, and maybe I went in for incest as well.

**[You are wrong about this. He was suggesting two possibilities, both of them dangerous. Maybe Anna is a relative of yours, in which case you ought to be loyal to her. No sane man would betray or abandon a woman of his lineage. Or maybe you are lying and she is not a relative. In this case you have obtained access to her rooms for a purpose which I am reluctant to mention. So either you are a traitor and not a pervert or else you are a pervert and possibly a traitor. But I do not think Lugala Tsu had the idea of incest in his mind.]**

"What did you do?" I asked.

"I said the future was in the hands of the Goddess, and we could never tell for certain how anyone is going to act; and then Vaihar told a long and boring story about one of his uncles, who had always been predictable; and then we left. I wonder if any of those young men will have the courage to tell Lugala Tsu precisely what he said to me."

"Most likely not."

He made a noise that indicated agreement. "I am going to talk to Ettin Per. Maybe she can find a way to restrain or delay the curiosity of the women. You will join me in the room where we talk to the enemy."

"Why?"

"I want the son of Lugala to see you next to me. You are the best translator we have and our first-in-front expert on humanity. I want that product of an ill-considered insemination to remember; and I want him to remember what you are to me."

From the journal of Sanders Nicholas, etc.

# VII

➤➤➤ THE NEXT DAY Nicholas showed her how to operate the kitchen. "The women want time to think about what you've told them. The general wants me back in the negotiations. So you are going to be on your own for a while."

She nodded, and he went over the instructions for use of the various—what ought they be called? Appliances? When he was done, he leaned against the nearest wall, folding his arms. There was a bracelet on his left wrist, made of heavy gold links, each one set with a dark green, deeply carved stone that looked as if it might be jade. A magnificent artifact, thought Anna, but it didn't go with his clothing.

"I brought the computer," Nicholas said. "It's not a new model. We take what we can get. But the software is friendly. In my opinion it's a little too friendly. I like more emotional distance in my software.

"I'll write down instructions on how to get hold of Vaihar and Matsehar. If you want to go anywhere, call them."

He paused and looked uncomfortable. "There's something I need to ask you, Anna."

She waited.

"Ettin Gwarha told you a story two years ago, before we left the last set of negotiations."

She nodded.

"Does anyone else know it?"

"MI grabbed me the minute your people were off the planet. I was questioned."

At first he was completely motionless. Then he asked, "How?" His voice was quiet.

"Drugs. I wasn't hurt, but they must know everything I know about you and the People."

"Ah." His gaze shifted. "Well, MI has never been generous about sharing information. Maybe they didn't tell the rest of your team."

"Do you care?"

"I guess I do. It's not a very nice story. I don't especially want to walk into that room tomorrow and have the other side think, Here is the poor bastard who works for the people who tortured him."

"Is it true?"

He was going to shut down. She could tell from his expression and the pose of his body. Shut down, shut up, tell her to mind her own business.

"Nicholas, I'm not going to tell you that you owe me an explanation."

"Good."

"But my career is a wreck, and I'm not sure I can put it back together. I almost ended in prison."

"Your choice, Anna. I asked you for nothing."

"The look you gave me in that room was a plea. I tried to help you. The general said it wasn't necessary, but I did what I could."

His expression said, So what?

"I knew they were creeps. I thought you were comparatively normal."

"You knew I had changed sides during a war. That leads us to a seven-letter word beginning with 't' which I have a lot of trouble saying: one who acts perfidiously or treacherously. You call that normal? Who do you hang out with, anyway?"

"Jesus Maria, you talk well. I'm never going to get you

in a corner. I do think you owe me an explanation. I said
I wasn't going to say that. I've gone back on my word.

"Do you think you can walk out on every obligation,
because you've done the thing that begins with 't'? Who
cares if you betrayed those crazy people in MI? I betrayed
them too. Everyone ought to. To hell with your feelings of
guilt, and to hell with your irresponsibility."

He looked around. "You know, I have very little interest in food, but this is not a conversation I want to have in
a kitchen. Let's get out of here."

They settled into chairs in the living room. Nicholas
pulled off his sandals and put his feet up on a pearlwood
table, then glanced at her. "What do you want to know?"

Anna fumbled around, trying to find the right words.
She wanted some kind of assurance that he was not as
crazy as the people from MI. What kind of person could
work for a man who had tortured him?

"It's been done before," said Nicholas.

She tried to explain about the abyss. It was the place
where you learned things about other people you really did
not want to know. You looked down into it, and you saw
darkness and ugliness and craziness and pain, and you
thought maybe it was too bad the dinosaurs had become
extinct. They might have done a better job.

He laughed. "I think you'd better tell me what the
general told you."

She did. He listened, his eyes half-closed and his face
expressionless. When she was done he said, "Well, he has
managed to make a nasty story even nastier, and I have no
idea why. I'm going to have to ask him."

"Did it happen?" she asked.

"Yes."

"The general said he was there."

"I don't remember him. Whenever they wanted to ask
me questions, they took me to a room. It was always the
same room. One wall was a mirror—the whole thing, top

to bottom, left to right. That is how my dreams usually begin, coming into that room and seeing my reflection and knowing something terrible is going to happen.

"There was an observation booth in back of the mirror. I could hear people moving around, and voices came over the intercom. Ask this question. Ask that. Stop. Go on. Gwarha must have been there. I never saw him in the room.

"I don't think I ever heard his voice over the intercom. He was not at all senior in those days, and his area of competence has never been interrogation. Most likely, he watched and listened.

"I don't think I could work for him if I had any memory of him in the room. I have no idea what I'd do if I ever met any of those guys. I haven't, except in my dreams, and usually—I have no idea why—I see them as reflections in the mirror. Something a therapist might be able to explain. There are none available. No one who understand humans, anyway. Going to a *hwarhath* diviner might be interesting, but I doubt that it would be therapeutic."

His elbows were resting on the wide arms of the chair, and he had clasped his hands together loosely. There was no evidence of tension in his pose or in his quiet, even voice. But she felt it.

"The first time I remember seeing him is when he came and told me it was over. The questions were going to stop. There wasn't going to be any more pain. And then—" Nicholas smiled. "Very formally, with his very beautiful manners, he apologized. Not for most of the questions or for most of the pain. That was necessary; and Gwarha does not apologize for anything that is necessary; but for the questions at the end. They produced nothing useful and were motivated, in his opinion, by the kind of malicious curiosity that is characteristic of small boys. Do you know the kind of thing? It's what I call the junior scientist stage. What happens if you pull one hind leg off a grasshopper?

What happens if you pull one wing off a fly? 'Hey, Nicky, wanna see what happens when you set fire to a frog?'

"I don't work for the man who tortured me. I work for the man who told me it was over and offered an apology."

He was still working for the enemy and for a group of people who had treated him very badly. What good was an apology, in a situation like this? "Gee, I'm sorry I made your life unmitigated hell"? It did not sound adequate to her.

"That is part of my explanation. The rest is—if I didn't forgive Ettin Gwarha, how could I forgive myself?"

"What do you mean?"

"Where do you think the information came from, that we used to break the *hwarhath* language? Do you think our prisoners gave it freely? And how do you think my knowledge of the language was used?"

"You were like him."

Nicholas nodded. He was still in the same pose and still without evident physical tension. His voice remained quiet and even. "I never got my hands dirty. I never touched a *hwarhath* prisoner; but I knew where the data I was analyzing came from; and I knew where the questions I wrote out were going."

The abyss again. She knew with a certainty that decent people did not get into these situations. Decent people lived law-abiding lives and never harmed anyone directly and never cooperated knowingly in the inflicting of pain.

"I had a good Midwestern Methodist upbringing," Nicholas said. "Church every Sunday morning after the bacon. I learned about evil, and I learned what pleases God most. God is most pleased when we care for the widow and the orphan, the poor and strangers. Well, no one could possibly be stranger than the *hwarhath,* and by the time we got hold of them they were certainly poor. They owned nothing, not even their bodies, and we would not let them do the thing they most wanted to do, which was die. That, for the People, is the most extreme form of poverty, when you do not own your own death. That is their dearest possession: the right to say 'This is enough.'

"Does any of this help? Or are you still at the edge of the abyss?"

"I'm still there."

"It isn't easy to understand people, and with that profundity I am going to leave." He stood and smiled down at her. "You know, you haven't touched on the real problem I have with Ettin Gwarha. It isn't the fact that he is alien or one of the enemy or that he was involved with the less than pleasant treatment I got when I was first captured. All of that we have managed to deal with.

"But there is one bit of advice that every mother ought to give her children, before she sends them out into the universe. Never fuck on the job, and never ever fuck the boss. Never get in a situation where you cannot separate your personal life from what you do at the office. The general and I have spent years negotiating and setting up rules for how to behave when the two of us are working and when we are not. It's never become easy.

"You've been asking me—very politely—how I can crawl into bed with the enemy. Well, enemies are not forever. One can always try to make peace. But consider what it is like to make love to the man who writes a semiannual evaluation of your performance at work. Now, there is a situation with ugly possibilities. Though there isn't a line on the form for sexual performance. I wonder how Gwarha manages to fit it in? 'Attitude toward those-in-front'?"

"Why do you do it?" she asked.

He laughed. "Anna, you are remarkable. The questions never end. But I have reached the limit of my ability to answer them." He left.

# VIII

➤➤➤ THE DAY AFTER that he appeared at the negotiations. She watched from the anteroom alone. He came in directly after the general, dressed in a grey space-cadet uniform, which looked good on him. She had never seen him with Ettin Gwarha before. He was almost a head taller. What an odd pair! For once he wasn't slouching, nor was he smiling. His pale thin face looked guarded, remote.

When everyone was seated, he introduced himself. "I think I met most of you during the last set of negotiations."

Charlie said yes and then offered an apology for the unfortunate turn of events that had ended and so on.

Nicholas listened and translated. The *hwarhath* stirred a bit, then Ettin Gwarha spoke.

"Your apology is not necessary," Nicholas said. "One was given and accepted before the People agreed to the current negotiations."

Charlie opened his mouth, then closed it. Clearly the apology had been given to Nicholas directly. Clearly the *hwarhath* were pretending that Nicholas was not there. Or had no existence as a separate entity? She wasn't certain.

Another game which made no sense to her.

Nothing much happened after that. The negotiators were discussing the possibility of exchanging prisoners, though neither side would admit formally to having any prisoners. The general continued to pretend that he didn't know English. What was the point of that? Maybe it gave him time to think about the subject being discussed. Nicholas translated in a quiet, almost expressionless voice, nothing like his usual speaking voice, which rose and fell, changed rhythm, did imitations, mocked.

She had lunch with the rest of the diplomatic team. She didn't tell them about her most recent conversation with Nicholas, though his name came up. They wanted to know why he was being used as a translator again. Anna shrugged. She had no idea. The general wanted him.

In the afternoon Hai Atala Vaihar came and escorted her back to the women's quarters. She checked out the computer Nicholas had brought. As he said, it was over-friendly, with a personality that set her teeth on edge. She got out of the learning program as quickly as possible, going to the quest game that Nick had mentioned.

It was based on the Chinese novel *Monkey*. The player (she picked the version for one person alone) was the title character of the book: a magical stone monkey who raised hell in Heaven, stealing the peaches of immortality and harassing the Chinese gods.

As punishment, Monkey was imprisoned under a mountain. In order to free himself and earn redemption, he had to escort the Buddhist monk Tripitaka to India and back, so Tripitaka could bring the Three Baskets of sacred Buddhist Scripture to the Chinese people, thus saving them from greed, lust and violence.

The journey to India was filled (of course) with perils, and she had to deal with a lot of monsters. Some turned out to be benevolent, after they had been defeated. Most remained evil. She had never been especially good at games, and she lost almost every fight. The game had an override. After Monkey had died for the umpteenth time, she would press a button and play on through, instead of going back to the beginning. The real Monkey cheated whenever possible. She figured she could do the same.

In the end, if she ever finished the game and delivered

the baskets of Scripture, she would (the instructions told her) achieve freedom and enlightenment, becoming a genuine Buddha. But it was going to take a long time, even with the override.

Her days fell into a pattern. In the morning she watched the human and *hwarhath* men negotiate. In the afternoon she talked with her colleagues. Sometimes she stayed in the human quarters through the evening. Often she went back to her own rooms and read or played *Monkey*.

The *hwarhath* women were still in the station, though she didn't encounter them during this period; and the frontman Lugala Tsu was also around and watching the negotiations as Anna did—from a distance, via holovision.

She learned this much from her escorts, but she couldn't find out anything else about what these people were doing or planning to do. Eh Matsehar said he didn't know, and Hai Atala Vaihar said it wasn't for him to speculate about what went on in the minds of women or frontmen.

She imagined the two Lugala as spiders squatting in the middle of their webs, alert and ready to act when the right moment came. Come to think of it, Lugala Minti looked more like a toad. But Anna had nothing against toads or any other amphibian. Fragile and sensitive, amphibians were dying off from pollution more rapidly than the members of any other animal order on Earth. Toads should be cherished and mourned, not compared to Lugala Minti.

Nor did she have any good reason to believe that there was anything wrong with the Lugala, except for the mother's overly gaudy sense of style and her tendency to pontificate about the awfulness of humans. Was this enough to condemn two people, one of whom Anna had not even met?

On the days when Vaihar escorted her, he and Anna

talked about human literature. He wanted another book to read. She recommended *Huckleberry Finn*. It would tell him about slavery.

"Oh yes," said Vaihar. "I have learned about that, though I can't say that I understand it. Why would anyone want to enslave—that is the right word, isn't it?—women and children? And why would any man ever submit?"

As always when dealing with the *hwarhath*, she had a feeling that she was missing important pieces. She couldn't answer Vaihar's questions, because she didn't really know what he was asking.

On the days that Matsehar was her escort, they talked about theater. Or rather, Matsehar talked and she listened. He had started work on his version of *Macbeth*. "I am beginning to understand how humans act when they are being devious. Nicky said it would be useful for me to come here; and he was right, as he so often is."

She saw Nicholas once in a corridor, talking to an alien with snow-white fur. There was something about the way that Nick was standing that was different, though she couldn't figure out what at first. Nick saw her and straightened up, smiling and lifting a hand in greeting. Then he went back to his conversation.

"I wonder what he sees in that furball," said Matsehar.

"What?"

"The snowy fool. The lackwit. The buffoon."

"Who is he?"

"The current champion of *hanatsin* at this station. It's his only accomplishment, unless you count having a good body as an accomplishment."

She asked about *hanatsin*. It was an activity in between a martial art and a form of dance. When it was done as a martial art, the two players were opponents, and one of them had to win over the other. When it was done as a dance, they were partners and could only win together. The snowy fool was a master of the martial-arts form.

"I don't know what Nicky is up to, though he does practice *hanatsin,* and he is good enough to need a good opponent." Matsehar paused. "But he is not good enough to need that opponent. Kirin would—give me a moment, I know there is a human phrase—have him as a midday meal. Your language has a remarkable number of figures of speech that derive from eating. At times it makes me queasy, though it is not, of course, as bad as the heterosexuality."

Of course not.

"Does Nick—?" She didn't know a polite way to finish the question.

"Sanders Nicholas is well known for his habit of looking around. He says it would be impious to do otherwise."

"What?"

"According to him, you humans have a number of unpleasant diseases that are sexually transmitted."

"Yes."

"Well, so do we, though nothing as bad as the wasting diseases that Nicky has described."

The HIVs. A new strain surfaced every four or five years, named—like a new strain of influenza—for the place where it was first spotted.

"But Nicky does not get our diseases. Not any of them. He looks like us, but that is appearance only. At the level where diseases live and reproduce, he is very different."

"What does this have to do with piety?" she asked.

"He says that he has come by accident to a place where it is possible to have sex with many people and not be afraid of dying. This is a gift from the Goddess. When the One who made the universe gives a gift, it is for use.

"Most likely, he is joking; though one can never be certain. He makes jokes that sound as if he is being entirely serious, and he is serious when you think he must be making a joke. But there is no question that he does look around."

They walked in silence through another corridor. Then Matsehar went back to his version of *Macbeth*. He explained how well Lady Macbeth worked as a mother full of ambition, pushing and cajoling her reluctant warrior son, who was going to turn finally—a judgment on ambition!—into a monster she could not control.

# IX

➤➤➤ I HAD MATSEHAR over for an evening. He was in a strange mood, both sad and catty. I couldn't figure it out, though he has always been moody: the price of genius and of being different.

Whenever something is bothering him—anger or fatigue or stress—he becomes even clumsier than usual. He dropped my little reading computer while trying to load in his version of *Macbeth,* and then we had to get down on our knees and look for the script, which had vanished into the carpet. I saw it finally, a crystalline gleam amid the fibers, picked it up and handed it over. He dropped it again and began cursing in English. I took the computer away from him and loaded in the script, then got both of us drinks: *halin* for him and a glass of water for me.

"How do you like Anna?" I had not seen him since he'd taken over the escort service, and as long as I've known him he's been interested in humans.

He turned the *halin* cup. In all likelihood, the way he was moving this evening, he'd knock it over.

Finally he spoke.

"Ettin Gwarha is more remarkable than I had realized. He can look at you and see a man. When I look at Perez Anna, I see an alien. I cannot look past the physical differences: the body with its strange proportions, the limbs that do not bend in the right places, the skin like tanned leather, the eyes—" He shuddered visibly, then glanced up, meeting my gaze. "I thought that I was open-minded,

Nicky. But no, I am as narrow as a dirt farmer on the plain of Eh. Hah, Nicholas! I feel trapped inside myself!

"And I feel lonely. I envy you, though envy is not an emotion I have any liking for. I saw you in the hall, talking to Shal Kirin. That is a great gift, Nicky, to look at people and find them lovable."

"Don't you start any ugly rumors, Mats. I want Gwarha to be able to concentrate on the negotiations."

"Then you aren't interested in Kirin?"

"Not at the moment. Though the Goddess knows that his body is wonderful, and I've always liked that kind of coloring, the white fur and the little areas of dark skin. There's a tree on Earth called the birch. It drops its leaves in the winter, and its bark is white and black. That's what Kirin is like, a birch tree in the snow."

Matsehar looked even sadder than before. I, of course, was angry with him. His reaction to Anna told me something about his reaction to me. I was another freak, another alien.

A line went through my mind, which I did not speak out loud.

Matsehar, I wanted to say, the universe is very large, and most of it is cold and dark and empty; it's not a good idea to be too picky about who you are going to love.

But the wisdom of one's elders is always boring, and Mats's problems are his own. There is no way I can help him, and one should never offer advice when angry.

I held out my hand. "Give me *Macbeth*. I'd like to see how you are doing."

He stood up to hand the computer over. In the process he knocked over his cup.

The first play I saw by Eh Matsehar was *An Old Woman Making Pots,* which was put on by the Arts Corps at a station festival. I no longer remember which station. Tailin, maybe. We've spent enough time there, and it's big enough to have people from the Arts Corps.

The play is in the modern or ambiguous form, which means it is not clearly a hero play or a woman's play or an animal play or anything else in particular.

A warrior traveling on business for his lineage meets a woman who is making pots by the side of the road. The warrior is young and proud and successful, from a lineage (the Eh) whose power is rapidly expanding. The woman is old and almost blind. She makes her pots by touch now and uses only a plain salt glaze. She can feel shape and texture, but cannot any longer see color or visual pattern clearly enough to use them. If she has a lineage, we do not hear about it. Maybe she is one of those women who cannot bear to be incorporated into another lineage, after their own has been defeated in a war, and who go off alone.

The two people converse, the woman about the making of pots—the technical problems and the difficulty of working as she does now, stiff with age and blind. The warrior speaks about the battles he's been in, the power of his lineage, his ambitions.

Gradually, the audience begins to suspect that the woman is a manifestation of the Goddess. One certainly realizes that the young man is a fool. The woman asks him questions, sharp and funny. The questions add up to: What do you think you are doing, anyway? He cannot answer, except with clichés out of the old hero plays and with a kind of childish greed.

In the end, the old woman asks, "Why don't you put aside those weapons and do something useful. Make a pot!"

The young man looks down, unable to answer further. The play comes to an end.

Gwarha hated it and went off with a couple of other

senior officers to get toxic and complain about modern theater. I went walking through the station.

The next day I looked for the author and found him at the Arts Corps theater, arguing with another man, who turned out to be the chief musician. Someone pointed him out: tall for a *hwarhath,* though not as tall as I am, big-boned and gaunt and very young. His youth explained the problems with the play. He glanced up as I came toward him. (The *hwarhath* usually look down when they are arguing seriously.)

"Hah," he said, a long exhalation. His blue eyes widened; even the long narrow pupils seemed to expand. He turned, moving clumsily. Later I discovered he'd been ill in childhood: some kind of infection of the central nervous system. The doctors never figured out exactly what it was.

The illness came at the right time to insure his survival. If he'd been younger, the doctors might not have worked to keep him alive. (The *hwarhath* do not believe that very young children are people.) If he'd been an adult, he would have been offered the option and might—especially at first—have taken it.

In the end, he made an amazing recovery, much better than anyone had expected. But there was permanent damage, mostly in the areas of balance and coordination. He was always a little ungraceful, and he dropped things a lot.

"I saw the play," I told him. "I liked it."

I don't remember his answer, but he was excited and interested. (Later I discovered that he was fascinated by freaks and outcasts.) We talked about the play and then about hero plays in general. By this time, I had lost my interest in them. He despised them.

"False and dishonest. Life isn't like that. We aren't heroes on a stage, nor do we make those kind of choices. Most of the time, we make no choices at all. We do as our mothers taught us and as the senior men order us."

The musician, who had been listening, broke in then. There was a problem about the music in the play.

He said, "I want to meet you again. Is that possible? I want to know what it is like to live among strangers. Why did you change sides? Do the humans have their own kind of honor?"

I said yes, it was possible to meet, and we did, though Gwarha looked surprised when I told him what I was doing.

"His work is insolent and impious. Why do you want to speak with him?"

I said I liked the play, and the kid was interested in learning about humanity.

"Material for another disgusting effusion," said Gwarha, or words to that effect.

(I may be making some of this up. It was over ten years ago. I could search my journal for the first reference to Mats. Maybe I'll do that, after I finish this entry.)

The kid took *hwarhath* directness all the way to the front. In less than half an *ikun,* he was asking me what it felt like to be a betrayer-of-the-lineage. How could I do it? Surely I had been offered the option? Why had I refused it?

"Is this going to turn into a play?"

"Not in a form that anyone will recognize. I am bold but not crazy. I don't intend to anger the favorite son of the Ettin lineage."

I fended off most of the personal questions, though I answered them later. Mats is persistent. But I told him something about humanity and something about my life among the *hwarhath.*

"You see the same thing I do," he said. "Everything has changed, but we continue as before. This is not the plain of Eh or the hills that belong to Ettin. This is space, and the enemy we fight is nothing like us. We will be destroyed, if we don't learn new ways of thinking."

After that I got in the habit of spending time with Mats.

He was the brightest person I had met since I came among the *hwarhath,* except maybe for Gwarha. Mats was more open-minded than Gwarha and had more imagination. Already, at twenty-four, he was the best male playwright of his generation.

When I left the station, I kept in touch via message probe. He sent me copies of his new plays, or holos if they had been performed.

I sent him information about theater on Earth and synopses of famous plays with translations of characteristic passages. It was a strange selection. I was limited by what I could find in the *hwarhath* information systems, and they were limited by what they had found on captured human ships.

*The Importance of Being Earnest* sounds flat-out stupid when reduced to outline form. The dialogue loses everything in translation. (The *hwarhath* are not a witty people.) Shakespeare, on the other hand, comes through splendidly. Mats was especially excited by *Othello.* It would make a terrific hero play, he said, the kind about the dangers of heterosexual love. I ended up translating the whole damn thing, and it was close to the hardest work I had ever done.

After two years we ended up on the same station again. This time I remember which one: Ata Tsan. I tracked him down to another theater. Once again he was arguing with a musician. By this time I'd heard his nickname, which translates (roughly) as The Man Who Raises Hell About Music, and I had learned the reason for it. His childhood illness had left him partially deaf. He wore a pair of hearing aids: plastic buttons that nestled out of sight in his large deep ears. When they were on, he had no trouble with conversation, but he heard music differently from other people. He knew he was a minority of one, but he also knew how he heard the music in his plays, and how— by the Goddess—he wanted to hear it. Musicians worked with him, because he was so good; but they always looked harried. One of them told me, "My job is not to compose music. It is to negotiate between Eh Matsehar and the rest of the species."

Mats stopped the argument and dragged me off to talk about the new play, which was a version of *Othello*. They were going to do it with masks like the ones in the animal plays. "Only these will be human masks. I am inventing a new art form, Nicky! With your help, and you will get credit, I promise you. Wait till you see the costumes! Everything is going fine, except the music."

He gave me a copy of the script. I read it that evening, while Gwarha fooled around with a board game, setting up problems and staring at them intently. A waste of time, in my opinion, but then I don't have a lot of interest in games.

*The Deluding of the Dark Man,* the play was called. It was longer than a traditional *hwarhath* play, and Matsehar had managed to include a lot of Shakespeare's language. His Othello was splendid: heroic and loving. His Desdemona was wonderfully sweet and gentle. I wasn't sure what the *hwarhath* would make of her. His Iago could have crawled under a snake.

When I was done, I gave the script to Gwarha. He went straight through to the end, saying nothing until he turned the computer off. Then he glanced at me. "It's wonderfully written. You are right about the boy. The Goddess has held out both hands to him. But the ending is wrong."

I asked him what he meant.

"A play about this kind of love ought to leave the audience with a feeling of horror and disgust. But I feel nothing like that. I am sad—and angry at this man of corrupt ambition. How do you say his name?"

"Iago."

"And there is something else—a feeling as if I have just stepped out of a place that is narrow and dark, a forest or the entrance to a fortified house. Now I am at the edge of a plain. There is nothing between me and the horizon. There is nothing above me except the empty sky. Hah!'' He gave the long slow *hwarhath* exhalation that can mean almost anything.

"Tragic catharsis," I said.

Gwarha frowned. I tried to explain.

"You use plays to clean out the digestive system?"

"I said that the wrong way."

In the end he understood me, though it would have helped if I'd had access to *The Poetics*.

"I still think the ending does not work. But if he does it in masks—if the characters are clearly human—maybe it will be acceptable."

Mats was busy with the production of the play, so I didn't see him much for a while—nor Gwarha, who had been called to Ata Tsan to arbitrate a really nasty quarrel between two frontmen. His great skill is negotiation, but—he said—he was reaching the limits of his skill.

"These two cannot be reasoned with, and they come from two lineages that have never been friendly. We are going to be here a long time, Nicky."

"I'll find something to do."

He gave me a considering stare.

A few days later I ran into Mats at one of the station's many gymnasia. I was there practicing *hanatsin* with one of the beautifully mannered, earnest and intelligent young men that Gwarha always has around him. (His ability to pick junior officers is remarkable.) I no longer remember which young man it was. Most likely, he was doing what most of them do: flipping me onto the padded floor, then helping me up and explaining what I'd done wrong with meticulous courtesy.

Matsehar did not practice any of the martial arts beyond the minimum required of everyone on the perimeter, and he didn't engage in competitive sports. His lack of coordination was too much of a problem. But he had the *hwarhath* obsession with physical fitness, and he worked out daily, swimming or using the resistance machines.

It wasn't surprising that we met in the *hwarhath* equivalent of a locker room, and it wasn't surprising that he'd forgotten to bring a long-handled comb. (Mats is not a detail man, except in the theater.) I found him sitting at the end of a bench, trying to reach the hair between his shoulder blades with a handleless comb.

I said, "Let me do that," sat down in back of him and took the comb. For a while, there was no problem. The *hwarhath* spend a lot of time grooming one another. It's a fairly impersonal activity, and I'd had plenty of experience with Gwarha.

The hair grows at different angles on different parts of a *hwarhath* body; I had learned how to deal with this by changing the angle of comb. I knew how to ease the comb through clumped and matted fur, causing no pain, and how to tease out tangles in the crest of longer hair that goes from the top of a *hwarhath* head to the bottom of the spine. I knew what kind of pressure was pleasant and comfortable.

My mind must have drifted to Gwarha or to whichever young man had been tossing me around the *hanatsin* room. All at once I noticed that my free hand was no longer resting lightly on Matsehar's shoulder. Instead it had moved in and down. I was rubbing—caressing—the thick shoulder muscle, moving toward the wonderful silky hair of the neck and spine.

Mats was sitting motionless, no longer leaning toward me. I could see discomfort in the way he held himself and feel it in the muscle tightening under my hand.

I was a little surprised by his reaction, but not much. Some *hwarhath* males are uninterested in sex. In their culture there is nothing shameful about this: they don't have to lie or pretend. Some are monogamous. Gwarha is, most of the time. According to him, promiscuity is too much work for a reward that is not commensurate. He can put the same energy into his career and get something of real benefit for himself and his lineage. And finally there are plenty of *hwarhath,* the overwhelming majority, who have no interest at all in me.

I muttered, "Sorry," and finished combing his back, working quickly now, with as much impersonality as I could manage, then stood and returned the comb. He thanked me, his head down, sounding unhappy.

"Don't worry about it, Mats. You know my reputation. It was close to inevitable that I'd make a try. It won't happen a second time."

He glanced up, looking miserable.

Touching was out for the moment. I said, "Lighten up," which can actually be said in the *hwarhath* main language, though for them it means "do not be dark" rather than "do not be heavy."

He kept giving me that look of dumb misery.

"I'll talk to you later," I said, and left.

I didn't see him for maybe twenty days. He was obviously avoiding me. I wasn't going to hunt him down. I put more time in at work, and with Gwarha, when that was possible.

One evening Gwarha said, "What is going on between you and Carrier Eh?"

I came up with some kind of evasive answer.

Gwarha looked at the table in front of him. He was playing another board game. I remember which one this time: *eha.* The board was a square, flat piece of wood, pale in color and fine-grained. A grid of straight lines had been carved in it. Where the lines crossed were hollows: the pieces rested there. They were small round pebbles, gathered from rivers in the land of Ettin. In a proper set, the pieces are always from the land of the player. Ideally, the player has gathered them. The masters of the game spend hundreds of days searching for the exact right stones. Gwarha is not a master and has never had that kind of time. One of his aunts sent the stones to him.

He moved a stone, then looked at me. "He is not the kind of man who usually interests you, and he— I have heard two stories. One is that he has no interest in sex. The other is that he likes the actors who devote themselves to female roles."

"You've been doing research."

"I like to keep track of what you're doing." He looked down at the computer on the couch next to him. The program re-created the style of a long-dead *eha* master. "Hah! I am in trouble."

I sat for a while, feeling angry. There are times when the constant struggling within the *hwarhath* male society— the gossiping and spying and maneuvering for position— is goddamn tiring, at least for me, though never for Gwarha.

Finally I said, "I made a try. I got turned down. At the moment, the carrier is ducking around corners when he sees me coming."

"A stupid little boy," said Gwarha, and moved another stone.

Mats called me sometime after that. "I have to talk with you, Nicky, and I need a safe place."

He meant a place without listeners—not an easy request, given the *hwarhath* mania for keeping track of one another. But Gwarha had his own security by then (he was far enough forward); and they had checked my rooms as well as his.

"Here," I said.

"What about the defender?"

"We came to an agreement a couple of years ago. I am almost certainly trustworthy, and I need privacy. Humans are not as social as the People."

"Hah!" said Matsehar.

He arrived at my door holding a squat jug. I knew what that meant. There were refrigerator coils inside the thick ceramic walls. They kept the liquid inside the jug below the freezing point of water: *halin* or *kalin*, depending on your accent. It's a very serious toxin, and I had never seen Mats even mildly drunk.

He came in and pulled a cup out of a pocket in his shorts, sat down and filled the cup with *halin*, transparent and as green as grass in spring.

"Are you certain you want to drink that stuff?"

"Yes. This is not a conversation I want to have while sober."

He drank the *halin* and refilled his cup, then started to talk. At first, he circled and jumped from one subject to another: the new play, various pieces of gossip. In back of him (I remember) was the monitor for my rooms. The lights were all on and colorless. This meant the doors were locked and the comm system was shut down. No one was listening, except me.

Finally, when I began to hear a slur in his voice, he paused and looked at me: a steady gaze, though his pupils were beginning to narrow. If he kept on the way he was going they would end as barely visible lines, and he would be thread drunk, a lovely term, exactly right as a description.

"It isn't you, Nicky. I have nothing against aliens. I consider you a friend. The problem is me."

I waited, saying nothing. He took a deep breath, exhaled and went on.

There have been times when I've wondered if I did the right thing when I took Gwarha up on his offer of a job. Maybe I should have been a hero and stayed in prison. But if I'd listened to Honor and Integrity, I would never have been in that room in the Ata Tsan station, listening to a very troubled young fellow explain that he had no interest at all in men.

No. I could not have missed that moment.

He'd never had any interest, Matsehar said. As far back as he could remember, all his sexual fantasies had been about women. There was despair in his voice. I had trouble keeping from laughing.

He had tried. The Goddess knew that he had tried to be like everyone else.

"If I think about the person I'm with, it doesn't work at all. I can't manage the act. If I imagine that I'm with a woman . . ." He stopped and shuddered. "I feel dishonest. I feel—" He used a lovely archaic *hwarhath* word that meant besmirched or perhaps, more accurately, covered with feces.

"Most of the time, it's easier to masturbate. At least then I don't involve another person. Except I get so lonely." He refilled his cup, his hand no longer steady. "I keep thinking—if only I hadn't gotten sick when I was young."

"Are you arguing that heterosexuality is caused by a viral infection of the central nervous system? It's an interesting idea, Mats, and it might be worth exploring."

He looked surprised. "No. I don't mean that. I mean— if I'd had a normal life, if I'd gone to school when everyone else did."

"You can drive yourself crazy trying to figure out why you're the way you are."

"You understand, don't you, Nicky? You come from a society where this kind of thing is normal. I would not be a pervert there."

I got up and got a cup and held it out. Matsehar filled it. I tasted the *halin*. It was ice cold, bitter and burning. If I was careful, it would make me a little woozy. If I wasn't careful, it would make me sick for three days. "Mats, I don't understand my life, let alone anyone else's. There have got to be other men among the People who are straight."

He looked puzzled. I had translated the English word directly into the *hwarhath* main language, where it meant straight as in a ruler, even, direct, upright and honorable. "Other men who are sexually abnormal. Why don't you look for them?"

"I've found some of them. They hang around the actors who play women. But what can they tell me? Only what I know. There is no solution to our problem."

He kept talking. He was no longer drinking, but the *halin* was having an increasingly obvious effect. He stumbled over words and paused sometimes, looking confused, as if he couldn't remember what he'd been saying. When he glanced up, his eyes were empty, the pupils contracted so far that I couldn't see them.

The two sides of *hwarhath* culture were too widely separated. There was no way for a man to meet women, except those in his lineage, and the People regard incest with profound horror. (Sex with animals is a comparatively mild form of perversion and—interestingly enough—the gender of the animal doesn't matter. It isn't worse to have sex with a mare or doe.)

There was no heterosexual subculture, no underclass of men and women who made love together.

Matsehar could masturbate while having fantasies about imaginary women, who often seemed disturbingly like his female cousins. He could hang out with the actors who played women and the men who were attracted to them. He did sometimes, but under the costumes and the mannerisms, the actors were men. Their lovers were self-deluded.

"None of it is real. No one is the person he wants to be. No one makes love to the person he dreams of."

He could think horrifying, terrifying thoughts about seduction and rape.

"I don't go home anymore. I'm afraid I will be like a man in a play. Violent. Crazy."

The situation had stopped being humorous. The poor kid was coming apart in front of me, and the thing I wanted to do—hold him and say, "There, there, life is hell"—was not a possibility.

"What do you want me to do?" I asked.

"Is there nothing you know, nothing you can say, that will make this bearable?"

Why me?

Because I had a perspective that no one else had; because I saw his culture from the outside; and maybe because he saw himself as an outcast—an outlaw—and saw me as being even further beyond the pale.

I looked up "pale" once. It's from *palus,* the Latin for stake. It means a fence, a palisade, any enclosing barrier or line.

"Mats, all I can tell you is to concentrate on what you have. In some ways we are opposites. I have Gwarha, which I guess is what you want: the great love—the fence against loneliness—and a warm body in bed. Believe me, I don't undervalue either. But I've lost my family and my nation and my species; and while I can still practice my craft, my skill with language, I can't give what I've learned to my own people.

"You have the People and your lineage and your art. Don't undervalue any of that."

He shook his head. "It isn't enough."

"It's all the comfort I can give you."

We talked a while longer. Mats was less and less coherent. Finally I told him I'd walk him back to his room. I don't think he would have made it on his own.

We got there. He palmed the door open, then turned back to me. "I wish I *could* love you, Nicky."

At the moment he wasn't especially appealing. I couldn't in honesty tell him I was sorry he was straight. I told him to go to bed. He staggered through the door. It closed. I looked around until I found the camera that covered this section of corridor. No question. It had got us.

I walked back to my part of the station. A light shone amber next to the door that led from my rooms to Gwarha's. That meant his side was unlocked. An invitation. I went in.

He lay full length on the couch in his front room, dressed in the standard at-home costume for a *hwarhath* male. It's in between a kimono and a bathrobe and as gaudy as possible. I don't remember which one he had on that evening. He has a lot, mostly gifts from adoring female relatives. Let's say it was the burgundy brocade, long since recycled, but very flashy in its time. The pattern was monsters twisting among flowers, and there was gold embroidery on the sleeves and hem.

He looked up when I came in and laid down a little flat reading computer. "What is the human phrase? If I didn't know better, I'd say you had been drinking."

"Matsehar was over. He got very toxic. I got a little toxic. I think I stopped in time, but Mats is going to be as sick as a small domestic animal on Earth."

"Your difficulties with him have been resolved." It was a question.

"I don't think he's going to be ducking around corners when he sees me, but he has no sexual interest in me. None at all."

"Good. It's never easy for me to hold back, when you are in the mood to look around."

I sat down on the edge of the couch. "You know, there are worse lives than the one I'm living."

"Assuredly," said Gwarha.

I took one of his hands and rubbed the fur on the back, steel grey and as soft as velvet, then turned the hand over and kissed the dark hairless palm.

> From the journal of Sanders Nicholas,
> information-holder attached to the staff
> of First-Defender Ettin Gwarha
> CODED FOR REVIEW BY NO ONE

# X

➤➤➤ SHE GOT BACK one evening and smelled coffee as the door slid open.

"Nicholas?" she called as she stepped in.

The room was dark, except for a single lamp that shone at the end of the couch. Nick was there, his feet up on a table as usual. (The wood glimmered pearl grey.) He held a mug in one hand. In front of him the wall had vanished, and a dark slope went down to a bay full of flashing lights.

She recognized the staccato rhythm and the colors: orange and pale blue. It was her warning in the I.E.C. *Danger. Strange friend. Danger.*

"What in heaven?" she asked.

"It's the *hwarhath* equivalent of vacation pictures. They take them every time they land on a planet. I knew there had to be something from your place. What did you call it?"

"Reed 1935-C."

"That sings. I thought you might like to see the recording."

The scene blurred: dark hill and luminescing bay. Anna said something, what she didn't know; but her throat hurt, and she had trouble speaking. A moment later she felt his arms around her.

"I didn't mean to hurt you, Anna."

His body was angular and muscular. His clothing had a sharp clean aroma that she did not recognize. Alien soap?

"Sit down." He guided her to the couch and was gone. She wiped her eyes. The ceiling light went on. The landscape in front of her vanished. "Back in a moment," he called.

He returned with another mug. "I added some brandy. The general managed to acquire a good stock of potables on Reed whatever. Now, what was that about? How did I manage to put my foot in?"

"They pulled us out. Not just me. Everyone. And they haven't let anyone go back. The planet is vulnerable now. The *hwarhath* can find it."

He nodded. "There are times I'm ashamed of my species. Why did they use that planet for the negotiations? Surely they could have found a world that didn't have anything worth studying."

"I don't know." She drank the coffee.

"Well, they've lost the planet, unless the negotiations here work out. Is that what you meant when you said your career was ruined?"

She nodded. "My field is nonhuman intelligence. What's left, if I can't get to the pseudosiphonophores? I can screw around, studying animals on other planets that aren't even as bright as dolphins. I can screw around on Earth, studying dolphins. That's assuming I can get a grant. Did you put brandy in the coffee or coffee in the brandy?"

"Do you want me to alter the proportions?"

"I think more coffee might be a good idea."

He brought the mug back, then said, "Do you mind if I turn off the overhead light? The People like a comparatively dark environment when they're relaxing, and I guess I've been conditioned. Bright lighting makes me think I have to go to work."

"Okay."

The light went off, and the room was dark again, except for the lamp at the end of the couch. He settled down where he'd been next to the lamp and picked up his mug. She saw the glint of metal on his wrist, the bracelet he'd worn the last time she had spoken to him. "So the general did you a favor, when he asked the humans to send you. Here you are, surrounded by alien intelligence."

"It's not what I expected. I'm spending my time listening to Eh Matsehar talk about *Macbeth* and Hai Atala Vaihar talk about *Moby Dick*."

"That will change," said Nicholas. "Vaihar has tracked down a copy of *Huckleberry Finn*. It was in the files that we cleaned out of your station. He has already started to ask me questions about the book. I told him to talk to you. I read your research notes. They also were in the files that we cleaned out of the station. I don't think your animals are intelligent."

"Why not?"

He was silent for a while. "Several reasons. Do you want me to talk about it? I don't want you in tears again, Anna."

"I won't be."

"Okay."

He gave his reasons. For the most part, it was the same argument she'd heard from her colleagues on Reed 1935-C. The pseudosiphonophores had no material culture. Their language wasn't a real language. It had no grammar; lacking a grammar, the aliens could not speak about sequence or consequence.

Nick said, "I guess I think intelligence had something to do with grouping and relating and maybe with cause-and-effect.

"I can't see any reason why they would need to develop a language. We use language to codify experience, put it in a form other people can understand. Once we've done that we can share what we know. That's how we teach and learn. But if one of your guys wants to learn something, all he has to do is eat another pseudosiphonophore. As far as

I can tell from your notes, this is the primary way they transmit information. It works, no question, and it means that they don't need complicated ways to communicate.

"Except at mating season. That's the only time they get close to one another. The rest of the year they are solitary for fear of being eaten; and the really big fellows, the ones who ought to be the smartest and best informed, because they have eaten the most relatives, those guys are always solitary. They no longer mate."

She was no longer unhappy. Maybe it was the brandy in her coffee or the pleasure of listening to Nick's argument, though she didn't agree with it.

"That leads me to my last reason for thinking your guys are not intelligent. They are not sufficiently interested in sex." He glanced at her. Anna saw the white flash of a smile.

"What do you mean? You saw the bay. You saw the ocean."

"That was during the mating season. But humans don't have a mating season, and neither do the People. We are sexually active and sexually interested all the time.

"I figure there is an evolutionary benefit to being horny all the time. It keeps you intensely interested in other people, and it gives you a reason to stay on good terms. It holds us together. We have to get along with one another, if we are going to get laid."

Anna shook her head. "There are plenty of animals that form communities."

"Not like our communities. I can't think of any animals that are as intensely and continuously interested in one another as we and the People are.

"If your guys lost their mating season, if they became interested in one another all the time, if their big fellows retained an interest in sex, then maybe they'd be forced to start creating a culture. Maybe they'd start to develop a genuine language. Maybe they'd begin to become intelligent."

"Are you serious about this line of argument?" asked Anna.

He laughed. "Most likely not. But I am serious about the lack of a material culture, and you might actually want to listen to me about the language. That's an area I know something about.

"I came to tell you something and got distracted. The *hwarhath* women are getting impatient. They want to talk to you again; but the general does not want to let go of me. So the women are bringing in their own translator, who is a woman. I'm going to sit in on a couple of discussions, to double-check her work; and then I will be out, which is too bad. My hunch is the women are going to be a lot more interesting than the diplomats. But the general has spoken. And that's what I came to tell you. I'm not entirely certain why I ended up analyzing your aliens." He set down his mug. Once again she saw the glint of the gold and jade bracelet. "No. That's a lie. I started talking about the aliens because you were upset by the recording, and your reaction made me uneasy. Knowledge is the only certain consolation. I think I told you that once. And there are only two activities that I have ever found that really distract one from the ordinary pain of life: sex and playing with ideas." He stood up. "Do you want me to take the recording?"

"No. Leave it."

He showed her how to operate the projector, then said good night. After he left, she turned on the recording. Once again the wall vanished, and she was looking down the hill on which the diplomatic compound stood. Had stood?

Her animals flashed their message. She drank the rest of the coffee and brandy. Nick was wrong, she thought, biased toward the kind of intelligence that humans had.

She imagined the adult members of her alien species floating in the ocean currents and trailing tendrils that extended a hundred meters or more. Their bell-like bodies contained a dozen brains, visible (dimly) through the transparent flesh. There had to be a reason for all those neurons and all that information. She imagined intellects that were huge, cool, solitary, devoted to contemplation, a species for whom nonattachment was natural. For them the Eightfold Path was unnecessary. The Four Noble Truths were irrelevant. They were not troubled by lust or greed. They had no need for Monkey to come with baskets full of Scripture. They had already achieved a kind of enlightenment.

At that point, she realized that the brandy was having an effect.

She went to the bathroom and took a shower. Then she went to bed. The ceiling was covered with a rose pink nebula, its filaments making it look—oddly enough—like a neuron. Beyond it and through it shone a multitude of stars.

# XI

➤➤➤ THE NEXT DAY she told her colleagues about the conversation.

"It's too bad you're going to lose contact with him," said Captain McIntosh.

"Why?" asked Anna.

"I'd like the chance to know him better," Mac said. "Directly or indirectly."

"No plotting, Captain," Charlie Khamvongsa said.

"I'm regular army, sab. We don't plot. We think strategically."

Charlie laughed. "All right. But let Nicholas Sanders alone."

Hai Atala Vaihar walked her back through the cool bright halls of the station. "Did Nicky tell you I found the other book?"

"Yes."

"Is the river real? Does it exist on Earth?"

"The Mississippi? Yes."

"I would like to see it."

She decided not to tell him how much it had changed: the forests cut down, the backwaters mostly dry, the river itself reduced (in many places) to a straight and narrow channel, just barely deep enough for traffic. The animals— the eagles and herons, fish, clams, bears, cougars, deer, raccoons and possums—were almost all gone.

Three hundred years of civilization. A hundred years of

the Great Midwestern Drought. It was painful now to read Mark Twain.

"My country lies inland," said Vaihar. "And I was raised near a river, though not such a big one. I used to explore the bottomlands and go out to the islands." He paused. "I don't understand what is going on between Huck and Jim."

"It's been years since I read the book."

"If they were members of my own species, I'd know exactly what is happening and say it's wrong. They are different ages. Children must always be protected. But—" He frowned and stopped in the middle of the corridor. "They don't seem to be different ages. The boy has not had enough care, and the man has not been given enough autonomy. So the boy is manlike, and the man has some of the traits of a child. Very strange! You humans mix everything together."

He walked on, Anna next to him.

When they reached the entrance to the human quarters, he spoke again. "There is a time when boys begin to fall in love with each other in the right and proper way. They dream of escape." He glanced at her briefly. "Usually we discover love at the same time that we realize how much we owe our families and the Weaving. Childhood is almost over. Adulthood lies in front of us.

"It is not an easy time. We want—" He paused. "—to run away, to escape all responsibility. We want to have nothing except our love.

"That is what this book is like. A dream of escape. But nothing is quite right. Nothing is exactly as it ought to be. I think I understand and then I don't. It is very disturbing."

He left her. She went to her rooms.

That evening she watched more of the recording. Her aliens had reverted to their own blue and green message. *I am me. I intend no harm.* It shone dimly through a misty rain. She could see the yellow lights of the research station at the edge of the bay. The *hwarhath* must have been there when this recording was made, searching through the computers and questioning her friends. She imagined the People, precise and polite, moving through the familiar halls, like so many dancers or accountants.

A few days later Vaihar reappeared in the negotiations, and that afternoon Nicholas stood at the entrance to the human quarters. He was dressed in his civvies: the oddly cut tan clothes.

"Tsai Ama Ul wants to talk with you."

"Okay."

They went to the same room as before. Two women waited for them. She recognized one: the woman of Tsai Ama, dressed this time in a white-and-silver robe. The second woman was the same height as Anna and slender. Her robe was blue-green and plain, not a brocade, though the panels had a silky shimmer. Her fur was as black as Tsai Ama Ul's.

"Don't meet Ul's gaze," said Nicholas quietly. "But the other woman is your equal. Look straight at her. Make sure you stay in front of me. I'm the junior person here and not related to anyone except you."

She was close enough now to see that the slender woman had blue-green eyes. Rows of silver studs went up the edges of her very large ears.

"Stop," said Nick.

She obeyed.

He said, "You have already met the woman of Tsai Ama. This other woman is Ama Tsai Indil. The two lineages are partnered. I will explain what that means some other time. This is Perez Anna."

"I am glad to meet you," said the slender woman. She had a deep, husky voice, and her English was excellent.

Tsai Ama Ul spoke in her own language. Anna under-stood only one word: Nicky.

"We are to sit down," said Nicholas. "And I am to mind my manners and not cause trouble."

Ama Tsai Indil said, "That is a free translation. My—what should I say? cousin?—is more polite than that."

"Try senior partner," Nick said. "There's no good translation."

They sat down, Nicholas in back of her and to the side, the two alien women facing her.

Tsai Ama Ul leaned forward and spoke. "Too much time has passed, and we are leaving too much to the men. I am not certain this is a good idea. It is the service of men to look for enemies. It is possible that they see enemies when enemies are not present. Certainly it is the nature of men to think of the danger that may hide in any new situation, and when they meet strangers they look for weapons.

"This may not be the right response, and while it is certainly the responsibility of the men to deal with your men, it is not their responsibility or their right to deal with you.

"I am going to ask you more questions about your people, Perez Anna. Please answer directly. I am afraid if we do not find a way to speak to one another, we will be left with the decisions that the men make out of suspicion and fear."

She spent the next couple of hours talking, once again, about life on Earth. For the most part, the slender woman translated. Now and then Nicholas corrected her or they discussed the meaning of a word.

Finally Tsai Ama Ul said, "It is clear to me that the old ways of understanding behavior are not going to work. You are too different.

"I thought I would not have a problem. I'm a scholar, and I have studied your culture. But I have to confess, I am unsettled, and it's possible that I am afraid." She paused, then added something, her voice rapid.

"The woman of Tsai Ama says it isn't human weapons that frighten her. She wants you to understand this. Our men have told us that they can deal with the violence of human men.

"But it's one thing to know about a strangeness in the far distance, and another thing to have the strangeness here in front of us."

The translator stopped, and Tsai Ama was silent. Anna got the impression she was brooding. Finally she spoke.

This time Nick translated. "The woman of Tsai Ama says that she has as much information as she can handle now. She needs to think. We are dismissed."

They stood. Tsai Ama Ul glanced up and spoke a final time. Nicholas laughed at what she said and nodded and then gestured toward the door. Anna walked out ahead of him.

Once they were in the hall she spoke. "What was that last bit?"

"With Ul? She was congratulating me on behaving myself halfway decently."

"Is she a friend of yours? She called you Nicky."

"We correspond. She's interested in humanity. We give her a comparison or a control, when she thinks about the history of her own people."

They reached her door. Anna palmed it open. Nick nodded farewell and left.

Anna went in and turned on the hologram: a sunny day on Reed 1935-C. The bay was blue, and the hills were golden. High thin clouds blew in from the ocean. What was that called? A mackerel sky? Her aliens were invisible, but she saw planes flying over the station and the compound hill. *Hwarhath* fanwings, going to and from their island base.

It ought to be possible to do a three-way comparison

between humans and the *hwarhath* and her aliens in the bay. Is a material culture necessary? What is language? How important is sex? There was enough stuff here for dozens of articles, and no human except Nicholas had access to more information about the *hwarhath*. Maybe he'd be willing to coauthor. Jesus Maria, to be able to use what he knew about the People!

But it would not be possible unless the negotiations succeeded. She began to feel a fierce determination. The negotiations had to be made to work.

# XII

➤➤➤ THERE WAS A note in my office. Gwarha had gone home. I could join him if I wanted. That meant it was an invitation, not an order.

I went home and got clean. He had unlocked his side of the door between our quarters. I went through into his main room. There was a hologram on: a landscape. Sunlight spilled from one end of the room, and I saw a wall made of rough grey stone, tall and broken. Pieces of rock lay on the ground in front of the wall; a gap opened, showing trees with copper-colored foliage that quivered in a wind.

The stone was mottled with a lichenoid plant. Most of the patches were yellow. A few were silvery. Here and there were spots and streaks of red.

I knew the place. I had been there with Gwarha on one of our visits to his home. It was an old fortress that stood in the wilderness on what had been the border of Ettin. The border was much farther out now. The fortress belonged to the days when Ettin had just begun to expand.

We'd climbed through the ruins, and Gwarha had told me about the builder of the fortress, who had been an ancestor of his, a bloody brutal determined man. In his time the lineage of Ettin had more than doubled in size. Two other lineages had been destroyed, their men killed, their women and children incorporated. Nothing could stop the ancestor except a word from his mother or his elder sister. He was a devoted son and brother. His female relatives were famous politicians. What he could not do with swords, they could do with language. What a combination! said Gwarha.

It was late spring, and the day was warm. The ruins were dry and dusty. We left them finally and went down to the stream that ran below the fortress, shaded by copper-red trees. We drank. Then Gwarha shucked his clothes and waded in.

I decided, no. The stream came out of the mountains. It was a lot too cold for me. He splashed and hunted around like a kid, looking for the usual things you find in a stream: rocks, fish and animals with too many legs. The fish got frightened off, of course, but he did manage to find something that was long and flat and segmented. Every segment had a pair of legs. Hey Nicky, look at this! Isn't it neat?

It twisted in his hand. There were mandibles at one end or maybe pinchers. At the other end were two long narrow antennae that waved in the air.

Very nice, I told him. The thing wriggled some more, and he dropped it.

Then he decided it would be funny to pull me into the stream. He didn't manage to do it, but I got pretty wet anyway. We climbed up to the courtyard of the fortress. I spread my clothes out to dry, and we made love. Gwarha dozed off. I lay in the sunlight, his body against mine, the fur still damp.

I had a sense that he'd brought me here for a purpose. Even the lovemaking had been planned. This was a show for his ancestor. "See where I have been, old man. To places you cannot even imagine. See what I have captured and brought home."

I drifted into one of those vivid, almost rational dreams that happen at the edge of sleep. There was someone in the courtyard. I got up on my knees. Gwarha lay next to me, asleep.

In front of me stood a *hwarhath* male, his fur silvered by age. He wore a chain-mail tunic that came down to his knees. A sword hung at his side. He carried a dagger, the blade bare and shining in the slanting late-afternoon light.

The ancestor, of course. He was an extreme version of the physical type characteristic of Ettin: short and very broad with thick arms and legs. A crest of dark fur ran over the top of his bare head. His face was wide and flat and ugly.

Gwarha sat up, looking frightened.

"What's wrong with you, boy?" asked the ancestor. He spoke the language of Ettin, which I knew; but I could barely understand him.

"If you want to fuck an enemy, fine. But you don't go to sleep next to him. This is how you should have ended."

He grabbed my hair and pulled my head back. Then he cut my throat.

I woke. A good thing, too. If I'd slept there much longer I would have gotten a sunburn. Gwarha was still out; he'd awakened only in my dream. I got up and checked my clothes. They hadn't finished drying. I hunkered down in a shadow by the wall, my back against the rough warm stone, and waited until he rolled over and groaned and sat up. All that time I felt nervous, as if the old man were somewhere nearby, still holding his knife.

That had been years ago; but I wasn't comfortable looking at the wall. The lichenoid—the red one—was the color of drying blood. The Goddess only knew why Gwarha had decided he wanted that scene at the end of his living room. I fooled around with the projector until I found something I liked better: whitecaps on the Round Lake of Ettin. A boat with red sails slid through the foaming water.

I sat down and watched. The boat was a pleasure craft, narrow and quick. It leaned over, pulled almost horizontal by the wind in the huge red sails.

After a while Gwarha came in and stood in back of me.

He was just out of the shower. I could smell damp fur and aromatic soap. "You did not like the fortress."

"No."

A hand touched my shoulder. "I went to a diviner after you told me the dream. Did I ever tell you that? She said I had angered the old man. I had ceremonies performed. He is not someone with whom I want a quarrel.

"She said another thing." The hand moved, ruffling my hair. "There is a gap between his world and mine that cannot be crossed. I tried to speak to him, to call across the void. Let the old ones be dead, she told me. Their way of life is over.

"I have been looking at the wall and thinking about her words. Hah! She is right. But I cannot see what the new way of life ought to be like. I don't know how to go forward. What am I going to do, Nicky?"

I didn't answer. Gwarha had already heard all my theories and all my advice.

In front of us the boat—the pleasure craft—went over. For a moment it lay flat in the water; then it righted itself.

"Is that an omen?" I asked.

"No. Omens happen in the real world. You ought to know that by now. No one ever sees the future in a hologram."

Okay.

From the journal of Sanders Nicholas,
information-holder attached to the staff
of First-Defender Ettin Gwarha
CODED FOR REVIEW BY ETTIN GWARHA ONLY

# XIII

➤➤➤ A COUPLE OF days later Anna stayed with her colleagues through the evening. Captain McIntosh walked her to the entrance. "If you see Holder Sanders, give this to him." He held out a paper folder.

"What is it?"

"A printout of his file. Look through it, if you want. There's nothing in it that's protected."

"Why do you want him to see it?"

"He might be interested. There is information about his family."

She took the folder, carried it back to her rooms and settled down to read.

Sanders, Nicholas Edgar, date of birth 14/7/89. His birthplace was DeCaugh, Kansas. His parents were Genevieve Pierce, D.V.M., and Edgar Sanders, a specialist in traditional technologies employed by the Agricultural Rescue Administration. He had one sibling, a sister three years younger: Beatrice Helen Pierce.

Education: the local public schools, followed by the University of Chicago. He obtained an M.A. in 2110. (She did some figuring and decided he must have skipped a grade or two.) His major had been linguistic theory; his minor had been in computer science. Immediately after receiving his master's, he joined the Unified Armed Forces. There was more education, this time at the University of Geneva. Again his area of specialty was linguistic theory. His record stopped in 2112.

Three years later he was on a spy ship that was captured in *hwarhath* space. The time in between must have been spent working on the *hwarhath* language.

An oddly bare history. There was no evidence of any personal life. Had he had one? Did she care?

She looked through the rest of the file. His sister had been educated at the University of Wisconsin, married and produced one child, a daughter named Nicole. The marriage had ended in divorce. The sister lived in Chicago and worked as a union organizer. There was a picture, a hologram of a tall woman in her forties, thin with unruly sandy hair. She squinted into the sunlight and smiled. It was Nick's smile and his posture, slouching a little, hands in pockets. The sister wore jeans, a faded red shirt and a denim jacket with buttons pinned to the lapel. Anna could not make out what the buttons said.

Next to her was her daughter: thin and gawky and café-au-lait-colored, her frizzy hair cut short, a girl of eleven or twelve who was very obviously going to be tall. She wore jeans and a short-sleeved black shirt. In red letters on the front was *Don't Mourn. Organize.*

She went on to the other picture, which was 2-D. A couple sitting in an audience. The picture had been taken from the side and was obviously a snapshot. A man and a woman, both tall and thin, sitting very upright. They both had white hair. The woman wore hers in braids wound around her head. The man's hair was shoulder-length and curly. They had a bony elegance that reminded Anna of herons.

She checked the file. They had retired to Fargo, North Dakota, and were still alive. (The picture had been taken five months before at a lecture given at the local university in honor of the North Dakota poet Thomas McGrath.) (Why would anyone retire to Fargo?) Genevieve was eighty-five; Edgar was eighty-three. They were active in the local Methodist church and in various other organizations concerned (mostly) with environmental and social issues.

Cause maniacs. Nicholas came from a family of good-deed-doers.

She looked back at the pictures: the sister with sandy hair blowing in the wind, the grave young niece, the parents like herons.

Did any of this fit with the man she knew?

She closed the file finally and went to bed. It was odd to lie in the darkness hundreds of light-years from home and think of people whose lives had been spent in the American Midwest, who might die in that dusty land that was slowly drying out, the rivers shallowing, the wells producing nothing, brown clouds filling the sky.

The next day she called Nicholas and asked him to come over.

He arrived in the afternoon, after the daily meeting had ended, still dressed in the space-warrior uniform with the high black boots.

She handed him the folder. He sat down and read. After he was done reading, he looked at the two pictures. Finally he looked up. His face was masklike. "Where did you get this?" She had never heard that tone in his voice. It was icy.

"Captain McIntosh gave it to me. He told me to give it to you."

"Why? What am I supposed to do?"

"Nothing. He thought you might be interested in information about your family."

"Why?"

"For God's sake, Nick, this is your family."

He gathered the pages and straightened them, so all the edges were even, then laid the pictures on top and closed the folder. Every movement was precise and angry. "I'm not certain what you expect me to do," he said, his voice soft. "Break into tears and say I'll do anything, if only I can see Mom and Dad before they die. Say I have to see the niece who is evidently named after me, if she exists, if she is not an invention of MI.

"I'm here. I am never going home. I have chosen my side. I cannot be bought or frightened or seduced or conned. There is no deal—absolutely none—that can be cut with me.

"So. Why does Captain McIntosh want me to see this folder?"

She felt close to tears. "Nick, I don't know."

He sighed and leaned back in the chair. "You probably don't. Anna, these people are poisonous. Don't let them use you. They never learn. They never get better. They keep playing their games. They keep thinking their games matter. I'm not sure what matters in history; but the games of spies are trivial and pointless and malicious and evil. Don't get involved with them." He stood and picked up the folder. "Thank Captain McIntosh for the information. I won't ask you to tell him to fuck off. That message ought to be delivered personally."

He left, and she did cry.

# XIV

➤➤➤ I WAITED TILL evening to talk with Gwarha. One of our rules was that in public and during office hours I had to behave approximately like an officer and a gentleman. I knew I wanted to be angry. I figured there was a good chance I'd want to pace and shout. So I waited till he was settled in at home, then brought the folder over.

He read through it, then laid the two pictures on the table in front of him. He looked at them and glanced up at me. "I have a hard time seeing resemblances among humans. But I think they all look like you, especially the sister and her daughter."

"They are trying to turn me. They tried kidnapping. Now they are trying to appeal to whatever. Family loyalty. Do you know what Lugala Tsu would think of this?"

"He is a malicious fool. His opinion cannot be changed by fact or reason, so there is no point in caring about his opinion. The important thing is this." He looked at the picture of Beatrice and Nicole. "You have a descendant, and the best possible kind. The daughter of a sister. A full sister." I thought I heard sadness in his voice. He is his mother's only living child. His closest relatives in the next generation are going to be the children of female cousins. His own children—and he is certain to have them—will not count, of course. They'll belong to their mothers' lineages. "Is she named for you?"

"Nicole? I think so. If she exists. Gwar, I want your

security people to look the pictures over. See if they can determine if they've been altered or faked.''

"Humans would lie about something this important?''

"Yes. For all I know, my entire family is dead. I have no reason to believe any of this.''

"Your species is contemptible. I will tell my people to do what they can. But I'm not certain they will be able to find any trickery.'' He touched the picture of Beatrice and Nicole. "You really think they would lie about this?''

I nodded.

He made a small unhappy noise, then put the pictures into the folder.

I sat down. "If we ever get out of this, let's go back to your home. I want to be outside.'' I stretched out my legs. "I think maybe a trip up into the mountains. A lot of exercise, as much sex as possible and no thinking at all. Jesus, I am tired of thinking.''

"Then don't do it. I will handle the problem of Lugala Tsu. The machinations of the humans can be ignored. Obey orders and do your job. That is always an alternative, Nicky. You do not have to plot. You do not have to manipulate. You do not have to play stupid games.''

"Goddess, it's tempting.''

"Then act, or rather do not act. Sit still and let events happen on their own. If something is important, if it needs to get done, it will get done without you scurrying around.''

Zen and the art of living among furry grey aliens. [?]
From the journal of Sanders Nicholas, etc.

# XV

➤➤➤ SHE SPENT ANOTHER evening with her colleagues. Etienne went to bed early, as did the little Chinese translator, Haxu. The rest of the men stayed up: Charlie, Sten, Captain McIntosh, Dr. Azizi and Dy Singh, who was a genuine practicing Sikh in a turban.

They drank coffee with or without brandy. After a while Anna told them about her conversation with Nicholas.

Charlie frowned. "I thought we had agreed there would be no plotting, Captain."

"I was not plotting, sab. I thought Holder Sanders might want to know about his family."

"Why give him a carefully edited version of his file?"

"I couldn't give him the full version. Much of the information is protected or private; and I couldn't see a reason to print out everything else. There's a lot of it. The people in Military Intelligence have an absolute mania for collecting information; and—as far as I can tell—no ability to discriminate. If I had been paying attention, I'd be able to tell you his shoe size and the results of every exam he's ever taken. None of it is interesting. He seems to have been an ordinary young man.

"MI worried about his family; his relatives are a little too socially active. But they found nothing in Sanders' personal history to cause them to worry about him as an individual; and in the end they took him."

"You have not answered my question," said Charlie. "Why did you give him a copy of his file?"

"I wanted to remind him that he used to be one of us, and that he still has family on Earth. I thought it might make him—not a friend, but more friendly."

"It seems to have made him furious." Charlie looked at her. "If you get the chance, apologize to him. Tell him we meant no harm."

"I'll do my best."

Dy shifted and looked restless in a grave and ponderous way. He had no interest in Nicholas Sanders, he said. But he wanted Charlie's opinion on the current state of the negotiations. So they talked about that. Charlie was cautiously optimistic. "We have only two goals at present. One is to establish a permanent line of communication. That is becoming more and more likely or at least possible. And we would like to recover any of our people who are being held by the *hwarhath*. This, I think, will happen. They are clearly interested in getting their young men back. Though I don't relish telling them how few are left alive."

There was silence for a while. Then Dr. Azizi asked how long the negotiations were likely to go on.

"I have no answer for that question," Charlie said. "But I'm reluctant to end them before something is achieved. We've already had one set of talks end in abject failure."

He looked down at his brandy snifter, frowning. "I keep getting a feeling that something is missing, some important piece of information. The image that keeps occurring is a station like this one, orbiting a singularity. We are pulled and guided by a huge fact that we can't see." He glanced up and smiled. "It's a dangerous sign when a diplomat becomes metaphoric. Maybe I'm wrong. Maybe we know everything we need to about the *hwarhath*."

Dr. Azizi leaned back, his expression resigned.

"But I still think we are making progress," Charlie said firmly. "And I intend to stay until I am able to report success."

Eh Matsehar walked her back through the bright cool halls. He was in a quiet mood—it happened occasionally—and she was tired. They hardly spoke at all.

She turned off the ceiling hologram in her bedroom and lay in darkness. Charlie's determination to stay made her all at once aware of being hundreds of light-years from the rest of humanity. The *hwarhath* station seemed fragile and alien. Outside was the void, immense and hostile. Inside were people she did not understand.

She went to sleep finally and dreamed of being lost in a labyrinth. At times she saw ahead of her a door that opened out on the golden hills of Reed 1935-C. But she could never reach the door. Instead she found herself in another grey hallway.

She woke feeling tired and mildly depressed. Coffee didn't help much. She put on a dark green pantsuit with a shirt of white cotton. Looking in the bathroom mirror, she regretted that she'd never learned to put on makeup. Her face looked unhappy. Lipstick would have helped, and something to hide the weariness of the eyes.

She drank another cup of coffee and then went out to meet Hai Atala Vaihar.

She asked him about *Huckleberry Finn.*

"I'm more than halfway through. It is a very strange narration. Almost all the people that Twain Mark describes are ignorant and mean. Is this an accurate description of humanity?"

She tried to explain that the characters were supposed to be funny.

"No," said Vaihar. "It is humorous when a single person is mean and ignorant. You hold him up as an example of the wrong kind of behavior. Everyone mocks

him. He is ashamed. But when everyone is like that—hah!
What a terrible society."

She tried to explain about the kind of people who are
likely to be found on a frontier.

"You send people out in fours and fives? Almost
alone?" He sounded horrified. "That's no way to settle a
wilderness."

"How do you do it?"

"A lineage divides, and the junior part goes out, many
people together. They can rely on each other and on the
senior part of the lineage. They don't lose everything they
had. They don't become like animals or like the people
that Twain Mark describes."

He was silent for a while, evidently thinking. Finally he
said, "The first thing they do is build a temple and perform
ceremonies. Then they build the other public buildings: the
meeting hall and possibly a theater. It depends on how
much the lineage likes to watch acting. They always put up
a gymnasium and a school.

"Religion, politics, art, exercise and education. These
are the bases of any community, and they must be laid
down as quickly as possible.

"After that the houses are built, the barns for animals
and the factories. The gardens are dug. The pastures are
fenced in. Then—it usually takes a year or two—the
women come out with the children.

"That is the proper way to do it. That's how my ancestors left Hai and settled in the valley of Atala. We still send
gifts back to our kin and perform ceremonies with them
and remember with gratitude and affection everything they
did for us in the early years."

"Do you do anything alone?" asked Anna.

"Not much. Nicky says that almost anything worth
doing takes at least two people. But this does not seem to
be a common opinion among your people. You are really
very solitary, in spite of your numbers. I see it in the books

I've read. Look at Huck and Jim. They float down the river like adolescent lovers who have actually managed to escape from obligation, as we never do, in spite of our dreams.

"Even in the other book, on that ship full of men, I had a feeling of loneliness. The captain is always alone, and the man who tells the story— Hah! What a people you are! So difficult to understand!"

She couldn't think of any comment, so asked a question. Vaihar wore three round metal badges clipped to the waistband of his shorts, and so did all the other men they passed. What did the badges mean?

"One is personal identification, one is rank, and one is lineage. Nicky has only two, because he has no family or at least no emblem for his family. I get used to seeing him; I don't think about what it means to have only two badges. Every once in a while I look at him and remember. It makes my hair go up on end." He glanced at her sideways, his expression—what? Serious? Unhappy? "I cannot imagine how he stays alive."

They reached the human quarters, and he left her. She went in and watched the negotiations. Nick didn't look unhappy to her, sitting next to his general. None of the People wore badges with their space-cadet uniforms, so his different status was not visible.

They were discussing the exchange of prisoners. Where to do it. How to be sure that no one tried a double cross. More than anything else, Nicholas looked bored.

# XVI

➤➤➤ I WAS SITTING on the edge of Gwarha's bed and putting on my socks, having found them in the corner on the far side of the bed, which was not the place I had left them, to the best of my memory.

He reached up and ran a hand very gently down my arm. "I have been looking at the humans, thinking how strange it must be to have no fur, to be so unprotected, so vulnerable."

I also didn't remember turning the socks inside out.

"No wonder you wrap yourselves in clothing from one end to the other. No wonder you move so stiffly, as if you are always expecting something to attack you. It must be terrifying to be so—" He hesitated. "—open to the universe. Is that what I want to say?"

"Maybe."

He was looking at me with almost-closed eyes. I couldn't see the horizontal pupils or bright inhuman color of the irises. There was only a liquid gleam between the dark grey lids. Even so, the face was alien: the features broad and blunt, the ears too large and set too high, and everything too furry. I notice the differences more and more these days, most likely because I'm seeing humans on a regular basis.

"But also interesting," he said. "To have one's entire body as sensitive as the lips and mouth or as the palms of the hands."

"And this is what you think about during the negotiations?"

"Only when you are translating me. I know what I've
said, and I know your translation will be accurate. I look
at the humans and think, What is it like when two people
like that make love? Both of them are unprotected. Both of
them are sensitive. Everything is exposed and erotically
accessible. Nothing—no part of the body—is safe."

Jesus H. Christ. I looked at the rest of my clothing,
folded over the clothing rack next to Gwarha's, and tried to
figure out how to get out of this conversation.

"Ask the humans what it's like. It'll make a change
from the usual subjects of discussion. 'What's it like when
you guys fuck?' Or ask them for pornography. Only decent
pornography, of course. That might be kind of amusing."

"Why?"

"They couldn't grab just anything and send it. It might
be truly disgusting, something that would make your people decide to have nothing to do with humanity."

"What could possibly be worse than what we have
already learned?"

I ignored that. "I like the idea of a bunch of people
sitting around on Earth, trying to decide what kind of
homosexual pornography will present humanity in the
best light."

"Why don't you tell me what it feels like to make love
with another human?"

"I don't remember."

"You are lying," he said after a moment. "It's not the
kind of thing a person forgets."

"We don't belong to the same species, First-Defender.
We have not had the same kind of sexual experience. Even
now we don't have the same kind of experience. What
makes you think you know what I do and do not remember? And I have told you over and over, humans need more
privacy than the People do."

He regarded me steadily, his eyes open wide now. "I think, because you talk so much, that you are actually telling me what is in your mind. I should remember your nickname. Under the noise is silence. You wrap yourself in it like a garment."

I said nothing.

"Because you have no natural protection." He reached out and touched my arm again. "What was the Goddess thinking of?"

I got up and finished dressing.

From the journal of Sanders Nicholas, etc.

# XVII

➤➤➤ Vᴀɪʜᴀʀ ᴡᴀs ʜᴇʀ escort the next day. When they reached the Talking-with-Enemies area, one of the *hwarhath* guards spoke to him.

Vaihar said, "I'm to take you to the observation room, then join the negotiation team. Hah! It's a good thing I'm wearing my space-cadet uniform."

"What happened?" she asked.

"I don't know. I don't want to rush you, Anna, but—"

They hurried to the observation room. He left her at the door. Inside, the hologram was on, showing the meeting room with its two rows of chairs. Anna sat down and watched. The humans came in, looking much the same as usual; but the *hwarhath* entrance was different. For once the People seemed awkward. After a moment she realized why. There was a new person, bulky and dark grey, his uniform a little tight. He and the general came in together, going around opposite ends of the row of chairs, trying (it seemed to her) to time their movements so they reached the middle of the row together.

When they met, they turned as one and stood together, facing the humans. The bulky man loomed over Ettin Gwarha, taller by half a head and far more massive. The other *hwarhath* came in on either side, moving reluctantly, it seemed to Anna, and keeping as close to the chairs as possible. Even Vaihar looked uneasy and almost clumsy.

The general glanced around. The bulky man nodded. Everyone sat down. The general, caught off guard, was a little slow and settled into his chair a moment after the others.

His body was rigid. Angry, thought Anna. Furious. Then he relaxed and leaned toward the bulky man, speaking in a low voice. The bulky man grinned. His teeth were large and square and very white.

"I am to introduce the Frontman Lugala Tsu," said Vaihar. "The man next to him is Min Manhata, who will be his translator."

Haxu introduced the human team.

Interesting, thought Anna. But what did it mean?

Trouble, she realized by the end of the meeting. Lugala Tsu had a hard time keeping still. The problem wasn't really conspicuous—it did not amount to open rudeness—but it was there: small shifts in position, especially when Ettin Gwarha was speaking, frowns and twitches of the lips. At times he leaned very slightly toward his translator, as if he was about to whisper something to him, but he never did. The general glanced sideways a number of times early in the meeting. Finally he spoke to the other frontman.

Vaihar said, "Ettin Gwarha has asked, 'Do you have anything to add, Frontman Lugala? What is your opinion?' "

No, the bulky man said. He had nothing to add. He was new to the negotiations. For the time being he was content to listen. He would speak later.

The general tilted his head slightly. One of the human translators had told her this could mean agreement or acknowledgment or consideration, depending. Then he leaned back in his chair. He had come to some kind of a decision, Anna thought, though she couldn't tell what it was.

After that he no longer glanced at the other frontman.

The mood in the room was changing. Something, an ease and confidence that had been growing over the past weeks, began to diminish now; and as it diminished, she began, for the first time, to notice it. It had grown so slowly! Though from the beginning the general and Charlie had been courteous and respectful. Still there had been a stiffness, that was gone—had been gone—and was returning.

Anna realized how rational and, comparatively speaking, clear the talks had been, when Charlie and the general had been in charge. Slow, yes, and maybe overcareful, though diplomacy was not her area of competence. Maybe diplomats had to circle that way.

Now she didn't know. Vaihar looked unhappy. Charlie—she had a side view of him—looked increasingly tense.

She ate lunch with the other humans. It was a vegetarian hash and exactly the right food for the situation. Her colleagues went over and over the meeting that had just ended, trying to figure out what was going on.

Charlie said finally, "My hunch is a power struggle between the two men." He used his fork to move the hash around on his plate. "I wish I knew what their positions were. Is Lugala Tsu hostile to us? Is Ettin Gwarha in any sense our friend? Anna—" He looked at her. "You have the best connections. See what you can find out from Sanders or the *hwarhath* women or those two young men."

She nodded. "I'll see what I can do."

She left the human quarters after lunch. Her escort was Matsehar. She asked him what was happening.

"Where?"

"In the negotiations."

"Exactly what you see. The son of Lugala has joined the negotiations, as is his right and responsibility. The Frontmen-in-a-Bundle should not be represented by only one person."

She was listening to the official version, the party line. Matsehar frowned, which might be a warning or maybe only one of his occasionally odd expressions. Then he began to describe the machinations of Lady Macbeth and her son. The mother was beginning to lose her confidence, and it was the bloody warrior who now took the center of the stage. "This is what happens," Matsehar said, "when women do not restrain their sons. Male violence must always be put in the right political context."

They parted at the entrance to the women's quarters, and she walked through the splendid lofty halls to her rooms. The holo was on and showed dawn over the ocean on Reed 1935-C. There was a pink glow at the horizon. High up, almost at her ceiling, was the morning/evening star. It was double at the moment, the two planets far enough apart to be visible as two points of light.

Other lights shone in the water of the bay. They flickered dimly, looking tired. It was the end of a long night of signaling identity and reassurance. She knew what that felt like. Anna rubbed the muscles of her face and neck.

After a while the primary rose. It was too bright to look at directly. She got up and moved to the intercom and called Ama Tsai Indil.

"I think I need a meeting with your people."

"You mean my senior partner. Yes, you do."

"And maybe Sanders Nicholas should be there."

"I am less certain about that, but let me consult with the woman of Tsai Ama."

The intercom went off. She fiddled with the holo, managing at last to fast-forward into the afternoon. The primary no longer shone into her room. Instead a long shadow stretched down the golden hill: some kind of artifact on legs. Maybe it was part of the equipment that had recorded the landscape. The sky was dappled with little round clouds. Whitecaps dotted the bright blue ocean. She imagined the wind that must be blowing, cold and salty.

Anna sat down and watched the shadow of the artifact grow longer.

Ama Tsai Indil called back finally and said the meeting with her senior partner was on.

# XVIII

➤➤➤ THE GENERAL SENT me a message at the end of the fifth *ikun,* asking me to come to his office.

He was sitting in his usual place, his arms on the table in front of him, hands lightly clasped, looking at the wall opposite, which was blank grey metal. I stopped inside the door and made the gesture of presentation.

He glanced at me. "You have remembered military decorum. Are you angry with me? Or do you think I'm angry?"

"Aren't you?"

"I was. Sit down. It makes me uneasy when you stand there looking like a soldier."

I took the chair in front of his desk. He leaned back and picked up his stylus. "Did you see the meeting?"

I nodded. "I went to one of the observation rooms." Not adding, after you told me I was off the negotiation team.

**[I had to do it, Nicky. He is a frontman. He cannot be ignored.]**

"I'm sending messages to the frontmen I trust and including copies of the meeting today. This stupid malice has to be stopped. Dealing with him is like walking through a field of burrs. I don't want to have to keep picking him out of my fur. I want him gone."

"Do you think you'll be able to get rid of him?"

"Yes. His intent is obvious; his manners are atrocious;

and he does not have enough allies in the Bundle." He laid the stylus down.

"What a man he is! So stupid and greedy! He's trying to grab more than he can handle, and he does not see the consequences of his actions."

" 'Vaulting ambition, which o'erleaps itself,' " I said in English.

The general frowned.

"It's a line from Matsehar's new play."

The general waved a hand, dismissing Eh Matsehar and Shakespeare William. "I did not ask you here to discuss Lugala Tsu. The woman of Tsai Ama has asked that you be present at a meeting between her and Perez Anna. Go and find a way to tell her what is happening. She is friendly with you, and she is an expert on humanity. Her opinion will be respected in the Weaving."

"I'm not sure about that. Most of the other experts think her theories are crazy."

He lifted a hand. I shut up.

"Her lineage has no close ties to either Lugala or Ettin. If she says I am right, that will be heard. If she says that Lugala Tsu is snarling up the negotiations, that also will be heard.

"And maybe it's time that we considered an alliance with Tsai Ama and Ama Tsai. They are not powerful lineages, but they have some importance, and the women especially in the past two generations have been of a very good quality."

He was silent for a while, drifting off into the kind of plotting that the *hwarhath* do, which combines politics with genetics. Which families have the power? Which families are producing strong and remarkable people? How can Ettin find the right allies and get the right genetic material?

Finally he looked at me. "I'd like your company tonight, Nicky. But I don't want to hear your opinions or your advice. I've done what I can today. I want to talk about something that has nothing to do with the humans or Lugala Tsu.''

''Okay,'' I said.

When I came over, we talked about hiking in the mountains at the western edge of Ettin. He had a hologram on: a slope that went up and up, covered with trees. Most were blue-green. Here and there I saw patches of copper red. In the distance were high white peaks. Gwarha named them: the Tower of Ice, the Blade, the Mother.

The hologram had been taken at the house of one of his cousins, he told me. She'd make us welcome. The climbing in the area wasn't especially difficult; there were places he wanted to show me: a famous battleground in a rocky pass and a famous waterfall, the Net of Silver.

''It covers an entire cliff. There have to be a hundred streams, and when the sun hits them—hah! We'll go when this is over, Nicky.''

He'd put on a dark blue dressing gown. There was a cup of *halin* on the table in front of him and a squat jug made of lumpy red clay. The glaze on the jug was clear and thin. I could see the marks left by the potter's thumbs.

Something in me said, Pay attention. See what is in front of you. Remember how intensely you love this person.

**[Hah.]**

From the journal of Sanders Nicholas, etc.

# XIX

➤➤➤ She woke in the morning to the aroma of coffee, gathered her clothing and went to the bathroom. She could hear Nick in the kitchen, whistling something that sounded as if it had come off a classical music net. Opera, maybe?

Anna showered and dressed in a caftan made of a handwoven fabric from Guatemala. It had narrow vertical stripes of red, green, blue, yellow, lavender, black and white. Her sandals (hidden under the caftan) were flat and comfortable. Her earrings were long and dangly. She looked at herself in the mirror, examining the round brown face that showed mestizo ancestry. Black eyes slanted over broad cheekbones. Her lips were full. Her nose had a Mayan curve. She didn't even regret her ignorance of makeup. This morning she looked *good*.

"Anna?" Nick called from the living room.

She went out. Breakfast was on one of the tables, and he leaned against a wall, holding a mug. He looked her up and down and said, "Very nice."

Anna felt a brief irritation. The look and the comment were absolutely typical of a human male. He ought to have learned better manners after spending twenty years among the *hwarhath*.

She sat down. Breakfast was coffee and toast and a bowl of grey stuff. Another kind of human chow, she thought, until she tasted it. It was oatmeal. She noticed the sugar bowl full of brown crystals and the pitcher full of thin bluish milk and added both. They helped a little, but the oatmeal still tasted like oatmeal. "What happened yesterday?"

"At the meeting? Lugala Tsu decided very suddenly that he wanted to join the negotiations. He has the right. He is a frontman."

"And you were pulled out."

"Yes." He drank some of his coffee.

"Why?"

"The frontman is not comfortable with me. He's willing to sit facing aliens. That must be done, if there are going to be talks. But he is not willing to see an alien out of the corner of his eye."

This was almost certainly a way of saying that Nick was unreliable and that he belonged on the human side of the room. "The man is an asshole."

"You might say that, but you'd be maligning a part of the body that is of unquestioned utility. I prefer to think of Lugala as a tumor."

She laughed. "Does that mean you'll be available for the women's talks?"

"Maybe. Tsai Ama Ul asked for me today, and here I am. But Lugala Minti is likely to feel the way her son does. That isn't a problem in this meeting. She isn't going to be present. But when she is—"

"They're trying to wreck the negotiations."

Nick was silent for a moment. "I don't think I'll comment on that. How did you like the uniform that the son of Lugala wore?"

"It needs to be a size bigger."

"Amazing, isn't it? The Art Corps is usually *so* reliable."

She had never heard that particular tone in his voice before: sweet and malicious. She remembered that he had worked on plays. Most likely he had friends in the Art Corps.

"Isn't that petty?"

"Anna, you have not yet seen pettiness. When a couple of tough guys like the general and Lugala Tsu decide to confront each other, vistas of pettiness open up that you and I can barely comprehend. Do you remember the first time you saw the Rockies? Or the ocean? Or Earth from space? If these fellows get going, it will be like that."

"Are they going to get going? Is there going to be some kind of internal fight?"

"I don't know."

She finished breakfast, and they went to the usual meeting room. The two alien women waited there, dressed in the usual splendid robes. Tsai Ama Ul's had panels made of a shimmery dark blue material. Ama Tsai Indil wore a bright yellow brocade. Rows of earrings hung from her large ears. This time they were fine gold chains that ended in gold beads. Each time she moved her head even slightly, the beads swung and glinted.

What gaudy people! And why—if the Art Corps was so reliable and the usual tailors capable of the kind of clothing she saw in front of her—did Nick so often look like a dorf?

They went through the ritual of greetings and then sat down, Nick as usual a little in back.

"My senior partner has instructed me to begin," said Ama Tsai Indil. "In her opinion the men—" Indil spoke in the alien language.

"The men are fucking up," said Nick in English.

Ama Tsai Indil inclined her head. The earrings swung. "In our language the metaphor is different. We say making a tangle.

"This is especially true now that the son of Lugala has decided to pick a fight with the son of Ettin. Tsai Ama Ul will not comment on this behavior, which is typical of males and which will not necessarily make either Lugala or Ettin look more desirable as sources of genetic material.

"But it's her belief that the present negotiations are

important and should not be pushed to the side, simply because a pair of men are trying to push each other back.

"The woman of Tsai Ama will not speak of war or any military matter. Fighting is a male skill. But the negotiations concern peace as well as war, and the skills of peace belong to women."

How definite these people were! Anna couldn't imagine speaking like this with hardly a modifier or qualifier, especially after spending years writing academic papers.

"Tsai Ama Ul wants to hear what happened yesterday directly from Sanders Nicholas, and then she wants your opinion of the negotiations, woman of Perez."

"All right," said Anna.

Nick spoke in the *hwarhath* language. She couldn't tell much about his tone, the sound of the language was too different from English. But his voice remained quiet. The alien women watched him intently. He looked down, except when Tsai Ama Ul spoke to him, most likely asking questions. Then he glanced up briefly before answering.

This language of gazes was more complicated than she had realized. Nick was making some kind of statement when he met the woman's eyes. "I speak the truth. I speak as an equal. I speak as a friend."

He ended finally.

Ama Tsai Indil said, "Now my senior partner wants to hear what you think is going on."

Anna glanced up very briefly, meeting the yellow gaze of the woman of Tsai Ama. "I'm not certain. My area of competence is not diplomacy. It's alien intelligence. I'm here more or less by accident, because of what happened during the last set of negotiations. What do I think is going on?" She looked at the wine dark carpet. "I think Charlie Khamvongsa is okay, an honorable man who would like to make peace. My hunch is that Ettin Gwarha is also okay, though I'm not sure I understand his motivations. I think Lugala Tsu is making trouble."

"You translate this," said Ama Tsai Indil to Nick.

He did.

Tsai Ama Ul answered.

"It is no accident that you are here. Your actions before have showed that you will act decently and with honor, even if it puts you in conflict with other humans; and it is good that someone is present at the discussions who is used to thinking about the question of intelligence. In order for us to talk, we have to be able to think about what makes people different from animals. Otherwise the differences between the *hwarhath* and humanity will seem enormous and impossible to cross.

"It's hard to describe how disturbing your behavior is to us. We have always thought that sex was one of the most important differences between people and animals. Animals have mating seasons. People do not. Among animals sex and reproduction are almost the same. Among people they are almost entirely separate.

"We thought this was natural and inevitable. Once an animal has intelligence and is able to make choices, it will not continue to live as its ancestors did, mixing everything together—fighting and breeding and raising children and seeking love all in one place. Hah! We have seen these things in the fields and on the shores of our planet. How the males beat on one another and tear each other with claws, how they mate in a frenzy, how children may be killed—"

Ama Tsai Indil stopped and drew her breath.

"Tsai Ama Ul has ended by saying, Now we have found creatures with a language and a material culture, who can travel through space, and they behave toward one another in a way that we thought was impossible once intelligence was achieved.

"That is why your skill is important, woman of Perez."

Jesus Maria. She glanced at Nick. "What am I going to say?"

"The truth, always, Anna."

She didn't know the truth. She glanced again very briefly at Tsai Ama Ul. "I'm not sure how to answer. I don't even know if you had a question. We always thought that heterosexuality was natural. It's what all the other kinds of animals on our planet did. We thought it was natural for men and women to live together and raise children together. That also was done by many kinds of animals.

"When we met you, we had a reaction that was similar to yours. I've talked to a number of experts in the past year. Most of them say your society makes no sense at all. It shouldn't exist. A number of them think it does not exist: there's something wrong with our information. The prisoners we've taken have lied to us or belong to an aberrant subculture. Something is getting lost in the translation. Maybe the translators are lying. One man actually told me that. He knew about Nick."

Nicholas laughed.

"We're in the same situation as you. We expected to find aliens who were different from us, really different. We didn't expect to find aliens who are very similar with some striking differences. It has us off balance; and there are people among the humans who— I won't say they want to fight, but they can't really imagine not fighting, and they're afraid to take the steps that lead to peace. They think we'll be cheated and betrayed. And the secrecy has not helped. How can we negotiate with so little information?"

Nicholas translated her speech.

Tsai Ama Ul tilted her head, a motion that could mean almost anything. Then she spoke.

Ama Tsai Indil said, "Do you think most of your people want peace?"

Anna said, "Nick must have told you something about our planet. We used to have many different societies—

many nations, and they have come together only recently. We do not yet have a single culture or a single government. Different groups want different things. Most humans want peace, but not all of us, and right now our government is so complicated—made of so many different pieces—that it's difficult to say what it wants, if anything."

Tsai Ama Ul listened to this, then spoke again.

"Do you think any harm will come from these negotiations, either for your people or the People?"

"I don't know. I think that knowledge is always better than ignorance, and that we'd both benefit from an exchange of information. Beyond that—who can say? It's possible that humanity needs an external enemy right now, since we are so recently united. If so, we may be harmed if we make peace. Maybe you are monstrous and evil. I can't tell. Though Nick says you're okay, and I trust him."

He laughed again.

"Maybe there is something about humanity that represents a serious danger to your society. Again, I don't know."

Tsai Am Ul listened, then spoke.

"We have always had enemies. Our men have always fought. It would be hard for them to give that up. It would be hard for us to know what to do with them, if our long history of struggle came to an end. Hah! A frightening thought! What are men good for, if there are no enemies and no borders to protect? How are they going to spend their time? How are they going to feel self-respect?"

She stared at Anna, clearly brooding. Anna looked down.

"And what would the universe be like with people like you in it? Not as rumors and as something dimly seen in the distance, but as neighbors. Already we have begun to question our own history and our own ideas of right and wrong.

"But I do not like the idea of a war fought with strangers out of ignorance with no rules established and no limits to the violence. This would be a return to the savagery of animals. It would be an abandonment of everything we have achieved since the Goddess gave the small black box of morality to First Woman and First Man."

She paused and then spoke again.

"The meeting is over," said Nick. "The woman of Tsai Ama says she's getting a headache."

She left with Nicholas. Outside the room he said, "You actually met someone who thought I made up the *hwarhath* society?"

"He didn't come right out and say it, but he thought it was really interesting—'suggestive' was the word he used—that a key person on the human translation team was . . ." She hesitated, trying to think of the right word.

"Your best choice is homosexual." His voice was cool and a little amused. "There are problems with it. I don't like the fact that it is an irregular formation, and it always seems to me to have a faintly antiseptic aroma, the stink of science and the intellect. I'd prefer a word that smelled of ordinary life. But there are never any really good words for a group that isn't liked."

She thought she heard anger in his voice, under the coolness and amusement.

"What do you mean, an irregular formation?" she asked.

"The root words come from two different languages. 'Homo' from the Greek for 'same' and 'sexual' from the Latin for sex. Someone in the nineteenth century coined it, and I can't imagine what he was thinking of."

They walked back toward her rooms. As they passed through the entrance hall, Nick said, "I've thought from time to time that it isn't the right word for me and Gwarha. We don't belong to the same evolutionary line. It could be argued—hell, I will argue—that we are members of similar or analogous sexes. In that case, the correct word would be 'homeosexual' from the Latin for 'sex' and the Greek for 'similar.'

"There's something pleasant about the idea of inventing a new form of sexual activity *and* the word for it."

He did sound pleased. The anger was entirely gone from his voice. They reached her door, and she palmed it open.

Nicholas said, "I have to report to the general."

"How do you think the meeting went?"

"I don't know. Things are getting complicated. Lugala Tsu has decided to move. Tsai Ama Ul has decided the women have to do something. The Goddess knows who's going to make the next decision."

He left, and she went in through the open door. It slid closed. She sat down on her couch, feeling exhausted. What time was it? The end of the morning. She ought to go over to the human quarters and join her colleagues for lunch. To hell with it. She went and took a shower and then a nap.

In the middle of the afternoon (if that was a term that had any real meaning in the station) she went and found Charlie and told him what had happened.

"I can certainly understand why Tsai Ama Ul got a headache. I'm getting one too," he said. "I think it is time to ask for advice from Earth."

The system had been explained to her. It was almost as complicated as the one they'd used coming to the station. The *hwarhath* would take a sealed message back to the first transfer point, then use one of their own probes to send the message back to a waiting Earth ship, which would open the probe and take out the message and send it on.

The reply would come the same way in reverse: by human probe to the first transfer point and then by some kind of alien conveyance.

The method eliminated various forms of double cross too elaborate for her to remember, and it struck her as amazingly tedious. Surely trust would save time and be more energy-efficient.

# XX

➤➤➤ THE GENERAL WAS busy till midway through the sixth *ikun*. I wrote a memo describing the meeting with Tsai Ama Ul, then went to the nearest gym and practiced *hanatsin* alone, doing sets of the slow motions in front of a mirror. Not easy. I don't like mirrors or moving slowly. But it's a good discipline, and I guess I'm in favor of discipline.

**[No. You endure it when you have to and avoid it when you can. You never take it in your arms.]**

After that I walked through the station until it was time to make my report.

The general had told me to come to his aunts' quarters. He was there in a wonderfully bare room. The floor was polished stone. The walls were plaster, painted yellow. No door was visible, though I had just come in through one. Instead, each side of the room had large, tall windows that overlooked a windy shore. On two sides was the ocean, cresting and creaming along a beach. On the other two sides were dunes covered with silver-grey vegetation. A tall bipedal animal stalked through the vegetation, its head—at the end of a long neck—poking under the silver leaves, obviously hunting. The animal had a shiny blue covering that might have been scales.

The room was empty except for five chairs made of wood and arranged in a circle. The general was in one. His aunts occupied three others. They wore robes made of plain dull fabrics: country clothing, the clothing worn at home.

I made the gesture of presentation. The room had sound. I could hear the low dull roar of the ocean and shrill cries that had to be animals, what kind I do not know. Not the blue hunter.

"Sit down," said Ettin Aptsi.

I took the unoccupied chair.

Ettin Per said, "Report."

I described the meeting between Tsai Ama Ul and Anna.

When I was done, Ettin Per said, "What is your opinion of the Earth woman?"

I glanced up briefly, not really meeting her eyes. In back of her was the top of a dune. Long narrow leaves bent in the wind. Clouds moved in a dark blue sky.

"I like her. I have since the first time I met her. The other humans were made uneasy by the People, and they had even more trouble with me. I saw the expression on her face, when she looked past me and saw Gwa Hattin. Like a kid at Christmas."

"You are using words we don't understand," said Ettin Sai. "Explain."

"It's a day when humans—some humans—give gifts to their children. It comes near the winter solstice in the darkest time of the year, and where I grew up—and Anna—it's almost always cold. The gifts are to bring joy. Anna looked at Hattin and saw a gift.

"When she looked at me her expression changed, and I'm not certain I know what she was thinking. But she didn't seem uncomfortable. Curious maybe, and watchful.

"I thought, this is a person who is not frightened of people she does not understand. It's a rare quality among humans."

"And among the People," said Ettin Per in her deep strong voice. "Do you think we can trust her, Nicky?"

"Yes."

Ettin Per continued. "And she believes the human ambassador is worthy of trust. Gwarha?"

"I agree, though I do not understand the ambassador's position. The human soldiers disobeyed him during the last set of negotiations. This argues that he is not in front alone. If we come to an agreement with him, what does it mean? I have no idea."

"Nicky?" asked Ettin Sai.

"There's an element of risk. As Perez Anna said, the human government is complicated and the various parts don't always agree. But my sense is, the ambassador has a better position than he used to. The military people really fucked up, and I think they've had to move a good distance back. There is no one among the people he has with him who's going to challenge him directly or—I think—disobey his orders.

"But I don't know about the situation on Earth, and even the situation here could change."

"Still," said Ettin Per, sounding thoughtful. "We have two possible allies among the humans. This is something to think about."

"There are three problems," said Ettin Sai. "The humans, the Lugala and Tsai Ama Ul. What Gwarha says about the Tsai Ama is worth considering."

"Nicky says that Tsai Ama Ul has given us a warning," said Ettin Aptsi. "This quarrel does not make either Ettin or Lugala look good."

"That may be true for the moment," said Ettin Per. "If Gwarha can manage to push the son of Lugala back and come to an agreement with the humans, he will be in front of all the frontmen. That's right, isn't it?"

"I will be in a good position," said Gwarha cautiously.

"He has no children, and he is reaching an age when children are appropriate. If the current problems can be settled well, Tsai Ama will be interested. The question is, will they help us now? And what can we offer them?"

That was obvious, even to me: first dibs on Ettin Gwarha's semen, plus a guarantee that the number of his children would be limited. A very good deal, and one that Tsai Ama Ul would be unlikely to pass up, unless she decided that she needed more information about Gwarha. If she had any serious doubts about him and his reproductive fitness, she'd wait until the current situation had been resolved. But then, of course, she'd lose her chance at the very good deal.

**[You are right about this.]**

Gwarha said, "Do we need anything more from Nicky?"

The aunts said no and thanked me graciously. Gwarha looked relieved. He knows what I think of genetic politics. If I'd wanted to listen to conversations like this one, I would have stayed in Kansas and gone to the College of Agriculture.

I left them to their plotting. I had meant to ask about the view out the windows, but didn't get a chance.

**[It is a recording taken at a house on the eastern coast of the Great Northern Continent. My aunts stay there when the Weaving has a meeting. As the poet says, "Other than mountains, there is the ocean."]**

Later in the evening I asked if those conversations ever bothered him. He was setting up the *eha* board, getting ready for another game with a long-dead master.

"I don't understand," he said.

"Doesn't it bother you that other people decide everything about your children, even whether you're going to have any?"

He finished setting out the *eha* stones and looked at me. "I have a say. I've told my aunts that the men of Tsai Ama and Ama Tsai are nothing special. If there is a child, it'd better be female. The kind of men those lineages produce will not increase our reputation, and I don't want lazy sons."

No, of course not, sweetheart. You want smart tough young men with good manners and a frightening drive to power. In twenty years, if I'm still around, I may see them coming out to the perimeter.

**[You will.]**

"I don't know what you are suggesting. That I should tell my aunts how to do their work? I wouldn't like it if they told me how to be a frontman."

How to explain? It bothered me to watch him sit placidly while his aunts discussed breeding him like a prize bull. It bothered me that something that belonged to him—his connection to the future, for the sake of the Goddess—became a chip or counter that the women of Ettin played.

He listened without moving, his expression grave. I wound down finally. He looked up. His pupils had expanded in the dim light, and I could see them clearly: wide black lines that lay like bars across his irises.

"You seem to think that I have a right to everything my body produces. It's a right I'll give up gladly. I have no desire to keep my shit. I don't much care what happens to it, so long as it's properly disposed of."

He paused for a moment. "And in what sense is my genetic material mine? I did not create it out of nothing. It came from a woman of Ettin and a man of Gwa, and they got it from their parents, so going back—generation after generation—to the time before all lineages.

"It seems to me I have as good a claim to own the hills of Ettin or the rivers that run through them or the sky overhead or the house where I was born."

From the journal of Sanders Nicholas, etc.

# XXI

➤➤➤ Nothing much happened for the next few days. She watched the negotiations, which continued badly. Lugala Tsu was no longer shifting and grimacing. Instead he sat back in his chair, motionless and looking glum. The other people—*hwarhath* and human—looked uneasy, except for the general, who seemed tranquil.

The intercom woke her one morning with its sound like wind bells in a light erratic wind.

It was Ama Tsai Indil. There was going to be another meeting with the *hwarhath* women. Nicholas would not be present. Lugala Minti objected to him.

"Okay by me," said Anna.

"What?" said Indil.

"I have no objection."

"It would be hard for you to object, Perez Anna. Lugala Minti is a senior member of a very powerful lineage. You, as far as we can tell, have no real family at all."

"Hey," said Anna. "I am of Chicago and Illinois. That ought to count for something."

She turned off the intercom before Indil could ask her about the lineage of Chicago and went to get dressed. Too bad about Nick. She liked having breakfast ready, and she had never been much good at making coffee.

She ate peanut butter on a bagel and drank alien water out of the tap. It was from the recycling system, distilled and pure.

Then she walked to the meeting room.

The women—all the women—waited there: the three sisters in gold-and-crimson robes, Tsai Ama Ul in silver, Lugala Minti in black and Ama Tsai Indil in pale grey.

They spoke again about the condition of women on Earth. The conversation went more slowly this time. Ama Tsai Indil was simply not as good a translator as Nicholas.

She had the feeling she often got when talking to Vaihar. Even though they were speaking the same language (she and Ama Tsai Indil, at least) and even though they seemed to agree on what the words they were using meant, communication was fragmentary; and she had a feeling that important questions were not being asked. The *hwarhath* were circling around some really big topic. Maybe she was imagining this, influenced by Charlie's image of the singularity.

Finally she said, "I've told you about Earth to the best of my ability. I'd like to know about your home planet."

Lugala Minti answered. "Our society is organized properly, according to the rules which the Goddess has given the People."

That seemed to be an adequate answer, as far as the women of Lugala was concerned. She leaned back and folded her hands over her belly. The light was hitting her robe just right, and Anna could see the pattern of the black-on-black brocade: a network made of narrow branches. They crossed and recrossed one another. Large delicate flowers bloomed at the points of intersection; elsewhere the branches were bare, except for long sharp thorns.

Ettin Per frowned and spoke, her voice rumbling.

Ama Tsai Indil said, "The woman of Ettin has reminded us that the Goddess is not simple. We know it takes more than one theory to explain her universe. Maybe there is more than one way to be right."

Lugala Minti looked angry.

Tsai Ama Ul leaned forward and spoke.

"There is much that cannot be told, according to the woman of Tsai Ama. Remember that we are enemies, at least for the time being, and it is the men who decide what is strategic information.

"She—the woman of Tsai Ama—says that she will tell a story about the origin of the world. Even the men can't object to this. Everyone agrees that it isn't literally true, and it is very old, which means it tells you nothing about our current situation. But it does tell you something about our world.

"Originally nothing existed except the Goddess and a monster. The moment they looked at each other they were at odds, and they fought until the Goddess killed the monster.

"When the monster was dead, the Goddess cut out its ovaries, and she fertilized the eggs in the ovaries, using her own semen."

What?

"Then she took the body of the monster and made the world. The high mountains are what remains of the creature's armored and spiny back. The plains and valleys come from its broad creased belly. The monster's teeth became the stars. Its eyes became the four main planets. The sun is its brain, full of violent ideas.

"When she had finished making the world, the Goddess took the monster's eggs and shaped them into living creatures. The eggs from the right ovary became animals; but those in the left ovary became the ancestors of the People. At this time they had neither judgment nor the ability to make distinctions. They were only another kind of animal, weaker and more miserable than most. But the Goddess knew what they would become. She placed them tenderly in the world. At once they began to crawl and walk over the huge body of the monster. The Goddess looked down at them with love."

There was silence. The women shifted a little, adjusting their robes, smoothing out wrinkles.

Anna said, "You said that the Goddess fertilized the eggs. I thought she was a woman."

Tsai Ama Ul spoke. Ama Tsai Indil translated.

"As the woman of Ettin said, the Goddess is not simple. She has many forms and guises. Usually, when she fights, she is male."

What did the myth tell her about the People? The world came out of violence and death. The Goddess was ambiguous. The sun—the light of the world—was a monster's fiery mind.

This was not a nice species.

The meeting ended. Anna walked back to her rooms. She palmed the door open. Nicholas was there, sitting on her couch. "How did it go?" he asked.

"Just a minute." She went in the kitchen and filled a couple of glasses with wine: red this time, an L-5 Burgundy with a flavor she liked.

She handed one glass to Nicholas and sat down opposite, taking a sip before she told him about the meeting. She was tired of distrust, and he would almost certainly learn what had happened from the general, who would learn from his aunts.

"I felt robbed," she said when she was done. "I've told them a lot about Earth and what have I gotten in return? A lousy myth."

"An interesting myth, and one I didn't know. But Tsai Ama Ul is a fund of information." He looked at the opposite wall. "Violence and procreation. I wonder who she was talking to? The women of Ettin or you? The story does tell you something—maybe a lot—about the People."

"It does?"

He nodded. "Though I'm not sure that I can explain how. It's a complicated story, and a lot of things in it are the reverse of what they ought to be. The mother of the

People should not be a violent monster. The Goddess should not be male—at least, not in a creation myth." He was silent for a while. "The People are great believers in judgment and discrimination, but they also believe that some things cannot be understood through analysis. So maybe I shouldn't try to analyze the story. Anyway, I have to go." He got up.

"You came to find out how the meeting went."

"Of course. I told you I can never leave well enough alone, and I'm seriously angry at the Lugala. I'm not going to let them push me to the side or back."

She finished her wine. His glass stood on one of the tables, untouched. She picked it up and took it into the kitchen, pouring it back into the container it had come from.

# XXII

&gt;&gt;&gt; The general wasn't in his office, so I waited, looking at the tangled purple jungle that filled one end of the room. Flying things flitted through the shadows. Animals like huge bugs crawled up the stalks of trees. I knew the place: a hellhole that the People had finally pulled out of, though they hated—absolutely hated—to ever admit defeat. Ettin Gwarha had been there to negotiate the withdrawal, not with the natives—the People had never been able to establish any communication with them—but with the various senior officers, who had turned on each other in frustration.

I'd gotten restless one day during the negotiations, taken a walk at the edge of our camp and encountered one of the truly remarkable biological weapons that the natives created or maybe were. The thing almost killed me.

Why was the general looking at his species' most conspicuous failure? Though he had done well on the planet. The various senior officers were persuaded to cooperate. The retreat took place in an orderly fashion. He got a promotion, and I got a little more careful about what I touched.

His door slid open. I glanced at him, then at the jungle.

"They were almost certainly not intelligent," he said.

"Which species?"

"All of them. What we thought was cooperation was symbiosis." He turned so he was facing the purple jungle. Something with many legs crawled over the ground. As

nearly as I could tell, it was a couple of meters long. "I
have been thinking, maybe it is not possible to fight with
another species, certainly not with anything like the creatures on that planet. One can only kill them like animals.
And why bother? There was nothing on that planet that we
needed, except an enemy, and they did not understand the
rules of war." He sat down behind his table, waving toward the only other chair in the room. I took it and told
him about the meeting between Anna and the women.

"That myth is one I've never heard before," he said
after I finished. "Most likely it belongs to one of the cultures she has studied. As far as I know, my aunts have not
spoken to Tai Ama Ul. Clearly they should. She is thinking
about procreation, which means she is thinking about alliances. It's an interesting story. It unfolds into many different shapes." He looked past me at the jungle, and his
eyes opened wide. I turned in my chair.

There was something new in the clearing: a round body
balanced on six stilt legs. It stood over the centipede creature, which had stopped moving. Two other limbs unfolded, reached down and began to stroke the centipede,
first the top of the head and then the large and scary-
looking pincer jaws.

"It's getting food, I think. I remember one of the reports said the many-legged creatures produce a substance
like honey." He glanced at me to make sure he'd used the
right word in English. "The animal will regurgitate the
substance, if it is approached in the right fashion.

"Our situation has gotten increasingly complex. Lugala
Tsu is not much of a problem. To be a frontman one must
deal with frontmen. But the women! Hah!" He was silent,
obviously brooding but unable to say anything. There are
*hwarhath* men who complain about their female relatives,
some of them loudly and at length. The general thinks this
is the worst kind of bad manners, not to mention evidence
of a weak and unmanly character. "It seems to me," he

said finally, carefully, "they could have struggled with Lugala Minti and negotiated with Tsai Ama Ul at home. They did not need to come so far."

"You can't tell the Weaving what to do."

"I know that, Nicky. You can go. I want to sit and look at my jungle and think."

I glanced back from the door. Long Legs had finished whatever it had been doing. It folded up its arms and walked delicately away. The centipede remained motionless. It looked dazed.

"Go," said Ettin Gwarha.

# XXIII

➤➤➤ HE WAS HAVING a party that evening. I stayed in my office, going over recordings of the humans: their private conversations in the rooms they thought were safe. We had no visuals, only their voices, talking about almost anything. Most of it was of no strategic importance. *Hwarhath* intelligence had been over it already. I was the double check.

There are times I think humans talk for the same reasons that monkeys groom. It isn't communication, it's contact. It says, "I'm here. I'm friendly. You aren't alone."

Maybe that's why the People seem to babble less than humans. They can groom. They don't have to talk about the weather or how the local team is doing or, in this case, what they missed about Earth—playing cricket, a garden in Sweden, food in India, the theater in New York.

I guess I can tolerate nostalgia, but it seems damn close to regret.

I stopped finally and went to my quarters, took a shower, fixed a sandwich and settled down to read.

At the end of the eighth *ikun* Ettin Gwarha called. "Nicky, come over."

The voice of command. I got dressed and went.

The stink hit me the moment the door opened: the bittersweet aroma of *halin* mixed with the sour aroma of *hwarhath* bodies trying to get rid of toxins. There must have been a lot of people there at some point in the evening. The tables were littered with *halin* cups and jugs.

Three people were left. Hai Atala Vaihar glanced up at me, looking sober and worried. Shen Walha sat next to him in a chair opposite the general. His shoulders were slumped, and his head was down. He held a cup of *halin*.

"Nicky, here." Gwarha tapped the couch next to him.

I sat down, glancing over as I did so, meeting his gaze. His pupils were narrow but still visible.

"We have been talking about humanity." Gwarha spoke carefully, making sure that he articulated every syllable. "I thought you might be interested. Wally—"

Shen Walha lifted his head. His yellow eyes were blank. Thread drunk. I glanced at the floor.

"The first-defender raised the question." He was much more toxic than Gwarha, but speaking beautifully. "How can we fight with people who do not understand the rules of war? How can we make peace, if we cannot interbreed? I said, there is no way. I said, we must kill the humans like animals."

"And I called you," said Gwarha. His deep voice was very soft.

"Maybe this is not a conversation for this late in a party," I said.

Wally emptied his cup with a gulp and set it down on the table in front of him. He leaned forward, resting his elbows on his broad furry thighs. "You are right, Nicky, it isn't. But if I am sober, I will not say what I have been thinking, and if I don't say it, I will not be serving the first-defender or the People.

"I will speak directly to Ettin Gwarha and to you. The humans are not real people, and if we think they are, we are deluding ourselves and entering a dangerous trap."

"What is Nicky, if not a person?" Gwarha asked.

I looked at Vaihar. He was sitting upright and motionless, his gaze down: the posture of a junior officer who is present at the fight of senior officers. You do as little as possible to draw attention and nothing that can make you vulnerable to criticism.

"You know the answer, First-Defender. He is an animal, a very clever one, able to mimic the behavior of a person. If I had known him only, I would think he was a person. But think of the rest of his species!" He refilled his cup from a square black jug: a very good piece that came from the pottery in the Asuth station. Why in hell had Gwarha put that out for drunks to play with?

"They mix everything together. We all agree on that. But we also agree on what makes us people. Judgment and the ability to make—" For the first time he hesitated, as if he couldn't think of a word. "—distinctions. That is what makes us different from animals and the Red Folk.

"These creatures can't tell men from women or children from adults. They kill each other and have sex with each other, as if there are no differences. How can any man kill a woman? Or have sex with a woman?"

"Men have done both," said Gwarha.

"For procreation! And that is something else that the humans can't keep clear. They don't seem to understand the difference between having sex and having children. Nine billion of them! Are they crazy?"

He paused and drank, then set his cup down firmly. "They don't even seem to understand the difference between real people and those who are people in appearance. I've seen the reports. They will struggle to keep something alive that isn't really a person: a child born wrong, someone who has been damaged beyond repair by illness or injury. They say—hah!—this is because the lives of humans are sacred. But then they let other humans die from hunger or diseases that can be cured, and not only men, though that would be bad enough. But to let a healthy woman die of hunger or a child die of a minor illness—" He stopped, as if overcome by horror, and I think he really was overcome. Wally is a very traditional guy. The idea of killing women and children or letting women and children die of neglect was probably enough to make his hair stand up, though I couldn't see that happening. Did he look a little fluffier than usual? He glanced at me. "It's true, isn't it?"

"Very few humans die of hunger, except when there is a disaster of some kind, a flood or an earthquake," I told him. "But given the size of Earth's population, it's difficult to keep everyone adequately fed. I think it's fair to say that at least part of the population is undernourished, and people who are undernourished are vulnerable to disease."

And there is pollution, overcrowding, a medical system that just barely works, even in the most prosperous countries. The kind of medical care that Wally was describing does exist, and it shows up on the news nets, but most humans don't have access to it. I kept quiet about all this.

Wally kept going. "If life is sacred, why has the Goddess given us death? Do humans set themselves up against her and say that she is wrong?"

"Both are sacred," Gwarha said. "They are both great gifts."

"Then why can't humans treat both with respect? And with judgment, as the Goddess instructed the parents of all of us? They kill when they should not. They do not kill when they should. There is no way to have a decent war with creatures like these."

Gwarha leaned forward and picked up the cup on the table in front of him: a personal favorite, round and smooth. The glaze was pure white. "Tell me again what Nicky is."

"It's no secret to you," said Wally. "Everyone knows about the bracelet you gave him."

I wasn't sure where I'd put it, when I took it off. Somewhere in my quarters. But I had no trouble remembering the look of it.

Each link is shaped like a vine coiling in a circle. In the middle of each link, nestled among the golden leaves, is a piece of jade carved in the shape of a *tli*. Gwarha gave it to me years ago, after a trip home on which I had not gone. At that time I had never seen a *tli*, but I knew what it was: the little trickster of the animal plays.

"The liar," Wally said. "The cheat, the animal who makes fools of the large and noble animals."

"Hah," said Gwarha. He sounded angry. It was time to end the conversation.

I reached over and began to rub the muscles at the base of his neck.

"What?" he asked.

What do you think you're doing, Nicky? That was the rest of the question. I dug in with my thumbnail. He glanced at me briefly and shut his mouth.

Good man! He could still pick up a signal. I kept rubbing his neck. The muscles were like rocks.

There was silence for a while. Wally had finished making his speech on what was wrong with humans and especially with Nicky Sanders. He sat in a furry heap, staring at nothing.

Vaihar lifted his head, encouraged by the silence or made curious about it. Our gazes met. I glanced toward the door. That lovely intelligent fellow yawned and said he was almost asleep. He really ought to go. He stood, as graceful as ever, and thanked the first-defender for the evening. He didn't even lie. He called it interesting, which it no doubt had been.

Then he turned to Wally. Would the advancer go with him? He'd be *most* grateful for the company.

As if the trip home were some kind of epic journey, instead of a short walk—or, in Wally's case, shamble— through well-lit corridors.

Wally looked up. The *halin* had finally gotten to him. That was obvious, and it must have hit like an express train. I don't know if he could see Vaihar's smile or hear what was in his voice: deference and friendliness mixed with a very slight amount of seductiveness. Vaihar does everything right. The seductiveness was just enough to make his request for company interesting, but not enough to commit him.

I don't know if Wally was taking any of this in. He looked barely conscious; but he managed to pull himself out of his chair and mumble thanks to Gwarha. Vaihar got an arm around his broad furry body and guided him to the door. I followed. As the door opened Vaihar said in English, "You owe me, Nicky."

"What?" said Wally.

"I'm saying good night to Nicky."

"Not a person," Wally said, and with that they stumbled out.

The door closed. Behind me something shattered. I turned. Gwarha was standing. His hands were empty, and *halin* ran down the wall opposite him. On the carpet at the bottom lay pieces of his favorite cup.

"Why'd you do that?"

"I was angry. I *am* angry. What is going on between Vaihar and Wally?"

"You're angry about that?"

"No. Of course not."

"Vaihar was getting Wally out before he lost his job, and you lost the best chief of operations on the perimeter."

"I have lost him," Gwarha said. "I will not have anyone on my staff who says things like that about you."

"We can talk about it tomorrow."

"It is not your decision."

"Yes, First-Defender."

He looked at me. His pupils were narrower than before, even though he hadn't had anything to drink since I entered the room. "How can you endure it? Why aren't you furious?"

"I don't want to talk."

"Then go."

"I think I'd better make sure that you get to bed, unless you'd rather spend the night next to the organic waste disposal unit."

"I am not going to throw up. I'm not nearly drunk enough."

"Good for you."

For a moment I thought he was going to get stubborn or pull rank on me again. Then he made the little coughing noise in the back of his throat that indicated amusement. "I don't want to argue any more. Not with you. Not over this. Good night." He walked almost steadily toward his bedroom.

He could make it on his own, I decided, and looked around. I really ought to leave everything the way it was: rings and pools of *halin* on the tables, the long smear down the wall and the sticky mess in the carpet. Let Gwarha come out in the morning and see the kind of swine he was.

But neatness is the curse of my family, and it felt painful to leave a room like this. So I cleaned up, leaving the cups and jugs stacked in his kitchen, everything washed, even the pieces of the cup he'd broken. Then I checked on him. He was asleep, making the noises he always makes when he goes to bed drunk.

What an evening. I filled a glass with wine and sat down in the living room opposite the newly washed wall. The air system was on remove and replenish. The foul odors were abating. I listened to the hum of the fan and thought about *tli*.

I'd seen at least one animal each time I'd been to the home planet, usually in the country at dusk or very early in the morning. I'd be out walking. It would be digging in a compost heap or snuffling through a garden, looking for something to eat: a little round furry thing, midway in size between a rat and a possum. Its snout is pointed. Its ears are large and tufted. It has a long, narrow, furry, prehensile tail.

Once I had seen a very large specimen scuttling down an alley in the middle of the *hwarhath* capital city.

It lives everywhere. It eats everything. There is no way to get rid of it. The People regard it with exasperation and respect.

When Gwarha gave me the bracelet, he told me the jade was the color of my irises. That was the only reason he'd given for buying it, though I'd asked him more than once. Why the *tli?* Which kind of *tli?*

In the animal plays for children, which are invariably moral, the *tli* is a liar and thief and troublemaker. His schemes are always foiled, and he is always punished at the end of the play.

The animal plays for adults are obscene and mock all the basic values of *hwarhath* society—even, on occasion, homosexuality, though that is done very carefully. In the adult plays, the *tli* is like Brer Rabbit: a clever little fellow who tricks and exposes the big animals, who are bullies and hypocrites, not heroes.

So what was I? The *tli* of real life, eating garbage and living under houses? The coward and criminal of the children's plays? Or Brer Rabbit? And did I like any of these roles?

Gwarha asked me why I wasn't furious. Because I can't afford to be. The *tli* does not fight, unless it's cornered or made crazy by illness.

I finished the wine and washed the glass, setting it next to the pieces of Gwarha's favorite cup. Then I went home to bed.

I left the door unlocked. He came over in the middle of the first *ikun*. I was sitting in my main room, having a cup of coffee. Gwarha entered wearing a robe made of a plain, rough, dull brown material. Country clothing. He smelled of damp fur and looked considerably less than wonderful.

"Look what the small domestic killer of vermin has brought me as a gift."

He sat down and rubbed his face, then massaged his forehead and the area around his ears. "You are being a smartass," he said in English. "Don't."

"Do you want to know what happened last night? Or do you remember?"

He rubbed his neck. "I had an argument with Shen Walha."

"Bingo."

"Don't do that, Nicky."

"What?"

"Use words I don't understand. The Goddess knows, I can barely understand the language of Eh and Ahara this morning."

I switched to his native language and described as much of the evening as I'd seen.

When I was done, he said, "I remember most of that. I will have to find a replacement for Wally."

"I think so, though I may be biased, and you have to find a new job for him. He's very good. You don't want him going to an enemy, and you don't want to punish him for speaking honestly."

"Don't tell me how to be a frontman."

"Yes, First-Defender."

"Jesus, what a mess," he said in English.

"How much of this kind of thing has been going on?"

He looked at me, puzzled.

"How many people are saying that humans are animals?"

He was silent for a moment, then answered carefully. "Wally is not alone. I think there's a lot of talk like this— far more than I ever learn about. I am the Human Lover. There are things that are not said in my presence. My male relatives have told me part of what is going on, but I think even they are afraid to tell me everything.

"I think the talk is increasing. A lot of men believe the negotiations are going to fail. We are going to have to fight the humans, and if they will not fight like people, we'll have to butcher them."

Butcher. Hew down. Hack apart. All three translations are possible. It's an ugly word, full of violence, and it is not used to describe the way men deal with one another.

"Why haven't you told me about this?"

"It's not my obligation to tell you everything I know."

"This is my species, Ettin Gwarha. If they are animals, then so am I."

He was silent again, gazing at the carpet. Finally he lifted his head. "What good would it have done? You'd have looked around at your fellow officers—the men you live among—and asked yourself, Who is saying this? Which of these people think I am not a person?"

"Fuck it all."

He sat for a while longer in glum silence, then got up and went back to his quarters.

I got another cup of coffee and drank it slowly, thinking about the last time I'd been on the *hwarhath* home planet, after we had gotten back from the disastrous first set of negotiations with the humans. There was one morning in particular. I was in the gardens that lie between Ettin Per's great house and the river, breathing the cool air and getting my feet wet in the dew, admiring the gaudy leaves of Per's ornamental plants and the equally gaudy plumage of her *halpa*. She raises them for eggs and appearance. They stalked everywhere, too heavy and too confident to fly. I turned a corner past a bush with green and scarlet leaves. There was a *tli:* round and fat with rusty fur and white rings on its tail. It was taking apart a *halpa* nest. Bit of egg dripped from its muzzle and covered its little clever front paws. I stopped. It looked up at me. For a moment or two we both were motionless. Then it trundled away. I was left looking at the broken eggs.

It was definitely time for another trip home. Time to be in the open air, away from the endless power struggles of the perimeter.

The endless power struggles of the center belong to women. Gwarha is sometimes invited to sit with his aunts while they plot. I'm called in very occasionally as an expert on the human enemy. I give my report and am sent away, having no further responsibility.

Goddess, that sounds appealing. But not yet. There are problems to be dealt with here.

From the journal of Sanders Nicholas, etc.

# XXIV

➤➤➤ A BELL CHIMED. It took her a minute to realize it was the door and not the intercom. She hit the inside plate, and the door slid open. Nicholas stood there. His pale face was masklike.

"What's going on?" she asked.

He stepped in. The door closed. "Anna, I have something to tell you. It's going to take time, and you're going to have to pay attention."

She'd heard this tone of voice before, usually when someone was about to tell her about a death in the family. "I have nothing planned. We won't be interrupted."

"Why don't you sit down? I'm going to want to pace."

"Nick, what is this about? You're making me nervous."

He had made it over to the other side of the room. He turned now and grinned at her. "I'm terrified, Anna. Please sit down."

She did. He stood for a moment, looking past her at the door that led out of her quarters. "First of all, this has nothing to do with the first-defender. This is from me, and he does not know what I'm doing."

She opened her mouth, then closed it.

"There's information that your side needs to know. It's up to you to figure out how to get it to the ambassador. Here in your rooms would be safe, if you can figure out how to get him in here. Better yet would be on board your ship. The human quarters are out of the question. Even the johns are bugged."

"Our people checked, and we were told—"

"Believe me, the People have been listening. I've been listening. I go over the recordings every day or so. The People don't like to lie, but they will, especially to an enemy, and they do not give up advantages." He was moving around the edge of the room. She had to turn to keep him in view.

"Can't you sit down? I'm going to get a sore neck."

He dropped into a chair and looked at her, his expression grim. "I think we're at some kind of turning point. If something goes wrong with this set of negotiations, there may be no recovering what's lost; and I don't think your people realize how dangerous the situation is. You have to make this work."

He paused for a moment. She waited. Finally he said, "The information. When the People fight a war, they follow rules, and the rules are absolute. They cannot be broken. The first rule, the most important one, is that no *hwarhath* male can do physical harm to a woman or a child.

"They are very good fighters, and they have a long and bloody history, but almost never has a *hwarhath* army attacked civilians. Men, yes. No man is a civilian after he leaves childhood. He's always fair game, even in a sickbed, even if he's an old man of a hundred. But women and children can't be touched. Not physically." He smiled. "I've read some of the women's plays. They tell what it's like to belong to a lineage that has been defeated. All your male relatives who are over twenty—or sometimes fifteen—are killed. Your brothers, your uncles, your cousins. You and your children become members of the lineage that has destroyed your family. Some women take the option, but that is not an entirely respectable thing to do. You're supposed to stay alive for the sake of the children.

"And the children are supposed to forget their uncles and older brothers. Once the war is over, once they are adopted, revenge becomes murder-within-the-family, and that's a terrible crime."

"Nick, is this relevant?"

"Am I drifting? I'm finding this difficult. I was saying that the People do not kill women or children. It has happened, though not often. When it does happen, it generates a kind of holy war. All the neighbors get together and destroy the outlaw lineage." He paused and looked straight at her. "Humans attack civilian populations. It has been the main way we've fought in the past two or three centuries. The *hwarhath* know this. They know they'll be at a terrible disadvantage, if they keep to their rules in fighting us.

"Humans can attack their cities, but they can't reciprocate. I'm assuming that we're going to find each other's home planets. Hell, the People are almost certain they know where Earth is. They could take out our home planet now, except for their rules.

"They also know it's only a matter of time before the humans figure out the *hwarhath* rules of war, and then some clever fool among the humans—some group of clever fools—is going to say, 'We have the enemy. We know how to destroy them.' And I think when this happens, it's likely that the humans will decide on war. I have told the general this, and I've told him that I think the People have a year or two at most. There is information in the files we took from your planet, Reed whatever-it-is."

"1935-C," Anna said.

He nodded. "Some of your people are very close to understanding the *hwarhath* rules for when it's right to kill. But there are other things about the People that are going to take longer to figure out, and humanity is likely to be in a full-scale war before we begin to understand— You know, Anna, I think I'd like something to drink, and not coffee."

She went into the kitchen, bringing back a bottle of Rose d'Anjou and two glasses, filled the glasses and handed one to Nick. He set it down.

"The *hwarhath* say, in order to be a person you have to be able to judge and make distinctions. Especially, you have to be able to judge and make distinctions in the area of morality.

"They don't think appearance has much to do with being a person. For one thing, they have close relatives still living: the Red Folk. They are the equivalent of—oh, I don't know. *Homo habilis?* Something like that. They've managed to survive on a handful of islands, like the orangutans on Earth, until whenever-it-was."

"A century ago," Anna said, feeling a bit of the familiar grief: another species gone.

"The People know the Red Folk are close relatives, but they aren't people. They don't have a moral system that the People can recognize as such.

"And some of the *hwarhath* are not real people, either. According to the People, it isn't murder to kill someone who's in a coma or whose brain does not work properly, for whatever reason. Accident. Disease. A birth defect. When you do in someone like that, you are putting an animal out of its misery. They think we're crazy for thinking that a person is human, simply because he or she looks human."

Anna felt a bit sick.

"The same is true for criminals. The People have them, though not as many as we do, at least as far as I've been able to determine. But they definitely know there are members of their species who are normal as far as intelligence goes, but have no moral sense. They prefer it if these people commit suicide. So they give them the option and some time. If the criminals remain alive, they may end by killing them. It depends on the crime. It's never done for punishment. The *hwarhath* are not especially vindictive, and they don't have our idea of justice. To them killing a criminal is like killing a dangerous animal."

He picked up his glass of wine and turned it between his hands, watching the pale red liquid move, but not drinking. Apparently he'd wanted something to fiddle with.

"Some of the *hwarhath*—I don't know how many—are arguing that humans are like the Red Folk or the members of their own species who can't make reasonable decisions about morality. We look like people, but we aren't people. Instead, we are some kind of clever animal, able to do a pretty good imitation of—what can I say? Right behavior. The careless observer is fooled, but if you look closely—

"Anna, the People do not negotiate with animals. They are careful in their dealings with other life-forms, especially on their home planet, but they have nothing like the Gaia religion. If an animal is dangerous, one gets rid of the danger, and the rules of war do not apply. I don't think they are likely to stop short of a final solution."

"Shit," said Anna.

He grinned. "My thought exactly. That is the first point. The second is—the *hwarhath* have a very serious problem. They haven't fought a war in over a century."

"That's a problem? I wish we could say the same."

He set down the wineglass and leaned back. Anna had the impression that he was forcing himself to relax. "The People believe that men are innately violent and innately— what word do I want? Hierarchical. They are obsessed with front and back, obsessed with winning and losing. Left to their own devices, they will try to dominate every situation. They will do physical harm. I have to say, I think this is a crock; but there is no question that *hwarhath* males are socialized to be intensely competitive and to think that violence is no big deal.

"Anyway—" He paused. "The People try, as much as possible, to keep men away from home. They don't want their children or their women to be afraid. They don't think continual fear is healthy, even continual fear at a low level—for example, never knowing when someone in the family, Uncle or Elder Brother or whoever, is going to blow up and strike out. My father has a temper. A very civilized man, but I can remember being afraid of him, when I was a kid. Not often. Now and then.

"*Hwarhath* males are sent to the edges of their society, where their violence is useful and where they'll only kill other adult men."

"This really sounds like a very unpleasant culture," Anna said.

Nick shrugged. "In a lot of ways, they're kinder than humans. In some ways, I guess they're more brutal; or maybe they're more clear and honest about brutality. I love them." He smiled briefly. "As you may have noticed, I'm betraying them. Everything I'm telling you is protected information."

"Why are you doing this?"

"Things can't go on this way, and I can't think of anything else to do. Let me finish, will you?"

Anna nodded.

"I told you their history is long and bloody. It led to the creation of the Weaving, which became a world government. There are obvious benefits to world peace, and they don't really want to give it up. But they don't know what to do with their men. They think, and they are almost certainly right, that they can't maintain their society the way it is without an enemy. What is going to happen, when the young men stop believing in war? What if men begin to say, There is no point in training for battle and no point in living on the perimeter? Jesus Christ, they might want to come home and not just for a visit. A frightening idea. It certainly frightens the *hwarhath*.

"One thing went right for them. They discovered FTL. That made it possible for them to send the men—a lot of them, anyway—into space to explore and establish colonies and to look for an enemy." Nick glanced at her and smiled. "They wanted a war that was big enough to keep the men busy and out of the women's fur. Far enough away so the home planet would not be threatened, but a reasonable commute. An enemy they could beat, but not easily. I don't think they ever really figured out what they were going to do with the alien women and children, after they'd done in all the men.

"They found humanity, and we were almost exactly what they wanted, except we don't play fair. We don't know the rules of war."

He had picked up his glass a second time. He tilted it, and the pale liquid gleamed. Like what? wondered Anna. Blood mixed in water?

"There is one other thing you ought to know about the People. I have been in a human ship under attack—the *Free Market Explorer,* when the People captured me; and I have been on a couple of *hwarhath* ships in the same situation.

"Once I was on a ship that reached a transfer point at the same time as a human ship. It was an unpleasant surprise for both of us, but more unpleasant for the humans. The other time I was traveling with Ettin Gwarha, and there was a failure in communication. Our nice little transport ship ended up in the middle of a practice battle. The *hwarhath* believe in making their practice wars as realistic as possible. The ammo is live." He smiled. "The soldiers—very often—end up dead.

"I may be the only person who has seen both human and *hwarhath* soldiers in a combat situation. They are much better than we are. As far as I can tell, humanity is not even in contention."

He stopped talking.

"If the pressure on them is so strong, how can we make peace?"

"Talk to the women. I think that's the only hope. There has to be a way to tell them— The People will be destroyed, not physically, but morally, if they fight a war of extermination. It's going to corrupt them. No matter what kind of sophistries they come up with, they are going to be killing off another intelligent species. We're not as rational as the *hwarhath,* nor as moral, but we are capable—sometimes, now and then—of reason and morality. Genocide is wrong. They're going to fuck their whole society if they go ahead with this.

"But I'm not sure that any of the men, not even Ettin Gwarha, understands the risk they are running. Talk to Charlie, either here or on your ship, and figure out what you are going to say to the women." He drank half the glass of wine in one swallow, then set the glass down and stood. "I'd better get going. You will talk to Charlie?"

"Yes."

He walked to the door. It opened. A pair of soldiers stood outside.

Nick spoke in the alien language, his voice rapid and sharp. One of the soldiers answered.

He turned and looked back at her. His face was paler than before. "They are asking you to come with them."

"Why?" There was fear in her voice.

"The general wants to see both of us." He smiled. "I doubt that it's anything important."

"Tell them I need a moment." She got up and went into the bathroom. Her heart was beating more rapidly than usual, and she could feel herself beginning to sweat. Don't be foolish, she told herself. She used the toilet, then washed her hands and face in cold water. That helped. She didn't look especially frightened. She combed her hair and went back out. Nick was standing, hands jammed in his jacket pockets, looking impatient. The soldiers looked calm.

They walked through the station. The soldiers stayed with them. Nick asked another question in the alien language and got an answer.

"They're supposed to escort us. He doesn't know why."

"Doesn't this strike you as odd?" she said.

He shrugged.

They reached a door. It opened, and they entered a small square room with nothing in it except carpeting. The soldiers stayed in the hallway. The door shut, and Nicholas looked around. "We're here," he said in English.

Another door opened. Nick led the way into a second room. This one contained a table, three chairs, the usual grey carpeting and a tapestry: a fire, surrounded at a distance by a ring of swords.

There was an alien standing behind the table: Ettin Gwarha. He spoke to Nick in the *hwarhath* language. She'd been listening to his voice for weeks. Usually it was deep and soft with a slight roughness: a furry voice, not at all unpleasant. Now it sounded hoarse and harsh. The man was furious.

Nick stood without moving until Ettin Gwarha was done, his hands still in his pockets, his head slightly tilted, listening courteously. "He bugged your room, Anna. I don't know how he got Gwa Hu to do something like that."

"She is not one of the People," the general said in English.

"I thought of having the conversation in my rooms," Nick said, his voice quiet and even. "I figured I could come up with a reason to invite you over. But I decided your place would be safe enough. Gwa Hu has been doing regular checks."

"It would not have mattered where you decided to

perform your act of treason," the general said. "I would have heard."

"My rooms are bugged? You had that done?"

"Yes."

"For the sake of the Goddess, Gwarha, we talked that one out years ago. You told me I could have that much privacy. You gave me your word."

The general looked at him, a steady gaze that did not seem friendly. Nick met the gaze for a moment or two, then glanced down.

Ettin Gwarha glanced at Anna. "This man—this treasonous being—has put us both in an uncomfortable situation, Mem Perez. I'm not sure how to resolve it. I cannot let you give the information you have just gotten to the other humans."

"Kill her," said Nick. "Accidents happen. You've already started to break the rules, and what is going to be left when you are done? Of you or the People?"

The general answered him briefly and harshly in the alien language.

Nick said nothing.

"You don't need to worry, Mem Perez," the general said in English. "I would never think of harming a woman, and there is no way to do it that wouldn't lead to further complications."

Nick laughed.

The general glared at him. "You have destroyed yourself, you stupid piece of shit, and almost certainly me and quite possibly any chance we may have had for peace. For all I know, you have destroyed your own species. How could I have ever trusted you?"

Nick answered him in the *hwarhath* language, speaking quickly and angrily, moving closer to the table. His hands were out of his pockets now, and he was leaning on the table, still speaking angrily.

"Shut up," the general said in English.

And then Nick was over the table. It happened so quickly that Anna didn't really see what happened. One moment they were shouting at one another, the table between them. A moment later, the general was down, and Nicholas was standing over him. All the noise had stopped, except for the sound of Nick's breathing, rapid and shallow. The general lay motionless. His chair had fallen over and lay next to him on its side.

Nick straightened and pulled off his jacket, then picked up a knife that lay on the table.

"What are you going to do?"

"Tie him up. Get you on your way to the human ship." He cut the jacket and tore it into strips. "Shit. This stuff is going to make lousy rope. Damn all synthetics."

"Is there anything I can do?"

"Not that I can think of. Unless you have some duct tape on you?"

"No."

He crouched and stuffed a piece of the fabric into the general's mouth, then rolled the limp body over and tied the hands. "This crap isn't going to hold. I remember my mother told my sister, never go anywhere without at least two safety pins. I figured it was one of those female mysteries and didn't pay attention. I wish there'd been something comparable for men. 'Go nowhere, my son, without a roll of really good adhesive tape.' " He tied Ettin Gwarha's feet, then stood up. "It really isn't going to hold. Be quiet for a while. I need to do some talking."

He touched the surface of the general's table and spoke, first to one person, then to another. His voice had a sharp authority that she'd never heard before. Finally he looked up. "Mats is coming over. He is going to escort you to the shuttle, and the shuttle will take you out to the human ship. I don't know what to suggest after that. Tell the captain what's going on. I don't think he can make a run for it. I doubt that he'll want to abandon the rest of the negotiating team. I can't think of anything better. It will buy some time, and it will mean that Gwarha can't stop the spread of information, unless he wants to take out the human ship. Shit. I don't know if I'm making this situation better or worse."

"What are you going to do?"

"Stay here and make sure that Gwarha doesn't get loose."

"Come out to the ship, Nick."

"Don't be ridiculous. I'm not putting myself in the hands of human Military Intelligence."

"Do you think they'd be worse than what is going to happen to you here?"

"I really don't like to answer questions, and the People aren't going to ask me any."

A voice said, "I'm here, Nicky."

"Come on," said Nicholas, and moved toward the door. "He can't see any of this, and don't tell him about it. I don't want him in trouble."

He waited till she was at the door, then opened it and pushed her out, stepping after her. The door into the general's office closed.

Matsehar glanced over. "What's the hurry?"

"Anna needs to see a human doctor."

"Nothing serious, I hope?"

There was something surreal—was that the right word?—about this situation, and Matsehar's polite question. Such a nice young man! A little furry maybe, and socialized to think that there was nothing wrong with violence; but nonetheless, an addition to any party. His English was so good!

"No," she said. "Nothing serious. But I do have to get going."

"Of course."

The door into the hall opened. The soldiers were gone. One less problem. She walked out, Matsehar behind her.

Nick stopped in the doorway. She glanced back once, when she was halfway down the corridor. Nick was still in the doorway, hands in his pants pockets now, looking only a little worried.

Matsehar started telling her about his version of *Macbeth*. He was almost to the end. All the plans of the ambitious mother and her son were failing. The mother was dead, having taken the option and not in a good and decent way, but out of craziness and to escape from guilt.

Her bloody son was now alone, struggling against the consequences of his actions. He had reached the point of complete despair.

"Listen!" said Matsehar.

" 'Tomorrow, and tomorrow, and tomorrow,
Creeps in this petty pace from day to day,
To the last syllable of recorded time;
And all our yesterdays have lighted fools
The way to dusty death. Out, out, brief candle!
Life's but a walking shadow, a poor player
That struts and frets his hour upon the stage
And then is heard no more; it is a tale
Told by an idiot, full of sound and fury,
Signifying nothing.'

"What splendid language! I only hope I can translate that passage as well as it deserves. If there is one thing you humans can do, it's write." He paused for a moment. "And I have to say, I like Macbeth. His courage is beyond question. He never gives up, even after he has reached the point of complete despair. This is what happens to people when they ignore ordinary decent behavior. Macbeth and his mother should have entertained the old king properly and sent him on his way."

"Huh," said Anna.

"Is something going on?" he asked.

"I don't want to talk about it."

He was silent for a while, leading her through a series of corridors that did not look familiar. "Is Nicky in trouble?" he asked at last.

"Yes."

"What kind?"

"I can't tell you."

"Should I go back and ask him?"

She thought a moment. "He doesn't want you involved."

"Then it's serious. I had better go back, after I have seen you where you're going."

They reached an elevator. It carried them to zero G, and they floated into the shuttle, watched by a pair of *hwarhath* crewmen, who were anchored to the floor by their sandals. Anna found a seat and strapped herself in.

Matsehar said, "Goodbye. I hope your problem, whatever it is, is easily resolved."

He left. Anna heard a door slide closed.

One of the crewmen said, "Mem Perez, we ought to tell you. There is another passenger."

# XXV

➤➤➤ I CHECKED GWARHA. He was still unconscious, which was worrying. He should have come to by now. Then I prowled around the room, trying not to think about the future. I knew I wouldn't take the option. It was available the whole time I was in prison—over three years—and it never seemed even mildly appealing, though the alternative had been a lifetime spent in twelve small rooms with six men from the crew of the *Free Market Explorer*. Career military. It was like a ring in Dante's hell, or like the play by what's-his-name, the French philosopher.

A voice said, "Nicky."

Matsehar. He was in the anteroom.

"Why'd you come back?"

"Anna said something was going on."

"She's wrong. She isn't feeling well. Everything is fine."

"Come out here," he said. "You know I like to see people when I talk to them."

Shit, yes, I knew it, and I also knew that Mats could be as stubborn as a pig. There was a good chance he wouldn't leave until he'd had his say. "Wait." I rechecked Gwarha. He was still out. The knots were tight, and his pulse was strong and even.

I went into the anteroom, moving quickly so Mats wouldn't get a chance to see anything in the office.

He was standing erect, his shoulders back, and wearing the expression he always had when arguing with actors and musicians: grim determination combined with a sense that he was in the right. Mats does not see the world in shades of grey, except—at times—when writing a play. "I don't believe you. I'm no expert on humanity, but Anna seemed in good health, and I don't think she's a liar."

I was a liar, as everyone knew. My reputation!

"She's wrong, Mats. I promise you."

He kept the look of grim determination.

"The first-defender is not in a good mood today." A slight understatement. "I think it'd be a good idea if you left, before he gets angry."

Mats glanced at the door into the general's office. "He is in there."

"Yes."

"I would like to see him."

"Why? You have no business with him, and the two of you have never had any use for one another."

"I am assigned to his command. I have the right to see him. I want to."

At that point I became acutely aware of the surveillance equipment in the anteroom. Most likely no one was watching, except for a computer program. But if the program decided that something odd was happening, it would alert a person, and I would be up the creek. Not that I wasn't already.

Damn the People and their mania for keeping track of one another. Why couldn't I have gotten involved with a less paranoid species? Or a less paranoid sex?

"Mats, I am in the middle of an argument with the first-defender. It's a private argument. I would like to be able to finish it without interruption."

Now he looked uncertain. "Is that what it is? One of your quarrels? Why didn't you tell Anna? She's acting worried. I think she's acting worried. It isn't always possible to tell with humans."

"You know what humans think about decent behavior.

If I do anything to remind her of what I'm like, it makes her uncomfortable.''

He frowned, looking unhappy. ''I don't like to think she is as narrow as the rest of her species.''

''No one is perfect.''

(Gwarha, if you can figure out a way, tell Matsehar this was a lie. I don't want him to think badly of Anna.)

''You should have come up with something to keep her from worrying, especially if she's ill. Why did she have to know it was a lovers' quarrel? There is more than one kind of argument.''

''You're right, I should have, but I didn't, and I have to get back into the office. Surely you have something better to do than stand in Ettin Gwarha's anteroom.''

He tilted his head in agreement. ''Tomorrow and tomorrow.''

''What?''

''Nicky, what's wrong with you? You ought to recognize that. It's *Macbeth*. Are you certain you're all right?''

''You would not believe the argument I'm in. But it's for me to handle. Get going.''

He left, and I returned to the office.

The general was standing at his table, one hand on the intercom. He glanced up at me, then lifted his other hand. It held the knife: the emblem of his office, as sharp as a razor.

I stopped and made the gesture of presentation and acknowledgment. The door slid shut in back of me.

The general turned off the intercom. ''That was security. They wanted to know if they should investigate the situation in my anteroom. I said no. Sit down, Nicky.''

I went to one of the chairs in front of his table, sat down and leaned back, stretching my legs in front of me and crossing them. A difficult position to get out of, and a signal that I had no further violent plans.

''You have never been good at practical detail,'' he

said. "When you tie someone up, don't tie around the outside of his boots. It isn't possible to tighten the bonds sufficiently. And don't leave the person in a room with a knife."

I looked down. He was in stocking feet. "I certainly should not have left the room; but Mats showed up, and I had to get rid of him."

"Is he involved? Have you involved a major playwright in treason? That is contemptible."

"He has no idea what is going on. Matsehar would never have anything to do with betraying the People."

He laid the knife down, but kept his hand close to it. "Now, where is Anna?"

"You find out."

He turned the intercom back on and called security. It took them a couple of minutes. She was on the shuttle, and the shuttle was halfway to the human ship, which knew it was coming with Anna on board. Even worse, there was another human on the shuttle with Anna: Etienne Corbeau.

"A courier," said the intercom. "The humans requested passage to their ship for this person on the regular shuttle trip, which is tomorrow. We told them the shuttle was making a special trip today."

He made an angry hissing sound and hit the flat of his hand on the table next to the knife. I looked down at my feet.

The person on the intercom said, "I did not understand your last order, First-Defender."

"Get me the pilot of the shuttle."

They did, and the general asked for Anna. There was silence for a while after that, except for the noise that the singularity made as it broke matter apart.

Then she spoke. "First-Defender?"

"Is the other human with you?"

"No. They told him to stay in the passenger cabin."

"Have you spoken to him? Does he know what's going on?"

More silence, except for the crackle of the singularity, doing its work.

"Mem, I am going to tell the shuttle to return here. As a courtesy and in the hope that we may yet have peace, say nothing to Etienne Corbeau."

"Is Nick okay?"

He gestured. I got up and came over. "I'm fine, Anna."

"Should I do as Ettin Gwarha asks?"

"I don't know."

The general made another angry hissing sound. The knife was between us. I thought of grabbing it. Why? So I could kill him? I put my hands in my pockets. He noticed that and smiled: a brief unfriendly flash of teeth.

"Anna, do what seems right to you. But remember that Corbeau is a serious dorf. I don't think he can help you."

The general said, "When you return, I want you to speak to my aunts. It is possible that they will be able to find a way out of this situation."

"Now, that is a good idea," I said to the intercom.

There was more silence from Anna. The singularity did more work.

The general added, "This is a conversation that should take place knee-to-knee."

And not over a radio, with other people listening. But he couldn't say that part.

"Nick?" asked Anna.

"It's your decision."

"I'll cooperate," she said.

The general said, "Tell Corbeau that the women of Ettin have asked for a meeting, and that is why the shuttle is turning back. If he asks—what is the term you humans use?—what the hurry is, tell him you don't know. Hai Atala Vaihar will be waiting to escort you."

She made some kind of acknowledgment.

He spoke to the pilot in the language of Eh and Ahara, then turned off the intercom and said, "Now, Nicholas, we will go to see my aunts. Do I have to tell you not to play tricks?"

"I'm out of tricks."

"Good."

We walked to the women's quarters in silence. I was over my initial response, which had been panic. Now I felt the remote dread you feel when you're going in for some kind of medical test that might have unpleasant consequences.

I'd been in an accident during the summer of my first year in college and gotten a transfusion. They decided some of the blood might have been contaminated, and for a year I went in for tests. Most of the time I was able to believe that everything was fine. I was magic, meant for the stars, and nothing on Earth could slow me down. But on the days I went to have blood drawn and saw how very careful the techs were, I felt terror. As it turned out, I was okay. The disease they were looking for never appeared.

We passed through the door marked with the emblem of the hearth (the soldiers guarding it made the gesture of presentation) then across the bare and shining floor of the entrance hall. The tapestries showed people on the home world, engaged in various kinds of agricultural labor.

There was one in particular: a woman fixing a tractor. I saw it with the lucid intensity that fear can sometimes give. The tractor was burgundy red. The woman was large and solid and grave, with pale fur, dressed in a bright blue tunic.

It was like something out of the early Renaissance, done by the Master of Equipment Maintenance.

We went down a corridor into an anteroom. Gwarha spoke to the air, and the air answered. We waited. A door slid open. He led the way to the room where I had last spoken with the aunts. This time the holograms were off.

Instead of windows opening onto the ocean, there were blank walls. The door through which we entered was visible: a slab of wood as black as coal.

Seven chairs were arranged in a circle in the middle of the room. The aunts occupied three of the chairs, dressed in robes the color of fire. A fourth woman sat with them, big and gaunt, with fur that had gone white with age. Her robe was green, embroidered in blue, white and silver. Most likely it was a traditional design with some kind of elaborate name. "Climbing higher into the mountains we come at last in sight of the high ice-covered peaks." I looked down.

"Lift your head," the old woman said. "I want to look at your eyes."

I met her gaze. She stared intently. "White and green. Strange, but lovely—like branches in the snow. Is that why you fell in love with him, Gwarha? The eyes?"

"This," said the general with restraint, "is my grandmother. I don't think you have met before."

But I'd heard about her. She was tougher than any of her daughters. It was in her time that Ettin had become a genuine power. At the age of eighty, she had retired to a house in the far south, saying that she was fed to the teeth with people. For more than twenty years, she had devoted herself to various hobbies: watching animals like birds and raising animals like fish, composing music and writing her memoirs. The music was competent and minor: not bad for a retired politician. The memoirs were awaited with fear by everyone. I had no idea what she was doing here.

"Sit down," the old lady said. "And keep your head up. I have never seen a human before, not in person. This is most interesting."

I obeyed. Gwarha sat down in a chair across from me, as far away as possible.

"You did not answer my question, Gwarha."

He glanced at the old lady. "It's not easy for me to remember why I ever loved him."

The old lady frowned. "That's still not an answer. What has happened to your manners?"

"Mother," said Per, sounding diffident. "Gwarha said he has a problem. Maybe we should ask him to explain what it is."

"Very well," said the old lady.

The general glanced at me. "Pay attention to what I say. If I miss anything that's important or if I misrepresent any part of what has taken place, interrupt me."

I nodded, and he described what had happened. He was beautifully in control, his posture relaxed but not sloppy, his voice quiet and even. As well as I knew him, I had trouble hearing any emotion. This was an officer giving a report. Now and then he glanced at me to see whether I had any comments. I nodded each time: Go on.

When he was done, he said, "You haven't said anything, Nicky. Is there nothing you want to add?"

"Not really. There's a bit at the beginning of my conversation with Anna that you missed; that must have been before the computer alerted you; and you missed a little more when you were unconscious."

"Anything important?"

I shrugged.

"I take that as a negative." He glanced around at his female relatives. "I have a recording of all of this. But most of it is in English."

Per said, "Make sure that Sai gets a copy."

"Yes," said Ettin Gwarha.

The intercom rang. Aptsi answered it. Vaihar. He had arrived with Anna.

Per glanced at me. "Go out and ask her to be patient. We have to settle this first. Tell her there is no need for her to be afraid. She won't be harmed. I promise."

Ettin Petali said, "The women of Ettin promise."

She was in the anteroom. Most of the time I forget that Anna isn't a very large woman. I'm misled by something in her, which I'm not entirely certain how to describe. Intensity? Force of personality? Solidity of character? In any case, Anna usually seems to take up more room than she actually does.

But not now. Sitting in one of the wide low *hwarhath* chairs, she looked frightened and small.

Vaihar stood nearby. "What's going on?" he asked in the language of Eh and Ahara.

"Ettin Gwarha will tell you later, if he thinks you need to know."

He looked worried. "What should I do?"

"Stay here. Keep Anna company, and make sure she does not leave."

"Is she a prisoner?" He sounded shocked.

"No. But the first-defender and the women of Ettin don't want her wandering around the station."

Now he looked dubious, but said nothing further.

Anna glanced up. Her expression was dazed, like an animal hit with a sudden bright light.

"Ettin Per sent me," I told her in English. "You don't have to worry. You aren't going to be harmed."

Vaihar started at the word "harm." Anna stayed motionless.

"She wants you to wait here, until we've settled some other things. Believe me, you can trust her word."

Again there was no reaction from Anna.

"I can't remember if I ever told you Gwarha's nickname. He has a couple, but the one that is friendly and can be used in front of him, and in front of me, is The Man Who Is Run By His Aunts. He won't act in opposition to the women of Ettin."

"You're talking to me as if I were a child."

"I didn't mean to. I apologize."

"You say I'll be all right. What about you?"

"I don't know. No promises have been made. But that is my problem, not yours."

"Nicky," said Vaihar. "Something bad is happening. What is it?"

"I don't have time to explain. Watch Anna." I got out.

Gwarha and his relatives were still in their circle in the room with no windows, waiting patiently, except for Grandma, who looked restless.

"It's taken care of," I told Per, and sat down.

"Thank you." She folded her hands and glanced at her sisters. "We have not had a chance to discuss the situation, but—"

"I will begin," said Ettin Petali, her voice loud and definite. "And I will not discuss the errors and failings of Sanders Nicholas. That I will leave to others. I will begin with my grandson." She turned in her chair and glared at him. "You put listening devices in the rooms occupied by a woman. You deliberately involved a female in the struggles that go on between men. This is shameful, Gwarha!"

"She is not one of the People," the general said.

"That is a dangerous argument," said Ettin Sai.

He glanced down, then up at his grandmother. "What are we to do? How can we deal with people who don't know how to behave? If they are people."

"Do I have permission to speak?" I asked.

"Yes," said Ettin Petali.

I looked at the general, meeting his gaze. "Do you think I'm not a person?"

"You betrayed me."

"What did you expect of Nicky?" asked Ettin Per. "That he would choose you over a female relative? Did you expect him to stand by quietly when the woman of Perez was threatened? It seems clear to me that you were threatening her."

"I threatened her after Nicky had given her the information and because he had given her the information. It was not the threat to her that made him betray me."

Grandma snorted. "This is a time of war. Men have made suggestions that threaten the lives of every human woman and child. Did you expect him to ignore this? What kind of lover did you think you had?"

"Shall I tell you what this sounds like?" asked Ettin Sai. "It sounds as if you think that nothing ought to matter to Nicky except you."

"We should never have permitted them to stay together," said Aptsi. "Look at the result! Why couldn't Gwarha have found a nice young man from a lineage we like?"

There was silence, and the women of Ettin looked uncomfortable. I couldn't tell if Aptsi was out of line or if she had said what everyone was thinking.

The general broke the silence finally.

"You asked me a question, Grandmother, and I refused to answer it. I will answer it now. You asked if I fell in love with Nicky because of his eyes. No, and not because of his hair either. It was as red as copper when I met him, and it shone even in the light of the station. If I had seen it in sunlight on a planet, I think it would have blinded me. And not because of his strange naked skin, which has always made me feel tender, the way one feels when faced with the vulnerability of a child. None of these, not any of the things about him that are foreign and unusual."

He paused for just the right length of time and then went on.

"Shall I give you five reasons? Everything comes in groups of five or used to, in the old stories."

"Yes," said Ettin Petali.

"He is intelligent, though not always in the way that the People are intelligent. He is curious—even now, when he ought to be afraid and ashamed. Watch him, how he keeps turning his head and glancing at one person, then at

another. He never loses interest in what's going on around
him."

Obedient to his suggestion, the women looked at me,
and I looked down.

"He never gives up. When you think he is retreating,
he is only moving to a new position to rest or to find a new
way to resist or attack. I saw this in the interrogation room.
If there is a good form of *rahaka,* this is it.

"And he refuses to hate. He doesn't even like to be
angry. When he was in prison, and I came to visit him, he
was willing to talk to me, even though he knew I had been
involved in what had happened to him."

(I'm reluctant to say this, but I was really bored, and
you were a lot more interesting than the rocket jockeys I
was in prison with. But I will treasure this speech. I've
tried to get it down exactly as you spoke it.)

"That is four reasons," said Ettin Petali.

"I had another one. It's gone."

Ettin Sai leaned forward. "That was well said, Gwarha,
and it explains why you picked Sanders Nicholas rather
than someone more appropriate. But it does not explain
why you thought you had the right to all his loyalty. You
never would have expected anything like this of any man
of the People."

"You thought, because you loved him and he was foreign and trapped behind our border and alone, that you
had the right—" Per hesitated.

"To own him," said Grandma. Her voice was full of
contempt. This was not the verb "to hold," which is used
for houses and land and the other kinds of wealth that
families have in common. This verb was the one that refers
to personal belongings: clothing, furniture, maybe a pet.

"You have always had this fault," said Per. "Even as a
child. You did not simply want to be first, which is a fine
ambition. You did not simply want to make the other boys

back down. You wanted to grab and keep for yourself. Greed and sullenness have always been your faults."

There have been times when I've wondered what made the general what he is. This did. These terrifying women. He sat with his shoulders hunched, enduring.

"May I speak again?" I asked.

"Yes," said Ettin Petali.

"Perez Anna is still waiting, and when I left her, she was both frightened and angry. You may not want to leave her waiting too long."

The old lady stared at me. "You are right. We should not spend too much time on the failings of Ettin Gwarha. There is still the question of your behavior, and whether that miserable oaf Lugala Tsu will be able to use this situation to harm us."

"Do you understand what you've done, Nicky?" asked Ettin Sai.

"I have given information to one of the enemy in time of war. Humans would see the act almost the same way as you do."

"Have you offered him the option, Gwarha?" asked Ettin Petali.

"No," said the general. "And I won't."

"Why not?" asked Aptsi. Her voice was plaintive.

"He is *rahaka*. He wouldn't take it, and I promised myself years ago that I would never again be part of harming him."

Did you?

"A pity," said Grandma.

"Why did you speak to Perez Anna?" asked Per.

I looked down at the bare polished floor, trying to assemble an argument that would make sense to the women of Ettin. Finally I looked at Per.

"I saw the son of Lugala doing his best to destroy the negotiations. I heard Gwarha's own chief of operations argue that my people were not people; and I knew that the

human negotiators did not know—could not possibly
know—how serious the situation is. I thought, Nothing is
made better by ignorance."

"I told you I could handle Lugala Tsu," said the general. "And Shen Walha."

"But what about the humans, First-Defender? Can you
handle them? Do you have any idea what they're going to
do? This is not an ordinary struggle among men of the
People, each one trying to push the others back. This is not
an ordinary conflict between enemy lineages. You are facing beings you do not understand, and they are ignorant.
They have no concept of the consequences of anything
they do."

Grandma lifted a hand, demanding silence. "I have no
interest in the arguments of men. The accusations can
wait; so can the explanations. We have three problems
which must be dealt with now."

Not five?

"One is you, Nicky. You have shown yourself unreliable. We can't let you remain here or in any place of
strategic importance. You might betray us again. But how
can we remove you, without letting other people know
what you have done?

"The second problem is Perez Anna. Is there a way to
keep her quiet?

"The third problem is Lugala Tsu. So long as he is here,
the negotiations will be in danger. In this I think Nicky is
right and you are wrong, Gwarha. I have watched the
Lugala for eighty years. They are all similar: greedy and
narrow-minded, but with a dangerous cleverness and very
great persistence. They never give up. They never learn
anything important. There is no argument that can make
them change, once they have decided what they want."

She paused and drew a breath. "There is a fourth problem, which occurs to me now. The humans as a species.
You asked, Gwarha, how we can deal with creatures like

these? That is a question that must be considered. We have left it to men, and this has been a mistake."

Grandma paused a second time, then said, "Leave us."

"What?" asked the general.

"Go out and speak with Perez Anna. Tell her something reassuring, and take Sanders Nicholas with you. I want to speak with my daughters, and I don't want to be distracted by the voices of men. Go."

Ettin Gwarha stood and so did I.

"Don't leave the women's quarters," said Ettin Per. "Either one of you."

We walked back to the anteroom, where Anna waited, still hunched in a wide, low chair. Vaihar had taken a seat opposite her. He glanced up at the general, then at me, then at the floor. Anna said, "Well?"

"We have been sent out," the general said. "The women of Ettin are conferring."

He sat down. I leaned against a wall.

"Vaihar, could you leave for a while? I need to speak with the first-defender. Stay in the corridor."

He left. The general lifted his head. "I'm not in the mood for conversation," he said in the language of Eh and Ahara.

"I can imagine," I said in English, then told Anna that I was going to be speaking one of the *hwarhath* languages. "I know this is rude, and I apologize. There is something I have to talk about."

She nodded.

I switched to the language of Ettin. "I have a favor to ask."

"Now? After the way you've acted?"

I waited.

"I make no promises, Nicholas. Tell me what you want."

"My journal. If anything happens to me, get hold of it

and destroy the parts that are coded for review by no one. Do it without reading them."

He gave me a long considering stare.

"Or have you read them already, First-Defender?"

"No. I have not interfered with any of your programs or unlocked any of your files. Should I have?"

"There's nothing in them that is—" I was back to the *t* word, which I really don't like to say. "—disloyal to you or to the People. But there are secrets. If they were my secrets only, I could live with the knowledge that you had read them."

Something happened to his expression. He was thinking about something not entirely pleasant.

"Or die with the knowledge," I added.

He kept quiet.

"The files I've secured contain secrets that belong to other people. I know the members of your species don't need much privacy. But you do need some, and these people trusted me."

"I will destroy the files unread, if it proves necessary to do so. But I don't think it will. What about the rest of the journal?"

"Whatever you want, though I always wanted to publish it."

The general hissed. "Memoirs. Like my grandmother."

"You would have to be the editor," I said.

He hissed a second time. "I make no promises at all."

"Okay." I glanced to Anna. "Give us a couple more minutes, will you?"

"Yes." She looked tired and depressed. I wondered how Vaihar was doing in the corridor.

"There is one other thing," I said in the language of Ettin. "Another favor."

His expression was that of a man pushed to the limit, but he didn't tell me to shut up.

"If the worst happens, don't keep my ashes in the hope that you can return them to my family. I don't want to be buried on Earth."

"Why not?"

"My parents live in North Dakota now, if the humans are telling the truth. I don't want to end up in some prairie graveyard. Goddess, I was so happy to get away."

He considered that. It was incomprehensible to him, of course. Every man—every person—must want to return to the home country, to be buried among relatives. "Where do you want to be buried?"

I shrugged. "Ettin, if you're willing. Otherwise, in space."

"This conversation is not necessary. You are not going to die." He paused. "Not in the near future. But given the difference in life expectancy between our species, you will almost certainly predecease me. I will take your ashes to Ettin, when the time comes, if that is still your wish." He looked up, meeting my gaze. "Don't be so frightened, Nicky, and don't say things that frighten me."

"Okay," I said. I glanced at Anna again. "We are waiting for the first-defender's aunts and his quite amazing grandmother to decide what to do."

"His grandmother? You brought your grandmother to the negotiations?"

"She began falling down," the general said. "We thought it was no longer a good idea for her to live alone. So Per—my aunt Per—has offered her a home." He switched to the language of Ettin and said to me, "They threw dice, and Per got the least auspicious combination. Doubtless it was the doing of the Goddess. Aptsi could not possibly handle my grandmother, and it would be a pity to ruin Sai's good disposition."

"Can that be said in English?" asked Anna.

"No," said Ettin Gwarha. "I'm sorry, Mem Perez. I am being discourteous. She is not used to living with other people, and my aunts thought it would not be a good idea to leave her in Per's house with only junior members of the family around her."

"She'd eat 'em for breakfast," I said.

"So you brought her to this place."

"Where she will probably eat us for breakfast."

He glared at me. "Do not mislead Perez Anna or malign the people who have sheltered you for over twenty years. We are not—what is the word for eaters of one another?"

"Capitalists," said Anna.

"Is that right?" Ettin Gwarha asked me.

"In this context the right word is cannibal."

"Hah."

After that we waited in silence. I looked down at my feet. A hole was forming in one of my socks in the usual place, over one of my big toes. Odd, what one notices and when. Like the tapestry in the entrance hall. I could close my eyes and see it now: the big square burgundy-red tractor, the woman like a column, blue and grey. She was holding a wrench, no different from a perfectly ordinary human wrench. I'd used ones just like it as a kid.

Finally Ettin Gwarha spoke in English. "Why have people told you secrets?"

I opened my eyes. "Because I listen. Not all the time, but often."

"Then why didn't you listen to me, when I told you to keep back?"

"I had to do something. 'There is only hope in action.' "

"What?"

"I'm quoting someone. A human philosopher."

He frowned. "That is absolutely wrong. Is it a common human belief?"

"Why is it wrong?" asked Anna.

I could see him shifting position, getting more comfortable, settling down for a discussion of his favorite topic: morality. "Everything has consequences, inaction as well as action. But as a rule, it's better to do nothing rather than something, and better to do little rather than a lot.

"To say that action is the cause of hope is to encourage people—fools like Nicky—to thrash around and do something, anything, rather than endure despair.

"This does not mean that we ought to be lazy. Obviously there is much that has to be done. But we ought to be careful, especially when we do something new. The Goddess has given us the intelligence we need to think about what we're doing, and she has given us the ability to distinguish between right and wrong. We can't expect any more from her. She will not rescue us from the consequences of our folly.

"What is needed—always—is patience and persistence and caution and trust. We must believe that the universe knows what it is doing, and that other people are not entirely stupid."

"But you don't trust Nick, do you?" said Anna.

Gwarha opened his mouth, but said nothing. Instead the air spoke. It was Ettin Per, summoning all of us.

We entered the room with blank walls: Anna first, then Gwarha, then me. The women looked up.

Per said, "Nicky, you translate. Tell the woman of Perez to sit down next to me."

Gwarha and I settled into our former chairs. The circle was complete now. There were no empty places.

"I will take care of introductions," he said in his deep soft voice. The edge was gone now. He was no longer furious. Tired, maybe, like Anna and the old lady, who seemed to be sagging a little.

But Petali straightened up after the introductions were complete, and spoke. "We have a solution to three of our problems. The first-in-front problem remains. It is you, Perez Anna."

I translated.

"You said I wouldn't be harmed," said Anna. "And I want to know about Nicholas. What's going to happen to him?"

"Do you understand how serious this is?" asked Petali. "He has given information to you that we—that our men— do not want humanity to have. If he were one of our own People, Ettin Gwarha would have asked him to kill himself. He would have offered to do so, without being asked."

The old lady paused, and I translated. Anna looked worried.

"If this story becomes known, he will die. This is beyond question," Petali said. "If we can manage to keep the situation in the family, then I think we'll be able to save Nicky."

Anna asked, "Is this true?"

"More or less," I said. "Though you have to remember that Ettin Petali is trying to cut a deal. What kind I don't know at present."

"Be careful," the general said in the language of Ettin.

"What do you want?" said Anna to the old lady.

"We want you to keep quiet. Don't tell the other humans anything about this."

"I can't promise," Anna said. "If Military Intelligence gets hold of me, I'll tell everything I know."

"A pity that she isn't a man," said the old lady after she heard this answer. "There could be an accident."

"But not to a woman, Mother," said Ettin Sai.

"I haven't lost my mind yet. I know right behavior."

Ettin Per said, "We will have to make certain that you stay here for the time being. If you cooperate, I think that can be arranged. We'll insist that we have to negotiate with you."

"For how long?" asked Anna.

"We don't know," said Per. "But remember the situation is dangerous. If you don't cooperate, Nicky will almost certainly die. Ettin Gwarha will be forced back. Humanity will be dealing with the son of Lugala and his repulsive mother. If they take over the negotiations, there will be a war. Nicky has told you that humanity will not win."

I translated.

"Nick?" said Anna.

"How can you ask me to comment? I'm in the middle of all this, and I'm having trouble being objective."

She waited.

The general said, "Things may not turn out as badly as my aunt suggests, but I don't think they will turn out well if I'm discredited, and I will be if this story comes out."

Gwarha always has such a clear sense of his importance.

"We are asking for a year or two," said Ettin Sai in English. "We think."

"And you're asking me to side with you against my own species," said Anna.

"Yes," said Ettin Sai.

"Nicky is almost certainly right," said the general. "If there is a war, we'll be forced to decide that you are not people. We have no choice. We cannot break the rules if you are people. But if you break the rules, as you clearly will, then we'll be destroyed. Not simply the perimeter; we could endure that; but the center.

"In order to survive, in order to save our homes, we will have to fight you as we would a—" He switched to his own language and spoke one word.

I translated. "Small vermin. A destructive bug."

"Mem, I assure you, we will destroy you," the general said. "If we have to."

"What's the alternative?" asked Anna.

The women shifted position. Like Gwarha getting ready to discuss morality, they made themselves comfortable. They had the beginning of a deal.

"The question of what humans are has to be resolved," said Ettin Per. "And it is not a question for men. They have never decided who is a person and who isn't. That task has always belonged to women. We are the ones who examine newborn children and decide whether or not they are going to become real people. We are the ones who examine those who have fallen sick and decide whether a true spirit remains.

"We have learned how to look in back of appearance. That is our skill, and not a skill of men. They cannot possibly decide this question."

Ettin Petali said, "We will take the problem back to the Weaving, away from the son of Lugala. Let the woman of Lugala follow us! We can deal with her at home."

"And we are going to take Nicky," said Ettin Sai in English.

"What?" I said.

The general said, "Why?"

Ettin Per answered. "We have to get him away from the perimeter and away from the other humans. Surely you see that, Gwarha. And he is our first-in-front expert on humanity. Obviously, the Weaving is going to have to consult him. So he will come with us, and we'll keep an eye on him, and no one will be surprised."

"Do you want me to translate any of this?" I asked.

"No," said Ettin Petali. She looked at her grandson. "This has to be done. If it is decided that he's a person—I make no promises, but we'll try to find a way to send him back."

"And if not?" asked Gwarha, his voice harsh.

"We will not look that far ahead," said Per.

I'll probably be put down like a dog that's developed the habit of biting. A lovely thought.

"What is going on?" asked Anna.

"A family dispute."

The general looked at me. "Nicky—"

"Can you think of any other way out?"

"No."

"Maybe this is for the best. I've told you for years that the frontmen were fucking up. Maybe the women can do better."

"Of course we can," said the old lady.

Per leaned forward. "Ask the woman of Perez if she is willing to keep quiet and stay at this station, until we have a grip on the situation at home."

I translated.

Anna said, "What do you think?"

"Do it."

"Okay. I will. But if this turns out all right, I want to be the first human after you on the *hwarhath* home planet."

As soon as the old lady heard that an agreement had been reached, she leaned back, sagging and growing smaller. All at once she was a bundle of bones covered by white fur. The splendid embroidered robe looked grotesque now. Her eyes closed. Her daughters looked anxious.

"Mother?" said Per.

"Do you want to take a nap?" asked Aptsi.

"Get these people—if they are people—out of here. I have done as much as I am able to."

We left. Vaihar was still in the corridor. The general dismissed him. Then Gwarha and I walked Anna to her rooms.

She stopped at her door and said, "This has been an outstandingly awful day."

"You can thank Nicholas for it," the general said.

"You really do speak English very well," she said. "I'm going to have a drink and then take a nap like your grandmother, who probably grinds bones to make her bread."

"Fee fi," I said.

She added, "Fo fum," and went in.

"What was that about?" asked the general.

"A children's story, and a way of reminding each other that we are both human."

We went back through the station. I told him about Jack and the Beanstalk.

"Hah," he said at the end. "It's interesting how similar you are to us, except in the areas where you are different. This story is like our stories about the Clever Little Boy and the Clever Little Girl."

We reached his rooms.

"There's a question I want to ask you, First-Defender, and I really don't want to be overheard."

"Do you have to ask it now?"

"How much time do we have?"

Blue eyes regarded me, the pupils like bars. He exhaled softly and palmed the door. "Come in."

He settled on the couch. I found a comfortable section of wall in a place where I could watch his expression.

"Ask your question."

"I have never known you to do anything dishonorable until now. You've broken a promise to me, and you have broken one of the rules of war. I'd like to know why."

"Surely it's obvious. I thought you were going to betray me." He paused, then added, "and the People."

"Why did you think that?"

"Does it matter? I was right."

I waited. He glanced down.

"Gwarha, when you are ashamed or embarrassed, you might as well wear a sign."

He glanced up, meeting my gaze. "I have been wondering about you and Anna. She isn't a relative. This story about the kinship between Kansas and Illinois is a lie."

At that point the money dropped, and I knew what he was thinking. "You stupid piece of shit."

"I have been remembering you are human." His voice was plaintive.

"What were you looking for, when you put bugs in our

rooms? Evidence of treason? Or evidence that I was crawling in bed with Anna?''

He stared at the carpet.

"You fool, I don't find *any* human sexually interesting. I sit in that meeting room and look across at the human men and think, 'I ought to find these guys attractive.' But I don't. I can remember that humans used to seem beautiful to me. Not anymore. Not in comparison to you and Vaihar and even poor Matsehar. But they are my people, and Anna is my friend, and I am too angry to continue this conversation.''

I went to the door. He stayed on the couch, shoulders hunched and head down, silent.

Time for a walk. I took my usual route, away from the part of the station that is inhabited.

I told Anna the station is mostly empty: a shell. This may be true, but a network of corridors covers the entire inner surface of the station cylinder.

Some go the length of the cylinder. I prefer them when I'm feeling trapped. I can look ahead and see rows of lights going into the distance.

Others ring the in-theory-empty central space. I don't like them as well. The curve of the floor and ceiling is obvious, and there are no long vistas.

It's possible the corridors are left over from construction. They are usually empty and always cold. But why are they all kept pressurized, and why do so many of the doors have security emblems?

I know you're not going to answer these questions, Gwarha. In all likelihood, I'll be gone from the station before you read this. I'll tell you my theory.

The doors lead to airlocks, and beyond the airlocks is another one of Advancer Shen Walha's ugly surprises. What kind I'm not certain. Maybe a *luat*-class interstellar warship with all its attendant scouts and scavengers. When I'm walking in the corridors, I imagine it floating in the middle of a station devoted to diplomacy: huge, blunt and brutal-looking, its little scouts like nursing cubs.

The scavengers are (almost certainly) on top: flat and spear-blade-shaped, like scales covering the *luat*'s wide back.

That's how I imagine it, Gwar: an armored monster-mother, like the one in the story that Tsai Ama Ul told. If events take a bad turn, it can be used to evacuate the women or to destroy the human starship.

Maybe I'm wrong. Maybe there's nothing beyond those doors. You've told me often that I have too much imagination.

I walked for some time, feeling angry. I'm not going to tell you what I was thinking: the ideas that come from anger, petty and self-defending. Finally I came to an area where the ceiling rods were dark; only the little floor-level lights were on. I stopped at an intersection. One corridor ran straight in both directions. The other curved gently up. The air was even colder than usual and smelled of the chemicals used in laying carpet.

I began to do a set of *hanatsin* exercises: slow ones, concentrating on getting each motion exactly right. That helped. I went on to the second set, which is even slower, and then to the third set, which incorporates held positions. It's usually at this point that I get my breathing right.

In the third set, minor irritations vanish. In the fourth set, one is no longer aware of self. At the end of the fifth set, one has reached the proper condition of rest. The practitioner no longer moves. He is empty, open, quiescent, ready and *chulmar*, a word I've never been able to translate properly. When it's used in ordinary conversation, it means being pious or having a good sense of humor. When it's used in *hanatsin*, I just don't know.

I reached the end of the fifth set and stayed there for a while, then came to. The corridors hadn't changed, and I was cold. I glanced around and found the cameras that watched the intersection: two of them, high up and almost hidden by the shadows. There were probably guys in some security post, looking at their screens and wondering what Sanders Nicholas was up to this time. If he wanted to practice *hanatsin,* why didn't he go to a *hanatsin* room?

A place for everything and everything in its place, as my father used to tell me, speaking about the toolshed and his library.

When I got back to my rooms, the amber light was on next to the door that led to Gwarha's quarters. The door was unlocked. He wanted me to come over. I was no longer angry, but I was tired, and some of the mood created by the *hanatsin* exercises remained. I didn't want to lose it, listening to Gwarha accuse or explain. I took a shower and went to bed.

There was a message on my computer in the morning: from Gwarha in the *hwarhath* main language, very formal and very polite.

He would prefer that I have no contact of any kind with the humans.

He would prefer that I not access any file that required a key, except my own personal files, of course.

He would prefer that I not go to my office.

There had been, he explained carefully, no change in my status. I still had my security rating. He had issued no orders. (Nor could he, if we wanted to keep what happened private.) But as a favor to him, could I please spend the day doing something that was harmless?

Sure, I told the computer.

He knew I liked to walk in the empty sections of the station, and he knew how important walking was for me. But could I please confine myself to the parts of the station that were currently in use?

And he would be grateful if I'd join him in his quarters in the evening.

Sure, again.

\*   \*   \*

I've spent the day working on my journal, trying to get everything down before I start to forget it and before the information starts to change, as it always seems to. There are problems with the human brain as a data-storage unit.

I can tinker later, changing words, trying to make things sound better. Though that's dangerous: reality turns into art.

The light next to Gwarha's door has just turned amber. He's home and waiting for me to come in. Most likely he's gotten out a jug of *halin* and is sitting on his couch with a cup in his hand and the jug in front of him, feeling hurt and sorry for himself. The little shit. How could he spy on me?

Why did I betray him and the People? All I can see right now is how stupid I've been.

And which of us is more of a rat? Which one has done the greater injury?

Not that it matters. I think the women of Ettin are going to pull me out of here quickly. If Gwarha and I are going to make peace, it will have to be now. Maybe the Goddess will be kind to us, and we'll have time later to argue and recriminate: time for a hundred visions and revisions. But at the moment I want peace.

For some reason I'm thinking of Anna's animals: the giant jellyfish, caught between fear and lust, desperately signaling their good intentions while poisonous tendrils float around them.

*I am me. I intend no harm. Let me come near. Let me touch you. Let us exchange what passes for love.*

After I finish this sentence, I'm going to turn off the computer and get up and go to the door.

From the journal of Sanders Nicholas, etc.

# PART III

## RETURNING

# I

➤➤➤ NOTHING HAPPENED FOR several days, at least as far as Anna knew. She watched the male negotiations, which continued as before, and spent time with her human colleagues. None of the *hwarhath* called her. She didn't hear from Nick, and he put in no appearance at the negotiations.

Remain calm, she told herself.

Her escort was Vaihar or a new young man, a Chaichik with lovely smoke-grey fur. He spoke English with a thick accent and the usual alien courtesy. His eyes, which she rarely saw—he kept them properly averted—were pale grey, almost colorless.

"What's happened to Matsehar?" she asked Vaihar.

"Don't you like Chaichik An?"

"He appears to be a sweetie, but I miss Matsehar's blow-by-blow description of the most recent scene in his play."

Vaihar laughed softly. "He has almost finished the play, and he's run into trouble at the end. He asked for time off, so he can devote himself to writing."

"And that's all right? He's excused from his duty for that?"

"The play is his duty, Anna. Remember that he belongs to the Art Corps. His assignment here is only temporary."

A couple of days later, Vaihar met her at the entrance to the human quarters. "We have to make a—what is the term?—detour on the way back to your rooms."

"Why?"

"The first-defender has asked to see you."

No question about which first-defender. When Vaihar spoke, he always meant Ettin Gwarha.

"Why?" Anna asked again.

"I am a junior officer and not a relation. The first-defender doesn't tell me what is in his mind."

He led her to Ettin Gwarha's office, which looked the same as when she'd last seen it, except that now there was only a single empty chair in front of the table. Ettin Gwarha sat behind the table, dressed as a space cadet. "You needn't remain, Holder. I'll see that Mem Perez gets back to her quarters."

Vaihar left. The door slid closed, and Ettin Gwarha nodded toward the empty chair. "Please sit down."

Anna settled into the chair.

He folded his hands and looked at her. The room was brightly lit, and his pupils had contracted to narrow black bands, surrounded by blue. The eyes bothered her more than anything else about the *hwarhath,* except maybe their hands.

"I've been neglecting you, mem. I apologize. A lot has been happening."

She waited.

"A ship has arrived. It will take my female relatives home; Lugala Minti has decided to go with them. Tsai Ama Ul and her translator will remain here; no woman should be alone on the perimeter." He paused briefly, still regarding her. "Nicky will go with my aunts. You and I will be left here to—what is the term?—hold the fort." He unfolded his hands and picked up something that looked like a metal pencil. "This is a situation that makes me very uncomfortable. A woman should not be involved with the struggles on the perimeter."

"But I am."

"Yes, and therefore we need to discuss what is to be

done. Your role and mine. I think we've already gone over most of it in our previous discussion, the one with my female relatives; but I want to be absolutely certain that we both understand and agree."

He was speaking more carefully than usual, more slowly and with a pedantic precision. As he talked, his long, narrow furry hands turned and re-turned the metal stylus.

"My aunts will make certain that other women are sent out here to speak with you. Most likely, they will be people sent by the Weaving to ask questions about humanity. If the Weaving is going to decide what humans are, it will have to gather information. These women will provide a reason for you to stay in *hwarhath* space. Speak to them as honestly as you can. If you feel there is something you can't—in honor—say, then tell them so. The People understand honor.

"But please be careful. I am not sure I can explain to you how dangerous this situation is for Nicky and me and my aunts. If you have any problems or questions, call me. Hai Atala Vaihar is absolutely reliable, and Eh Matsehar is a good friend to Nicky; no one has ever questioned the integrity of the woman of Tsai Ama. But I do not want any of them knowing what has happened.

"That's as much of a plan as I have, Mem Perez. You will talk to the women who come out here. I will continue the negotiations. We'll hope that everything goes well at the center, and that no one finds out what has happened." He laid the stylus down and refolded his hands, meeting her gaze again. He had not been kidding. This was one extremely uncomfortable *hwarhath*.

"I feel as if I've been tested like a hero in one of the old plays, and I failed. I could not let Nicky be destroyed."

"What should you have done?" asked Anna.

"Told him to kill himself or turned him in. Either one would have been acceptable, though the first would have done less damage to my career, provided—of course—that no one found out why he'd killed himself."

She shook her head. "Nope. You'd still have been left with the problem of me. I wouldn't have cut a deal with you, except to save Nick. The complexity of the bind you're in is quite wonderful, First-Defender. I can't see any way out that preserves honor."

"You sound amused. Is that right? Or am I hearing anger?"

"I don't have much use for concepts of personal honor. I think when people start talking about their personal integrity, they are trying to distract attention from their lack of compassion and ordinary human decency." She paused for a moment, considering. "And their lack of belief in any kind of moral or political system that says the community is important and other people matter. This is only my opinion, and it's limited by what I know. Where I come from, the people who talk about honor tend to be right-wing assholes."

"This is interesting," he said after a moment. "Maybe it explains something about humanity."

"We have a lot of right-wing assholes," Anna said. "And at least some people who'd understand your concern with honor. Don't think everyone is like me."

He was silent, looking past her at the tapestry on the far wall: the fire and the ring of swords.

"I have another concern," she said finally.

"Yes."

"I don't like the idea of humanity being judged in absentia."

"I don't understand."

"The Weaving is going to decide whether or not we are people. But we don't know about it. We aren't going to have a chance to defend ourselves. That isn't right."

"Hah! Now you speak of rightness, after telling me that you don't believe in honor."

"I believe in justice, at least part of the time; and I certainly believe in people having a say."

"You want the Weaving to tell your government what is going on. You want the Confederation to be able to present an argument for humanity."

"Yes."

Ettin Gwarha sighed. "I'll ask my aunts. But I am not certain this will be possible, mem. In order to explain to your people what the problem is, we'd have to explain what we are trying to keep secret. Remember that Nick will be on the home world, and the Weaving will send people here to speak with you, and we do have human prisoners. Humanity will not go entirely unrepresented."

"I'm not sure that I want that kind of responsibility," Anna said.

"You think a group of human politicians can do a better job than you and Nicky?"

"I didn't say that. I said I didn't want the responsibility."

"Maybe you will have to take it." He stood up, and she began to rise. He lifted his hand in a gesture that clearly meant "stop." "Please wait here." He walked to the door, which opened, and went out.

Nicholas came in past him. The door closed. Nick strolled to the general's table and leaned against the front of it. He was dressed in his usual tan civvies, his hands in the pockets of a new jacket which looked identical to the one he'd cut up. His face was paler than usual; his expression was remote and grave. After a moment, he took his hands out of his pockets. He glanced back to make sure the area behind him was clear, then lifted himself onto the table and sat there, his hands on the table's edge, his feet swinging.

"Are you ever planning to grow up?" Anna asked.

He grinned, and the remote expression vanished. "To become what? A pillar of the community? And which community? I think not. Ettin Gwarha decided we ought to have a chance to speak before I leave."

"Why?"

"I didn't ask him. I'm not going to question the pedigree of a *sul* that's been given as a gift."

"A what?"

"It's a domestic animal, used for hunting, about the size of a shetland pony. You don't ride them. You send them after whatever you're hunting. They have teeth like this." He held his hands about fifteen centimeters apart. "The teeth are sharp; and there really is a proverb about how it's bad manners to ask too many questions about the breeding of a *sul* that has come as a gift."

"Ah," said Anna.

He put his hands back down on the table. "I ought to thank you. If you had not agreed to help the Ettin out, Gwarha would have had no choice. He'd have had to throw me to the wolves. I'm using animal metaphors. I wonder why? Maybe because I'm not entirely certain of my status."

"Have you straightened things out with the general?"

Nick smiled briefly. "We have a truce, and we have begun negotiations. There's a lot to forgive. I'm really angry that he bugged my rooms and your rooms, and I can't say that he's especially happy that I turned a second time. The damn *t* word. It keeps coming back to haunt me."

Anna waited for him to go on. He didn't. "My mother was a psychologist. Did I tell you that?"

"It's in your file," Nick said.

"She told me in every relationship, if it goes on long enough, things happen—things are done—which are unforgivable, and then the problem becomes, How do you forgive what can't be forgiven? How do you get past betrayal and pain? You have to find a way, she told me, or you end up alone."

"Ah." Nick looked past her at the tapestry that had fascinated Ettin Gwarha. "Why haven't you ever married? Not that it's any of my business."

Anna shrugged. "No luck; or maybe a solitary nature; or maybe I've never accepted how imperfect people are."

After a moment he said, "I think the general and I will be able to work something out. The aunts are a help. They keep hammering at Gwarha. How could he ask any man, even a human, to turn away from a female relative? That's what they see, when they look at the situation—a man acting to protect a female relation; and as far as they're concerned, that's right behavior. You should have heard Ettin Per. 'May the Goddess forfend that any son of Ettin ever do what you expected Sanders Nicholas to do.' "

Anna laughed. "What about Matsehar? Have you talked with him?"

He nodded. "I told him something was going on, and he should keep as far away as possible. He owed it to his art. The little shit started talking about loyalty and honor, as if he hadn't been attacking them for the past ten years in his plays. 'You're my friend, Nicky. I can't leave you alone to deal with whatever is happening.'

"So we had an argument, and now he's sulking. When he starts coming out of it, tell him—hell, tell him I love him, and he should do what he's good at, and let me deal with my own problems."

"You really want me to say that?"

"You like him, Anna. Gwarha doesn't. I can't use Gwarha as a messenger. He'd deliver any message I gave him with meticulous care and obvious disapproval." Nick slid down off the table. "I think we ought to end this. Gwarha's waiting to escort you."

She stood. He gave her a quick hug and kiss, then stepped back. "*Courage, ma brave.* I think—I hope—this is going to work out."

She couldn't figure out what to say. She grabbed one of

his hands and squeezed hard, then let go and walked to the
door. It slid open. Ettin Gwarha was in the anteroom, his
stance alert and relaxed, as if it wouldn't be any problem
for him to wait all day.

"Mem?"

She went with him back to the women's quarters. He
escorted her all the way to her room. She opened the door
and hesitated, then asked, "Can you come in?"

"Yes."

He did. The hologram was on and showed the hill
above the human research station on Reed 1935-C. This
time it was late afternoon. Rain fell slanting. A few lights
shone among the buildings. The mating bay was dark: no
messages gleamed in the steel grey water.

Anna waited till the door had closed, then said, "Nick
thinks things are going to work out."

Ettin Gwarha made the coughing noise that was *hwarhath* laughter. "There is no way to push Nicky back. He
steps to the side and then he's ready to go forward again.
He always thinks he can see a new path in front of him."
He was silent for a minute or two, looking at the rain
falling on Reed 1935-C. "I don't know, Mem Perez. If we
are careful and lucky, if my aunts are skillful, if my grandmother collects the obligations that have been owed her for
sixty years and more, if the Goddess decides not to give in
to her love of malicious jokes—then, maybe everything
will turn out. All we can do is to go forward."

He paused, then said, "I ought to get back to my office.
If you want to talk, if you have any problem, tell Hai Atala
Vaihar to get hold of me. I will respond."

Anna said thanks.

He walked to her door and then looked back. "And I'd
better get you some new holograms. You can't want to
spend the next year looking at that scene."

# II

➤➤➤ THE SHIP LEFT, and Matsehar reappeared a few mornings later. The play was done, he said as they walked through the corridors of the station. "No thanks to Nicky. It wasn't easy for me to concentrate on my writing after the quarrel we had."

Anna gave him Nick's message. It was typical, said Mats. Nicky always became affectionate after he became stubborn. "He pushes you away from him, and then he talks about love and friendship, as if any of that will make up for what he's done."

Anna kept quiet.

"And now he's gone, just when I needed his opinion on the new play." He glanced at her sideways. "Do you think you'd be willing to read it?"

"I don't know your language."

"You really ought to learn it, Anna. It's not easy, but it's very beautiful! In the meantime, I can make a translation. I really would like your opinion."

How could she resist the look he gave her? Like a wistful werewolf. Poor fellow! He wanted so badly to show his play to a human. Anna nodded.

"It won't be as good as the version in my own language," said Mats. "But I have a firm grip on English. It won't be able to wriggle free."

"Uh-huh," said Anna.

It took him a couple of weeks to get the play to her: fast work for a man who was not a professional translator. The title was *The Gate of Punishment*. She spent an evening reading.

He'd redesigned the play so it centered around the gate to Macbeth's castle, which was also the gate to hell. There was a doorman, who was sometimes an ordinary human being, a comic drunk, and sometimes a monster or demon. All the characters in the play moved around the door and through it in a kind of dance: witches and warriors, ghosts, the terrible mother and the murdered frontman. At times they spoke to the doorman. At other times he described what was happening as they danced.

Jesus Maria, this would be a thing to see! She imagined the witches in black robes dancing around Macbeth in blood-red armor, and the monologue in which the doorman (now a demon) described the banquet. Of course that would be done offstage. The *hwarhath* were bored by eating; or was it disgusted?

She didn't stop reading until she reached the end. Macbeth lay dead in the middle of the stage. The doorman, dressed at the moment in the splendid garb of a supernatural being, pulled off his robe and dropped it. Underneath was the drab costume of the human doorman. His task was over, he told the audience. The gate had become once again an ordinary doorway, which led nowhere except into the castle. Remember the rules of hospitality, he said, and the evil consequences of too much ambition. He picked up his jug of *halin* and shambled off. *Finito*.

"Wow," said Anna, and turned off the play. She stared at the wall opposite, not seeing the grey wood. Instead she visualized the gate and the doorman, changing back and forth from a human in dark clothing to a glittering gold-and-silver demon. The stage directions said the actor was to increase in size when he became a demon. How was that done? Padding in the demon robe? Or special shoes? She'd ask Matsehar.

The English was awkward in places, and it was odd to

read the famous monologue, Macbeth's final speech: "To-morrow, and tomorrow, and tomorrow." Going through the *hwarhath* language had changed it. It was like a famil-iar object seen through water or in a distorting mirror.

Amazing! She went to bed.

The next day Matsehar was her escort. "Did you read it? What did you think?"

"Why are you walking me back and forth? What are you doing in this station? You are some kind of genius."

He stopped in the corridor and looked at her, their gazes meeting. "Does that mean you liked it?"

"It's wonderful. It's splendid."

He must have remembered they weren't related. He glanced down quickly. "I'm here to study humans, and I am acting as your escort because Nicky asked me. I think he wanted someone he trusted, and someone who does not play politics, and someone who is not repelled by the known habits of humanity."

Heterosexuality rearing its ugly head again.

They resumed walking.

"I had to compress it," Matsehar said. "Your plays are so long! I tried to make it simple. There is power in sim-plicity, and the play is about power. Hah! It rushes like a torrent of blood!"

He was settling into a lecture on the play. Clearly a man who appreciated his own work.

"What has to be kept—aside from the violence—is the feeling of horror and strangeness; and the moral has to be kept and made obvious. Even the stupidest person in the audience has to understand the play is about greed and bad manners."

"Bad manners?" asked Anna.

"Can you think of a worse host than Macbeth?"

Anna laughed. "I guess I can't. So that's how you'd describe *Macbeth*? This is a play about a man who was a terrible host?"

"Yes, and it's a play about violence that has not been contained within a moral framework."

They reached the entrance to the human quarters. Matsehar stopped and frowned. "I'm not happy with my translation of the title. 'Punishment' is a good strong harsh word. I like the sound of it. But it doesn't have exactly the right meaning. *The Gate of Retribution* might be more accurate, though the sound is less good. Or maybe *The Gate of Consequences.*" He tilted his head, obviously thinking. "No. I will stay with 'punishment.' It's the right name for a gate that opens into hell. An interesting concept. We have nothing like it. Maybe we ought to. Our ghosts and malevolent spirits wander free and get into dreams and make the living uncomfortable. We could use a repository."

"Do you believe in ghosts?" asked Anna.

"Yes and no," said Matsehar. "But whether or not they are real, it would be nice to have a place to keep them."

Damn these people! Had they never heard of the excluded middle? How could he answer yes *and* no?

A few days after that, the first delegation from the Weaving arrived at the station: five large women of middle age, dressed in rich robes. They brought a new translator: a tall, gaunt woman with steel grey fur and an air of absolute seriousness. Her name was Eh Leshali, a first cousin to Eh Matsehar.

According to Leshali, Matsehar had told his relatives to learn English. "As many of us as possible, he said. It's the only piece of advice that Matsehar has ever given any of us. He said it was likely to be a useful skill. So we did it. Mats is odd, but no one would ever say that he is stupid."

Now, that was true, though Anna didn't find him especially odd. In a lot of ways, he seemed to be the most normal alien she had encountered, maybe because he lacked the certainty the others had. Mats saw the universe as full of ambiguity. Vaihar didn't; he knew right from wrong; and her sense of Ettin Gwarha was that he could have seen the universe as Mats did, but refused to, like a man averting his eyes from something huge and terrible.

But maybe she was wrong. What did she really know about the aliens? More than when she'd arrived at the station, but a lot less than the *hwarhath* women knew about humanity. Anna was surprised at the amount of information they had. After she thought about it, she realized there was no good reason for her surprise. For more than twenty years Nicholas Sanders had been doing his best to spill all the beans.

The aliens had plenty of facts. Now they wanted an explanation. How could humanity be this way? What did it feel like to be a human? What was it like to be a woman on Earth?

She answered as best she could. At least she didn't have to worry about letting go of information that might be strategic. For the most part, she found herself explaining things like child care or human ethical philosophy or her own work in animal behavior.

Harmless, said Cyprian McIntosh.

More women arrived at the station, and the first group left. Tsai Ama Ul went with them.

She was needed at home, Ettin Gwarha told Anna. The discussion of humanity was progressing, though no one could tell how it might end, and the women of Ettin decided to bring in every possible ally.

The two translators stayed behind. By this time, Anna had gotten friendly with Ama Tsai Indil. But she wasn't crazy about Eh Leshali, who appeared to be absolutely humorless.

Women continued to arrive. Some stayed a few days, peered at her as if she were something truly strange—an exotic bird, a thing from under a rock—asked a couple of brief questions and left. For the most part, these were politicians, Indil said. The scientists and philosophers and theologians stayed longer. When Anna talked with them, she had real conversations.

Now and then she spoke with Ettin Gwarha in his office or her rooms, places where they could talk safely.

His aunts had raised the question of whether humanity ought to be invited to defend itself before the Weaving; the *hwarhath* government decided no. They were reluctant to bring humans to the home world, and they really didn't want to explain what was so frightening to them about human behavior.

Anna was it, along with Nicholas and the various human prisoners: a motley collection of spies and career military and people like her, scientists who'd been caught up somehow in the war.

The discussion in the Weaving was fierce, the general told her. His aunts were not yet willing to predict the outcome of any vote.

"They do not tell me everything, mem, and they tell me even less when sending messages. There is no such thing as a line of communication that is absolutely secure, especially if it reaches to the perimeter."

It was creepy when the People said things like that, reminding her of how competitive they were, how violent, how disrespectful of personal freedom and privacy. Nonetheless, she liked them. Why? Was it their fur? Or their large ears? Their honesty? Or their reluctance to hurt women and children, a trait which she found extremely endearing?

The *hwarhath* were still being careful about what they told her, though the women were less careful than the men. Nonetheless, she was learning about their culture. The questions the women asked her were informative, and so were their responses to her answers.

Maybe they didn't entirely understand what she had done for a living, before the events on Reed 1935-C. She was trained to observe societies made of animals who did not use language. There was more than one way to communicate, though verbal animals tended to forget this. There was motion, posture, intonation and glance. The *hwarhath* were very physical. The women did not have to speak in words in order to give her information. Anna felt the excitement that always came when she was finally able to make sense of her observations.

The other members of the human team were getting restless. No one had expected the negotiations to go on this long; the last set had been over comparatively quickly. Charlie said he couldn't ask the Confederation government to call them home. Too much progress had been made. The negotiators had worked out all the details of a prisoner exchange, and were now discussing ways for the two species to police their borders in the event of a treaty. Not easy, Charlie said. The borders went through too many dimensions, and they were not continuous in a way that was understandable to ordinary people.

How, he asked, does one police something that one cannot visualize or imagine?

Anna had no answer for this question.

Midway through the year, Charlie asked for permission to send part of his team back to human space and bring in new people. He needed physicists.

The two frontmen looked uncomfortable and said they needed to discuss the problem. When they came back a day later, Lugala Tsu said, "If we let you send your ship home, the position of this station will be known. It was built for these meetings, and we can afford to lose it. The men in it can all be replaced, even Ettin Gwarha and myself." He glanced sideways at the general. "Isn't this so?"

"The place of frontmen is in front," said Ettin Gwarha. His tone was one of comfortable agreement.

"But there are women here," said Lugala Tsu. "And we cannot risk them."

Very well, said Charlie. End the discussions between
Anna and the women. The humans would send Anna back
to human space. The *hwarhath* could send their women to
a place of safety.

Oh, shit, thought Anna, watching from the observation
room.

The two frontmen looked at one another. Ettin Gwarha
inclined his head. Lugala Tsu leaned forward and spoke in
his deep harsh voice.

Anna waited for the translation.

"There are things you don't understand, Khamvongsa
Charlie. We don't tell the women what to do. We can relay
your suggestion to them, but I don't think they'll pay a lot
of attention. What they are doing is important. What they
decide about humanity will influence and possibly decide
what happens in this room. If they stop, I don't see any
way for us to go on."

Charlie looked puzzled, and Anna got the impression
he didn't really understand what Lugala Tsu was telling
him. Finally he said, "If the problem is our ship, we'll be
willing to go on one of your ships."

Ettin Gwarha leaned forward slightly. This was something to consider, he told the human team. Frontman
Lugala and he would have to talk.

The two men were getting along better, Anna decided.
Maybe is was the absence of Lugala Tsu's mother. Without
her, the frontman seemed more malleable, less certain.

The meeting ended, and the humans had lunch: noo-
dles and pickled vegetables. They were starting to run low
on supplies.

"If we can't get out of here soon, we're all going to
have to get hardship pay," said Sten. "The union will
insist on it."

"As well they should," said Dy Singh.

"Don't worry about that," said Charlie. "What I'm
puzzled by is this: if we had wanted to send the location of

this station home, we could have done it in a diplomatic pouch. That's obvious. They must've seen it."

Cyprian McIntosh nodded. "I think they don't want us to see whatever they've been doing at the various transfer points along our route. I assume they've moved equipment in, certainly to the first transfer point, in case our people decided to follow us."

Charlie thought for a moment. "We'll press to go home in one of their ships. I won't be going, of course. This is the most important work I've ever done. But the rest of you—" He looked at Anna. "Don't feel obligated to stay. If the conversations with the women are so important, we can bring in new people."

Anna shook her head. "I'm not giving up this chance."

"You don't miss Earth?" asked Etienne.

"No."

"I can't understand that," said Etienne.

"You haven't spent enough time on the edge of the Con," said Cyprian McIntosh. "There are plenty of humans who'd be just as happy if they never went back to Earth or even to the Earth system. I'm right, aren't I, Anna?"

"Yes."

"Though most of them still like to be around other humans." There was an edge to Cyprian's voice. He had made advances toward Anna—a wonderful old term! It reminded Anna of the behavior of many of the animals she'd watched, who actually did advance and retreat in the early stages of courtship. A couple of the other men on the diplomatic team had indicated a similar interest in her. It was hardly surprising, given the amount of time they had spent in the *hwarhath* station.

Charlie had discouraged visits to the human starship. The *hwarhath* might become uneasy if there was a lot of traveling back and forth. In any case, the women on the ship had formed their own relationships with other members of the crew. For all intents and purposes, Anna was the only human female in light-centuries. Uncomfortable, but she had been in similar situations while doing field-work. Her answer to everyone had been no. She liked Cyprian, but he reminded her a bit too much of the people in MI; the other men did not interest her; and the human rooms were bugged. She got chills, thinking of someone like Ettin Gwarha listening to—for all she knew, watch-ing—a recording of her having sex with a man.

No. There was more to life than desire and its gratifica-tion. She was not going to ruin her credibility with the aliens.

Two days later, the frontmen gave their answer. If the humans were willing to travel in the *hwarhath* ship, and be closely confined during the trip, they could go, and more humans could be brought back. But no other alternative was possible. The station and the women had to be pro-tected.

The human team agreed, and most of them left. Charlie stayed, as did Cyprian.

"I'm going to see this through to the end, and if I'm lucky I'll be home in time for next year's Test Matches. But I have to tell you—" The island rhythm in his voice grew stronger. "The loveliest things in the universe are green grass and white flannels and the women of the Carib-bean." He paused for a moment. "And music, island music. I've been dreaming of cricket and carnival."

Anna laughed.

For a while, they were alone: Anna and Charlie and Cyprian and Haxu, the little translator. Then the *hwarhath* ship returned with a load of physicists and fresh new dip-lomats. Anna felt remote from these unfamiliar humans. Their news did not especially interest her. What did she care about the latest hit series on the drama nets? Her interest in politics, especially Earth politics, had never been strong, and there was always a new environmental crisis. After a while, it was hard to get upset or angry. Humanity survived as best it could, with intelligence and courage, cursing the ancestors who had made this mess and left it for future generations to deal with.

Soon after the humans arrived, a group of *hwarhath* women left. Eh Matsehar went with them, called home by something he could not discuss. Eh Leshali stayed behind, looking satisfied, though she would not say by what.

Anna went to Ettin Gwarha.

"What's going on? Mats left without telling me anything, and Eh Leshali looks like the cat that ate the canary."

The general frowned and asked for an explanation. He knew about cats, a small domestic killer of vermin, but what was a canary? A kind of vermin? In what sense could Eh Leshali be said to look like a vermin eater that had just done its job?

Anna explained about cats and canaries.

"Hah," said the general and explained about Mats.

The Weaving had decided they needed information about human morality as it was depicted in human art. They wanted to see all the plays of Shakespeare William that had been translated into the *hwarhath* main language; Eh Matsehar was going home to work on a Shakespeare festival.

Nick was going to handle the discussion with the audience after each play. Anna had a sudden wonderful vision of a theater full of furry matrons with Nick on the stage answering questions, strolling around, hands in pockets, or slouching in a chair.

"What will happen if the Weaving decides that humans are not people?"

"That's a large question," Ettin Gwarha replied.

"What will happen to Nick and you?"

They were in his office. The tapestry was gone, replaced by a hologram which showed a yellow desert under a dusty

green sky. Two moons hung in the sky, pale in the sunlight. One was a crescent. The other was half full. Ettin
Gwarha looked at the hologram, then at her, meeting her
gaze. "I think I will be able to save his life. But it's a
perversion to have sex with animals—though not, of
course, as bad as having sex with women or children; and
we do not keep pets on the perimeter; and dangerous animals cannot, of course, be allowed to wander free in areas
inhabited by people."

Her skin was crawling.

"I can tell from your expression that you find what I'm
saying unpleasant. That's what happens when you ask
questions, Mem Perez. You find things out and they are
often unpleasant. Leave the activities of men to men."

More women came and went. But the groups were
smaller now and contained no politicians. The Weaving
had the information it needed, Ettin Gwarha said. Now the
arguing would begin and the watching of Shakespeare.
That had been saved till last, to give the Art Corps time to
rehearse.

Anna began to feel nervous. She disliked waiting for
results of any kind of examination, and this was a really
big one. The entire species could flunk. She needed something to distract her. She got out her field notes from Reed
1935-C. For the past two—no, almost three—years she had
carried them around, thinking that she really had to get to
work on them. At first, she had been busy dealing with
human MI; after that was over, she had been busy trying
to find a way to make a living and get back in space; and
then she'd been busy here. And maybe she hadn't thought
there was any point. Her career had seemed ruined. But
that situation had changed. She already knew more about
the *hwarhath* women than any other human, except maybe
Nicholas Sanders, and if she made it to the *hwarhath* home
planet, she was going to be unbeatable. No human scholar
would be able to come close.

But she had to write and publish.

First, a few articles on the pseudosiphonophores, then the real stuff: the culture of the *hwarhath* women.

Anna settled down to work.

# III

➤➤➤ ONE AFTERNOON SHE returned to her rooms. As the door opened she smelled coffee.

Nick was standing in her living room, holding a mug, which he lifted as she came in. "Hello, Anna." His face was tanned, and his long curly hair was almost pure grey. A mustache covered his upper lip. It was thick and surprisingly dark.

She felt an odd joy that she could not articulate and said, "Why did you grow a mustache?"

"It was something to do. I felt the need to do something. What do you want? Coffee or wine?"

"Wine." She sat down and put her feet up. She'd been in the swimming pool provided for women, swimming laps until she was too tired to go on.

He went into a kitchen and came back with a glass, giving it to Anna. She took a sip: an okay red.

Nick went to the wall that faced her couch and leaned against it, touching his mustache with one finger. "Gwarha doesn't like this. I think he's in no position to complain about a little extra hair."

"Are you back for good, or is this a visit?"

"Every post that Gwarha has is temporary. So there is nothing permanent about my stay here. But I don't have to go back to the home planet, and I don't have to worry about ending in a zoo." He looked at her, smiling. "The Weaving made their decision. We are people."

Anna exhaled. She could feel tension easing. "That is excellent news."

He nodded. "It's an interesting decision. Humans are people, but not the same kind of people as the *hwarhath*. We have our own moral system, which is—the Weaving says—almost impossible for them to understand. We can't be judged by the standards which the People apply to one another. The Weaving has advised the frontmen to try for peace, since it would be difficult to fight a war with humanity.

"But they haven't eliminated violence as an option. They've asked their philosophers and theologians to consider the various moral and religious problems that would result from a war with humanity and to find solutions. Moral ways to fight us; or do I mean them? The People like to be prepared for any contingency, and the Weaving thinks this is a problem that's likely to come up more than once. If humans exist, who knows what other ugly surprises are waiting for the People among the stars? Maybe the next set of aliens will be even more disgusting. The People have to find new ways to think about morality and war."

"What does this mean for the Lugala?"

He laughed. "They lost badly. There were issues of prestige, and they have got damn little left at the moment. Lugala Minti should not have taken such a hard line. She tried to make it sound as if humans lived in damp places under rocks. She ended up sounding like a fool and a bigot. I'm going to refill my cup."

He carried the mug into her kitchen. When he came back steam rose from it. He settled in a chair and put his feet up on the same table she was using.

"I'm tired. I got in this morning." He sipped the coffee, then set the mug down. "And it hasn't been an easy year. I don't know if you ever dreamed of being important when you were a kid. You know, saving the universe, saving the

human species." He grinned. "A stupid dream. I thought
I'd grown out of it, but the women kept asking questions,
and I kept thinking, What if I say the wrong thing?"

"The Man Who Does Not Like to Answer Questions,"
Anna said.

Nick laughed. "There's a line from a poem. I don't
remember who wrote it. 'Others abide our question, thou
art free.' Well, that was certainly not me. I felt as if I spent
the entire year waiting for the next person to ask the next
question; and I had to reply promptly and honestly and
courteously. No lies. No tricks. No silence. I don't know
why it was so difficult, but it was.

"Gwarha told me something about what's been happening out here. I wouldn't mind hearing more."

She told him about the *hwarhath* women, especially the
two translators, since she knew them better than anyone
else. Eh Leshali was interesting, but too serious and ambitious. Anna liked Tsai Ama Indil a lot.

Nick grinned. "I've been hearing rumors about that."

"What do you mean?"

"The *hwarhath* know that it's possible for their people
and humans to become romantically involved, and they
love to gossip."

"I like Indil. I consider her a friend, but nothing like
*that* is going on."

Maybe she spoke with too much emphasis. He gave her
an odd look, but said nothing.

She hurried to another topic: Eh Matsehar's new play.

"It's absolutely terrific," said Nick. "We didn't have
time to get a full production ready for the Weaving, so we
did a reading, which for this play is a serious problem. It
really needs music and dancing. But even so, it was a hit.
He showed me his translation, the one he did for you. Not
bad, though I can do better. Go on. Tell me more."

She described the papers she had written, reporting her
work on Reed 1935-C. "Ettin Gwarha read everything to

make sure I wasn't sending any kind of protected information back to human space. He said"—she grinned—"the papers seemed to be entirely harmless, and if my animals were intelligent, he'd eat one of them, like a cat eating a canary."

Nick looked surprised. "What is he trying to do, master human figures of speech?"

Anna shrugged. "Must be."

Charlie had sent the papers back in a diplomatic pouch. *The Journal of Extraterrestrial Behavior* had accepted one. The other had been turned down by *The Journal of Theoretical Intelligence.*

"The ignorant fuckers," said Anna. "What do they know about intelligence? None of them has met intelligent aliens. I have. I'm starting on my first paper about the People."

"You've learned that much?" asked Nick.

"I think so." She leaned back in her chair. The wine was starting to have an effect. "All in all, this has been a good experience, except I can't see a way to go home—for me or you. I thought about that, Nick, when Charlie told me that they'd worked out an exchange of prisoners. There is no way to include you, is there?"

"I am home, sweetheart. But you are not; and that's the next project."

"MI is going to grab me the minute I get into human space, and nothing has changed about the stuff I know. It can still do the People harm."

"Not so much the People as the Ettin and me. You understand that, don't you, Anna?"

"No."

"I explained most of it to you. I think I did; it's been a year. The humans are going to figure out the rules of war. The Weaving knows that, so does the Bundle. The most they can hope for is a little more time. If they get it, they

will thank the Goddess. If they don't get it, they'll make
do.

"The real problem—and the dangerous secret—is this:
you know I'm unreliable, and you know that Ettin Gwarha
protected a man who should have been killed. If human
MI gets hold of this information, they'll try to do something stupid with it, if not at once, then sometime. Gwar
is not going to live with the knowledge that his enemies
have that kind of weapon. He says he's *rahaka*, which
means he'll go to the other frontmen and tell them what
has happened, and they will deal with the problem."

"Shit," Anna said.

He nodded. "The aunts checked with various scientists
to find out if there was a way to remove information from
a human mind. I thought I was up the creek then. I figured
they'd try the process on me first, though maybe Gwarha
could have talked them out of it. But there's nothing. Their
medical technology isn't as good as ours, especially in the
areas of psychology and neurology. They aren't interested
in messing around in one another's minds; and they tend
to believe that most mental problems are moral or spiritual
rather than physiological. They haven't been trying to find
medical cures for sadness or evil.

"But if they could remove the information you have
about me and Gwarha, we'd all be happier. I am never
going to forgive myself for panicking that way. If only I'd
kept my mouth shut."

"You told me that you don't believe in regret."

"You're right. I don't." He stood up. "I'm going to bed.
I'll see you in a day or so. Whenever I get up." He paused
at the door. "Would you consider changing sides, Anna?
Then we could use diplomatic immunity to protect you."

"No."

"It was only a thought." He glanced at her, smiled and
left.

Anna finished her glass of wine and then refilled it and

turned on the latest hologram she had gotten from Ettin Gwarha: a planet seen from space. It had rings more spectacular than Saturn's, braided and broken, and at least a dozen moons. Huge storms coiled and flashed in the planet's atmosphere. The rings shone in the light of an invisible sun. Anna drank her wine.

The next morning Matsehar was her escort.

"I'd like to hug you," Anna said.

"That isn't possible, as you ought to know. But I will take your wish as an expression of decent affection."

They walked together through the cool bright halls. Anna mentioned that she'd seen Nick and that he liked *Macbeth*.

"My best work so far. I think I've finally made a breaking-out, a coming-forward. What is the right term?"

"It depends on what you're trying to say."

"I feel as if I've been in one place too long, and it has become like one of those rooms in the old stories that shrink and darken and become a trap. But now—hah!— I've come out of the room, and it seems as if I'm standing at the edge of a plain."

"Breakthrough," said Anna. "That's the word you want."

He repeated it, sounding thoughtful.

She asked him about the Shakespeare festival. He gave her a sideways glance. "Nicky told you about that? It happened too quickly; we didn't have time to rehearse properly. The audience was difficult; and the music sucked. I am using 'suck' as a human would. It's interesting what one can learn about a culture from its figures of speech."

"Nick said the festival worked. It did what it was supposed to do."

He gave her another sideways glance. "Yes, but it did not happen the way I imagined it. If we'd had more time, if the chief musician had not been an idiot, and if we'd been able to make new costumes—"

He stopped at the entrance to the human quarters. She went into the observation room and watched a meeting that was as boring as usual.

Afterward she had lunch with the other humans. She told them that Nick was back.

"Did he tell you where he'd been?" asked Cyprian McIntosh.

"The home world." She picked through her tofu and defrosted broccoli in red pepper sauce, looking for a truly crisp piece of broccoli.

"Why?" asked Cyprian.

"They were doing a Shakespeare festival and they wanted Nick to do the question-and-answer period after the plays." Having said that, she glanced up.

"They pulled their best translator out of peace negotiations to work on a Shakespeare festival?" asked Cyprian. He sounded incredulous.

Anna looked back down at her broccoli. "They take art very seriously."

Mats escorted her to the women's quarters and stopped at the door.

"Aren't you coming in?" asked Anna.

"To see my cousin? Not today."

Anna went to her rooms. Once again she smelled coffee the moment her door opened. Two heavy white ceramic mugs stood on one of her tables. Nick was at the entrance to her kitchen, holding a coffeepot. This time he was wearing a space-cadet uniform. There were three badges clipped to the belt, though her memory was he didn't wear badges with this costume; and she had never seen him wear three badges.

"What's that about?" asked Anna.

He filled the mugs, then looked at the table. "I really can't set the pot down, can I? Just a moment."

She settled into a chair. The red pepper sauce at lunch had an aftertaste, and she wondered about her breath.

Maybe coffee would help. She picked up one of the mugs. He came back and sat down. Anna asked about the badges.

He smiled. "Now that is a question I actually enjoy answering. The Weaving decided that my position needed to be regularized. I am now officially a person; all doubt has been removed. And I have been working for the People for twenty years. It's wrong for me to be treated like an outlaw or a beggar, a member of a destroyed lineage. So they created a lineage for me. It happens about once in a generation, usually when a big lineage splits or when two small lineages decide they'd do better together. But this—" He tapped one of the metal disks. "—is the first time it's been done for any human or group of humans."

"You sound happy."

"I feel for the first time in years, maybe in my life, that I belong somewhere." He paused for a moment, then said, "The aunts think I ought to get a promotion. I've been a holder for a long time. It's embarrassing for me to be stuck in a low rank, especially now that I'm a real person with a lineage. People will think Gwarha lacks confidence in me, and that will cast a shadow over all the arguments the women of Ettin made in front of the Weaving.

"No woman is ever going to tell a man what to do on the perimeter—not directly, anyway. But they've made a suggestion, and he usually listens to his female relatives; though I am not entirely certain he will this time."

Why not, Anna asked.

"Gwarha will do a lot of things for me, and almost anything for his aunts, but he won't endanger the People. I have shown myself to be unreliable."

"Is that why he didn't give you a promotion before this?"

He picked up his mug and held it with both hands, as if warming the long narrow fingers. "No. We talked about it. It was too likely to anger the other senior officers. I am—I was—an enemy alien. There were always people who were willing to argue that I was not reliable and maybe not even a real person. It would have been like Caligula's horse. Remember? Caligula made him a consul. It did not go down well with the Roman aristocracy.

"And there was the question of my security rating. It isn't especially high. It would have been embarrassing to have a high-ranking officer who wasn't allowed access to protected information.

"The problem now is that Gwarha is not certain how far he can trust me. If I could betray only him, he'd take the risk, he's told me. But he will not put me in a position to do serious harm to the People. So—we'll see what happens."

"Jesus Maria, you've had a strange life."

He tilted his head, considering. "Maybe. I certainly found human Military Intelligence pretty damn peculiar, and there are mysteries about the American Midwest which I've never fathomed, such as why anyone stays there."

Anna laughed.

They talked a while longer, mostly about her year. Finally he stood up. "I have to get back to the office. The general let my work pile up while I was gone. I can't say I blame him. There is no one who's my equal as an analyst of human behavior." He walked to the door, then paused, looking back at her. "Are you certain you don't want to change sides, Anna? We could use another expert on humanity."

"No," she said.

"Most likely you're right. We need people on the other side who are sympathetic to us."

Then he was gone. She carried the two mugs into the kitchen. He'd washed her breakfast dishes and left them neatly stacked, clean and dry but not put away, a silent reproach. For a moment, looking at the dishes, she felt pity for Ettin Gwarha. Imagine spending your life with someone who could not leave anything alone, but had to be—always!—neatening.

A new group of women had come out on the same ship as Nicholas and Matsehar. She had no idea why they'd come. To speak with her, yes. But why? The big discussion was over. The decision had been made; and the human diplomatic team still did not know that humanity had been judged and found more or less adequate. This struck her as funny now.

She was most impressed by a Harag politician, a woman the size of Lugala Minti, with thick fur, more brown than grey, that made her seem even larger than she was. The fur was striped, and the lines on her face made a kind of devil's mask. Pale yellow eyes shone out of the mask. The woman's voice was deep, slow, rasping and metallic. She sounded like a piece of machinery in need of lubrication.

She was the representative for a large and sparsely populated region on the southernmost continent, Indil told Anna. There were a number of lineages in the region, all of them small and none clearly in front of the others. The woman had her job because she was able to argue them into a kind of cooperation.

"Watch out for her," Indil said. "There are people who move to the front on their own, dragging their lineage after them. This is one."

As it turned out, they got along fine. The woman was genuinely curious about humanity and willing to believe that there was more to the universe than her windy plain. Behind the frightening face was an acute mind and a good—if flat—sense of humor.

Anna settled down to learn about Harag and the Northwest Cooperative Region. Harag am Hwil saw no reason to be shy or secretive. "There is nothing I know which can be turned into a weapon against me. How disturbing it must be to have that kind of information."

She was the only woman that Anna had met so far who did not wear a ceremonial robe. The costume she preferred looked very much like a pair of overalls cut off at the knees. The fabric varied in color, but was always plain and rough. The adjustable straps had fasteners that looked as if they were gold.

"It's the fur," the woman said, speaking through Ama Tsai Indil. "My home is cold, and I am very well insulated. If I wore the same kind of clothing as the other women, I'd be panting all the time."

She looked at Anna, yellow eyes gleaming from the devil's mask. "Life is short. There is plenty to do. The best way to save time is to deal plainly and directly and don't worry about how you look or what might be happening in other people's minds."

"How do you get along with the women of Ettin?" asked Anna. She was trying to imagine this lady in the cut-off overalls up against the Three Norns.

"Well enough, though they are not, of course, half of what their mother was. Now there was someone with whom you could make an arrangement!"

They spent one afternoon in Anna's rooms along with Ama Tsai Indil. The woman of Harag had arrived with a ceramic pot full of something like tea. Anna drank wine. Indil drank a little water and looked nervous. It must be a strain translating for someone as blunt as Hwil.

Anna talked about the various research stations where she had spent much of her adult life. Hwil listened with interest and drank her tea, which must have been mildly narcotic. Her posture eased a little. She looked as if she might begin to purr.

Finally she spoke. "I don't know if I'd be willing to travel as far as you have, Perez Anna, especially at my age. The little trip out to this station has unsettled me. My digestion isn't back to what it ought to be. I think the spinning of the station keeps the liquids inside me stirred up. But you! A traveler such as you are ought to be willing to go a little farther. Come to Harag!"

"I can't," said Anna.

"Do you mean the war?" She made a gesture of dismissal. "That is going to have to end. Can't you tell your men to get busy and finish whatever they are doing here?"

Anna looked at Indil. Her dark velvety face wore an expression of shock.

"Can you tell Ettin Gwarha that?" asked Anna. "Or Lugala Tsu?"

"Yes, though it won't do much good in the case of Lugala Tsu. He listens to his mother and no one else. Now, if you are going to listen to only one person, Lugala Minti is a good choice. She is powerful and clever, though I have not been impressed by her behavior recently. She's afraid because the universe is changing in ways that are noticeable to her, as if the universe is not always changing! As if the Goddess does not love change! Ettin Gwarha has told me that he's doing the best he can."

"How can you talk to him? Are you related?"

"One of my brothers is the father of two of his cousins, and I wouldn't mind having some of his genetic material for Harag. But—" Hwil glanced at Indil. "It may be that another lineage has gotten ahead of us."

Huh?

The woman of Harag spoke again, and Indil translated. Her voice was as calm and melodious as it always was, a striking contrast to the grating baritone of Harag am Hwil.

"I'm wandering from the subject in front of us. You have traveled much, Perez Anna. Think of traveling more. If we are going to share the universe, we had better come to an understanding."

"I'd like to come," said Anna, and was surprised by the intensity in her voice.

By this time she had heard a lot about the Northwest Region: a dry plain with mountains to the east and south that cut off rain. Their white peaks shone like clouds in the dark blue sky, and the old stories said that ghosts and spirits lived there. Now aqueducts brought water down to cities built of adobe. Some of the people still lived by herding. Others fished. The polar ocean was very rich.

A bleak land, but tempting, like Samarkand or Timbuktu. The woman of Harag spoke about wonderful embroidery, fine metalwork, mines that produced green and blue stones, the fish-drying racks in the coastal cities with the fish swinging in the wind and gleaming like—what was the figure of speech that Hwil had used? "A forest of silver leaves."

She also spoke about the Water Resource Regulation Authority (always a center for conflict in the region) and the Making-All-Eyes-Bright-and-Clear Project, the Fishing Authority, the co-ops for buying and selling. (Some of these names Anna had to make up, after Hwil described what the organization in question did. Indil had trouble when it came to translating bureaucratese.) The woman of Harag had as much interest in these—maybe more—as she did in the land and the cities, though she clearly loved the land and the cities.

The end of it was, Anna wanted to go. She imagined herself wandering in marketplaces or taking a tour of a desalinization plant. (That was not optional, as far as she could tell from Hwil.) Or driving along some dusty highway, past animals she did not recognize.

Their conversation wound down finally, and the woman of Harag left. Tsai Ama Indil stayed behind. Anna groaned and put her feet up on a table. "Jesus Maria, what a woman!"

"I warned you," said Indil.

"What did she mean about the genetic material?"

Indil was silent for a while. Finally she said, "I have

been intending to speak to you, Anna, since it isn't our custom to have children in space, and that means I will have to leave here and go home."

Anna glanced at her. "Are you saying that you're pregnant?"

"Of course not! How could I be? I haven't been home in a year." Indil sounded shocked. "And I would never travel in space after insemination."

The People used artificial insemination. Anna remembered that now. There must be sperm banks on the home planet. Or did the donors have to make a special trip home? She'd have to ask Nick. She certainly was not going to ask Indil. She was feeling embarrassed already.

After a moment or two Indil said, "My lineage and the Tsai Ama have come to an agreement with the Ettin. It happened before Tsai Ama Ul left here, but it was decided that I ought to stay and keep you company." She paused. "There wasn't any hurry, and if something really unpleasant happened, if the Lugala managed to seriously embarrass the Ettin, then we could always draw back. Though Tsai Ama Ul did not think this would happen. She has a great respect for the Ettin, and Ettin Gwarha is certainly the best male in his generation."

"You are going to go home and become pregnant, and Ettin Gwarha is going to be the father."

"Yes," said Indil. "A girl. It's part of the agreement. I would like to give her two names. That's sometimes done in my lineage. I'd like your permission to make one of the names Anna."

She felt honored and also frightened.

"You don't have to say anything now," said Indil. "There is plenty of time. But Tsai Ama Ul agrees with the woman of Harag. If we are going to share the universe with your species, we must find ways to get along."

She left then. These terrifying women! They were making Anna welcome. She imagined a furry grey baby—

Indil's child, Ettin Gwarha's kid—with her name. They'd probably shift the pronunciation of the first *a* in Anna to 'ah.' Ama Tsai Ana. It made the skin on her back prickle.

A couple of days later she met Nick at the entrance to the human quarters. Vaihar was escorting her. "I'll take over," Nick said, and walked with her to the observation room. There were two chairs; Nick settled into one. "I thought I'd see how everything is doing."

"You haven't gone back to translating."

"I wasn't kidding you when I said that the general let my work pile up. I don't have the time for this crap. It's almost done, anyway, or haven't you noticed?"

"I've been dealing," said Anna, "with a grey tide of matrons. There's a lady here from Harag who could take on the aunts and win."

Nick laughed. "Maybe not. But she is formidable. She's been telling Gwarha to stop screwing around and make peace, so people can go about their business without having to think about this utterly tedious war. There's real work to be done!"

"I know," said Anna. "Eye diseases to be eradicated. Oceans to be desalinated. She's invited me to Harag to see the fish-drying racks."

Nick looked surprised.

"And to tour the new desalinization plant."

Now he looked thoughtful. "I don't think that's possible at the moment—for you to go to the home planet, I mean. But it's an interesting invitation."

"How secure is this room?"

"Come on." He stood.

He led her down a series of unfamiliar corridors, past several guard points. The guards recognized Nick and made the gesture of presentation. He nodded in reply. They came to a door. He palmed it open and waved her in.

She was in a living room: grey carpet, tan and grey furniture: a couch and two chairs, a couple of low metal tables. It was much more spartan than her own quarters— no touch of color or luxury anywhere, and it seemed utterly impersonal. There was nothing that indicated the room was occupied.

The door closed.

"Sit down," said Nick. "Ettin Gwarha has decided to trust me again. These rooms are not bugged, not even by him."

"These are your quarters."

He nodded.

"What are you, a monk?"

He laughed. "Hardly." He glanced around, still standing, his hands in his pockets. "I don't like thingies."

"What?"

"You know. Whatnots, bibelots, clutter, stuff. The crap you have to pack when it's time to move. There's a proverb I read once in some book or other. 'He who furnishes his mind will live like a king. He who furnishes his house will have trouble moving.' Words to live by, and I have. So the woman of Harag wants you to come visiting. Do you want anything? Coffee, tea, wine? I even have a new kind of human chow, which is good for a laugh."

"No," said Anna. "Ama Tsai Indil has asked permission to give my name to her child."

Nick turned and stared at her. "Jesus God, these people move quickly when they've decided it's time to move." He went over to one of the tables, touched it and spoke in the alien language.

The table replied in the same language. Nick spoke some more and got another answer, then straightened up and turned back to Anna. "What did you say to Ama Tsai Indil?"

"Nothing, yet."

"I'll have to do some checking, but I don't think you'd be stuck with any responsibility. It'd be good manners to pay some attention to the kid. Look on her with kindness, give her an occasional bit of advice. But mostly, it's a compliment to you and an attempt to create a connection between you and her family—not a big connection, a thread, not a rope. But definitely something. This is very interesting news. I'm going to pace. I hope you don't mind."

"Go ahead," said Anna, and settled into a chair.

Nick moved around the room. "One problem—I have to say—with owning almost nothing is, I have nothing to fiddle with when I'm trying to think. On the other hand, it takes me half an *ikun* to pack. Whenever Gwarha moves, it's a production." He settled against a wall and folded his arms. For a minute or two he was quiet, staring past her, his green eyes unfocused.

Finally he looked back at her. "The Tsai Ama and the Ama Tsai and the Harag have decided it's a good idea to start getting close to humans, and especially—apparently—to the one human female who is available. I really wasn't expecting this. They must have started thinking in this direction the moment that the Weaving decided we were people. I'm tied to Ettin, as everyone knows. There's no way that I can operate on my own. But you're different. As far as they know, you're independent, and you are clearly important: the only woman on the human negotiating team. Looking at this situation from the point of view of a *hwarhath* woman—Anna, you must be the queen of Earth." He sounded really happy.

Anna was starting to get nervous. "Is Harag friendly with Tsai Ama?"

"Not especially. They're both—how can I say it?—less important lineages, who are looking for a way to become more important. They might work together, if they could see a good reason."

"Indil warned me about the woman of Harag."

"So." Nick looked past her again. After a moment he grinned. "They're fighting over you. I think it ought to be possible to cut deals with both of them. The thing I'm trying to figure out is how we can use this to solve your problem."

"MI?" asked Anna.

He nodded. "Gwarha and I have been talking about it. We think the answer is diplomatic immunity."

"I won't change sides," Anna said.

He shook his head. "I'm not suggesting that. How would you like to be an ambassador?"

"What?"

He lifted a hand. "I'm exaggerating. I don't think we can convince the Con to make you an ambassador. Maybe a special envoy. You did say you wanted to be the second human on the home planet. Now you have an invitation. Most likely, two invitations. The child will have a naming ceremony. I expect you'll be invited."

"When do I get home again?"

"When you are so important that no one can touch you. Even those idiots in MI aren't going to use drugs to deback-ground a senior diplomat." He grimaced. "Debackground. What an ugly word! How could I work for people who used language like that?"

She frowned, feeling that too much was happening way too quickly.

"Anna, I'm offering you—the People are offering you—a research opportunity that many people would kill for, *and* money. The Con will have to cough up a decent salary. If they don't, the Weaving is loaded. You'd be surprised how wealthy a society can be, if it's properly run. You won't have to worry about grants. You won't have to worry about your articles getting turned down by asshole scholarly journals." He grinned at her. "All you'll have to do is deliver whatever tedious messages the Con wants delivered to the Weaving."

"I've never wanted to be a dip."

The door to the hall opened, and Ettin Gwarha came in,

dressed as a space warrior. "Mem," he said as the door closed, then glanced to Nick, who spoke rapidly in the *hwarhath* language. The general stood listening with the remarkable alert patience of the *hwarhath*. Finally, Nick stopped.

"Anna is a good name," Ettin Gwarha said. "I've come to like it, though it has the wrong kind of ending for a woman's name in the languages I know; and the woman of Harag is a valuable friend; and I think, Mem Perez, that you would be a good envoy.

"The problem that Nicky and I came up against was this: how could the Weaving be convinced to ask for you as an envoy? We didn't want my lineage to bring up the subject. We are already too closely connected with humanity. But if Harag will suggest that you ought to be invited to the home world—hah!" He tilted his head, considering. Nick was watching him, smiling faintly. It hit Anna that these two guys loved to plot. Maybe that's what held them together.

"I think I need some time to think," she said.

The general glanced at her. "Yes. Of course, Mem Perez."

Nick straightened up. "I'll escort you."

They left Ettin Gwarha and walked through the station. She'd become so familiar with it that she no longer noticed anything strange about the place. The furry soldiers looked ordinary. The cold air that smelled of *hwarhath* seemed like the air in—how many other stations where she'd spent time?

But she was tired of stations, all stations. She wanted to be on the surface of a planet.

After they reached her rooms, she said, "I'll do it. I can't pass up this kind of research opportunity. I wish, though, that I wasn't carrying secrets."

He nodded. "I can understand that. A heavy burden. But the alternative is an ending like one of Gwarha's beloved hero plays. You know, the problem surfaces, and it's insoluble, and there is nothing to do except die. I've spent a lot of time thinking about this mess. I like neatness. You may have noticed."

"Uh-huh."

"The problem *is* insoluble, at least in the short term. You and I and Gwarha are caught between loyalties in the conflict." He grinned. "Matsehar would love this situation. I wonder what he'd do with it? Nothing ordinary.

"But I don't want to involve him, and I don't have his kind of imagination. I can't think of anything to do, except dig a hole and bury the problem, and hope like hell that no *sul* with a keen nose comes around to sniff.

"The other solution—the neat one—is for me to die, because I can't choose between Gwarha and humanity, and Gwarha to die, because he can't choose between me and the People, and you to be left to clean up the mess like Fortinbras, Prince of Norway."

"No, thanks," said Anna.

"Well, it would look good in a play. But I can't say that I've ever wanted to be in a tragedy. Do you remember the story about the actor who was dying, and someone asked him if dying was hard? He said, 'Dying is easy. Comedy is difficult.' "

Anna smiled politely.

"Comedy is difficult, life is messy, and Gwarha and I are *rahaka*. So where does that leave us?"

"With a mess," said Anna. "That may or may not be funny, and with a lot of secrets that may well bite us in the ass."

Nick walked to the door that led out of her rooms. "Right you are, Anna. You're going to love the *hwarhath* home planet. You may even like the miserable cold plain where the Harag live.

"What else can I tell you? They're planning to redo Matsehar's festival—the whole thing, in the capital city, with *Macbeth* done properly. Costumes and music. They are even planning to use male actors in front of female audiences. That is very unusual; but the general opinion is, women can't possibly understand those plays well enough to act in them. Maybe we can get you there in time to see the festival. I guarantee, it will be splendid.''

The door opened. He glanced at her, smiled and left.

## APPENDIX A: ON TIME

&#10147;&#10147;&#10147; THE HOME PLANET of the People has a rotation period of ten *ikun* or 23.1 hours.

One *ikun* = 100 *ha-ikun*.

One *ikun* = 2.31 hours.

One *ha-ikun* = 1.386 minutes.

One minute = .7215 *ha-ikun*.

15 minutes = approximately 10 *ha-ikun*.

One *hwarhath* year = 402.2 *hwarhath* days.

The year is divided into ten units of forty days each, with two days left over, which are ghost days and do not appear on the calendar. No business takes place in this period, unless it is absolutely essential and cannot be deferred. It is considered especially bad to do anything violent or hostile. Wars stop. The pious attend religious ceremonies. The adventurous do things they wouldn't normally do. (Make peace with an enemy. Make sexual advances to someone they have been afraid to approach.) The superstitious do nothing at all.

The *hwarhath* schedule inseminations so that no children are born on a ghost day. It is believed that anyone born on a ghost day will be not entirely in this world. A ghost child may be a power for good or a power for evil. Whatever he or she is, it won't be ordinary.

Every fifth year has an extra ghost day.

On the perimeter the day is divided into fifths. Each fifth = 4.62 hours.

One fifth is devoted to work that is of immediate social utility: i.e., your job.

One fifth is devoted to activities that increase one's social usefulness: study in one's area of competence, the acquisition and improvement of skills.

One fifth is devoted to activities that improve one as an individual: exercise, meditation, going to the theater, acquiring knowledge that does not pertain to one's job.

One fifth is free time.

One fifth is sleep.

Most *hwarhath* need more than five hours' sleep, so free time tends to be reduced.

The only part of the day that is formally scheduled is the work shift, but the *hwarhath* log in and out as they go from one activity to another, and computers monitor the time that each individual spends in the gym, at the theater, using learning programs and so on. Anyone who is conspicuously out of line will hear from a superior officer.

The *hwarhath* women do not schedule their lives with this kind of precision. Remember that they live on the surface of the home planet. They have to make allowances for the planet's seasons and the changing length of real (as opposed to artificial) days, also for the vagaries of weather and children.

## APPENDIX B: ON RANK

≻≻≻ In ascending order, the ranks in *hwarhath* male society are as follows:

Carrying-for-the-People (Carrier).

Keeping-Watch-at-the-Edge-of-the-Army (Watcher).

In-the-Great-Darkness-Holding-a-Sword (Holder).

Advancing-Toward-the-Enemy (Advancer).

Defending-the-Hearth-with-Honor (Defender).

There are three divisions within each rank: the rank itself, the rank one-in-back and the rank one-in-front. So the ranking within Carrying-for-the-People, again in ascending order, would be:

Carrier One-in-Back.

Carrier.

Carrier One-in-Front.

In total, the *hwarhath* male society has fifteen ranks, which satisfies their need to count in groups divisible by five or ten. Their foremost rank is not counted with the others: Defending-the-Hearth-with-Honor First-Ahead, i.e., a first-defender or frontman.

Actual position within *hwarhath* male society is determined by a combination of rank, lineage and personal connections. In battle or any kind of emergency, rank has absolute priority. There isn't time to consider the other factors when giving orders, and the junior officers must obey.

But in the day-to-day struggle to move forward within the military organization, lineage and connections count for a lot, and officers consider who they are talking to before they give an order. Nicholas, despite his low rank, is given a lot of space and hears few orders, except from Gwarha and (occasionally) other frontmen.

Gwarha is a triple-threat officer: high-ranking, from a powerful lineage and with excellent personal connections. Only a few individuals give him orders, and they are all senior members of his lineage. Otherwise, he listens to organizations: the government of the Weaving and the Frontmen-in-a-Bundle.

## APPENDIX C: ON THEATER

➤➤➤ THERE ARE (broadly speaking) three kinds of *hwarhath* drama: Dark Plays, Bright Plays and Plays of Uncertain Light. The Dark Plays are (very roughly) equivalent to human tragedies. The Bright Plays are comedies, and the Plays of Uncertain Light are whatever is left.

There are two main kinds of Dark Plays: the hero plays, which are written and acted by men, and the women's plays, which (as you might expect) are written and acted by women.

The Bright Plays are animal plays, of which there are two kinds: the moral ones, for children, and the obscene ones, for adults.

Until recently there was only one kind of Play of Uncertain Light: the modern or ambiguous play. But recently—due largely to Eh Matsehar—a number of plays about humanity have been produced, and these may represent a new and separate type.

Men are never involved in the production of women's plays, and women have nothing to do with the hero plays, but both sexes write and perform Bright Plays and Plays of Uncertain Light, though never together.

The different kinds of plays vary considerably in their staging, their costuming and their style of acting.

The hero plays use a bare stage, limited props, much music and splendid, richly colored costumes. The acting is stylized and has many of the qualities of mime or dance.

In the women's plays the costumes (as a rule) are simpler than in the hero plays. Colors tend to be muted and subtle, even drab. Sets are painted curtains and banners, often on very thin cloth that becomes transparent when lit from behind. There is considerable visual complexity. The curtains and banners hang in front of one another, and since they are—at least part of the time—transparent, complicated layers of pattern are created, which change as the lighting changes. Actors disappear into the background, then reemerge. The plays do not use much music. The acting style is quiet and natural.

The animal plays use masks, elaborate animal costumes, bright colors, broad acting and a lot of physical activity: dancing, tumbling, mock fights, and so on. In the adult animal plays the costumes are grotesque and often obscene. In the plays for children the animals look (for the most part) pleasant and friendly.

Hero plays and animal plays are performed on an open thrust stage. Women's plays are performed on a stage enclosed in a cage of wood beams to which the curtains and banners are fastened.

Eh Matsehar is responsible for the human play as an art form, though he had (as he is usually willing to admit) extensive help from Sanders Nicholas. These are mostly retellings of human plays and/or stories, done with masks and more or less realistic human costumes. Use of music varies, as does use of props. Most use sets: human scenes painted on curtains and banners. (This has necessitated the use of a modified women's stage—a shocking innovation, since the plays are written and acted by men.) The acting style varies, but is often quiet and natural, another shocking innovation.

## APPENDIX D: ON THE SOCIAL THEORIES OF TSAI AMA UL

➤➤➤ FOR THE MOST part the People have assumed that their behavior is in accordance with nature, reason and religion. But some scholars (not many) began to wonder after they learned about humanity, was homosexuality inevitable? If so, how could they explain human behavior? (The religion of the People is rigorously monotheistic, and it is an offense to the Goddess to suggest that she would deliberately create a perverse or wicked people, or so these "radical" scholars argue.)

The most radical thinker about the "human problem" is Tsai Ama Ul. What follows is a synopsis of her theories. Remember that most scholars and scientists disagree with her.

First of all, the woman of Tsai Ama points out the extraordinary similarity of the two species. Both are warm-blooded and hairy, bear their young alive and produce milk to feed them. Both have two sexes, though this seems to be the norm for the universe. Their bodies are almost identical: one head, four limbs, five digits. Their organs are similar. Almost all the important differences are at the level of cell and molecule. As far as the unaided senses can tell, the two kinds of people are alike.

And they have similar histories. Both had arboreal ancestors. From these came grasping hands and bifocal vision. The *hwarhath*, with their slit pupils, probably came from ancestors active at night.

Both species are bipedal. The origin of this is not en-

tirely clear. Humans believe their ancestors moved out of
the trees and onto a grassy plain, where they needed to
stand upright in order to see danger above the vegetation.

The *hwarhath* are not as certain. They have a near relative still surviving: the Red Folk, who inhabit four islands
in the Great Southern Chain. The Red Folk are upright,
though the islands they live on are heavily forested. Some
scientists argue that the Red Folk evolved their current
physiology in open country and then retreated into the
forest, when the People began to proliferate and spread.
(There is some evidence that the People used to kill the Red
Folk. The bones of Red Folk have been found, mixed with
the bones of other animals, at early campsites of the People.) Gradually, the Red Folk migrated south onto the island chain, which may have been a land bridge at the time.
When the water rose, they were isolated and protected.

Other scientists believe the Red Folk and the People
both evolved in forests or at their margins. The Red Folk
were never able to adapt to any other environment, these
scientists argue, and have managed to survive only in a
few isolated areas: i.e., the island-forests of the south.

There is a final remarkable similarity between the People and humanity. Neither one has a mating season. The
females do not go into heat. Women and men are sexually
interested all the time, and the sexual interest is diffuse.
No special cues are necessary. The objects of lust are many.
Society, not biology, determines which are appropriate.

So, asks Tsai Ama Ul, why do two species that are
almost identical in physiology and history develop two
different kinds of sexual behavior?

The answer lies in the function of sex and especially in
the nonspecific and continuous sexual interest that is characteristic of both the People and humanity.

The first thing to understand, says Tsai Ama Ul, is that
sex has very little to do with procreation.

If the purpose of sex were procreation, then both the

People and humanity would have a mating season. It works just fine for most animals. It maximizes competition and selection; it insures that most of the young are born at the time of the year when they are likely to survive; and it gets sex out of the way for the adults. Most of the year, they don't have to think about it. They can concentrate on making a living and raising the young.

So why have the People (and humanity) developed their never-ending interest in sex? What is the evolutionary advantage?

Obviously, says the woman of Tsai Ama, it serves to keep the People (and humanity) continuously and intensely interested in one another.

Most animal communities are built on kinship, usually around groups that consist of mothers and children or siblings. This is true, to take a couple of examples from Earth, of elephant herds and termite hills.

But the problem with kinship as a basis for community is twofold. (1) There are size limits, at least for mammals and mammal-like animals. Such creatures do not produce very large families. It is possible to extend the concept of kinship beyond the immediate family, and both the People and humanity have done this through adoption and interbreeding and by stretching out the idea of the family, until it becomes the *hwarhath* lineage and the human clan or tribe. But this involves abstract thinking. One is no longer responding to memory or perceptions of genetic similarity. The woman of Tsai Ama does not believe that the concept of extended families was an early one. (2) Kinship gives people no way to relate to strangers and to other communities. But sex and sexual love enable people to be interested in everyone. Communities can be any size. It is always possible to integrate new people.

Those who ask questions about religion might be inclined to ask, *what* was the Goddess thinking of, when she used one set of organs and one group of hormones for two such different purposes? But, as the woman of Tsai Ama points out, the Goddess is famous for using whatever is available; evolution is full of strange transformations; and no one has ever been able to figure out what the Goddess is thinking, if anything.

So a drive designed for procreation became a way to bind the People together. But this led to a problem: if people are continuously engaged in heterosexual behavior, they are going to produce children, and it's likely that they will produce more children than they want or can support.

What is to be done? asks the woman of Tsai Ama.

Humans found one solution, according to Ul, and they found it early: in their Neolithic at the very latest. There were three aspects to the human form of population control. One was infanticide and especially the killing of female children. (If you want to limit population, it makes much more sense to kill females than males.) A second aspect was the control and limiting of female sexuality. In order to do this, women must be enslaved, at least to some extent. (And in what sense, asks Tsai Ama Ul, can slavery be partial? Slavery is slavery, a concept of unimaginable horror. A little slavery is like a little incest.) The final aspect is the systematic devaluing of the lives of women and female children. This may be a result of infanticide and the enslavement of women. Humans, like the *hwarhath,* need to feel their behavior is right. If one harms other people, one needs a justification: the people one harms are bad or not really people. As a result of this devaluation, human women and female children have been systematically underfed and overworked. This also works to reduce population. A woman who is exhausted and malnourished is less likely to bear a healthy child or survive childbirth.

All of this is ghastly beyond belief, Tsai Ama Ul says. But it worked better than nothing, though not nearly as well as the People's solution: to make heterosexuality taboo, except for the purpose of procreation.

Why did humans use the murder and oppression of women to control population? Why did the *hwarhath* use decent sexual behavior?

There is one important difference between the two species. Among humans, males are larger and stronger than the females. The opposite is true among the *hwarhath*. Tsai Ama Ul argues that among the People women have always controlled mating, while among humans it was most likely the males who decided when to have sex.

(Tsai Ama Ul's argument is more complicated than this. Among most of the People, the size difference between men and women is not dramatic. They are close to equal in height and strength, though the women are usually taller than the men and tend to put on weight in middle age, and the men do not. The woman of Tsai Ama argues that sexual dimorphism among the People has diminished over time. In part she argues from fossil remains, though it is not always possible to determine the sex of bones. She also argues from "anthropology." Among the Red Folk, who are very similar to the pre-moral ancestors of the People, the difference in size between men and women is marked. The Red Women are much larger than their men and definitely control mating. And there is one group among the People that has a number of physiological and genetic [and possibly intellectual] differences from the rest of the species. The members of this group tend to have thick bodies, short arms and legs, prominent crests and flatter than usual faces. They are legendary for toughness and produce many fine soldiers, politicians and farmers, but they seem to lack something in the areas of creativity and imagination. They almost never produce a great artist or a truly original thinker. A number of the lineages on the Large Southern Continent belong to this group, which [the woman of Tsai Ama argues] is an actual subspecies that has retained a number of primitive traits. Among these primitive traits is a marked sexual dimorphism. In this group [which includes the Ettin and the Gwa] the women are significantly larger than the men. It was people like these, possibly even belonging to this subspecies, who created the original culture of the *hwarhath* and established female control over mating. The *hwarhath* women have never lost this control.)

This is an extremely controversial theory. Most of Tsai Ama Ul's fellow scientists think it is completely wrong.

Human males were unwilling to give up heterosexuality. Why is not clear to Tsai Ama Ul. It doesn't sound especially attractive. Maybe it was the weight of habit or the force of animal drives.

*Hwarhath* women were unwilling to lose children or the right to control their own bodies and lives. So they (the woman of Tsai Ama argues) limited population by denying men sexual access.

As a result, two different styles of child rearing developed. The People severely limited the number of children they had and made every effort to nourish and care for their children. They also made every effort to nourish and care for their women. There are no healthy children without healthy mothers.

The humans used poverty, oppression and violence within the family to limit their population. In the end, this technique did not work.

The *hwarhath* drew a clear line between sex for procreation and sex for affection or fun. The latter was encouraged. The former was carefully controlled. For the most part, they were able to keep violence out of the family. They drew a clear line between those-who-fought-and-killed and those-who-are-nourished-and-loved.

This was done rationally, according to Tsai Ama Ul, by the women of the People. It was not "natural." To provide this, she has hunted for examples of heterosexuality-for-purposes-other-than-procreation among the *hwarhath*.

Thus far she has collected over a thousand examples

from history and ethnography, including entire societies that were predominantly heterosexual and that even—in some cases—imposed sanctions on homosexual behavior. Reports of these societies all come from historical sources. None survived into modern times. Various reasons are given: (A) Their populations grew until they became a problem to their neighbors, who destroyed them. (B) They controlled their populations in the human way, through infanticide or the enslavement of women. This enraged their neighbors, who destroyed them, or (in several cases recorded by historians) their women left, taking the children.

More common were societies that allowed limited heterosexual behavior, usually at festivals and almost always for religious purposes.

There have been societies that allowed heterosexuality among children, but forbade it once the girls began to bleed, usually between fifteen and twenty years of age.

Other societies allowed a certain number of "licensed perverts": people who were permitted heterosexual behavior so long as they dressed in distinctive clothing and acted in odd (and often self-mocking) ways. The children of these perverts were taken away in infancy and raised by relatives in the traditional manner. Most became homosexual and productive members of society, though they did not usually become parents. Their genetic material was suspect.

These limited forms of heterosexual behavior survived into the recent past, though only in remote areas. They may still survive, the woman of Tsai Ama argues. Evidence for this is not good.

Tsai Ama Ul has also found evidence of many covert heterosexual cults and subcultures. The Dark Goddess religion, which flourished on the Great Northern Continent in the Era of Warring Alliances, seems to have had a distinct heterosexual element. Enemies of the religion certainly accused its followers of indecent sexual practices, as well as infant sacrifice. These may be the lies of enemies, but it is almost certain that the Dark Goddess herself had a consort or male twin, and that her religious ceremonies were led by a couple called "Mother" and "Father."

The Dark Goddess was suppressed at the end of the Era of Warring Alliances by the Ten Wound Together, led by Eh Manhata, known to history as the "Bloody Sword of Eh." The extreme brutality of the suppression and the destruction of many records for that time suggest that the followers of the Dark Goddess were doing something especially horrific.

The Ten Wound Together were the beginning of the system of alliances that led first to the Net of Lineages and finally to the Weaving. Tsai Ama Ul suggests that the extreme (as she calls it) heterophobia of modern society derives from the Ten and from the struggle against the Dark Goddess. She believes that Eh Manhata in particular is the source, and that there may be some connection between his famous violence and his equally famous hatred of any kind of deviance. "No man in history has been more moral, pious and destructive," the woman of Tsai Ama says.

There is no question that many earlier societies were more relaxed and permissive. Of course, as the woman of Tsai Ama also points out, the world used to be emptier. The People could afford some accidental children.

## APPENDIX E: MISCELLANEOUS FACTS ABOUT THE PEOPLE

➤➤➤ THERE ARE A little over eight hundred million *hwarhath*. The majority are in the home system and on the original planet, the Hearth of the People, but there are *hwarhath*—almost always male—on tens of moons and planets outside the home system, in hundreds of deep-space stations and in thousands of ships.

The People are able to sort sperm well enough to determine the sex of their children. Prior to their first encounter with humanity, they were producing far more girls than boys. The species was sixty-five-percent female, and the People were aiming at a seventy-five-to-twenty-five ratio.

As soon as they encountered their first human ship, they began to produce more sons. At present, the species is sixty-percent female. The split will be fifty-fifty in another generation. Depending on events, the percentage of males may continue to increase.

The reason for this ought to be obvious. Women are more useful on the home planet and in times of peace. Men are more useful for space exploration and in times of war. It took the People more than a century to find humanity, and they had begun to despair of finding another intelligent species with whom they could fight. The only way they could see to deal with the problem of no war was to produce fewer men.

There are almost no women outside the home system, and the overwhelming majority of the female population live on the Hearth World itself. The majority of the adult men are in space or in settlements on worlds other than the home world.

All the adult men are in the *hwarhath* armed forces. They enter at the age of twenty and stay in until retirement, which is usually at eighty. Everyone is trained in warfare, but only a minority are full-time professional killers-of-other-people. The rest explore, mine, build, farm, do research, move goods from station to station, make pottery, do theater and so on.

The male society is organized in a military hierarchy. At the top (or the front) are the first-defenders: twenty frontmen who are something like the joint chiefs of staff. The *hwarhath* do not have a single commander. The frontmen have different skills and areas of competence. Different frontmen speak loudly at different times.

The female society is organized around the lineages, which are extremely large extended families. There are just under a hundred thousand lineages. The largest is a huge anomaly with a hundred and twenty thousand members. A few families have under a thousand members. They are too small to be important, and it would be common sense for them to join another lineage. But some families cannot bear to have their name go out of existence. Most lineages have between two and twenty thousand members.

The lineages are connected by interbreeding and by political alliances that are often centuries old. One of the main functions of interbreeding is to form new alliances or to make old alliances stronger. Some families have been interbreeding so long that they regard each other (more or less) as cousins. The Ettin, for example, regularly exchange genetic material with their neighbors. They are especially close to the Gwa, Hwa, Hattali, Hu and Tesh. Over time, the physical boundaries between such closely allied lineages become less clear. They move into each other's territories and share (at least to an extent) each other's resources. The Land of Ettin is inhabited by many people who do not have the family name Ettin, but all are tied to Ettin by centuries of interbreeding, and they all know exactly how they are related.

Among the People land is held by families, not by individuals. Manufacture tends to be controlled by specific lineages, but trade is carried on by coalitions of families, for obvious reasons: one lineage cannot control both ends of a trade route, and a long route will go through land held by many different families.

The basic political unit is the lineage. Political parties are coalitions of lineages. Lineage alliances are the basis for almost all regional governments.

There is only one exception to this: the great cities. There are too many different people in these. No single lineage or alliance of lineages can possibly dominate. The cities are independent of any lineage and ruled by councils that are elected by their adult inhabitants: one person, one vote. There are urban political parties. In some cases, these are lineage-based, but often they are based on neighborhoods, interest groups and even on political and economic theories.

Each of the three largest cities has its own representative in the Weaving. The smaller cities have formed alliances, which elect representatives to the Weaving.

The ruling body of the world government is called either the Weaving (which is the name of the entire government as well) or the Gathering of the People. It is a legislative body with a thousand members, each representing a region and/or group of lineages. Nine members represent the cities. (They form a group called The Ten Less One, which is almost always radical, though humans would have trouble deciding whether they leaned to the left or the right.)

Lineages vary in how they pick their representatives and how they run their own internal affairs. Some are rigorously democratic. Others tend to pick their leaders from specific genetic lines, known to produce good politicians and administrators. A few have hereditary rulers. The Ettin in theory are democratic, but Ettin Gwarha's particular subfamily has been dominant for several generations and will probably continue to be so, until they make a major mistake or until the Ettin forget how impressive Ettin Petali was.

## APPENDIX F: ON THE PRONUNCIATION OF THE *HWARHATH* MAIN LANGUAGE

➤➤➤ CONSONANT SOUNDS ARE about what one would expect from English, except that the *h* sound is always noticeable. You ought to hear the *h* in Gwarha's name clearly, as if it were spelled Gwar-ha.

Vowel sounds are pronounced as follows:

*a* is approximately 'ah,' though modified by the following consonant;

*ai* as in hay;

*e* as in pet or (sometimes) pear;

*eh* as in feh;

*i* as in tin;

*long i* (which should be spelled í) as in tea;

*u* as in hull;

*long u* (which should be spelled ú) as in hue.

Tli has a long *i*.

The first *i* in Minti is short; the second is long.

The *u* in Tsai Ama Ul's name is short.

Lugala Tsu's name has two long *u*'s.

The language is accented, and the accent tends to fall on the first syllable of any given word.

The double *t* in certain names (Ettin, Hattin) reflects an orthographic peculiarity present in the written versions of several related languages on the *hwarhath* Large Southern Continent, and has no effect on pronunciation.